“ENJOYING YOURSEL

“No.”

His answer, a chuckling snort, brought heat to Jacey’s cheeks. But that warmth was nothing as to what slipped over her skin when he sent her a raw look that said he saw past her bravado, a look that said he’d peered into her soul. Completely unnerved, Jacey could only watch as he raised her hand to his mouth, cupped open her palm, and kissed it with a whole lot of slick daring.

Simple reflexes reacting to the foreign sensation jerked Jacey’s hand. Zant’s grip tightened. Trapped, caught in his web, she submitted. With a sinking feeling, knowing just how forbidden this one man was to her, she admitted to herself that she didn’t want to pull away. A shallow, bated breath escaped her in a whisper. “What . . . are you doing?”

Zant angled his heavy-lidded, black-eyed gaze up to her face. His strong, handsome features suddenly seemed all masculine angles and planes. “You tell me, Jacey. What am I doing?”

Jacey flicked her gaze down to her hand in his. “You’re kissing me.”

“Uh-uh.” He let go of her hand and, with his hand now cupping the back of her head, he pulled her to him. “Now I’m kissing you.”

The Lawless Women Series
by Cheryl Anne Porter
from St. Martin's Paperbacks

HANNAH'S PROMISE

JACEY'S RECKLESS HEART

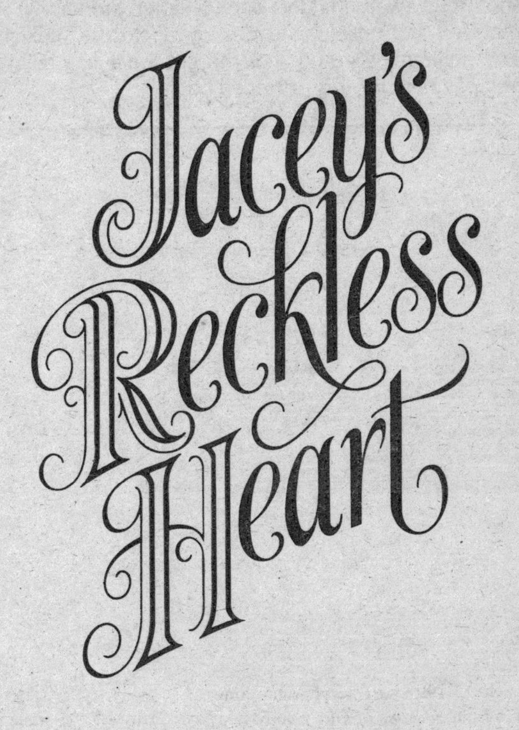

Jacey's Reckless Heart

CHERYL ANNE PORTER

St. Martin's Paperbacks

JACEY'S RECKLESS HEART

ISBN: 0-312-96332-7

Printed in the United States of America

St. Martin's Paperbacks edition/December 1997

St. Martin's Paperbacks are published by St. Martin's Press, 175 Fifth Avenue, New York, NY 10010.

10 9 8 7 6 5 4 3 2 1

The *Lawless Women* trilogy is dedicated to the memory of Jimmie H. Deal, Sr., my beloved father who passed away on December 24, 1995.

PROLOGUE

"That thieving, no-good polecat will pay. I swear he will. I'll find him, whoever he is. And with my boot on his neck, with my name being the last words he hears, and with Papa's gun in my hand, he'll die. No one steals from me. He'll die, and I'll be glad. Do you hear me, Glory? I'll be glad."

Hannah's letter fisted in her hand, Jacey paced her ranch home's great room. With every turn that brought Glory into view, she glared her anger at her younger sister. "I know I promised Hannah I'd stay here with you and Biddy while she's in Boston. And I have for the last month. But this letter"—she shook it—"this letter changes everything. Tomorrow, I ride for Tucson."

Jacey watched as Glory's green eyes filled with tears. *Here it comes,* she sighed. Sure enough, Glory put a hand to her mouth and shook her head. "Please don't go, Jacey. If you leave, I won't have any family here. None."

"Oh, for—Quit your crying. I have to go. Besides, you won't be alone. Biddy's here. And Smiley and the men are back from the cattle drive."

Glory nodded and swiped at her eyes. "I know all that. But Jacey, first Mama and Papa are . . . murdered. And then Hannah leaves for Boston. And now you're going to Tucson. What am I supposed to do?"

For a long moment, Jacey stared levelly at her sister. "I don't know, Glory. You're a grown woman now. You tell me what you're supposed to do."

Glory's pouting doll-face only made Jacey more impatient.

Mama'd babied the nineteen-year-old girl until she couldn't do a thing for herself. That perfect little form, her auburn hair, her wide green eyes, and her helpless pose always got her what she wanted. Well, not now. Times were different. Mama and Papa were gone. Glory'd just have to get tough to survive. Starting now. "Glory, I don't mean to hurt your feelings. But I'm leaving tomorrow, and I have plans to make. I don't have time to stand here holding your hand."

When Glory's pouting frown only deepened, Jacey took a deep breath and let it out slowly. Shaking her head, feeling her heavy black braid swing with her movement, she fought for calm. "Try to understand. I *have* to do this. It's killing me to sit here, Glory. I should've gone to Boston with Hannah. She's all alone with those murdering Wilton-Humeses." Jacey pounded her fist into her other palm. "Those rich, uppity snakes-in-the-grass. Mama's own family. And then to have her and Papa killed . . . And what do I do about it? I sit here like a clucking hen on a nest. Well, I can't do it anymore. I'll go crazy."

Glory's tears dried instantly. Her face darkened with . . . could it be? . . . anger. "I'd rather you go crazy here than go get yourself killed over a missing keepsake and a piece of spur. That's all you really have, Jacey. A piece of silver spur and a sliver of wood frame from Great-grandmother Ardis's portrait. With nothing more than that, you're going to race off to Tucson?"

Astonished at Glory's tirade, Jacey could almost smile at this first sign of gumption from the family's youngest. But she didn't dare. Not in this instance. So, with slow, measured steps, her booted feet scuffing across the wood floor, she advanced on Glory. "You're danged right I am. This piece of spur"—she held up the spikelike rowel she'd just strung through the silver chain around her neck—"is an exact match with Papa's. And I should know. Which one of us three girls spent the most time listening to his stories of his outlaw days? Who's held and admired his silver spurs maybe a thousand times? Me, Glory."

She paused to allow that to sink in before going on. "And now this broken-off rowel turns up here. In our house. It's not off Papa's. I've got his up in my room. So it's got to belong to someone else in the Lawless gang. And where are those men still? In Tucson. So, that's where I'm headed."

Again, she paused, staring at Glory. "The same son of a gun who left his spur calling card also took that portrait. You know he did. We—you and me, not ten minutes ago—searched Mama's room and didn't find it. And where were you when I tripped over that rug by the fireplace and came up with these things tangled together? Wasn't that you standing next to me? So, how'd they get there, Glory? Was there a fight? If so, who was in it, and why? All I've got is questions. You got any answers?"

Glory's chin came up a notch. "No, I don't. But what does it all prove? Please—just once, Jacey—*think* before you go off half-cocked. Read Hannah's letter again. It's just a passing notion that makes her even mention Mama's keepsake. She's not asking you to look for clues. All she wrote was she saw the original portrait at Cloister Point. And it started her thinking . . . where was Mama's copy?"

With her last words, Glory's face darkened. She spun around, fisting her hands at her sides. Her voice choked with emotion. "For God's sake, Jacey, Hannah was only curious. Nothing more. Why can't you let it go?"

"Let it go?" Jacey stalked over to her sister and spun her around. "I cannot believe we read the same letter. Don't you get it, Glory? The portrait is *gone*. And it's the *only* thing missing from . . . that day. Why is that, do you suppose? I'll tell you why—because someone from the old gang came here and stole that keepsake. The spur proves who it was. Trust me, this is no coincidence. It happened *the same day,* Glory. It had to have, because we were gone only that one night."

Jacey searched Glory's eyes for understanding. "Aren't you the least bit curious about *why*? I know I am. I've got to go to Tucson—to find out the why of it. And mark my words, I'll get my keepsake back and make some sorry old outlaw pay with his life for ever taking it in the first place."

Glory's frown creased her brow. "I understand how you feel, Jacey. I do. No one knows better than me what that little oil painting meant to Mama. And I know what it means to you. I do remember her saying that when she died, she wanted you to have it. But you can't—"

"I can't what? Get back what's rightfully mine? That little oil painting, as you call it, is of the only Wilton-Humes that

Mama gave a fig about. And she wanted me to have it, Glory. Me." Jacey swallowed around the sudden constriction in her throat. "She said I have Ardis's spunk. Her fire. Mama loved that old woman, and I reminded her of her."

Jacey's face worked with the depth of her emotion. When she could safely speak again, she went on. "But now, she and Papa have been taken from us. There's not a blamed thing I can do to bring them back, but I can sure as shooting get back her keepsake. And I will. It's mine now. So whoever took it, stole it from me." Her chest rising and falling in the deep, even breaths of firm conviction, Jacey awaited her sister's response.

For long moments, Glory stared at her. Then, without a word, she stepped around Jacey, who turned to watch her go. Head erect, her bearing queenly, Glory walked across the big comfortable room that retained the memory of the Lawless girls' childhood laughter and tears. When she reached the stairs and put her foot on the first riser, then laid her hand on the railing, she finally turned to face Jacey.

"You *are* trying to bring Mama and Papa back, Jacey. That's what this is all about, even if you won't admit it. But I know you—you're still going to try. Once you set your mind to something, no one and nothing—not God, and not reasoning—can stop you. So, go. And don't worry about me or Biddy or the ranch. Like you said, I have to grow up."

Tears stood again in Glory's eyes, and then spilled unheeded down her steadily pinkening cheeks. "But don't expect me to see you off tomorrow. Don't expect me to wave as you ride off to what could be *your* death, and not some sorry old outlaw's." She glared for a moment and then added, "I, for one, have had enough of death."

With that, she ascended the stairs. Jacey watched her all the way up, but not once did Glory hesitate or look back. When she was out of sight, when her footfalls no longer echoed upstairs in the hallway, and a door could be heard closing, Jacey looked down at her hand, at her older sister's now crumpled letter. Dry-eyed, she lifted her gaze to the impassive stairway, set against the great room's far wall.

She relaxed her fist. Hannah's letter fluttered to the floor. Jacey then clasped the jagged piece of spur on her chain. She gripped it so tightly that its edges cut into her palm.

* * *

The next morning, in the middle of a blustery October in 1873, Jacey raced away from the Lawless spread out in No Man's Land. She urged Knight into a thundering gallop. His black mane and tail flying, his neck stretched out, the gelding's muscled body sped over the familiar terrain in long, ground-covering strides. Jacey tautened the reins, twisting them around her hands as she hunched forward in her saddle to ride low over her mount's neck.

Farther and farther away his thudding hooves carried her, farther from the safety of the ranch. From Glory and Biddy. From the hill out back of the house. From the weeks-old graves and white crosses there. From her grief and her broken heart.

Knight's coarse mane whipped across Jacey's face and stung her cheeks. When her gelding capped the hillock that would give her a last view of her home, she reined her laboring mount to a halt. Straightening in the saddle, she turned him in a tight circle, controlling him with her knees and the reins until she could see her home. As she swept her gaze over the shallow valley, her only thought was . . . if things didn't work out the way she hoped in Tucson, she may not see this piece of land or what was left of her family ever again.

Blanking her mind to such notions, Jacey settled her gaze on the Lawless cattle ranch, situated deep in the desolate and windswept plains west of the Cherokee Strip. She picked out people made tiny by distance, but people no less precious to her, even if she never could find the words to tell them so.

There stood Glory. She'd said she wouldn't see her off. But she had at the last minute. Next to her was Biddy. The two stood on the verandah. Tiny, alone, and staring after her, they waved. Jacey raised her hand in a final farewell. A twinge of guilt pricked at her and brought her hand down.

She *had* to do this. Didn't anyone else besides her realize that? She had to. With her anger and grief all knotted up in her soul, Jacey reasoned that if she didn't do this one thing, if she didn't right this one wrong, then she couldn't call herself the daughter of J. C. Lawless, the most notorious outlaw in the West in his day.

Papa. Jacey's throat worked convulsively. *I'll find him, Papa, and I'll take his life, and I'll get Mama's precious keep-*

sake back. I know you'd do the same thing for her if you were alive. She coughed hard and scrubbed her sleeve under her nose. That infernal dry wind was blowing the dust around. Always made her tear up something fierce.

Fighting the . . . prairie dust, Jacey blinked wetly. *Not accomplishing a danged thing sitting here.* But still, she sat there, not turning Knight, not urging the black horse toward the trail that led to Tucson.

Just then, she saw Biddy hug Glory. Jacey's chin quivered. She was going to miss her sister. And too, their old nanny's lectures to her about her cussing and about how she never acted like a lady. Biddy always said that she and Mama'd done the best they could with such a tomboyish child. Always carrying on about how Jacey should wear a dress and act like the lady she was raised to be.

A lady. From under the brim of her black felt slouch hat, Jacey looked down at her split riding skirt, loose blouse, leather vest, and boots. Papa's Colt nested in its holster low on her hip. A beaded knife sheath, encasing a long, thin blade, snugly encompassed her right thigh. And her thick black braid trailed past her waist. Be a lady. Ha. Where she was headed, being a lady could get her killed.

Jacey thought of the long, lonely trip ahead of her to Tucson in the Arizona Territory. She steeled her resolve by pressing her thumb against her left middle finger and rubbing over its pad in slow circles. She'd pricked this finger for the blood oath with her sisters on the day they buried their parents. The wound in her finger, unlike the one in her heart of hearts, was healed.

Jacey saw again herself and Hannah and Glory making the simple pact, promising that the cold-blooded murderers would pay. With their lives. Hannah'd see to her end of the bargain in Boston, where she went with her evidence to confront Mama's family. And as for her?

Jacey turned Knight, urging him down the far slope of the hill. As for her—Jacey Catherine—the one most like Papa, the one named after him—she was riding for Tucson. Papa's old stronghold.

And when she got there, somebody was going to die.

Chapter One

"For J. C. Lawless. For Catherine Lawless. Vengeance."

Like stones, Hannah's remembered words pelted Jacey's spirit. Trail-worn and saddle-weary, she pulled herself upright when, rounding the pass in the Santa Catalina Mountains, Tucson took shape down on the desert floor.

As Knight continued his plodding pace alongside a caravan of wagons, Jacey let out the breath she felt she'd been holding all the way here. There it was. Tucson. The city that'd been a Lawless Gang refuge over twenty-five years ago. The city where Papa'd kidnapped Mama for ransom, but had instead fallen in love with the Boston debutante and married her. He'd even, over the protests of his gang, returned the ransom money to her family.

"Vengeance." That one word had sustained Jacey all the way from No Man's Land to the Arizona Territory. And now, here was Tucson, the city that harbored men who had some answering to do. And answer they would—to her, the daughter of J. C. Lawless. They'd find no refuge in Tucson now. Not so long as there was breath in her body.

She'd come a long, hard way for answers. Every mile imprinted itself in her bones. From home, she'd ridden over the waterless Cimarron Cutoff and connected with the long lines of wagons on the Santa Fe Trail. After resting a day in the adobe town of Santa Fe, she'd set off on Cooke's Route, which meandered southward alongside the Rio Grande. Then, northwest of El Paso, she'd finally joined up with the California-bound folks taking the Apache Pass on the Gila Trail.

And she'd ridden that trail all the way to Tucson. Jacey's

dusty clothes and slumping spirit testifed to the weeks of hard trudging, weeks of low prairies and high mountains, and weeks of rain or relentless sun that she'd lived through just to get here. They were weeks of danger, weeks of wariness. Weeks of mourning for Mama and Papa. But finally, they were at an end. Except for the mourning. That would never end.

Jacey reined in Knight, off to one side of the trail. Several wagons passed her, a few folks called out their good-byes. Jacey waved a hand in farewell, at once grateful for their company and grateful for their leave-taking. From here on out, she needed to be unknown. When her big black gelding shifted his weight and pawed the sandy desert ground, Jacey smoothed a hand over his withers.

"You hankering to ride into Tucson, Knight? Well, let's look it over and see what we're in for," she crooned softly to him.

Lifting her black felt hat and rubbing her sleeve across her sweating forehead, Jacey made an assessing sweep of the village below her. There was the army fort folks'd spoken of. Fort Lowell, they'd called it. Wasn't much to see. Mostly just wood sheds. Moving her gaze on, she focused on Tucson's cluster of adobe buildings that squatted staunchly in the afternoon's hot sun, their dried-mud roofs blending with the surrounding desert. Jacey then made a sweep of the narrow, twisting streets below her and dismissed them as not looking much different from Santa Fe's.

She next looked to the south, spotting a starkly white mission church. Like those she'd seen in Santa Fe. Shifting her gaze back northward, back to Tucson, she focused on impressive stands of huge cacti—those saguaros Papa'd always talked about. Like sentinels with their arms raised in challenge, they stood protectively around the city.

When Knight again shifted his weight and shook his head, Jacey resettled her hat low on her brow. "You're right. We're not gaining anything sittin' here."

She urged her restive mount forward. From the relative sanctuary of the foothills, horse and rider moved out onto the open valley floor. While glad to be at trail's end, Jacey nevertheless felt exposed, felt like hidden eyes were watching her. Like they knew the daughter of J. C. Lawless was coming for them. They'd not greet her with a warm smile and a welcoming wave, either.

That was fine with her. She wasn't here for a homecoming. But she'd be willing to bet that Tucson would be glad to see her leave.

"Hey, Chapelo, take a look at what's riding up the street—and all alone, too."

His booted feet crossed on a rough-hewn table, a half-empty bottle of rotgut whiskey in one hand, a shot glass in the other, Zant Chapelo turned his blurry gaze to Blue. "Give me more of a reason to get up, *amigo*."

Blue stepped back from the swinging doors and turned to Zant, showing him an eager-eyed expression. "There's a woman just ridin' into town. She's a good-lookin' woman, from what I can see."

Zant snorted his opinion of that as he measured out a stiff shot of the liquor. "Good-lookin', huh?" He then hoisted the bottle by its neck, using it as pointer. "So's Rosie, and she's right over there. Now *she* doesn't require me gettin' up to look at her."

He tossed his drink back and contorted his face into a grimace. He eyed the bottle as if it were responsible for its contents. "This stuff tastes like panther piss. Don't know why I keep drinking it."

When Blue, his spurs jangling, strode noisily over to Zant's table and flung himself into the chair opposite him, Zant looked at the kid the same way he had the bottle.

The lean, blond and blue-eyed, sober *pistolero* crossed his arms on the table and leaned forward. "Zant, I been sittin' in this saloon for the past two days watchin' you drink yourself stupid. Now, this ain't what Señor Calderon told me to do. He told me to find you and bring you home pronto. But I ain't takin' you back to Sonora in this shape."

Zant eyed him silently. Blue smacked the table and leaned over it. "Look at you. Pigs wouldn't be seen in your company. You need to get yourself sober and get a bath, a shave, and a decent meal. If you don't care about yourself, at least give a thought to your grandfather."

"To hell with my grandfather." Zant's flippant tone of voice belied his curse. "Which one of us, me or you, just got out of that Mexican prison after serving five years for something he didn't do?''

Blue huffed out a breath and answered, ''You.''

Zant nodded and quirked a cock-eyed grin. ''That's right, *amigo*. And which one of us hasn't seen the inside of a cantina or tasted liquor or seen a woman for those same five years? Me, right? So, one thing you need to know, Blue—I'm just gettin' started.''

The kid huffed out his disgust and shook his head. ''Is that all you got to say for yourself?''

Zant shrugged. ''It's enough. For now.'' He then narrowed his eyes at his childhood friend. ''No, I've got one more thing to say. Don't ever throw Don Rafael up to me, Blue. I've already been home and paid my respects to the old man. So, for the last time—I'm not going back. And don't push me. Because I'm in no mood to be pushed.''

Zant outstared Blue. The kid made a disgusted noise and pulled his weight up out of his chair. He hitched at his gunbelt and turned his head to spit on the scuffed, tobacco-stained wooden floor. ''Suit yourself.''

Zant set the bottle on the table and raised his next drink like a toast. ''I always do.''

Blue scowled and shook his head. ''Yeah, you do, don't you? Can't nobody help Zant Chapelo. I don't think those five years in a cell taught you anything. Señor Calderon should've left you there to rot. He never should've hunted all over hell and half of Mexico to find you and then pay your way out. Because you're still hell-bent on destroyin' the old man—''

''You shut your damned mouth. You don't have any idea what you're talking about because you don't know him like I do.'' The chair's two front legs hit the floor, the table scraped forward, and Zant was on his feet, the bottle and shot glass forgotten as they both spilled and rolled across the floor.

He heard Rosie gasp, saw her, from the corner of his eye, duck behind the long bar with Alberto. The other customers sought their own refuge wherever they could find it. But not Blue. He didn't flinch. He stood his ground. Which made Zant see red.

He flipped the table out of his way and stepped up to the kid, getting in his face, his nose practically touching Blue's. The two, both six feet tall, stood eye to eye. ''If you're so all-fired determined to preach, Blue, then heist your sorry butt on down to the mission church. Otherwise, shut the hell up and let me drink in peace. You got that?''

Blue shook his head. ''No, I ain't got that. But you got this—and you've had it comin' since we were kids.'' With that, Blue stepped back and punched Zant in the jaw, sending him staggering back and sprawling over tables.

Zant ended up on the floor, sitting on his own sorry butt. ''Son of a bitch,'' he muttered, rubbing his jaw. Then he was on his feet and launching himself at Blue. Who sidestepped neatly, soberly.

This time, Zant met the floor hard in a belly slide across the greasy wooden floor, only to roll and collide, back first, with the bar's wooden base. He heard Rosie screaming, and he heard Alberto fussing in Spanish about damage to his place of business.

His ears ringing, his head throbbing, Zant pulled himself up drunkenly to lean his elbows on the bar behind him, and saw . . . two Blues. Three Blues. Shaking his head, blinking rapidly, he finally got the three Blues to become one. He then pointed at his friend, who had his fists raised, and bellowed, ''You had enough, boy?''

Blue coiled up like a rattlesnake. ''Who you calling a boy? You're twenty-two—the same age as me. And hell no, I ain't had enough. 'Cause I'm the one kickin' your ass, *amigo*.''

''Like hell you are,'' Zant slurred. He pushed away from the bar and went in a lurching run across the saloon, avoiding cowering patrons and correcting course and grasping at empty air each time Blue danced or darted away—after getting in a lucky punch or two. Dizzy from spinning to hunt Blue and reeling from his punches, Zant grimaced. ''Stand still, you stupid blue-eyed—''

''Why don't you make me? You're too drunk to even defend yourself against someone who gives a damn about you. What if some quick-draw hears Zant Chapelo is out of the hoosegow and decides to come try his gun hand against you? Until last week, you ain't had a gun on in years. You're still rusty. So how're you goin' to be able to outgun him?''

The kid has a point. Zant weaved to a flat-footed stop. And reached for his gun. He didn't have to fight all the Blues. He could just shoot 'em.

He raised his pistol in a wavering aim and . . . couldn't find any Blues. He turned to his left, only to have Blue wrench his gun out of his hand and shove him, with a boot against his butt, right out the saloon's bat-wing doors. Right out into the parched late-afternoon heat of a Tucson day.

Trapped in his own bumbling momentum, Zant careened about with a windmilling of his arms and got his booted feet all tangled in each other, finally stumbling and tripping until he lost his balance. The rock-hard, dusty street collided with him in a solid thud of bone and muscle.

Lying sunny-side up and right under the hooves of a rearing black horse, Zant froze and stared up at death.

"Zant! Get the hell outta the way, man!"

Blue's shouted warning galvanized Zant into doing just that. Two deft rolls saw him beyond the reach of the horse's stiff-legged, dust-stirring crash back to earth. Just then, a woman screamed. Zant sat up and flipped back around. A black hat went flying through the air. A flurry of unseated arms and legs and long black braid followed it as the horse's rider was thrown over its bucking head. She hit the ground hard and rolled three or four times, finally pitching onto her side, still and lifeless.

Too stunned to do much but stare, Zant flicked his gaze to Blue as he barreled through the cantina's bat-wing doors. He jumped clear of Zant and grabbed up the panicked black's trailing reins. With hushed and soothing sounds, the blond kid quieted the animal and backed him a safe distance away. As if he'd been ordered to, Zant numbly watched as Blue tied the horse to a hitching rail.

"La muchacha. Señor Chapelo, la muchacha!"

Zant turned to Rosie when she cried out. The pretty little Mexican barmaid stood next to her father and clutched at his sleeve. They both stared wide-eyed, looking past Zant and pointing out into the street.

He spun back around. *La muchacha.* With her back to him, the girl still lay on her side. And she still wasn't moving. Cussing and suddenly sober, Zant jumped up and ran to her. A month out of prison and he'd already caused the death of an innocent woman. *Great.*

When he reached her, he went down on one knee behind

her and put his hand on her shoulder, thinking to turn her toward him. *She surely is a slender little thing. Biggest thing about her is that black braid of hair*—Two shadows fell across him from behind. From long gun-fighting and prison habit, Zant jerked to his feet, his hand on his . . . empty holster. Luckily, it was only Rosie and Alberto. But behind them was a gathering crowd. Just what he needed.

When Blue ran up, skittering to a crowd-parting stop and squatting on one knee in front of the woman, Zant turned his attention back to his friend. Frowning, Blue looked the woman over without touching her. He then looked up at Zant. "Damn, man, that was a close one."

Zant raised an eyebrow. "Close? That horse is a gelding. That's how *close* it was."

"You ain't lyin'." Blue shook his head and huffed out a breath, finally pointing to the girl. "Is she dead? That was a mighty mean spill she took."

Zant put his hands to his waist and frowned down at Blue. "You're just a regular ray of sunshine, aren't you? No, she's not dead."

"How do you know?"

"Because I—" *How did he know?* Zant looked down at Blue's earnest face and then lowered himself again to squat on his haunches. "Because her heart's still beating."

To prove it, he felt for her pulse, but couldn't locate it what with her blouse and vest and her sideways position. Sighing and rolling his eyes, he worked his hand inside the neck of her blouse, around a silver chain tangled in her underclothes, and finally found . . . her breasts . . . *Nice* . . . and then her steadily beating heart between them.

Before he could even sigh in relief, the woman sucked in a huge breath and swung her gloved fist back in an upward arc as she blindly struck out. Zant tried to rear back, but his too-big hand wouldn't come free. Her small fist connected with his nose, forcing an involuntary yell out of him as he jerked backward and tore his hand loose. And tore her blouse open. Cussing for all he was worth, Zant sat down hard on the sandy street, amid the retreating and shocked gasps of the spectators.

"That's the least of what you've got coming, mister, if you ever lay a hand on me again."

He heard her words, heard her scrambling movements, but his eyes remained closed as he braced himself with one hand while he held his other to his aching nose. When Zant finally opened his eyes, when the stars and tears cleared from his vision, he became aware that Blue was now sitting in the dusty street with him. And was laughing like a jackass—while he pointed at him.

"Pretty damned funny, ain't it, Blue?"

Blue grinned and nodded. "Pretty damned funny, *amigo*. I believe the little lady bloodied your nose."

Frowning, Zant swiped his hand under his nose as he looked up and then all around him. *Where the hell is she?* The wide-eyed but hushed crowd began backing up, leaving one lone woman in the ring with him and Blue. Still not facing him, she was on her feet and dusting her clothes with her felt hat.

Zant finally looked at his hand and verified what Blue'd just told him. Blood. He looked up again at the woman's slender back. "Lady, I was trying to help you. You've no cause to bloody my nose like that."

With no reaction to indicate that she'd even heard him, she pushed her way through the curious crowd. *Is she deaf?* Raw anger tugged Zant's mouth down as he wiped his sleeve under his nose and looked at it. No more blood. But that didn't change things. Nobody—man or woman—just poked Zant Chapelo in the nose and walked away without accounting for it.

Zant hauled himself up and made a swiping gesture at the crowd. "Get the hell out of my way."

They did, moving aside to open a wide corridor between him and the swaggering female. Her thick black braid hung down her back and swung like a pendulum back and forth over her split-skirted bottom.

"Now, Zant, don't do anything stup—"

"Shut up, Blue. This is between me and her."

Blue grinned good-naturedly as he rested his arms on his bent knees and shook his head. "All right. But somethin' tells me you're gettin' in over your head."

Zant watched the woman take another step or two before looking down at Blue. "Yeah, well, it won't be the first time."

He then pointed at the woman's back. "Hey, you, I'm talking to you, lady."

All heads turned to stare at the lady. Who kept walking. Like she didn't even hear him. All heads turned back to Zant. He eyed the sober, wide-eyed crowd and felt a heat that had nothing to do with Arizona climbing up his face. A muscle twitched in his jaw. He called out to her again. "Turn around and answer me, woman."

She did neither of those things. Instead, she stepped around to her mount's left, which put the big horse's bulk between her and Zant. All he could see was her black hat. She moved to the horse's head, unhitched him, and easily swung herself up into the saddle. Still not acknowledging him, she silently turned her mount away from the crowd and urged him into a canter.

Frowning like a prison warden, Zant turned to Blue and put his hands to his waist. "She can't just ride away like that. Doesn't she know who I am?"

Once at the other end of Tucson, Jacey slowed Knight to a walk. Shaking like a scared dog, her whole body aching as much as her right hand, she transferred the reins to her left hand and slowly worked her leather riding glove off. She stared at her swelling knuckles. *So that's how it feels to hit a man.*

It hurt. That's how it felt. But it didn't hurt as much as being thrown from her horse. Good thing Papa'd raised her in the saddle and taught her how to land and roll when thrown. Otherwise, she might not be alive right now to moan like a baby over her aches and pains.

Threading her way through the wagon traffic, and keeping an eye on the folks afoot out in the street, she urged Knight into a relatively cool and shaded alley between two adobe buildings. There she turned him and reined to a stop.

She worked her gun hand, fisting and unfisting it. Not five minutes in Tucson before she'd gotten into a brawl out in front of a saloon. *Damn!* She'd hoped to slip quietly into town, get an out-of-the-way room, and put her plan into action. If putting out the word that J. C. Lawless was back in town worked the way she hoped it would, she'd be riding for home in a few days.

But now? Well, now word would spread like wildfire about the woman who'd bloodied some drunk's nose when he shied her horse, got her thrown, and then stuffed his hand down her blouse. Jacey fumed as a blaze of heat suffused her cheeks. Again she felt the indignity of the thrusting hand on her flesh, heard her blouse tearing.

Lucky for him she hadn't pulled her thigh-strapped knife. Because she'd have been more than happy to bury it in the same place on him where his hand had been on her. If she ever saw that no-good, low-down—*No*. She took a deep breath and willed her thoughts away from the rough moments she'd just survived.

She then looked again at her puffy knuckles and groaned. That lousy drunk's nose surely was hard. By tomorrow her whole hand would be stiff, most likely. And that would considerably slow down her quick draw for days. *Dang him!* Now she'd have to lie low while she healed. Just hole up in some stuffy room and mend. And hide from the world. Angry, close to defeat, Jacey put a hand over her eyes, hitching irritably at Knight's reins when he balked suddenly.

"*Señorita?* Are you hurt?"

Jacey started and lowered her hand from her face. There, standing about a pace or two in front of her and Knight, was a pretty Mexican girl dressed in a loose white blouse and brightly patterned skirt and a bunch of silver jewelry. A half-smile rode her lips as her wide brown eyes invited trust.

Unsmiling, Jacey eyed her. "I'm fine."

"*Que bien*. My father and I were afraid for you when you took that fall from such a big horse."

So she'd seen that. And followed her. "I'm fine," Jacey repeated, wanting like crazy for this nice, concerned girl to clear out of her business. She wasn't here to meet folks.

The girl's smile faltered, but still she nodded in a friendly manner and didn't go away. "That man back there"—she jerked her thumb over her shoulder to indicate the street behind her—"he is not so bad."

Jacey snorted her opinion of that as she pointedly tugged her blouse closed. "I was in a better position to judge that than you were."

Now the girl laughed. A pleasant sound. *Go away*. "Perhaps

you are right.'' She shrugged her slim shoulders and took hold of her skirt. ''But I am bothering you. I will go now.'' She started to turn away, but immediately turned back to Jacey. *''Me llamo Rosarita Estrada.''*

Jacey frowned and shook her head. ''I don't speak Mexican. What'd you say?''

''I said my name is Rosarita Estrada. But the men, they call me Rosie. You can, too.''

''Row-cee?'' Jacey tried the name, giving it the same inflection the girl had. It sounded funny on her tongue. ''You mean . . . like Rosie?''

''*Sí.* Like Rosie.''

When Rosie stared at her and smiled, Jacey knew she was expected to give her name in return. But it was too soon for that. So, instead, she just said, ''Well . . . thank you for checking on me.''

Rosie nodded. ''I will thank my father for you. It was he who sent me.'' She then cocked her head as she looked Jacey up and down. ''He says there is something about you, something he knows.'' In another quick change of mood, she roused herself with a dismissive gesture and laughed. ''You must think us *loco,* eh? *Por nada*—it was nothing, my seeing to you. You would do the same for me, no?''

Jacey almost said no right back to her. She knew she wouldn't have come to check on this girl, had she been the witness and not the one thrown. But she caught herself and nodded. ''Yeah.''

Rosie put her hands to her slender waist and grinned. ''You are lying to me, *mi amiga.* It is written on your face.''

Jacey stiffened. ''I wouldn't be calling me a liar, if I were you, sister.''

The girl ducked her head in apology. ''I meant no harm. Perhaps I should go now. My father will be worried.''

Finally. But when she turned away, Jacey surprised even herself when she called out. ''Wait!''

Rosie faced her again and raised her finely arched black eyebrows in a wordless question.

Jacey firmed her lips into a frown. ''That man . . . back there. You said he's not so bad. How do you know him?''

Rosie's expression changed to one of amused disbelief. ''I know him from my father's *cantina,* where I work. But I also know him by his reputation. The nose you bloodied belongs to Zant Chapelo. And he will not soon forget it.''

And he will not soon forget it. Jacey's stomach wrenched at those words, but she focused on the man's name. What with Rosie's heavy accent, all Jacey could do was frown and repeat, ''Saint Sha-pellow? What kind of a name is that? He didn't look or act much like a saint to me.''

Laughing, Rosie wagged a finger at Jacey, which upset Knight into snorting and backing a step or so. Jacey reined him in and frowned at Rosie's amusement. ''Did I say something funny?''

''*Sí.* Very funny. That one—he is no saint. The holy cross itself would fall off the wall at San Xavier del Bac if Zant Chapelo were to darken the mission's door.'' She made the sign of the cross on herself.

Jacey watched her go through the motions and swallowed. If all that was called for, then the man was pretty bad, no matter what Rosie'd said a minute ago. Something wasn't adding up here. And now that she kept repeating the name in her head, kept sounding it out, his name was beginning to sound familiar. Too familiar.

Saint Sha-pellow. Saint. No, she said it more like Sant. Sha-pellow. Sant Cha-pellow. Zant Chapelo. Zant Chapelo? Jacey jerked upright and stared straight ahead, barely able to get a breath past her aching lungs.

''*Señorita,* what is it?''

Jacey held up her hand. ''Hold on a minute. Don't say anything. And don't leave.'' Staring at Rosie, but not really seeing her, Jacey gave herself over to the memory which flooded her with Papa's voice. She again heard him talking about Kid Chapelo. The Kid rode with Papa in his outlaw days. But Papa'd always talked the man down, said he was a hothead, had a real nasty streak. The way Jacey remembered the story was the Kid had forced Papa to—

A sinking feeling, like she'd been exposed to too much heat, swept over Jacey. The Kid had forced Papa to shoot him dead. Papa had killed Kid Chapelo. *Oh, Lordy.*

But Papa never would say exactly what had happened to make them draw on each other. He and Mama would just exchange a serious look when it came up. Could this Zant—a man she'd just humiliated—be some of the Kid's family?

Jarred by that thought, and blinking as if just waking up after a long sleep, Jacey focused on the quietly attentive Mexican girl in front of her and dismounted as she spoke. "Rosie, where's this Chapelo from?"

Rosie shrugged as Jacey approached her. "Sonora. Just across the border in Mexico. His *abuelo*—his grandfather—is a very important man there. He owns *mucha tierra*—much land. And much cattle. Very rich. Do you know him?"

Jacey nodded before she could stop herself. *So this Chapelo is from Meh-hi-co,* pronouncing it for herself as Rosie'd said it. *Papa'd said something about the Kid and Mexico. But what?* Not able to come up with it, Jacey again focused on the girl, shook her head, and cleared her expression. "No. No, I don't know him."

Rosie cocked her head and pointed that wagging finger at Jacey. Again. "*Sí.* You do know him. You are not a good liar, *mi amiga.*"

Jacey put her hands to her waist. "I tell you what, Rosie—one more time you call me a liar, and you better be danged sure you're armed and ready to back it up. Now, what's that other name you keep calling me?"

Rosie smiled. "'*Amiga*'? It means 'friend.' I'm calling you my friend. You do not tell me your name"—she shrugged with graceful nonchalance—"so I must call you my friend."

Jacey snorted her opinion of that. "You've no cause to call me friend. You don't know me."

Rosie laughed. "Eh, you are a hard one, *no, mi amiga*?"

"No," came Jacey's immediate response. Then she frowned. "I mean yes. Yes, I am."

Her words denied it, but Jacey was intrigued by this notion of a friend. Especially someone who knew the lay of things in these parts. So, making her mind up, she quelled the tiny voice of protest in her head, a voice that warned she knew nothing of this girl, and stuck her hand out. "Sorry for being so rude a minute ago. I'm pleased to meet you. My name's Jacey Lawless."

Rosie's smile, which began when Jacey stuck her hand out, ran away from her face. The girl slowly lowered her hand to her side and stared wide-eyed at Jacey. "*Madre de Dios.*" She then crossed herself—twice. "Ay-yi-yi." She shook her head slowly and blinked more than once. Then, looking all around, she whispered, "We got to get you out of here. *Ahora*—now! You and your *caballo* must come with me." She reached out toward Knight's bridle.

Jacey could have kicked herself. She should have listened to that voice in her head. Not surprised but still stung by the girl's reaction, Jacey stepped back. "Me and my . . . *caballo* aren't going anywhere—with you or anyone else."

Rosie firmed up her expression, even narrowing her eyes like a mother to her naughty child. "*Sí*—yes, you are. If Zant Chapelo learns that a Lawless bloodied his nose, he will kill you." For emphasis, she drew her finger across her throat, like a knife slitting it.

Jacey raised an eyebrow at this bit of theatrics. She'd just learned two things. One, the Lawless name still held sway in Papa's old stomping grounds. And, two, it meant something to Zant Chapelo. She was right, then—he was related to Kid Chapelo. Closely related, she'd bet. *Does he have on his spurs?* she wondered.

But out loud to Rosie, she challenged, "So you think he'd slit my throat? Well, you tell him for me that had I known it was a Chapelo sticking his hand down my blouse, I would have killed him right then and there. Better yet, I would've let my . . . *caballo* stomp him to death before he ever got the chance."

Rosie began backing up and shaking her head. "No. I cannot tell him these things. You do not understand this man, *mi amiga*."

Jacey advanced a step on the girl, holding Knight's reins tighter than necessary as he trailed behind her. Pressing Rosie, hoping she'd reveal more about this Chapelo, Jacey taunted, "Maybe I'll just tell him myself."

Rosie shook her head with enough emotion to swing her unbound, waist-length black hair all around her. "You cannot. I say this for your sake. You are as good as dead if you challenge Chapelo. And it will not matter to him that you are a woman—because you are also a Lawless."

"Good. Because it won't matter to me that he's a man. Or a Chapelo."

Rosie didn't end her retreat until the afternoon's sunshine spilled across her. Jacey, undecided about following her or not, stayed deep in the alley's cool shadows. Frowning, she tried to keep Rosie in her sight as folks ambling by stepped between her and the other girl. Finally catching sight of her, Jacey saw Rosie look both ways out in the crowded street and then elbow between two sombreroed misters and return to the alley's mouth.

Looking mighty vexed, the Mexican girl leaned toward Jacey and spoke in a low hiss. "*Por favor*—please. If you won't come with me, then you must leave Tucson now—while you can. Forget that he is here."

Her comeback to that already on the tip of her tongue, Jacey opened her mouth. But the words never left her throat because Rosie darted a glance to her left, gasped, and abruptly turned around, only to smack into two bonneted women behind her. What happened next was blocked from Jacey's view by the passing crowd. Frustrated, more than a little concerned, she kicked at the sandy ground in frustration.

And then froze when Rosie reappeared at the alley's entrance, just as suddenly as she'd disappeared. Only this time, she wasn't alone. Zant Chapelo was with her. Shock sucked the juice out of Jacey and dried her mouth. The man's back was to her, but if he turned the slightest. . . .

She didn't even dare finish her thought as, hand over her own mouth, she helplessly watched the scene between Chapelo and Rosie. The man, who no longer moved or spoke as if drunk, stood with one knee bent and his thumbs hitched in his gunbelt. "Did you find who you were huntin', Rosie?"

Jacey didn't hear Rosie's answer because her mind was screaming, *Rosie'd followed her, and he'd followed Rosie*. But how long had Chapelo been standing off to a side before Rosie'd spotted him? Long enough to know she'd been speaking to someone in this very alley?

Fear-induced sweat meandered down Jacey's spine. Her heart pounding, her clothes clinging damply to her, she forced her attention back to the scene before her. She saw her new friend grab Chapelo by his arms—effectively holding him in place. Relief swept over Jacey with the thought that the man probably would not have left his back open to a bullet, if he thought he wasn't alone with the girl. She relaxed and lowered her hand to her side.

God bless Rosie, she was flirting outrageously. And obviously protecting Jacey's presence. That said something about the Mexican girl. "Señor Chapelo, shame on you. Why are you following me? You better not let my father know you do this. He will get his gun to you."

Señor Chapelo didn't say anything for a moment. But when he did, his tone of voice clearly said he wasn't the least bit sidetracked. "Well, we wouldn't want that, now would we? Where is she, Rosie?"

When Jacey was suddenly nudged forward, as if in answer to the man's question, she swallowed a startled breath and clamped her hand back over her own mouth. *Who—?* But then she remembered who was behind her. Knight. She quickly stepped back farther into the shadows, pulling down on the reins and putting a hand over the gelding's muzzle to keep him quiet. If Zant Chapelo turned around right now, she would be trapped. And from what Rosie'd told her, he wouldn't hesitate to shoot her.

With that thought, her gaze slipped down to the man's hip. That was a pretty big Colt strapped there. She then looked him up and down. He was big, too. That sinking feeling swept over her again. He was really big. Why, his shoulders came close to rivaling the alley's width. His lean waist tapered to narrow hips and muscular legs under his close-fitting denims. He was most certainly a powerfully built man. He looked like he could snap her in two with one hand. Then, biting at her bottom lip and fingering the bit of broken spur on the silver chain around her neck, she looked to his boot heels.

And sucked in a breath through her dread-pinched nostrils. No spurs. On her way into town, Jacey'd observed that nearly to a man, the gunslinger types she'd passed wore spurs. So why wasn't Chapelo sporting any? She glanced up at the back of his head, as if she could read his mind for her answer. But all she saw, under a wide-brimmed black felt hat, was hair as black as her own that lay over his shirt's collar.

Zant Chapelo. He had more reason to want her dead than she did him, she figured. After all, if he wasn't the thief she was after, then she had no quarrel with him. But, on the other hand, she was Jacey Catherine Lawless, daughter of J. C. Lawless—the man who'd killed his kin, maybe his father. And like Rosie'd said, it probably wouldn't matter to him that she was a woman, if it was vengeance he was after.

Suddenly wanting to be as far away from Zant Chapelo as

she could get, Jacey looked back over her shoulder to the other open end of the alley. She swung her gaze back to Knight, then to Chapelo, and then back down to the alley's exit. And slumped. She didn't dare try backing the cantankerous gelding all the way to the next street. The big horse, never too well behaved for long, wouldn't go without a fuss if she forced him blindly backward.

And Zant Chapelo was kicking up enough of a fuss right now for both of them. Jacey forced a calmness on herself that she didn't feel, and listened to Chapelo's raised voice. "Dammit, Rosie. I saw you take off after her. I swear I'm not going to shoot her. Just tell me where—"

"No, I will not. I mean—I cannot. I do not know where she is." Rosie, all but lost to view on the other side of the big man, didn't sound the least bit afraid of him. But then again, she wasn't the one who'd bloodied his nose and then turned her back on him. And her last name wasn't Lawless.

Chapelo exhaled noisily, effectively signaling his disgust. "Fine. I'll find her myself. But when you see her, tell her I'm looking for her."

Rosie didn't say anything. Jacey figured that wasn't a good sign. Shouldn't she have been protesting that she didn't know where she was, that she wouldn't be seeing her? "Tell me this, Señor Chapelo. This *muchacha*—what do you want with her?"

Again, Chapelo took his time answering. In those few seconds, Jacey's heart didn't beat—she was sure that Rosie's question was a tactical error. To add to her mounting dismay, Jacey was sure she could hear the wheels turning in the man's head.

He chuckled—and proved her right. "Just as I thought." He nodded several times, and moved his hands from his gunbelt to cross his arms over his chest. "We both know you know where she is. Now, why don't you do me a favor and just tell me?"

Rosie backed up a step. "No. I cannot. I do not know. I must go now." With that, the little barmaid turned. Chapelo grabbed at her, but he was no more successful in keeping her there than Jacey'd been. With a flash of color, she was gone.

Surprisingly, Chapelo didn't give chase. He simply put his hands to his waist and muttered, "Damn." Then, he stepped out of view, going back the same way he'd just come.

Exhaling, Jacey slumped against the adobe wall behind her. Flexing her knees, she leaned her head back against the sun-dried bricks' warmth and closed her eyes. *That was close. Too damned close.*

Just then, Knight snorted and whinnied out his impatience. Jacey sucked in an agitated breath and grabbed for the horse's bridle. In the next instant, she came close to jumping out of her skin when, right behind her, Chapelo asked, "What's wrong? Can't find anyone to poke in the nose?"

Chapter Two

Her heart pounding, her bones liquefying, Jacey jerked around.

Chapelo snaked a big hand out and grabbed her arm. His grip was tight, painful. "Uh-uh. You're not going anywhere, little lady. You and I've got some unfinished business to attend to."

Almost before the whiskey-scented words were out of his mouth, Jacey had her Colt out and the tip of the barrel jutting into the soft flesh under his chin. With his combined scents of sweat, liquor, and male flaring her nostrils, she cocked her gun with more canyon-sized bravado than she felt. "Take your hand off me. That's twice I've had to tell you in one hour. I won't warn you again."

He let go of her. Like he would a scorpion. And raised his hands high. "Easy does it, ma'am. No harm intended." His voice was somewhat garbled, having to talk around the business end of a Colt like he was.

"Yeah, I'll just bet. Now, you listen carefully to me. We don't have any unfinished business between us. So don't follow me anymore. And don't try to find me. In fact, if you see me coming up the street, you cross to the other side. Now . . . do we understand each other?"

In the gray-black shadows, Jacey thought she saw the man grin. *With a Colt stuck up under his chin, he grinned?* That chilled her more than any January blizzard back home could. She stepped back, keeping her gun aimed at his heart. Chapelo kept his hands raised while he answered. "We understand each other, *gringa.* Completely. There's only one problem."

Jacey cussed herself for letting her danged curiosity get the better of her. "What problem is that?"

"I don't know what you look like—other'n black hair and one hell of a right hook. But hell, that describes me, too. Now, that being the case, how will I know for sure it's you, so I can cross the street? All I've seen is your backside, lady, and right now I can't see you clearly for your hat and the shadows in here."

Jacey quirked her mouth. "Sounds like a personal problem, Chapelo."

She'd said his name. *Mistake.* In the ensuing quiet, Knight again whinnied out his impatience. Passing conversations, mostly in Spanish, wafted into the alley. The sounds of laughter and distant gunfire joined them. Wagons creaked by, horses' hooves thudded in the dusty street. And the rising heat between her and this man's closeness permeated every pore.

"So you do know who I am."

Jacey's mind raced to what Rosie'd said about him. "Everyone knows Zant Chapelo."

Now he chuckled. "So it seems. But I don't know you."

"And you aren't goin' to, either. Now, leave this alley the way you came in. You walk straight across that street so I can see you. And while you're walking, you count to one hundred before you turn around." Already playing with fire, Jacey lit another match. "You *can* count that high, can't you?"

He made a choking noise and then laughed out loud. A clear, ringing, masculine sound that made Jacey jump. "I can. And higher, if need be."

Jacey sobered and let him know that, "One hundred's plenty. Now, go. And keep your hands up and keep facing me until you get out in the street. Then you can put your back to me."

"Yes, ma'am." Briefly ducking his head as if showing respect, he began backing up. But then he stopped.

Jacey tensed her gun hand. "What now?"

"I've just thought of a way for me to know it's you."

Dang him. She was the one with the gun aimed at his heart, and yet he was the one playing with her. "So what is it?"

"Those sweet breasts of yours. They're pretty nice. I feel I'd know you anywhere. But of course, you'd have to be naked—and I've have to have my hands on 'em."

Jacey sucked in a breath of outrage. And squeezed the Colt's trigger.

"Chapelo, it's after suppertime. Where the—? Man, what the hell happened to you?"

"That *gringa* shot me. Help me, Blue. My arm hurts like hell. She shot me in my gun arm."

Leaning weakly against the doorjamb, Zant raised his uninjured arm. Blue immediately draped it around his shoulders and put his other arm around Zant's back. He kicked the door closed behind them and helped Zant to the one chair in his hotel room. "The *gringa* shot you? What *gringa*? Oh, hell, not the one who bloodied your nose?"

"The same," Zant said, groaning as he settled himself on the chair and then gripped his right arm.

Blue put a steadying hand on Zant's shoulder. "She *shot* you? What'd you do?"

Zant chuckled . . . painfully. "I told her she had mighty nice tits."

"You what?" Blue then strung together a random sampling of cuss words before observing, "I'll be taking a dead man home if you run into that woman one more time. Now, sit still. Let me look at it."

"I lost a lot of blood. Ouch! What are you doing? I said it hurts like hell. See if she broke the bone." Zant grimaced and gritted his teeth as he watched Blue tear open his bloodstained shirtsleeve and probe the wound. "My damned gun arm, too."

"I can see that. Now, hold still and let me look. . . ." Blue's voice trailed off as he felt around some more. Done with his examination, he snorted his estimation of the wound. "Nah, you're fine. The bullet just grazed you. Tore out a chunk of hide, but you're okay." He picked up an open whiskey bottle and upended the fiery liquid over Zant's raw wound.

Zant sucked in a huge breath, stared wide-eyed, and then catapulted out of the chair, cussing and yelling and dancing around the room. In his frenzy, he managed to kick over the chair, roll on the bed, hold his arm, and call Blue every name he could think of. But his friend remained unperturbed as he tilted the same bottle to his own lips and drank deeply.

When Zant could breathe and talk again, he was sitting on

the floor with his back against the closed door. "You trying to kill me, Blue?"

Blue wiped at his lips. "No. I'm gonna let the *gringa* do that. You'd already be dead, if her aim was any good."

Zant snorted his opinion of that. "She's got a damned good aim, from where I'm sittin', *compadre*. She meant to shoot me right through the heart, but I jumped out of the way."

Blue laughed. "Not far enough, from the looks of that arm." He then righted the bedside table and set the bottle on it. "Come over here. That rotgut ought to've cleaned your arm up good. Sit on the bed and let me see if I need to sear it."

Zant stayed where he was. "You don't need to sear it."

"I think I do."

"Like hell you do."

Blue shrugged. "Suit yourself."

"I always do."

"At least let me bandage it, Zant. Hell, you're getting blood everywhere. Look at this mess. I gotta sleep here."

"Well, pardon me for being shot. I'll sleep here, and you take my room, if you're that fussy about a little blood."

"Like hell I'll take your room. That little lady might come huntin' you and, thinkin' she has your room, haul off and shoot me. Uh-uh. I'm stayin' right here."

Zant shrugged. "Suit yourself."

Blue's eyes danced with his chuckle. "I always do."

A grimace capped Zant's features. "You're just having a high old time at my expense, aren't you? Some damned woman shoots me—"

"Now that's what I can't figure, Zant. Why do you keep messin' with her? There's a whole lot more willin' women around this town."

"I wasn't looking for her for anything to do with *willing*."

"Yeah? Then why were you? Because she walked away from you?"

"Something like that."

Blue shook his head. "If you don't beat all. Now, do you think you can behave long enough for me to go get some clean bandagin' rags from the clerk?"

Zant nodded, feeling suddenly queasy. "And ask that

Nancy-boy down there to get me a bath sent up, too, and something to eat, will you?''

Zant watched Blue staring at him. With a shake of his head, Blue started across the room. ''Danged nursemaid, that's what I am. I grow up on Señor Calderon's land, hire on as a ranch hand, end up a *pistolero*''—he nudged Zant with his boot's toe, wanting him to move out of the way; Zant scooted over against the wall—''and then I become a nursemaid to the old man's drunken, son of a—'' The door closed behind him.

Zant slumped over to the floor, out cold before his head hit.

Sleepless and edgy, Jacey reflected on her day. Let's see, she'd ridden into Tucson, gotten thrown from Knight in front of a saloon, been groped by Zant Chapelo, bloodied his nose for him—with the entire town as witnesses—then had a confrontation in the alley with first Rosie and then Chapelo, and then she'd shot him—one of the most notorious guns in the whole West—and left him for dead. And then, skittish as a colt, she'd come back here—to the very saloon, or cantina as folks here called it, where all her troubles began. But also where her only friend was.

She quirked her mouth in a self-deprecating gesture. All in all, not a bad way to keep her identity a secret—especially in a town where her life depended on not drawing any attention to herself. And a town where anyone could have a reason to hate the Lawless name. This was all she needed right now—some yahoo with a grudge to sidetrack her from her own mission here.

Jacey groaned and rolled onto her back on her narrow bed, kicking at the entangling covers over her legs. The danged sheets kept snagging on her knife sheath. Too bad, because as long as she was here, she wasn't taking it off except to bathe. Still, she gave up on sleeping and sat up, looking all around the small, stuffy room. Moonlight shining in through the one closed window forbade the room's shadows to come out of the corners.

With nothing but her own problems to occupy her mind, she retreated to an inventory of her room at the back of Rosie's father's noisy business. Let's see, there was this bed, herself, that rough-cut table and chair, the washbasin and chipped pitcher on the table, three crucifixes, and a couple of wood hooks for her clothes. That didn't take long. Now what could she do?

Someone knocked on the door. *That was a pretty quick answer.* Jacey slipped her Colt out from under her pillow, bent her knees, and rested her arms atop them with the Colt pointing at the door. "State your business."

"My beez-ness? Señorita, my beez-ness is to be the owner of this cantina. It is I—Alberto Estrada. Rosarita's *padre.* I have some news for you. About *el desperado*—Señor Chapelo."

He sounded breathless, conspiratorial. The little man was getting the biggest kick out of being involved in her predicament. Jacey relaxed her arms, allowing the Colt to dangle from her fingers. "All right. Hold on a minute, Mr. Estrada."

She hid her gun under the pillow again and swung her legs over the side of the bed. Standing up, she smoothed her chemise down and then grabbed at the bed's top sheet. She drew it Indian-style around her shoulders. Then she crossed to the door and opened it, which only intensified the sounds of glasses clinking, men laughing and swearing, and the scraping of chairs coming from the cantina. Yep. Just like he'd said—it was Señor Estrada, cantina owner. "Yes?"

Mr. Estrada ducked his head in greeting and smiled broadly under his mustache. "I hope I have not awakened you. No? *Bien.* I have just checked out in the corral, and your horse—he is fine. Not like earlier when he bit at me. And how are you, señorita? Is everything to your liking?"

Before Jacey could say a thing, he bowed low and spoke very formally. "I am honored to have a Lawless in my home. *Mi casa es su casa.*"

Jacey fought her urge to chuckle at his elaborate manners, especially in light of his stained shirt, dirt-shiny pants, and the bar towel slung over his shoulder. "Thank you, and yes, everything's fine. Now, what about Chapelo? Is he dead?"

Alberto's eyes widened. "No, no." He crossed himself and mumbled something in Spanish, which sounded like a hasty prayer. Then, to her, he said, "No, he is only wounded—here." He pointed to his right arm. "He rests now at La Casa Grande. Tomorrow—a *pistolero* such as himself—he will be fine."

"Good." But she wasn't sure if she meant it. "Thank you,

Mister Estrada.'' Then, feeling obliged, Jacey added, ''I apologize for coming to you and Rosie like I did tonight. And I appreciate your letting me put up here. I just wish you'd let me pay you. Come tomorrow, I'll get a room—''

Alberto raised a quieting hand and pulled himself up to his full and proud height—no taller than Jacey. ''No. You must stay here. No money—not from you. Besides, this room is much safer for you, *chica.* The hotels in Tucson—?'' He made a dismissive noise that adequately expressed his contempt. ''They are not as nice as what I offer you.''

Jacey raised her eyebrows and then did a half-turn to stare at the bare furnishings behind her.

''Or as clean. Or as safe and as private, señorita. Private for you, and a good place to hide such a big, bad animal like that black horse of yours who repays my many kindnesses with a bite.''

Jacey made an apologetic face. ''I'm sorry about Knight. I should have warned you.''

''It is nothing—only a finger or two. Eh, I have eight others.''

Jacey laughed with Rosie's father, liking him more and more. She looked into sincere jet-black eyes, the same color as her own, and finally nodded her consent to stay. ''I'm much obliged, Mr. Estrada. I'll try to take care of my business in Tucson quickly and clear out without involving you and Rosie any more than I already have.''

He bowed slightly. ''*Por nada*—it is nothing. Rosarita and I will help you in any way we can.''

Jacey cocked her head at a questioning angle. ''Are you and your daughter always this helpful to strangers, Mr. Estrada?''

He grinned, showing gleaming white teeth against his olive complexion. ''No, Señorita Lawless. But then, you are no stranger.''

Jacey narrowed her eyes. ''How's that?''

''Your papa—he is known to me.''

Something quivered in Jacey's belly. ''My papa's known to a lot of folks in Tucson.''

''This is true. But especially to me. I am happy to say your father is my friend. Perhaps he has mentioned me?''

Jacey hated to hurt the man's feelings, but she couldn't recall a single instance of Papa mentioning any Estrada in Tucson. Still, she hedged, "He probably did. It's just been so long, and he didn't talk much about his outlaw days."

Mr. Estrada nodded sagely. "This I can understand. But many times, as a young *desperado,* he slept right here in this room when he wished to hide from the world. You also hide from the world, no?"

"No. Yes." The way these folks phrased things kept tripping her up. "Yes, I'm hiding from the world. For now." But what he'd said was tripping her up more than the way he'd said it. *Papa'd slept here—in this very room?*

Jacey felt a sudden warmth spread through her. She hadn't once thought of encountering people and things here that her father'd touched and loved. She didn't think of Tucson that way. Not since someone from here had stolen from her—and, she supposed, from Papa. In a way. With that thought, she roused herself enough to stare somberly at Rosie's father. She had to tell him.

She tried to get the words out, but they wouldn't come, not on the first try. This would be the first time she'd said them out loud. She cleared her throat and willed a flat steeliness into her voice. "My father's dead, Mr. Estrada. He was murdered."

Alberto froze, but then his expression and his posture crumpled. "I am sorry to hear this, *chica.* Your father was a great man, a man of heart and soul. He helped me many times. Please tell your beautiful mother of my pain."

Jacey swallowed hard and sniffed, raising her chin a notch. "I can't do that. She was murdered, too."

Alberto stared at her somberly for a long moment. When he looked as if he might hug her, Jacey stiffened and raised her chin another notch. Alberto retreated. His gaze then flicked up and down her. "And that is why you are here?"

Jacey shook her head. "Not so much. The killers are in Boston. My sister's there taking care of that business. I'm here because some thieving scum from Papa's old gang stole from me, stole something I hold dear. And I aim to get it back."

"Ahh." He considered her a moment and then spoke abruptly, as if the words came out of him at the exact moment he thought them. "You are very much like your father. I said to my Rosie earlier that there is something about you that I know. I was not wrong."

Then, Alberto worked his mouth, twitching his drooping mustache, giving the appearance that he weighed something in his mind, something he wasn't sure he should tell her. Finally quirking his mouth, and apparently deciding, he said, "We are not so busy tonight. Put on your clothes. I will check on Rosarita, and then I will come back and you will go with me. There is something I must show you."

For no reason she could fathom, Jacey's throat threatened to close as a cold shiver slipped over her, tensing every muscle. "Show me what?"

He shook his head and put a staying hand on her arm. "No. I must show you. I cannot just tell you. I have something . . . something that belonged to your father. You should have it."

With that, he turned and left, striding quickly down the short, dark corridor and then out through the heavy wooden door that would see him back in the cantina. Jacey stood there for the longest time, just staring down the empty, musty hall at the barrier the closed door made.

She should be getting dressed, she knew, but somehow she wasn't sure she wanted to see what Mr. Estrada had. Would it be the portrait of Ardis? Was he the one she sought? But that was silly. Mr. Estrada? Hardly. But whatever he had, it belonged to Papa. Those were his words. And the portrait was Mama's. It belonged to her now, the only thing Mama'd ever said she wanted Jacey to have. Because she was so much like her great-grandmother. Feisty. Independent. Beautiful. No one had ever called her beautiful before. No one but Mama.

Blinking and frowning, Jacey hastily stepped back inside her room and closed the door. She drew the sheet from around her shoulders and tossed it onto the bed. Within moments she had on her split skirt and boots and blouse. Turning her nose up at the sweaty, dirty state of her attire, she tucked the blouse into her waistband and turned toward the door at the sound of knocking.

"Coming," she called out. Hurrying to the door, with only a passing thought of her Colt still hidden under her pillow, she opened it. And froze. It wasn't Mr. Estrada. Or Rosie. Or Zant Chapelo. It wasn't anyone she knew. But he was big, heavily armed, and mean-looking. And his eyes had almost no color to them.

Her heart in her throat, Jacey fought to keep her voice from cracking with fright. "You got the wrong room, mister. You better clear out now."

"I got the right room. . . . Miss Lawless."

The man's voice was a threatening drawl that stood the hair up on Jacey's arms. She sucked in a breath through her flared nostrils. The only two people in Tucson who knew her name were Alberto and Rosie Estrada. She'd been set up. She knew that as surely as she was standing there facing a big, ugly man.

Jacey's right hand went to her hip. No Colt. She met his gaze and saw the deadly gleam in his eyes, like a snake that had cornered a meal.

Well, this dinner isn't going down without a fight. Jacey tried, with a mighty shove, to fling the door closed, anything just to give her a second to hike her skirt and reach her knife or get to the bed and her gun.

But the big man was quicker. He shoved a hamlike hand against the door's wood and pushed inward, sending Jacey spiraling backward into the room. Stumbling, she nearly fell but finally managed to keep her feet as she grabbed at the wooden chair behind her. The man grinned and stepped into the room. Terrified but determined, Jacey swung the chair at the man's head. He raised his arm to block the blow. The chair caught him on his forearm and hand, and broke apart, its pieces clattering to the floor.

Jacey was left holding one end of the slatted chairback. The man held the other end. Jacey looked at his hand. Scratched and bloody knuckles. She then met his gaze. Again, he grinned at her. "What now, Miss Lawless?"

Immobilized in a frozen moment, Jacey stared at him. She instinctively knew that any movement on her part, whether it be a blink or a breath or a raised hand, would set him in motion. He indicated he was waiting for her. He was playing with her. And then he meant to kill her. *Think, Jacey.*

Knowing her gun was out of reach, knowing he'd never let her reach the bed, Jacey made her move. Releasing her grip on the splintered chair, she hiked up her split skirt and went for her knife.

But she never even got it out of its sheath before he flung the broken chair aside and backhanded her, sending her reeling toward the bed. She landed hard on the floor, her back hitting the hardwood bed frame and knocking the air out of her.

Stunned, numb, staring straight ahead, she sat with her legs sprawled out in front of her.

Until the man stepped up and punched her in the jaw. The world receded.

When Jacey awakened, it was to the smell of cheap whiskey and the sensation of throbbing pain—in her jaw, her ear, and the side of her head. She felt like somebody'd hit her. Then it came to her. Somebody had. Remembering that, she lay perfectly still and kept her eyes closed. He might still be here.

Allowing her other four senses to work, she noted that she was lying on a bed, and that her surroundings were perfectly quiet and cool. Risking discovery that she was awake, Jacey finally opened her eyes. To moon-filtered darkness. But even that hurt. Getting another whiff of the whiskey, she grimaced, a motion that hurt worse. She closed her eyes, wondering what was going on here. She'd expected to be . . . what? Dead? Hogtied? Thrown over the back of a horse? Surrounded by hostile Indians? Abandoned out in the desert? Anything but what she actually was.

Which was alone and in her bed at the back of the cantina. Clutching at the sheet under her, Jacey opened her eyes again. Blinking back the pain, she raised up on an elbow, worked her jaw with her other hand, and looked around. The door was closed. There was no sign of the big ugly man. Pieces of the chair still littered the floor . . . which was wet, smelled of liquor, and sparkled with bits of . . . Jacey looked closer . . . broken glass?

She cupped her swollen, tender jaw and worked it gently. Almost crying with the pain, she sent up a silent thanks that at least it wasn't broken. She then smoothed a hand under her pillow. More than likely, he'd taken her Colt. No, there it was. She drew it out and checked the cylinder. It was still loaded. She laid the gun down in front of her and felt along her thigh. Her knife was still there. This didn't make any sense. Who was that man? And why would Alberto and Rosie be in cahoots with him?

The door latch clicked. Jacey snapped her attention to the slowly opening door. She quietly raised her gun in both hands. Whoever this was would receive a welcome he wouldn't soon forget.

Rosie and her father, both shushing the other one, stepped into the room. Jacey cocked her pistol. And caught their attention.

"*Madre de Dios*. Don't shoot, señorita." Alberto Estrada's hands went straight up in the air.

Rosie's hands joined his. "It is only us, *mi amiga*."

"Don't you call me friend." Talking hurt. Jacey grimaced, taking a hand away from her Colt to cup her jaw. Looking at the frightened duo through pain-slitted eyes, she then mumbled on. "You let that man in here, and he knew my name. You're—"

"He knew your name?"

"Yeah, he knew my name. Because you told him." Jacey bent her knee to rest her gun arm atop it.

Rosie exchanged a startled look with her father, who began shaking his head and protesting. "No, Señorita Lawless, you are mistaken. We would never—"

Jacey swung the big Colt to sight on Alberto. "I'm doing the talking here. So, where is he? And I mean that mangy coot who hit me. I owe him something." To prove it, she frowned horribly and touched the warm and swelling knot that rode her jaw.

With her hands still raised, Rosie managed to jerk a thumb back over her shoulder. "*El malo* . . . I mean, the bad man is out there. Outside."

Jacey stared hard at the girl she'd thought was her friend. "And what's the bad man doing out there, outside?"

Rosie shrugged as best she could and exchanged another look with her father before looking again at Jacey. "*Nada*. Nothing. He is just lying there."

"He's just lying there?" Jacey heard herself repeat. "Why's he just lying there?"

Rosie dared grin. "*Porque mi padre* . . . um, because my father hit him hard on *la cabeza*"—she tapped herself on her head—"with a whiskey bottle. What is left of it, you see and you smell here."

Jacey looked askance at Rosie. All the evidence seemed to be in their favor. She swung her gaze to Alberto. "Why'd you knock him out?"

His black eyes were big and rounded. "I was sure you would want me to, *querida*. I checked on Rosie, like I said, and then came to my back storeroom for the whiskey she needed for the bar. But then I heard the noise in here, and me and my bottle, we come running. I saw the *malo* bending over you. So, I hit him. I''—he briefly lowered a hand to thump himself on his chest—''I, Alberto Eduardo Luis Estrada, will not allow anyone to harm you. Then, Rosarita and I dragged him outside. And now we have come to see to you.''

Jacey stared at the father and daughter. All of a sudden she didn't care if this was a trick and they did kill her. Her jaw hurt like hell, her head was killing her, she was dangerously close to tears, and her arm, despite her leg's support, was shaking from holding the Colt up. Relenting, Jacey uncocked her gun, straightened her leg out, and let her gun arm fall limply onto her lap. ''Put your hands down.''

They did. But they didn't move, either. Jacey looked from one to the other of them. ''Who is that man?''

Alberto shrugged dramatically. ''*¿Quien sabe*? Who knows? Tucson is full of bad men.''

Jacey wasn't convinced. ''Maybe so, Mr. Estrada. But it's not full of men—good or bad—who know I'm here. And that man called me Miss Lawless. And you two are the only ones I've told who I am.''

Rosie shook her head. ''And we have told no one. So maybe you bring this bad man with you, no? You have come a long way and have met many people. Did you tell no one your name?'' Her tone of voice and raised eyebrows plainly said that Jacey had some apologizing to do.

Feeling suddenly too warm, Jacey looked away from Rosie's black-eyed, accusing stare. She focused instead on the gun in her lap and thought about what Rosie'd asked her. Had she told anyone her name? She didn't think so, but she couldn't be sure. She looked up again at Rosie and her father. ''I don't think I did, but I could have without realizing it. Maybe I did bring him in with me.'' She looked from one to the other of their sober expressions and added, ''I'm sorry I didn't trust you.''

Alberto forgave her first. He waved her apology away. ''Eh, your fear is understandable. But, tell me, what will we do with him now?''

Jacey bit at her lip while she stared at Alberto. Rosie put her hands to her hips and waited, too. ''Well,'' Jacey began as she scooted off the bed, "let's go see him and see what he has to say for himself."

Rosie and Alberto nodded their agreement and preceded Jacey outside. She nearly ran into them when they stopped suddenly in a tiny, walled courtyard that enclosed one side of the cantina. Forewarned by their actions, she raised her gun. "What? What is it?"

Rosie turned to her. "He is gone. We put him right here. And now—he is gone."

Jacey lowered her gun, looking all around on the moonlit ground. "Gone? How can he just be gone?"

"*¿Quien sabe?* Perhaps the same way he just appeared," Alberto offered.

The three then stared at each other in the moonlight.

Zant figured that today just had to be a better day than yesterday. It sure as hell couldn't be any worse—if he expected to get to the end of it alive. At least he was sober, cleaned up, and rested. Sitting in a rickety chair out in front of La Casa Grande Hotel, his booted feet up and crossed on the hitching post, Zant enjoyed the relative coolness of the morning.

Then he felt his nose and his arm. That was another thing that would make today better than yesterday—he wasn't going anywhere near that crazy woman he'd had run-ins with yesterday afternoon.

Well, at least he wouldn't knowingly. But how the hell was he supposed to avoid her, if he hadn't gotten a clean look at her face? He knew other parts of her well enough. Again he saw her sweet little bottom sashaying away from him in the street. Then he felt again her full, firm, and warm breast in his hand. Oh, he knew her figure well. Very well. She was a fine figure of a woman. And she had long black hair. And a big, loaded Colt. And a big, black horse with a temper like hers.

And that was all he knew of her. No, wait. Despite her black hair, she wasn't Mexican. Her skin was too light, and she didn't speak with an accent. Pausing long enough to realize the drift of his thoughts, Zant had another question for himself. Why was he spending his first sober day in three weeks thinking about a woman who'd hit him in his nose and then shot him? Like Blue'd said yesterday, there were women in Tucson more willing than her.

Now, that was a pleasant thought. A willing woman. Maybe he'd go find himself one today. Then, he remembered and slumped, nearly upsetting his chair. Windmilling the least bit, he finally got all four chair legs down before it pitched over backward. Forget women. He was leaving today to go face Don Rafael Calderon in Sonora. Again. He'd never get up to No Man's Land and J. C. Lawless at this rate.

Letting out a long, slow breath, Zant tugged his Stetson down lower on his brow. Just then, someone stepped out of the hotel lobby and came up behind him to flip his hat forward, knocking it off his head and onto his lap. Only one person in the world would dare. "Cut it out, Blue."

Zant ran a hand through his hair and replaced his hat on his head as Blue, spurs ever jangling, walked around him to lean his butt against the hitching rail. "How's the arm today?"

"Why? You got more whiskey you want to pour on it?" Having said that, Zant worked his arm and shoulder. "Sore as hell, that's how it is. Same as my nose and jaw, thanks to you and some *gringa*."

Blue chuckled good-naturedly. "Yeah, me and the little lady pretty much kicked your tail, didn't we?"

"Enjoy it while you can, pardner. But just remember, I owe you one."

Blue made a fist and flexed his biceps. "Ready when you are."

Zant dismissed Blue's muscles with a snort and then slyly slipped in his question. "Did you get a good look at that woman yesterday? I never did."

Blue's blue eyes twinkled and his mouth fought a smirk.

Zant narrowed his eyes in warning. "I'm sober today, Blue. And I don't need but the one good arm to knock you off that rail. Now, answer me."

Blue performed a lazy imitation of a military salute. "Yes, sir." Then he looked up consideringly at the overhanging roof as he crossed his arms over his chest. "Let me see. Yep, now I remember." He looked down at Zant, revealing pure devilment in the sparkle of his eyes. "She has the face of an angel."

Zant stood up abruptly. "Don't start with that 'face of an angel' crap. You always start with that."

Blue stood up, too. "But it's true this time. She does have

the face of an angel. Big black eyes, fair skin, ruby-red lips, pink—''

''Ahh, never mind. Shut the hell up.'' Zant turned to go back inside the hotel.

Blue followed him. ''Pink cheeks, all soft and dewy. And her neck is white and slender. Looked soft to me—''

''You're not going to be able to look at anything, if you don't shut—''

''Chapelo!''

Zant and Blue stopped and turned around—with their guns in their hands. But when they saw who it was, they relaxed and reholstered their weapons. Zant stepped to the edge of the wooden boardwalk. ''What the hell are you doing in Tucson, Rafferty?'' Not giving the man a chance to answer, he turned to Blue. ''He come with you to get me home?''

Blue licked at his lips, like he was nervous, and cut his gaze from Zant to Rafferty and back to Zant. ''I don't need no help with you. And especially not from the likes of him.''

Zant squinted at his friend and focused on Rafferty. He'd never liked this big, ugly man. One day it'd be his turn to go around with this mean son of a bitch. And what a fight that would be, because no one had to tell him the nature of the man's work for his grandfather. It was enforcement, pure and simple. ''What's Don Rafael got you doing up here, Rafferty? Kicking puppies? Drowning babies?''

Rafferty marked Zant's insolence with only a slightly raised, bushy eyebrow. Then he pulled out his cigarette fixin's and began rolling one. ''Something like that. You on your way back to Sonora?''

Zant watched the man's hands move, and noted the fresh scratches and swellings over his knuckles. And wondered who today sported the bruises that'd caused them. ''What if I am?''

Rafferty, intent on his task, just shrugged. ''Seems to me Señor Calderon wanted you there, that's all.''

Zant stiffened. ''You got nose trouble, Rafferty? What I do and where I go is none of your business. So stick to your own.''

Rafferty focused his pale, almost colorless eyes on Zant. ''Usually I do, boy. But not this time. This time you *are* my business.''

Sudden wariness pulled Zant up taller. ''What the hell are

you talking about? How am I your business?"

"Easy now, Zant."

Zant heard Blue's entreaty from behind him, but ignored him. Locking gazes with Rafferty, he repeated, "I asked you how I'm your business."

The hired killer shrugged. "Señor Calderon has me tracking someone. Someone who's mighty interested in relieving you of your short, sorry life."

"Somebody wants me dead? Hell, that describes about a hundred people I can name. Is he going to have you kill 'em all?"

For some reason, that made Rafferty chuckle. "No. Not this one, anyway. This one he wants alive. For now. And I'd already be on my way to Sonora with my catch, except for some interferin' Mexicans. In fact, I'm on my way there now to set 'em straight."

"Is that so?" Zant exchanged a look with Blue and was surprised to see how round-eyed and frowning he was. If Zant didn't know any better—and it occurred to him that he didn't, having been in prison for the past five years—he'd say Blue looked guilty about something. Or like he was afraid of Rafferty. Well, hell, so was he. Any smart person was. Still, Zant looked back at the killer and asked him, "Don Calderon wants this one alive, huh? Who is he?"

"She."

"She? Don Rafael set you on a woman?" Zant straightened up. Blue put a restraining hand on his arm. Zant jerked his gaze to Blue's hand on his arm, and then to Blue's face.

Blue shook his head. "Let it be, Zant. I was there when the order came down. You weren't. You were in prison still."

"Order? What order?" Zant jerked his arm out of Blue's grip. "My grandfather's not some damned military general. He's a vindictive old son of a bitch who wants to control everything and everybody he comes into contact with. Now, who's going to tell me who this woman is?"

"It ain't no skin off my nose, boy. But the fact is, you weren't supposed to be here still." Rafferty's gaze accused Blue of not doing his job. Blue cut his gaze away from Zant and edgily shifted his weight.

Increasingly uneasy, Zant focused on Rafferty as the gunman stepped up to strike his match against the hitching rail.

He then lit his cigarette, shook out the match's fire, and took a deep drag. All while looking Zant in the eye.

Flipping the match out into the street, Rafferty pinched his cigarette between his thumb and index finger to remove it from his lips. He blew smoke all around Zant and grinned. "The old man didn't want you in town when I took this one in. She's supposed to be a present for you. But I guess it's too late now." He turned to Blue. "Ain't it, Blue?" Then he sighted on Zant again. "Seems you met the lady yesterday, boy. In fact, she gave you that arm."

Zant's surprise wrenched him up to his full height. "Who the hell is she?"

Rafferty grunted out a chuckle. "Now, this here's the funny part. Seems she's the daughter of the man who killed your pa, boy. The lady's name is Jacey Lawless. Same as her pa."

Chapter Three

Not too many streets away and dressed now in a full skirt and loose blouse borrowed from Rosie, Jacey sat cross-legged on her bed. At the narrow bed's other end, Rosie perched in much the same fashion. Between them and absorbing their attention was a time-yellowed packet of letters and a slim journal that Alberto'd given Jacey last night. Alberto stood beside the bed and pointed to the various items.

"Your father gave these things to me many, many years ago as he prepared to leave Tucson. For safekeeping, he said. He also said he would return for them one day. But as you can see, he did not. Still"—Alberto shrugged his narrow shoulders—"I keep them with me. Such was my friendship with your father." He placed a fisted hand over his heart for emphasis.

Jacey smiled at his sense of loyalty as she sifted through the pile of letters. "I'm much obliged, Mr. Estrada, but I can't make heads or tails of this. I tried to read some of it last night, but my jaw was hurting so much that I couldn't catch the meaning of all this to Papa."

Alberto reached out to lift one of the brittle envelopes. Peering at it, he questioned Jacey. "Then these people are not known to you?"

Frowning and shaking her head, she flipped through the pages of the journal she held. "No. Never heard of 'em. The woman signs her name Laura Parker at the front. And just like the letters, it's full of her trip out West."

"In this one," Rosie said, holding up a letter, "she writes of her husband and then calls him Seth."

Jacey nodded. "Yeah, I see that name here. And these letters—they're to folks back in Kentucky. Can't say why she never mailed 'em, though."

"Or why, *mi amiga,* your father had them."

Jacey looked at Rosie. She'd been thinking the same thing. Jacey looked away first, settling her gaze on the journal. She flipped pages and skimmed the words. "Hold on. Look. Here's another handwriting in here." She read the words silently and then shook her head. "Look what it says." She held the book out to Rosie.

Frowning in curiosity, Rosie took the journal and looked down at the page Jacey indicated. She read silently for a moment and then looked up at Jacey and then her father. "She had a baby. Seth must have written this." She looked back down at the journal, using her finger to keep her place as she read the entry. "A girl. Laura had a *niña.* On *nueve de Mayo*—um, you would say the ninth of May—in the year 1854. They named her Beatrice." She looked up at Jacey. "Do you know such a person? A Be-a-trice Parker?"

Bay-ah-treese? Jacey shook her head. "Never heard of her."

Alberto caught the girls' attention when he began pacing. Jacey looked over to see him pulling at his mustache. "Then I do not understand any of this, Señorita Lawless. Why would these papers be so important to your father?"

"I can't rightly tell you, Mr. Estrada. I was at home and only two years old when all this went on. You were here. Did you question him?"

Alberto stopped his pacing to pull himself up as stiff and as tall as he could. "Señor Lawless was not one to be questioned."

Jacey put up a placating hand. "I meant no offense. I was just wondering what might have been going on here when he gave you these. Do you remember anything about that day?"

Alberto nodded vigorously. "I remember everything. It was the day the Lawless Gang broke up. Your father gave these things to me—which I never read, such is my respect for your father. He told me good-bye, and I never saw him again."

Jacey frowned. "Was he alone?"

"*Sí,* señorita. Very much alone."

Into the ensuing silence, her head still lowered as she read,

Rosie cooed, "Aah, *pobrecita*—poor little thing. Listen to this. Seth writes that Laura had *mucho* trouble bringing the *niña* into the world. He says this is her first, and he is very scared because they are traveling alone." Rosie shook her head and quickly scanned the page. "But wait, he says on the next day that the baby is doing fine, and so is Laura."

Jacey stared at her new friend's beaming face. "I'm glad for them. But I still don't know who they are, what my father was doing with their letters, or what happened to these folks."

Rosie shrugged her shoulders. "It may forever remain a mystery, *mi amiga*."

Jacey's frown reflected her dislike of a mystery. "Well, flip to the last thing this Laura Parker wrote. Maybe that'll tell us something."

"As you wish." Rosie carefully turned the cracked and yellowed pages, the brittle edges of which tended to break off at her touch. She turned past a page, looked over two or three more, and then turned back again to the one she'd thumbed. "Here we are. Laura writes that the baby is a week old now." Rosie read for a minute and then looked up, her eyes shining with unshed tears. "She loves her baby very much. She says she has only one nice thing to give to her little daughter when she grows up. A ruby necklace."

Jacey frowned. "Ruby necklace?" She turned to Alberto, a question on her face.

"There was no necklace."

Jacey narrowed her eyes in thought. Just then, Rosie waved a hand at them, even as she kept her gaze on the yellowed pages. "*Oye*. Listen. This is not good. They approach Apache Pass on this day."

"Apache Pass? Through the San Pedros? I traveled those mountains myself coming here, but I did it with a wagon train for company. I wouldn't go through those gullies and slopes alone today, much less twenty years ago and without the protection of Fort Bowie."

Jacey's words were no more out of her mouth than Rosie and Alberto were crossing themselves and mumbling prayers. She almost joined them before she caught herself. "What does this Laura Parker woman write after that?"

Rosie looked at Jacey. "You asked me to read to you the

last thing. That was it. They were approaching Apache Pass. And Laura was scared for them."

For some unaccountable reason, Jacey's stomach did a flip-flop and she had to swallow thick saliva. She started to speak, but the words came out on a croak. Clearing her throat, she started over. "Then something bad happened to them and . . . their baby in Apache Pass?"

"*Sí.*" Rosie nodded grimly, staring hard at Jacey. "Something bad."

With abrupt movements, Jacey unfolded her legs and got up from the bed. She gathered up the journal and letters and set them on the table. Silence followed her to the window. She stood staring out at the hot, dry, bright and quiet morning. "And Papa ended up with their letters and that journal."

"*Sí, mi amiga.*"

"He'd never hurt those folks. I know my father." Jacey spoke as if she hadn't heard Rosie's soft words. Locking her knees to keep her moment of doubt from sending her limply to the floor, Jacey stood with her arms crossed defiantly over her chest. Finally, she turned back to Alberto and Rosie. "I need some fresh air. I'm going out to check on Knight. Alberto, can I ask you to put these . . . papers away again for safekeeping?"

Two sets of black and sympathetic eyes stared back at her for the longest of brief seconds. Then Alberto became animated. "*Sí, querida.*" He then turned to his daughter. "*Venga.* Come," he chirped, holding his hand out. "We must open *la cantina.*"

Rosie jumped up and preceded her father out of the room. Alberto stepped across the threshhold, but then he abruptly turned back to Jacey and put a hand over his heart. "There is one more thing. It could be nothing, or it could be *muy importante*. I tell you this now, so that you might have a care for yourself, *chica.*"

With that, Alberto paused dramatically before saying, "On the day that your father gave these things to me, he also killed Kid Chapelo."

Zant edged closer to the low adobe wall that surrounded the tiny courtyard beside Alberto's cantina. Although he'd had to practically hogtie Blue to get him to stay behind, it hadn't taken much prodding to get Rafferty to tell him where the Lawless woman was. Send her my regards, he'd said, tell her he owed her for the lump on the back of his head. The ugly bastard thought it was pretty damn funny that Zant had been shot by a Lawless, just like his father. One of these days, Zant promised himself, he was going to have to kill Rafferty.

Zant unclenched his jaw and relaxed his stomach muscles. One day, but not this day. Today was reserved for reckoning with a Lawless. With that thought, he bounded quietly over the adobe wall. And then stood still, staring straight ahead. At first, given her costume, he thought it was Rosie stretched out in a chair, her sandaled feet crossed at the ankles and resting on the cracked-tile fountain's rim. But on stepping closer to her and looking down at her face, he realized it was her. The Lawless woman.

Zant's gut tightened as a tormented grimace claimed his features. Her almost child-sized jaw was bruised and swollen. *That son of a bitch.* He ran a hand over his mouth, fighting back the faint images of his young mother looking the same way. More than once. Breathing deeply, Zant focused on the girl in front of him. That damned Rafferty could've killed her.

And just what are your plans for her?

Zant squelched his twinge of conscience. He didn't know what his plans were for her. All his life he'd known what his plans were for her father—the man who'd killed his father and thereby left his mother brokenhearted. But for the man's daughter? Well, whatever he intended, it sure as hell wasn't hitting her. His hand strayed to the butt of his Colt. Or shooting her.

Why not? Those are two things she's already done to you.

Zant barely stopped himself from turning around to see who was taunting him. What was this new voice in his head?

Just then, her sleepy sigh caught and held Zant's attention. He eyed her long black hair, which draped unbound over her wooden chair's back and trailed almost to the ground. He made a fist to stop himself from reaching out to stroke its silky length. Her face, in repose, was just as Blue said—that of an angel. Thick black lashes, pink cheeks, ruby mouth. That face was no place for a bruise.

Zant's anger only increased as he scanned his way up and down her length. Her hands were folded over her flat belly, and her chest rose and fell in even breaths. She didn't seem to be hurt anywhere else. But with Rafferty, it was hard to tell.

A bee buzzed in lazy circles around Zant's head. Somewhere a dog barked, a horse nickered. The morning sun beat down, its heat made bearable by a soft breeze. Zant exhaled sharply once he decided what to do next. Too bad, though, because she sure made a pretty picture, what with the morning surrounding her with peacefulness and quiet.

Zant reached out a booted foot, hooked a chair leg, and broke the reverent moment when he slowly tilted the chair over. Her squawk accompanied her windmilling arms and widened eyes and flying skirt as she hit the dirt with a dust-raising thump. Flat on her back and spread-eagled, half-stunned, the Lawless woman stared up at him, apparently not comprehending what had just happened.

Zant nonchalantly set her chair out of his way, drew his Colt, and squatted on his haunches beside her. Using his gun's barrel, he tipped his hat back and then pointed the Colt at her forehead as he cocked it. "Morning, Miss Lawless. I see you're not armed."

To her credit, she recovered from her shock and look of naked fear to settle her features into taunting lines. "Morning, Mr. Chapelo. I see you're not dead."

Surprised at her pluck, under the circumstances, Zant chuckled. "Yeah, lucky for me your aim was off."

"Depends on where you're sitting. Who told you who I am?"

"Rafferty." Then, using his gun as a pointer, he indicated her bruise. "He give you that jaw?"

She stared up at him, her black eyes radiating a wary bravado. "I couldn't say. The ugly polecat didn't introduce himself."

A guffaw escaped Zant before he could guard against it. "Well, his name's Rafferty."

"Rafferty. I'll remember that." Her eyes narrowed to slits as she edged up onto her elbows.

Tough, that's what she was. Tough as boot leather. He wondered just how far below the surface that toughness ran. When Zant realized he was grinning down at her and not saying anything, he sniffed and cleared his throat. Might as well come to the point and strike some fear into her heart. "Kid Chapelo was my father."

She didn't even blink. "I figured as much. Is that what all this is about?"

Zant clenched his hand around his gun. She might be all soft and womanly on the outside, but on the inside, she was one tough, cool gunfighter. Everything about her was a dare, a line drawn in the sand, a chip on a shoulder. Just waiting for someone to step over the line and knock it off.

Looking at her, Zant decided he just might be the one to do it. This Lawless woman needed to be brought down a notch or two. "Yeah, that's what this is all about. But not like you're thinking. I've got no quarrel with you personally."

She cocked her head to one side. "Is that so? Then why'd you pull my chair out from under me?"

"For my nose and my arm. Paybacks are hell, aren't they?" With that, he pulled his Colt out of her face and rose to his feet, stepping back. He reholstered his gun and held his hand out to her, offering to help her up.

She shot him a look that said she'd as soon bite his hand as take a hold of it. Zant chuckled again and shook his head, putting his hands to his waist as she rolled to her side and stiffly came to a stand. "Tucson's tough on its women," he felt compelled to add.

She nodded. "I'll give you an amen to that."

About shoulder-high to him and slender, but rounded in all the right places, she looked him right in the eye. Without knowing he was going to do it until it happened, Zant again smiled at her. She immediately looked down at herself and began shaking the dust out of her hair and brushing off her skirt. When she did, her loose hair cascaded forward, framing her face in its night-black sheet. Zant swallowed hard and just watched.

Done with her grooming, she finally met his gaze and proceeded in a very businesslike manner. "All right, Chapelo. What's it going to take to make you go away? I didn't come all the way to Tucson to be sidetracked by some two-bit gunslinger like yourself."

"Two-bit gunslinger?" Insulted, and instantly over his growing fascination with her, Zant glared at her. "You got a mouth on you, lady, you know that?"

The Lawless woman huffed out a breath. "Yeah, I do. Now state your business or move along because my patience is wearing thin. I've been thrown from my horse. I've been beat up and bruised up. And now I've had my chair pulled out from under me. And all in less than twenty-four hours. And all having something to do with you, the way I see it."

She then eyed him critically and sniffed the air in front of him. "At least you smell better today."

Beyond insulted, Zant shook a finger at her as he bellowed. "I'm about an inch away from turning you over my knee and pounding some respect into that backside of yours, girl."

The Lawless woman twisted her mouth into an awful frown. "You just step up and try it, Chapelo."

Zant fisted his pointing hand and came near to gnawing on his own knuckles. All hot and blustery, he threatened her with more words. "I'm not going to take any back talk from a Lawless pup. It's not you, but your father, that my quarrel's with. But that can change in a heartbeat. Now, I'm only going to say this once, so you listen up. You mount up—today, right now—and get on back home. Because Tucson's not big enough for both of us."

The Lawless woman cocked her head slightly to one side and planted her hands at her waist, looking like a frame-ready picture of sass and vinegar. "Then why don't *you* leave?"

Blinking and baffled, Zant truly didn't know what to do next. He'd never been faced with this before—a kitten arching its back and showing its tiny claws to a snarling wolf. Knowing he was dangerously close to flinging his hat to the ground and stomping it flat out of sheer frustration, he decided to point out the obvious to her. "Lady, has it occurred to you that I'm more than twice your size—and armed?"

She shrugged. "I've noticed. But you're also bluffing. If you were aiming to do something, you'd have done it yesterday."

"Why, I ought to just let—" was as far as he got before he reached out and grabbed her by her arms, yanking her to him. A part of his mind registered how delicate, how wrenchingly vulnerable her warm and slender arms were. "I didn't come here this morning to shoot you. But I'm getting awful close to doing just that. Now, shut your mouth and listen to me. Because the last thing I want to do is save your skinny butt, lady. But it looks like I'm going to have to do just that. And for no other reason than to spit in the eye of Don Rafael."

A frown flickered over her face. "I don't know any Don Rafael. And I don't know what your beef is with him, either. But I do know I won't be your pawn in some game you're playing. Nobody uses me—no-how and for nothing, you got that? If my skinny butt needs saving, I'll do it myself."

"Not this time, *gringa.* You're in way over your head." Angry breaths pushed in and out of Zant's lungs, giving him a noseful of her warm and clean smell. Being this close to her, looking deeply into eyes as black as his own, feeling her breath on his neck. . . . Just the idea of Rafferty getting his hands on her again sickened him. Don Rafael had gone too far this time.

"All right, you got my attention. How am I in over my head, Chapelo?"

Relieved that she was willing to listen, Zant freed her and stepped back.

"That jaw of yours was no random act. Rafferty meant to kidnap you last night, but apparently Alberto stopped him somehow. And now he and Rosie could die for helping you. Because Rafferty won't forget. He'll kill them both for interfering."

The Lawless woman gasped and went wide-eyed. "Kill them?" She then set her features in hard lines. "Interfering with what? What's this all about?"

Zant huffed out a breath. "It's all about you. And me. Somehow."

She shook her head. "Just like everything else that's happened to me since I rode into this one-horse town. Why don't you tell me where this Rafferty is, and I'll go settle my score with him myself?"

"I'm going to do better than tell you where he is. I'm going to take you to him."

She stepped back. "Like hell you are. You some kind of messenger boy, Chapelo?"

"I don't messenger for anybody. Right now, I've got Rafferty tethered on a short leash. But I don't know how long I can hold him. So, I'm riding for Sonora today with him. And you're going with us."

She took another step back. "You've been out in the sun

too long. Because you're plumb crazy if you think I'm going anywhere with you and that Rafferty skunk.''

Zant took a step toward her, surprising himself with the depth of his fear for her safety. ''And Rosie and Alberto'll be pushing up sagebrush if you don't. Make no mistake—your cooperation with me is the only thing standing between them and Rafferty. Now get your gear and saddle up that devil you call a horse. We ride this morning.''

''Now, just hold on a minute, Chapelo. You're not giving me time to think. I've got my own business to attend to right here in—''

''It'll just have to keep. Because you're up against Rafferty now. The man is a paid tracker. And a damned good one. He tracks people, and he kills them. He's been following you since you left home.''

She stood stock-still, as if someone had hammered her into the sandy ground. All the color drained from her face. ''I never saw—Following me? Why?''

''I don't know the whole story yet, but he's supposed to be taking you to Don Rafael in Sonora. But Alberto fouled him up. Rafferty doesn't like being fouled up. That means he doesn't get paid. He was on his way here this morning to right things when he saw me. I told him I'd get you to come willingly. If you don't, Rosie and Alberto are as good as dead. Maybe even you, too.''

She digested that for a moment and then turned those big black eyes up to him. ''Why is this happening?''

At her look, which was laced with no small amount of fear, Zant blew out a breath and shook his head. ''I don't rightly know. I just know who's behind it all.''

''Meaning Don Rafael? You don't care too much for him, do you?''

''No more than he cares for me.''

''Well, who the heck is he? I think I have a right to know. He did cause me to be sporting this lump on my jaw.''

''His full name's Don Rafael Calderon. He's Spanish nobility. He's rich as hell. He's a mean son of a bitch. And he's my grandfather.''

The Lawless woman stilled and stared up at him, her black-eyed gaze relentless. ''Your grandfather?''

''Believe me, I'm not any happier about it than you are.

But that being the case, Miss Lawless, the only way for you to save yourself and the Estradas is to ride with me to Sonora. Under my protection."

She eyed him coolly. "A Chapelo helping a Lawless? Why would you do that?"

"It's not out of love. And believe me, I never thought I'd live long enough to see it, either. But then"—Zant looked her up and down—"I never figured the Lawless I'd face would be a woman."

She pulled herself up, as if insulted. "When it comes down to that day, Chapelo, my being a woman won't be your worst problem."

Zant looked deep into her eyes, not speaking until she blinked first. Only then did he lower his voice to a throaty drawl. "We'll just have to see, won't we?"

She raised her head a proud notch. A telltale vein throbbed at her temple. "How do I know this isn't a trap? After all, the man is your kin. And this Rafferty is in your employ."

Zant chuckled in a way that had nothing to do with humor. "Not my employ. I wouldn't hire that son of a mule to dig me an outhouse. But this isn't a trap. You'll just have to trust me."

"Why should I?"

A huffed-out breath preceded Zant's terse words. "I didn't have to involve myself, did I? And I didn't have to come here to warn you, did I?"

She slowly shook her head, as if judging his words against his actions. "I suppose you're right."

Zant's eyebrows rose with his words. "I know I'm right. And the way I see it, *gringa,* we can do this the easy way, or do it the hard way. And the hard way will be with you tied up and thrown over your horse. So, it's up to you. I'm riding to Sonora for some answers. You coming?"

"Do I have a choice?" She raised a hand to shade her eyes as she stared up at him.

She was so damned little. And so damned ornery. Zant took a deep breath around the sudden tightening in his chest. "No. I don't guess you do. You've got five minutes to get what you need for a hard three-day ride. I'll wait right here for you. Then we'll join Blue and Rafferty at the hotel." Zant considered her a moment. "Do I have to tell you to stay close to me on this ride?"

Her eyes widened. "No." And then narrowed. "Just try to stay downwind for me, if you would."

Chapter Four

Two nights out, and just this side of the Mexican border, the four of them and their horses once again set up a rough camp in the cool desert night. With the silver-dollar moon throwing the encircling saguaros' tall shadows across them, it seemed to Jacey that they were surrounded, much as if they sat in the middle of an Indian powwow. All they lacked were the drums.

She looked up at the night sky. Pinholes pricked in black cloth and then held up to a light. That's what the stars in the sky looked like. Like a bad dream, like none of this was real. Without warning, a shiver escaped her.

"You cold, Miss Lawless?"

Jacey jerked her head to her right, to Blue, and shook her head. "No."

"You're shivering."

Jacey stared at the blond man for a long moment. "Don't you have something better to do than watching me to see what I might do next?"

"Yes, ma'am," he said, lowering his gaze to his coffee mug.

Jacey let out a breath. Now why'd she go and be mean to him? Of the three she rode with, Blue was the least obnoxious. Hadn't he come near to tripping over his own feet trying to help her unsaddle Knight and then set up her bedroll—both nights—before Chapelo'd warned him off? Speaking of Chapelo, where was he?

Looking around, she saw him wiping down that danged high-strung roan stallion he rode. As she watched Chapelo's practiced and loving motions, and noted again how big and finely formed he was, just like his horse, his words from yesterday morning mixed themselves up with Mr. Estrada's revelations, and they all came back to Jacey in a tumble.

Bestirring herself when she realized she was watching the man's every move—the same thing she'd accused Blue of with her—she pivoted back to face the campfire and poured herself a cup of strong black coffee. She settled back with it, bracing her spine against Knight's saddle and stretching her legs out in front of her. Somehow, staring at the mesmerizing leap and crackle of the flames helped her sort out her thoughts. And kept her from having to look at Rafferty's ugly face directly across the campfire from her.

Focusing on what she already knew, she realized it was a whole lot and not very much, all at the same time. Because all she had were events and no answers, and no one thing to tie them all together. Except perhaps those letters and journal that Papa'd given to Mr. Estrada—on the day he killed Kid Chapelo and rode away from his outlaw days. The two events had to be connected in other ways.

And what about the spur rowel she'd found with the frame fragment at home? How'd they fit in? Had she jumped to the wrong conclusion and then hightailed it here for no reason, like Glory thought? Could be. Because when—and why—would an old gang member have come calling? The broken spur and piece of frame indicated a scuffle. Anybody'd who'd scuffled with Papa wouldn't have gotten away alive. And Mama and Papa had died together. Papa'd been lying atop Mama, as if he'd been trying to protect her from the bullets.

As if that weren't enough to chew on, she had to consider that Kid Chapelo rode in the old gang. But he was dead. Well, his son certainly wasn't. Could it be he wanted revenge? Or maybe this Don Rafael, Zant Chapelo's grandfather, did. What had Chapelo said . . . she was a present for him? What did that mean?

Jacey shook her head at the convoluted mess in her head. And then realized, with a start, that at some point she'd again turned to watch Chapelo. Only now he was looking back at her. With his hands still resting on the roan, and a knee bent, he was soberly considering her. Jacey had the crazy thought that maybe she'd said some of her thoughts out loud.

That had to be why her heart was pounding and she felt all hot under her arms and at the back of her neck. She licked at her lips to wet them. But for the life of her, she couldn't look away from Chapelo's deep and disturbing black-eyed gaze. Jacey felt as if his hands had been on her, stroking her, instead of his horse.

Do you hear yourself, Jacey Lawless? Never in all her born days had she ever had a thought like that about a man. Unnerved, she set her mug down, sloshing the hot coffee over her hand. She yelped and wiped her hand on her skirt. What was wrong with her? Just then, Chapelo's words filtered through her consciousness. *Do I have to tell you to stay close to me on this ride?* Jacey remembered making some smart remark about him staying downwind from her.

But now all she could do was stare at his bedroll next to her own. *That was a mite too close, pardner.* Without preamble, Jacey got up and tugged his blankets more to the west of her southerly placed roll. Then, hands to her waist as she surveyed her handiwork—and ignored Chapelo's chuckle behind her—she figured that was much better. Now the four of them were aligned north, south, east, and west around the campfire.

Now, how was that much better? Jacey stopped herself just short of knuckling her own head. How could moving a bedroll keep her safe from these three yahoos out here in the birthplace of nowhere?

She couldn't believe this. What in the world was she doing here? And then she remembered—for Rosie's and Alberto's sakes. Going back to her own bedroll, Jacey sat down heavily and stared at her boots. For the sake of a day-old friendship, here she was on a dusty, almost deserted trail heading for Mexico with three men she had no reason to trust.

Under cover of her lowered lids, she considered her trail partners. For the past two days, Rafferty and Blue had flanked Knight as they fanned out behind her. These men, she reminded herself, were hired guns for a man who wanted her dead. Rafferty she knew only too well. And Blue was the handsome, yellow-haired man she recognized from three days ago at the cantina. He'd handled Knight and had laughed at Chapelo when she bloodied his nose. He couldn't be all bad.

Just for completeness' sake, Jacey cut her gaze over to Chapelo. His back was to her, but she didn't allow herself to linger on his broad shoulders and long legs. Because this man was the grandson of the shadowy Don Rafael, who seemed to be the one pulling all their strings right now. And she ought still to be mad at Chapelo. After all, he'd hustled her out of Tucson without giving her a chance to tell Alberto and Rosie that she was leaving, much less where she was going. And who she was with. He'd barely given her time to saddle Knight, pack a few things in her saddlebags, and change her clothes.

She lifted her mug of coffee to her lips and stared right through Rafferty when he sent her a leering look and winked and made little kissing sounds at her. She refused to give him the satisfaction of knowing how much he scared her. *Jacey, if this isn't a trap, as well as one of the most reckless things you've ever done, then I don't know what is,* she berated herself.

''Knock it off, Rafferty. Leave her alone.''

Jacey jerked her head in Chapelo's direction. She hadn't even heard him walk up. Only a second ago, he'd still been fiddling with his roan. Danged thoroughbred acted like it was too good to be strung on a remuda line between two saguaros with the other mounts. Jacey grinned to herself, remembering how Knight had bared his big teeth this afternoon at the prissy animal when it highstepped around a gila monster and bumped into the black gelding.

''What's so funny?'' Chapelo lowered his saddle onto his bedroll and then followed it, stretching out. With the casual elegance of a reposing panther, he crossed his long legs at his booted ankles and supported his weight on a bent elbow as he turned toward her and stared. And waited for an answer.

Jacey sobered and shrugged, lowering her gaze to follow her own motions as she set the mug next to her on the blanket. ''Nothing. I can't think of a thing to laugh about.'' She then looked over at Chapelo and caught him looking her up and down. First Blue, always Rafferty—and now Chapelo. ''Do I fascinate you or something?''

A soft chuckle came from the bedroll to her left. ''Don't flatter yourself, Miss Lawless. I'm just trying to see your father in you.''

Caught off guard by his words, Jacey blinked and looked away. One after the other she looked into Rafferty's and

Blue's eyes, those two being suddenly alert at Chapelo's words. The last thing she wanted to do was talk about her father with these men. But what choice did she have, if she wanted answers?

After a moment in which she composed herself, she peered over at Chapelo, noting his steady gaze and strong, unshaven jaw. "I take it you've met my father?"

"I was never introduced, no. But I've seen him."

Just for something to hold on to, Jacey once again picked up the tin mug of cooling coffee, took a sip of its bitterness, and then gripped it tightly. "You saw him? When?"

"A little over five years ago. In Santa Fe. I was no more than a raw kid with a gun back then."

"Santa Fe?" Jacey thought about that. Something about Santa Fe. Then it came to her. She leveled a mean-eyed look on the man. "I remember that trip. I was sixteen years old when Papa came back with a graze-wound to his arm. He said he never saw who took a shot at him."

Chapelo raised his head and showed her the leering grin of a wolf. "Is that so? Well, that's too bad. Only seems fair that a man know who's shooting at him."

Oppressive heat still rising from the desert sand commingled with the night's cool air to race a hot chill over Jacey. Chapelo'd all but said that he was the one who'd shot at Papa back then. Rage built slowly. She fought to control it, seeing as how she was outmanned and outgunned. She'd have to proceed cautiously. But only until such a time as the odds were more in her favor.

For once, Jacey settled on careful questioning rather than taking rash actions that could see her dead. "I guess you think you have good reason to want to see my father dead, don't you?"

"Think? No, Miss Lawless. I don't think it. I know it. And I'm betting you know why. Did your father tell you about him and the Kid?"

"Some. Not all. Not the why of it. I just know they didn't get along."

"No, they didn't."

"Do you know why they didn't?"

"Like you, I've been told some things over the years. And

I had five years in a Mexican prison to sit and wonder about it."

"Five years? What'd you do?"

He shrugged his broad shoulders and tugged his hat down firm on his wide forehead. "Some folks said I robbed a bank and killed a man. I didn't. At least, not that bank and not that man. Just was in the wrong place at the wrong time."

Jacey could only stare at him. Close up, he didn't look to be much older than her or maybe even Blue, but he'd robbed banks, killed men, and spent five years in prison already? He was truly an outlaw among outlaws. Clearing her throat and swallowing, she picked up the threads of their conversation. "How'd you get out? From prison, I mean. Did they catch the real robbers?"

Now he laughed, but it was at his own expense. "No. Don Rafael finally located which prison I was in and paid my way out. A month ago."

This Don Rafael he hated so much had apparently hunted all over Mexico to find his grandson and then had paid his way out? That didn't sound like a man who didn't care, which was what Chapelo'd said more than once. Then, something else he'd just said struck Jacey. A month ago? He'd just gotten out of prison a month ago?

She now realized that somewhere in the back of her mind, she'd been wondering—contrary to what Hannah'd written—if Chapelo was somehow involved in Mama's and Papa's murders, as well as in stealing the keepsake portrait. But he couldn't be anything but innocent. Because he was still in prison when they'd buried Mama and Papa. She looked over at the big man at her side. *He's innocent.* Relief, as terrifying in its intensity as it was in its unexpectedness, swept over her. *He's innocent.* Then her next thought dashed her giddiness. Was he telling the truth?

Jacey swept her gaze down the hard length of him. No spurs. She just couldn't get past that. Rafferty and Blue wore spurs. Not the right kind, though. What kind were Chapelo's? If he was lying about being in prison, then everything else about him was a lie, also. She made a mighty leap to the conclusion that his spurs were his father's old ones. And he couldn't wear them because . . . they were broken. Just thinking about the spurs made the piece of one around her neck suddenly feel too heavy against her skin. "Why don't you wear spurs, Chapelo?"

"Spurs?" His voice and raised eyebrows let her know he thought she'd asked a dumb question. "Why? Is it the law now, that a man has to wear spurs?" He rose up to look around Jacey. "Why didn't you tell me, Blue?"

Blue chuckled. "Didn't know, pardner."

Despite the creeping heat invading her cheeks, Jacey persisted. This was important. "There's no law to it. It's just that most men wear 'em."

Chapelo settled back down to his original position and picked up a pebble, which he lobbed at her. It hit her on her thigh, but she ignored it. Chapelo grinned. "I used to wear spurs. But it seems mine are missing."

Jacey's stomach muscles contracted. "Missing? How do a man's spurs come up missing?"

Chapelo leaned in closer to her. "For someone who doesn't like to be questioned, you've sure got your nose in my business."

Stung but still determined, Jacey countered with "Just trying to make conversation, Chapelo."

He leaned back again. "Fair enough. When I'd need them—and I didn't all the time—I'd wear my father's old silver spurs. The ones every member of the Lawless Gang wore."

Her mouth dry, her palms wet, Jacey said, "I've seen 'em."

"I figured you had. Well, I didn't have them on when I got thrown into jail. But when I got out and went home, and thought to look for them, they couldn't be found. So, I don't wear any. Happy now?"

Jacey nodded, knowing in her heart that another piece of the puzzle had just fallen into place. For as sure as she was sitting in the prickly desert at night and being all sociable-like with three killers, the piece of spur around her neck belonged to Kid Chapelo. Only he was long dead. And Zant had been in prison. Jacey gave him a sidelong glance. Or so he said.

But satisfied for the moment with his spur answer, Jacey went back to what he'd originally said. "You see my father in me yet?"

He snorted his opinion of that. "Yeah. In that hot head of yours."

Jacey grinned, despite herself and her circumstances. Everyone said she had her father's temper. "How about in my gun arm?"

Chapelo chuckled at that. "Your gun arm? You're just spoilin' for a fight with me, aren't you? What'd you ever shoot besides targets and maybe a bird or two?"

Smirking inside, her answer already in her head, Jacey first made a dramatic show of shifting her weight around on her bedroll, rubbing her hand under her nose, and looking off into the darkly silhouetted and sagebrushed distance . . . before she finally turned back to him. "Well, you, for one. I shot you."

That got him. Lines appeared to settle on his face, around his mouth, and at the corners of his eyes when Rafferty and Blue chuckled at his expense. Shooting the two men a warning glare that did nothing to stifle them, he turned his glare on Jacey. "You missed me more than you shot me."

"That wad of bandaging poked up against your sleeve doesn't look much like I missed you."

"Were you aiming for my arm?"

"No. I was aiming for your heart."

"Then you missed me."

Jacey allowed him his point. She gave herself over to the distant howl of a coyote, to the answering yowl of its mate, and to the nervous stamping coming from the tethered horses. But in the end, not able to stand letting him have the last word, she turned to him again. "I won't miss next time."

He burst out laughing. His hilarity slowly transformed itself into a wolfish grin. "Make sure. Because I never do miss what I'm shooting at, Miss Lawless."

Rafferty's guffaw, a raw sound that somehow put the lie to Zant's words, rang out. Jacey turned to stare at him across the campfire, and knew that Blue and Zant were, too. The ugly hired gun cut his pale gaze from one to the other of them but finally settled on Zant's face. "Never? You say you never miss what you're shootin' at, boy?"

From her left, Zant said, "Don't call me boy again . . . unless you aim to find out, Rafferty."

When Blue popped up from lying on his bedroll, Jacey turned to see him gesturing at her. "Why don't you come over here, Miss Lawless?"

No one had to tell her twice to get out of the line of fire.

Jacey shifted her weight to get up, but a warm, strong hand on her shoulder stopped her. She looked up to see that Zant was now on his feet and standing next to her. The man moved quicker than greased lightning, and he was staring thunderbolts at Blue.

"There's no trouble. She stays put," Zant told his blond friend. He then turned a mean, hard look on Jacey. "You understand?"

Much to her own surprise, Jacey nodded and stayed put.

"You, too, Blue."

Blue sat down.

Zant took his hand from her shoulder, stepped away from her, and turned again to Rafferty. "What about me is stickin' in your craw, Rafferty?"

Rafferty slowly stood up, distributing his weight evenly on his legs, his right hand hanging loosely beside his holster. Jacey looked from his heavy, craggy face to Zant's chiseled, dangerous one. With the campfire between them and casting shifting shadows over them, the two men looked like they'd just risen up from Hell. Hearing her own heartbeat in her ears, Jacey swallowed hard and kept very still.

"You're in the way of me doin' my job, boy."

Zant shifted his stance. "I told you not to call me boy."

"I heard you . . . I just don't take orders from you. An' you're makin' a big mistake right now, if you think bein' the old man's grandson will stay my hand against you. So, why don't you do yourself a favor and just sit down all nice-like right now?"

"Zant, why don't you do what—"

"Shut up, Blue. This isn't your fight." Zant spat his words out—all without looking away from Rafferty. "We've got a big problem, Rafferty. The way I see it, your orders this time just don't sit well with me. They've got something to do with me. I want to know what that something is. And I want to know from you. And I want to know right now."

When Rafferty curled his mouth up in a threatening leer that some would've called a grin and turned his head to stare at her, before cutting his gaze back to Zant, Jacey knew a moment of gut-wrenching fear. The man's almost colorless eyes made him seem not quite human. "Ask the Lawless bitch what she's doing in Tucson. She's your answer."

Jacey's heart tripped over its next beat. But Zant never looked away from Rafferty. "I'm asking you, Rafferty. What's Don Rafael up to?"

Still leering and not even blinking, Rafferty leveled his words at Zant. "Prison didn't teach you nothin', did it, boy? You're still a smart-mouthed, cocky little bastard, just like your worthless father."

Into the charged silence following Rafferty's insults, a tired-sounding "Oh, hell" came from Jacey's right. She jerked when Blue's hand closed around her arm. On all fours and frowning, he tugged at her arm and silently nodded for her to scoot back with him out of the way. Jacey quickly crabbed over to Blue's bedroll.

"I never could understand why the old man took you in," Rafferty was going on. "All that whore daughter of his ever gave him was grief. And a bastard for a grandson—"

The words hardly hit the air before Zant cleared leather. The first bullet took Rafferty in the chest, and stood him up straight and wide-eyed. "See you in Hell, you son of a bitch," Zant intoned, and then fired again. This time the bullet smacked into the big man's forehead, making a neat little circle there. Rafferty's hand was still on his gun in its holster as he spun around and fell to the ground with a dead thump.

Zant lowered his gun hand to his side and turned to face Jacey and Blue. "He had that coming."

Her mouth agape—never in her life had she ever seen such a quick draw—and feeling no sorrow, far from it, at Rafferty's death, Jacey stared at Zant and remained as silent as the stars overhead.

But Blue, most likely used to this display, seconded Zant's observation. "He surely did, Zant. Should have done it myself years ago, *compadre*."

Having said his piece, Blue got up and walked over to Rafferty, leaving Jacey to face Zant alone. From her seated position, she met his black-eyed stare. When he didn't say anything, she allowed her gaze to slip from his black hat, to the somber, shadowed face under it, down that bull neck of his, over his massive chest, down to the holster at his hip, and then back up to his face.

"You're the fastest I've ever seen," she heard herself say.

He shifted his weight on his denim-covered, muscular legs

and continued to stare down at her. "I made myself this way, knowing there was an old score I had to settle one day. But until then, I've had to be fast to stay alive."

Jacey nodded, not wanting to think about who that old score was with. "That's the way it is for some men. Got to make his point with a gun in his hand."

Zant slipped his gaze to the Colt holstered at her hip. "And some women, too."

Jacey stilled. "And some women."

"I don't like taking a life. But"—he looked across the campfire to where Blue was dragging Rafferty by his boot heels into the desert darkness beyond the campfire's light, then resettled his gaze on Jacey—"sometimes, some people just ask for it."

Jacey swallowed, not knowing which was dryer, her mouth or her eyes. She blinked rapidly and ran the tip of her tongue over her lips. "I'd have done the same thing in your place, Zant."

When his expression faltered and he cocked his head back, Jacey frowned. What had caused that? Then she heard her own words. She'd called him Zant. When had she even begun to think of him as Zant and stopped throwing Chapelo at him like it was an insult?

"Get up." His voice was no more than a growl.

Afraid she couldn't, not with her legs feeling like pudding, Jacey tensed her stomach muscles and rose in stages to her feet. Facing the legendary gunslinger only moments after he'd killed someone took all of Jacey's mettle. Because Papa'd told her that, just like a snake, a man who's just killed is at his most dangerous and unpredictable. "You aim to shoot me, Chapelo?"

His eyebrows rose a fraction, either at her words or at the Chapelo that came more naturally out of her mouth. "If I thought it would solve anything, I would. But it won't."

Jacey blinked and let out a deep breath. He'd just spared her life. He knew it, and she knew it. She was fast with a gun, yes. She'd shot at targets, like he said, and yes, she'd even wounded him, but there was no way on God's green earth she could take this man with a gun. Even Papa wasn't that fast. *Papa*. Even Papa wouldn't have stood a chance against the Kid's son. Jacey sniffed and kept her expression as sober as his. "With Rafferty dead, am I free to go on back to Tucson?"

"Yeah, you're free. Alberto and Rosie will be safe now. But you won't be. Don Rafael will send someone else after you. I'll try to stop him, but I don't know if I can. So, come sunup, I want you to hightail it on back to Tucson, get what belongs to you there, and then get yourself home to protection. I'll stall Don Rafael as long as I can to give you a chance to—"

Jacey held up a staying hand. Despite everything she'd just seen, she dared puff up like a toad at this man. "Now, just hold on right there, Chapelo. I appreciate your concern, but I've got business in Tucson."

Zant exploded into action, covering the ground between them in long, angry strides. Jacey had time only to tense before he grabbed her arms and hauled her up to his chest. "I said get the hell out of Tucson and get back home, gal. If I run into you again, if I have to keep looking at that Lawless face of yours, I'll have to kill you. Or worse. You take my meaning?"

Jacey couldn't imagine anything worse than being killed, but she wasn't about to ask what it was. "I take it. Now you take your hands off me. And don't call me gal."

He didn't take his hands off her. And he did call her gal. "Listen up, little gal, and listen good. You're toying with things here that I'm not sure you understand. Now, I don't know why your daddy sent you this far from home—"

"Nobody sent me anywhere. I go where I want. And Tucson is where I want to be." Jacey narrowed her eyes and fairly spat out her next words. "Don't you ever talk about my father, Chapelo. Ever. Not unless you want to end up like your friend over there. Because I'll back-shoot you if I have to. Believe me, it won't make a bit of difference to me."

Either something about her expression or something in her words, or both, stilled Chapelo. The moment seemed to hang on the edge of time. He eyed her askance. "What the hell *are* you doing here?"

Jacey wanted nothing more than to throw in his face exactly what she was doing here. But for the second time tonight, some new and cautious understanding in her, perhaps some new maturity, stopped her reckless tongue. When she spoke, she heard herself do so in a calm, cool voice, and wondered at its source. "My business is just that, Chapelo—my business. If and when it becomes yours, I'll look you up. You can count on that."

During the hard weeks of her trek to Tucson, Jacey'd gotten used to waking up to some mighty strange sights. But none compared to what greeted her when she opened her eyes the next morning. This time it wasn't the saguaros or the yuccas, or even the little cactus wren whose chirping had invaded her sleep. No, it was Zant Chapelo. The man was lying on his side in his own bedroll, but right next to her and facing her. His eyes remained closed in sleep. Deep, even breathing marked the rise and fall of his chambray-covered chest.

After her initial start of surprise, Jacey lay still, supporting her cheek with her bent arm, and stared at him. When in the night had he gotten up to put himself between her and the now-dead campfire? And why had he? Was it to hog all the fire's warmth for himself? Somehow, she didn't think so. For one thing, she didn't think the creosote-bush-dotted desert would dare chill him.

Jacey grinned at her own estimation of Zant Chapelo. To her, he could do anything. No, that wasn't it. To her, he was capable of anything. Yes, that suited him more. He was capable of anything. Using this rare opportunity to openly scrutinize the man, Jacey started with that black hair of his. Thick, wavy, somewhat longish and unruly. Somewhat like her own. Her grin at this comparison of the two of them froze when some quirk or sensation brought a grimace to Zant's sleeping face.

Jacey didn't exhale until she was sure he slept on. His broad forehead smoothed out, relieving the worry lines and resettling his black-winged eyebrows low over his deep-set eyes. Now Jacey frowned. The man had the longest eyelashes of anyone she'd ever seen. Their tips brushed against the high cut of his cheekbones and forced her attention to his straight but still slightly swollen nose and down to that square chin of his. She clutched at her bedroll to keep from reaching out to touch the raspy growth of beard that shadowed his jaw.

Then, another grin cut across her features when Zant's wide, firm mouth began to move, as if he were talking in his sleep. No words formed, no sound came out. Just movement. Something moved inside Jacey, too. Once again, her grin fled as she paid attention to her own body. Something low and deep, she realized, something gripped her, tightening her core and quickening her awareness of this man . . . as a man. And she didn't like it.

That was twice in three days she'd experienced womanly feelings for him. They were a first for her. Jacey narrowed her eyes in critical scrutiny of Zant Chapelo. Why him? What was it about him that, doggone it, appealed so to her? In a state of irritated agitation, Jacey shifted about under her blanket. In only a little while, the rising sun's fierce heat would render its cover unnecessary. But for now, Jacey stayed under its weight, as if the wool that covered her could protect her from Zant's nearness.

He was near enough to touch. Jacey swallowed against the sudden impulse that dried her mouth. She was going to touch him. Slowly, ever so slowly, she eased her hand out from under her blanket and slipped it across the thin line of sandy earth that separated her bedroll from his. When she touched his blanket, she bit at her lower lip and willed away the tremble in her fingers. Still, the twitchings persisted.

Unaccustomed to her body not responding to her will, Jacey stayed her hand, fisting it where it lay, only a breath away from the black and crisply curling hairs at his throat that peeked over the edge of his white combination suit. Not even a low grunt followed by a sigh from a little ways away, obviously Blue, could make her retreat now.

Inhaling deeply through flared nostrils, Jacey inched her hand forward. And came into contact with the foreign feel of a man. Instantly fascinated as much by the steady pulse at the base of his throat as she was by the curling hairs that danced under her feather-light touch, Jacey grinned with her discovery and moved her fingers to feel his skin. With a tentative touch, she explored the muscled expanse of his throat and found it to be warm and smooth where beard didn't cover it. His skin, brown and taut and yet silky, like leather tanned to a buttery softness, allowed her fingers to slip easily over it.

Jacey's wondering gaze flickered upward from his throat to his eyes. Now open and frankly staring at her. Startled, she froze, leaving her fingers still taking his pulse. Jacey wished she could be as sure of her own heartbeat. When mortification dropped over her like a cloudburst, she jerked her hand back. But not quite fast enough. Just like his lightning-flash quick draw, the man's hand covered hers before she got it back over the sandy line that separated them.

"Enjoying yourself, Miss Lawless?"

"No." Jacey prayed for a sudden third arm and hand to sprout up on her, so she'd have two free ones to dig herself a hole in the ground. Right now seemed as good and painful a time as any to die.

He leaned toward her and whispered, "I think you're lying."

Jacey's chin came up a notch, even as gooseflesh bumped her skin. First Rosie, and now Chapelo. Appeared to her that folks in Tucson had a fearsome bent toward calling other folks liars. "Don't flatter yourself. There was a . . . a bug on you."

His mouth twitched. "A bug?"

"Yeah. A bug."

His answer, a chuckling snort, brought the heat to Jacey's cheeks. But that warmth was nothing as to what slipped over her skin when he sent her a raw look that said he saw past her bravado, a look that said he'd peered into her soul. Completely unnerved, Jacey could only watch as he raised her hand to his mouth, cupped open her palm, and kissed it with a whole lot of slick daring.

Simple reflexes reacting to the foreign sensation jerked Jacey's hand. Zant's grip tightened. Trapped, caught in his web, she submitted. With a sinking feeling, knowing just how forbidden this one man was to her, she admitted to herself that she didn't want to pull away. Her mouth slacked open as she tried to pretend that her breasts didn't ache or that the vee in her thighs wasn't throbbing. A shallow, bated breath escaped her in a whisper. "What . . . what are you doing?"

Zant angled his heavy-lidded, black-eyed gaze up to her face. His strong, handsome features suddenly seemed all masculine angles and planes. "You tell me, Jacey. What am I doing?"

Jacey flicked her gaze down to her hand in his. "You're kissing me."

"Uh-uh." He let go of her and, with his hand now cupping the back of her head, he pulled her to him. "Now I'm kissing you."

Jacey opened her mouth to. . . . It didn't matter, because his head slanted down and his mouth took hers. His lips settled over hers as if they'd been formed to fit there perfectly. Jacey stiffened. Zant entreated, holding her more firmly to him. His tongue insisted, warmly and wetly, on entrance into her mouth. Sucking in much needed air through her nostrils, Jacey realized her eyes were closed, her hand was on his chest, and she was opening her mouth, giving him the access he wanted.

Still, when his tongue plunged into her mouth and stroked in and out, dueling with her tongue, Jacey's eyes flew open. Zant filled her vision. His eyes were closed. Jacey's fluttered closed and her hand fisted, knotting up a wad of his shirt in her grip. Sensations, new and hot and breathtaking, invaded her body. Parts of her that she'd never suspected could, came to life, and seemingly did so of their own volition.

After an eternity, Zant broke their wet kiss to trail nipping kisses over her jaw, down her neck. Lost in the flood of tingling nerve endings and belly-tightening tuggings, Jacey belatedly became aware that Zant's hand was on her breast. Through her blouse and chemise, he cupped it, softly kneaded it, flicked his thumb over the peak—

He'd done this before. Three days ago. Out in the street. Jacey stiffened and then shoved him away, shooting straight up to a sitting position. Staring at him as if she'd never seen him before, she scooted backward until she felt herself to be out of his range. She swiped her wrist over her wet lips and spat out, "Damn you, Chapelo."

Was that raspy, husky voice hers? Confusion, outrage, guilt, and awakened desire brought her dangerously close to reaching for her gun. She felt but couldn't control the twitching and trembling that claimed her face. "How dare you—?"

"Me?" Zant pulled himself up on his elbow and appeared completely unrepentant. "Put it any way you like to make yourself feel better, but we both know *you* started it." His black eyes slanted wolfishly at the corners, just as his mouth did. His voice became a damning hiss. "You asked for it. You got it. And you liked it."

Stung, guilty as charged, and sweaty with embarrassment, Jacey gasped and jumped to her feet. A movement on the other side of the smoldering campfire dragged her attention there. Her gaze locked with Blue's. Still in his bedroll, he immediately closed his eyes . . . and remained very still. Weak with mortification, knowing he'd seen and heard everything, Jacey looked down on Zant. And gave full vent to her anger. "I did no such thing. I didn't like anything about it. Just don't you ever lay a hand on me again, Chapelo. Because it'll be your last act on this earth, I promise you."

A dangerous glint came to his eyes, but he doused it as he rolled over onto his back, resting his head on his folded hands. His white and dazzling grin, itself a threat somehow, mocked Jacey's virtuous outrage. "Now, that's the difference between us. Because I'd love for you to put your hands on me again."

It was all Jacey could do not to kick sand in his hateful face. "Oh, I'll put my hands on you again, if you like. Only this time, I'll have a knife in one of 'em."

Now Zant laughed openly at her. "Is that so? And where are you going to get this knife?"

Aware of the show it'd give him to produce it, but not seeing any way around it, Jacey hiked up her split skirt, looked down at her own stockinged leg, and—over Chapelo's appreciative grunt—slowly unsheathed her long, thin and deadly sharp blade. Another grunt came from Chapelo, only this one had a more respectful sound to it.

Triumphant, Jacey held up the knife between them, turning it this way and that to allow its steel to catch and reflect the sun's hot rays. "Right here, Chapelo—that's where I'll get it. I always have it with me. Always. And don't think I don't know how to use it. Or that I won't."

With natural male grace, and undaunted spirit, Zant Chapelo rolled to his feet. Reaching behind himself, he produced a knife that made Jacey's look like a toothpick. Brandishing it in one hand, he hooked his other thumb into his waistband and considered her in a narrow-eyed way. "Don't think, Jacey Lawless, that you won't get a chance to prove your skill with that pig-poker, if you're still in Tucson when I get back from Sonora. Starting tomorrow, you've got two weeks. So consider yourself warned, little lady."

Chapter Five

This was about the last thing she needed, Jacey figured, an irritated grimace replacing her tired frown. She shortened the reins on a suddenly skittish Knight. Just then riding back into town from her desert nights with Chapelo, she could only wonder what was going on in Tucson this evening. Happy and drunk and lurching and war-whooping folks, men and women alike, soldiers and civilians, Indians, Mexicans and American outlaws, filled the dusty streets.

Torches blazed from makeshift sconces to light the desert night. Under the lights, cloth-covered tables littered the street on Jacey's route to Alberto's cantina, and boasted some of the most mouthwatering foods she'd ever smelled. Cheerful, chattering women presided over the tables and over the hordes of giggling, racing children underfoot everywhere. From a band somewhere around the next corner, lively rhythmic music could be heard. Whooping and whistling accompanied the cheerful strains.

When some exuberant revelers began firing their guns into the air—all too close for Knight's comfort—Jacey found herself suddenly forced into fighting a bucking bronco. Caught off guard and cussing up a storm, her felt hat flying through the air, her braid lashing her like the thick rope it was, she fought the reins, fought to get Knight's head up, all to the drunken delight of the celebrants. Jacey's determined efforts to stay in the saddle earned her sideshow status and drew a circle of clapping and cheering folks. Instant betting from the sidelines became the order of the day.

Finally, thanks to her superior skill as a horsewoman, or

maybe because Knight was more tired than she was—Jacey didn't care which—she was the victor. Within a few minutes of acting up, Knight smoothed out into a prancing canter around the inner perimeter of the circle that was their audience. Cheers and groans, apparently depending on which way the individual had bet, greeted horse and rider. Money exchanged hands as the big gelding heaved and blew and obeyed Jacey's every command. Sweating as much as her horse was, and feeling just as frazzled, she glared at the happy folks.

Reining Knight in at the center of her impromptu arena, Jacey remained silent as she looked around the circle. As if she'd commanded it, the revelers quieted, and then shushed those who weren't. When she had their attention, she called out, "Which one of you is holding the money?"

After a second's hesitation, a squat-legged old grizzled man came forward, a fist of wadded greenbacks held up high in his hand. "That'd be me, ma'am."

He stopped about twenty feet away on Jacey's right. Keeping her spine ramrod straight, and knowing another quiet entrance into Tucson was already shot as full of holes as Rafferty was, she transferred her reins to her left hand and rested her right on the butt of her Colt. "Good. I'll be taking my cut of the action, thank you."

At the groans and shouts of protest that stirred the night air, Jacey pulled her Colt and fired it in the air. Knight went stiff-legged, folks squawked and cringed and grabbed for neighbors. "Does that sound familiar to any of you yahoos? You made me lose my hat, and you like to've cost me my life. Could've seen my horse injured, too. Now, I'm tired, and I've had a bad day. So just hand over my share, or get ready for a shooting display the likes of which won't see all of you standing at the end of it."

A moment of strained silence, backed by the music on the night wind and the laughter on down the street, followed her words.

Then the old man holding the money stepped up another few feet and addressed the crowd. "I don't know 'bout the rest of ya, but I say the lady's right. I say we cut her in. Hell, I'll even give 'er my whole share—'cause I ain't seen but a handful of men as could keep his seat on a buckin' horse like she just did. Whadda ya say?"

Instantly won over, the crowd sent up a great cheer. And Jacey danged near had to fight Knight again. The mule-tempered gelding shied and fought to get his bit between his teeth. Again, Jacey prevailed and even managed to keep the horse mannerly while the money was counted and paid out. When the crowd finally began to disperse, she leaned over from her saddle to take her black slouch hat, full of greenbacks and held up to her by the same grinning old man.

"Ol' Deadeye found yer hat over there and handed it to me." Then, his rheumy blue eyes glinted and his gap-toothed mouth curled up in a grin. "I meant what I said—that was some mighty fine ridin', ma'am."

Jacey wadded up the money and poked it into her pocket. She settled her hat on her head and grinned at the old man. "Thank you. And I'm much obliged for the money. And my hat."

The old man patted Knight's shoulder. The gelding turned his head to warily eye the offender. "You and this here animal earned it. It was touch and go there for a minute, warn't it?"

Jacey nodded. "Yep. Especially from where I was sittin'."

The old man's shoulders and little potbelly shook with his cackling. "I'll warrant that's true enough."

"So, tell me, mister, which one of—"

"Name's McGinty. Ed McGinty."

Jacey ducked her head in acknowledgment. "Mr. McGinty, then. Tell me, which one of us—me or my horse—did *you* bet on?"

He eyed her a moment, then scratched at the white stubble on his cheeks. "Why, I bet on you, ma'am. I larnt long ago never to bet against a Lawless."

Struck mute at hearing her name fall from his lips, Jacey watched the old man turn and wander into the milling crowd. *Well, that did it.* She wondered if she was kidding herself—was she the only one in Tucson who thought her identity was a secret?

Finally, she nudged Knight into a walk. Skillfully and absently threading the gelding through the foot traffic, she gave free rein to her grumbing thoughts. She had less than two weeks before Chapelo showed up, hell-bent on showing her what was worse than being killed. No one told her what to do. Who did Chapelo think he was? Give her two weeks to clear out of town. Well, she'd just see his two weeks and raise him another one.

Then she blinked, first seeing him shoot down Rafferty, and then feeling his lips on hers, his hand on her breast . . . *Two weeks ought to be plenty of time to accomplish what I came here to do.*

Providing, of course, that Zant Chapelo didn't turn out to be the one she aimed to flush out.

After stabling Knight in the tiny corral behind Alberto's cantina, after brushing him down while he munched on oats, Jacey paced tiredly through the deserted and dusty courtyard, only to find herself faced with a locked back door. Her saddlebags slid from her shoulder in defeat. Making a face, she retrieved the leather pouches, flung them over her shoulder again, and set out for the front of the squat adobe building. Just what she wanted to do—wade through the happy citizens again.

With her chip firmly back on her shoulder, and daring anyone to say she couldn't set foot inside a saloon because she was female, Jacey pushed through the bat-wing doors to Alberto's establishment. Stopping just inside, she frowned, going narrow-eyed at the cheerful and chaotic scene that greeted her.

Loud-talkin', whiskey-drinkin', back-slappin', and card-playin' men. The place reeked with their sweat and exuberance. As she stood there, searching the crowd for a flash of color that would be Rosie, Jacey saw a few men catch sight of her, poke a neighbor, and nod toward her.

With studied indifference, she ignored them, sighting instead on Alberto. Dressed all in dirty white, bar towel over his shoulder, he chattered away and presided over the revelry. Finally he looked up from assisting a young, skinny Mexican male pour drinks up and down the length of the bar. Alberto glanced at her, looked away, and then swung his attention right back to her. His swarthy, mustachioed face lit up. "*Señorita Law—Señorita! Madre de Dios!* Where have you been, *muchacha*?"

Jacey tensed and then let out her breath when Alberto caught his own slip of the tongue. His arms raised in greeting, he stepped out from behind his bar, irritatedly shoving men out of his way, elbowing and fussing at others in rapid-fire Spanish. When a path finally cleared, he all but ran to her, enveloping her in his arms before she could protest.

Tired as she was, she wasn't sure she could've stopped him, anyway. Or would've, because it felt good, just for a moment, to have someone glad to see her and to let someone . . . well, mother her. Right now, she suspected she'd even let Biddy cluck over her.

Alberto broke his hug and stepped back. And realized, after exchanging a look with her, that the oppressive quiet in his very packed and stuffy cantina was aimed at them. "Come, *chica,* we will get you to your room. Let's go this way." To his customers, he waved a hand in the air and proclaimed something in Spanish which made them all cheer. He turned to her. "I tell them the next round is on the house."

Clapping and banging on the tables resulted from Alberto's generosity and got him and Jacey ignored in favor of the remaining bartender. As the swarming men tried to belly up to the bar with their glasses, Alberto put an arm around Jacey's shoulders and herded her, with loud fussing and a waving hand, through the sea of men.

"Where's Rosie?" Jacey called out over the crush of noise.

"My Rosarita is right over there." He turned Jacey with him to look. "No, she is over here, then." He turned her in that direction. "Ah, there she is. Rosie! Look who has returned to us, *mi vida.*"

"I don't think she can hear you," Jacey offered, watching Rosie serve a table of surprisingly respectful men their drinks from a big tray she balanced at her waist.

"I think what you say is true, no?"

"No. I mean, yes." Jacey shook her head in little mind-clearing jerks. "Don't bother her. I'll see her tomorrow."

"*Sí. Mañana.* Now we will get you to your room, and then I will myself bring to you a nice plate of enchiladas and tamales. That sounds good to you, no?"

"No—yes. I haven't eaten in so long that my belly thinks my throat's been cut." She then nodded in the direction of the street. "What's going on in Tucson tonight? I never saw the likes of this in my life."

Alberto shrugged as he switched his bar towel to his other shoulder. With his free hand, he opened the heavy oaken door into the short, musty hallway which led to Jacey's room. "It is called a *fandango*—a party, a dance. All over Tucson, the people are happy."

Accepting Alberto's gesture for her to precede him through the doorway, Jacey stepped through. "I can see that. But why?"

Alberto followed her and closed the door behind him, significantly muffling the revelry. "Oh, *mi querida,* there is no why. There is a *celebración* for—how do you say?—um, just because? Just because someone sets out *la comida*—the food—someone else strums his guitar, and yet another begins to dance. Before you know it, all of Tucson dances and eats and drinks. And some even fall in love. Perhaps you would like to join in?"

Darned if that Zant Chapelo's dark and grinning face didn't present itself to her mind's eye. Jacey shook her head, as much to rid herself of the image, as to turn down Alberto's suggestion. "No, thanks, Mr. Estrada." At the door to the room she thought of as hers, Jacey put her hand on the wrought-iron latch and depressed it. "I've already stabled Knight out back. So, if you don't mind, all I want is to eat and get some shut-eye."

Alberto patted her arm. "I will see that no one disturbs you—this time." He then drew himself up into a fine military stance, as if he were bravely facing a firing squad. "It is my fault that you have that ugly bruise on your jaw. I should cut out my own heart and—"

"Whoa! I hardly think all that's called for. But there is one thing you can tell me."

With his unblinking gaze focused just to her left, Alberto maintained his stiff pose and entoned, "Anything, *querida.*"

"Do you know an Ed McGinty?"

Alberto lateraled his gaze over to Jacey and then just as quickly snaked it away from her face. "*Sí,* he is known to me."

"Mr. Estrada, look at me."

He did. But his expression said he clearly didn't want to.

"I met him tonight, out on the street. He knew my name. How would he know my name?"

Alberto grinned in a sickly sort of way. "Because I told him?"

Disbelief widened Jacey's eyes. When she recovered, she asked, "Now why would you go and do that?"

"Because he is a friend of mine, and he always admired your father, as did I."

"Well, I appreciate that, Mr. Estrada, but you're not going to tell everyone in Tucson who I am, are you?"

"Oh, no, no, no. Just this one. You see, his son rode in your father's gang."

"He what?" Jacey's screeching tone didn't suffer any from her stiffening with her fisted hands at her sides. "His son? I never heard Papa talk of any McGinty. And I know all their names."

Alberto continued the humble nodding he'd been doing since his confession. "He was with them only for one summer. Did you hear your father speak of . . . how do you say . . . Rooster?"

Now Jacey's eyes narrowed. "Well, sure I did." Then she straightened and held up a hand. "Wait a minute. Ed McGinty—that nice old man—his son is Rooster? Papa said Rooster was just a red-haired kid who hated guns, but wanted real bad to be an outlaw."

"*Sí.*" Alberto nodded. "That was Rooster. Your father let him ride with them, but made sure the *muchacho* did not like the life. He came back to Tucson and married and gave my friend, Eduardo, many grandchildren. Señor McGinty always liked your father for what he did for his son. But poor Rooster. He is dead now. A fever took him."

"Well, I'm sure sorry to hear that." And she was. But her focus on the old gang being what it was, she mentally crossed one name off her list.

"No. I won't do it. It is *loco.* You will get yourself killed—like this." Rosie drew her finger across her throat and then hurriedly crossed herself. She next resumed her industrious sweeping of the cantina. Mid-afternoon heat mixed with the dispirited breeze coming in through the open windows and with the dust she was raising.

Jacey wrinkled her nose and swatted at the dry and choking miasma. "All I'm asking you to do is tell a few tall tales."

"These tales, they are called lies, Catarina. You will get yourself killed and send all our souls straight to *el diablo.*"

Her broom clattered to the wooden floor as Rosie reverently clasped her hands under her chin, closed her eyes, and sent a silent prayer heavenward.

Jacey stared levelly at her friend for a moment, looking her up and down from her tied-back black hair to her loose white blouse—what Rosie called her *blusa*—and plain, woven brown skirt. Jacey had on similar clothes, borrowed from Rosie. She slept in their bed, ate their food, and wore Rosie's clothes. She'd been accepted as family by them. And now she wanted to damn their souls to hell for all their hospitality. According to Rosie.

Jacey braced an elbow on the cantina table and rubbed in resignation at her forehead. There wasn't one dad-blamed thing that'd come easy here in Tucson. Not even her name. Jacey, as pronounced by these folks, was Hacey. And that was just plain dumb-sounding to her. So they'd settled on her middle name, Catherine. After a fashion. She was now Catarina to the Estradas and all of Tucson.

Jacey shook her head, hearing again their mid-morning breakfast conversation in the bright and airy little kitchen off their adjoining rooms behind the cantina. Over omelets heaped with ham and cheese and mild peppers, they'd listened to Jacey's lie of a story about her disappearing to check out some leads on the stolen keepsake. All clucking concern—reminding her of Biddy back home—they'd made her promise not to take off again without telling them. Jacey'd made an easy promise, knowing that she hadn't gone of her own free will to begin with. And didn't intend to go again.

Tired of Rosie's infernal praying and arguing with her, Jacey drummed her fingers on the table's rough and scarred surface. "You done praying yet?"

Rosie lowered her hands and opened her eyes. "Are you still asking me to lie?"

"Yes."

Rosie immediately raised her clasped hands again and closed her eyes.

Jacey banged a hand on the table. "Now, cut that out. Your father's already said he'd do it for me, so why won't you?"

Rosie again lowered her hands and opened her eyes. "Because, as you have seen, I must worry for my father. He is too kindhearted, and he tells everything he knows. My mother''—Rosie crossed herself—''God rest her soul, is not here to watch over him.''

Jacey quirked her mouth up in irritation. And maybe a little guilt. ''All I'm asking you to say is that you served a drink to J. C. Lawless. That's all. I'm not asking you to go up against the soldiers at the fort all by yourself.''

Rosie put her hands to her waist and stepped over her fallen broom. ''At least God could understand that.'' After that lofty pronouncement, she drooped her shoulders and came to stand in front of Jacey. ''All right, *mi amiga,* it is as you say. My father has already agreed—only because he feels so bad for telling Señor McGinty who you are. But now? If I do not also say that what he says is true—that Señor Lawless himself was in our cantina—then he will be known as a liar. And so''—she shrugged her slender shoulders, showing a wealth of natural feminine grace that Jacey found herself envying—''I will do this thing for you. But you must do something for me in return.''

Jacey cocked her head at a wary angle. ''Like what? Finish sweeping?''

''No. You must attend services with me at the mission church.''

Jacey came straight up out of her chair, causing it to thump over backward. ''Like hell I will.''

Rosie gasped and crossed herself, looking around the cantina as if she expected demons to pop up all about them. When they didn't, she arched a finely formed eyebrow and narrowed her eyes at Jacey. ''Like hell you won't, *chica.*''

''I will not. My sisters and I learned our Bible at home with Mama. And that was good enough for me. I've never set foot in a church in my life.''

''Then it is about time you did, yes?''

''Yes.'' Jacey heard herself. ''I mean no. And stop doing that yes and no thing. I haven't gotten one right yet.''

''Then you must learn to listen better. Now, will you go to church with me or not?''

Jacey quirked her mouth into a straight and exasperated line. ''Yes, I'll go. But I don't have to like it.''

''Ah, but you will.'' Rosie dropped her tough stance and laughed as she tugged a resisting Jacey into her arms. She even kissed her on the cheek, much to Jacey's outraged chagrin. And secret girlish delight. Rosie finally stepped back and sat down across from Jacey. "Now, Catarina. Tell me of this plan of yours to catch a thief."

Her passion for her mission leaned Jacey over the table toward Rosie. "Well, it's really simple."

"What is so simple, Catarina?"

At the sound of Alberto's voice, Jacey turned with Rosie to face him. He went behind the bar and began alternately checking his liquor stock and turning an expectant face to the girls. Jacey exchanged a look with Rosie and then turned to Alberto. "My plan to catch a thief."

Alberto straightened up like something had bitten him on the behind. He thumped a whiskey bottle down hard onto the bar. "Catch a thief?"

"Yeah. I think I'm close to doing that already. You see, I didn't quite tell you the whole truth this morning—"

Rosie gasped. "Do you see how it is with lying? You tell one lie, and then, the next thing you know, you are chasing off after dangerous thieves."

Jacey rolled her eyes at Rosie and turned back to Alberto. "Like I said, I was going after a lead. That part's true enough. But what I didn't tell you is . . . I was with Zant Chapelo." Jacey stopped talking. Even though neither Rosie nor Alberto had interrupted her, she felt their silence had somehow deepened. Looking from one to the other, and suddenly unsure of herself, she went on haltingly. "We were, um, riding for Sonora with his friend, Blue, and that Rafferty skunk—the one who hit me."

Again, she looked from one to the other of them. No response. Just black-eyed stares and a heavy, censuring silence. Swallowing, feeling the day's heat like never before, Jacey went on.

"Well, the second night at camp, somewhere out in the desert, Rafferty got into it with Zant and got himself killed for his insults. I tell you, I've never seen the like of that man's quick draw. He made greased lightning look purely sluggish." Shaking her head at the memory, she next recalled herself sleeping next to Zant and then kissing him the next morning. A sudden intake of breath forced on her by her conscience told her she'd best leave that part out.

But the rest of her words tumbled out of her like rolling

pebbles in a swift-moving stream. "And then, yesterday morning, Zant told me to go back to Tucson and take care of my business and get out of town before he got back in two weeks. He said he'd kill me or worse—but I don't know what that means—if I was still here. So, I hightailed it back here, and he went on to see his grandfather, that Don Rafael Cal . . . Calde . . . Calde-something."

"Don Rafael Calderon."

"Yeah, that's him." Grateful for Alberto's breaking his silence, but aware that he said the man's name like it was a sin, Jacey half grinned, half frowned. Clearing her throat, she added, "Now, from what I've learned so far, I think this Calderon is involved. I learned something else, too. Maybe you can tell me if it's true. Was Zant in prison for the past five years?"

Jacey watched Alberto look past her to his daughter. She spun to look at Rosie. She was looking at her father, so Jacey turned back to him. "Well?"

He finally focused on her. "*Sí,* he was in prison."

Jacey nodded, feeling one of the knots in her stomach unravel. She took a deep breath before asking, "And when did he get out?"

Alberto shrugged and shook his head. "Maybe a month ago? No more than that."

As Rosie walked past her to go confer in low tones with Alberto, Jacey almost slumped onto the table, so great was her complete relief regarding Zant. He wasn't a liar. He was innocent. Then, catching herself singing the man's praises, she conceded that even though he might have his good points, she couldn't forgive him for making her feel things for him she shouldn't. Or for making her think of nothing but him and his mouth on hers.

Jacey jerked upright, fearing she wore some cow-eyed look on her face, like the ones she teased Glory about having whenever some boy fell at her feet in worship—as they always did. Well, except for Riley Thorne. Now, there was a man Jacey could respect. Riley didn't let Glory get away with anything, and that just got Glory stomping mad—Jacey jerked upright again. *What in the world is wrong with me that I'm giving myself over to daydreaming?*

Jacey self-consciously looked from Rosie to Alberto, only

to realize, by their expressions, that her fears were well grounded. She had given something away. Dividing her wary attention between the two, she asked, "Why are you two acting so funny all of a sudden?"

Rosie came back to the table, sat down, and reached across the table to take Jacey's hands in hers. Unaccustomed to such intimacy, Jacey looked from their entwined hands, both sets small and long-fingered, to her friend's earnest face. "What?"

"Catarina, do you hear yourself talking? Señor Chapelo is now Zant to you. And your face, when you speak of him, is very soft, very *enamorada*."

Already fearing what that word meant, and afraid she knew, Jacey nevertheless sat back and pulled her hands out of Rosie's grasp. "What does that mean—that *enamorada* word?"

Rosie gave her a soft smile. "In love, I believe you would say."

A sudden hotness suffused Jacey's face, catapulting her up and out of her chair. "I'm no such thing." She turned at the sound of Alberto's approaching footsteps. "Tell her, Mr. Estrada. Tell her that's just crazy talk. Why, I care more about my horse than I do that polecat outlaw Chapelo."

Alberto stopped beside the table, putting himself between Jacey and Rosie. With a hand on Jacey's shoulder, he urged her to sit down. "Come, *querida*, what my Rosarita says is true for all to see."

Jacey sat, but she wasn't the least bit mollified. "Hogwash. The day I start getting all soft over the likes of Zant Chapelo—"

"Is already here, I am afraid," Rosie cut in. "And this worries me very much."

Jacey narrowed her eyes at Rosie. "You're gettin' a might too personal for me, sister. What I feel or don't feel is my business."

Mouth quirked into a grin, Rosie sat back and crossed her arms under her bosom. "Don't worry, *mi amiga*. I will keep your secret safe."

Angry heat exploded Jacey to her feet again and forced Alberto to step back. "I already told you—there is no secret. Now, I don't want to hear any more about it. All I need from you is a yes or a no on helping me."

Rosie's smirk faded to a gentle smile. "All right, *her-*

mana—sister, as you call me, I will speak no more of it. I will help you. Tell me what to do."

Jacey relaxed and sat down. She motioned to Alberto. "Get a chair and sit here a minute, Mr. Estrada. I'll tell you my plan. And how you both can help me."

Zant pushed his plate away and shook his head, signaling to Conchita that he didn't care for more. The round little maid made a dissapproving-mother face as she stepped back from the long table, taking the serving platter with her to the richly carved sideboard behind Zant.

The clinking of china accompanied her movements and mingled with the trillings of a songbird perched atop the high adobe walls of the bougainvillea-draped courtyard. With the room's double doors open to the afternoon breeze, the happy splashings of water in the tiled fountain kept the silence in the large, airy dining room from being oppressive.

For his part, Zant sprawled back in his chair, bracing an elbow on its armrest. Silently, soberly, he watched his grandfather's meticulous gestures as he finished his meal.

As if he sensed Zant's attention on him, the old man looked up, ran his gaze over his grandson, and then gestured with his silver fork, indicating Zant's still-laden but ignored plate. "Is something wrong with your food? I can have Anna cook you something else."

"No. Nothing's wrong with the food."

Don Rafael rested his wrists against the table's edge and stared pointedly at Zant. "Then perhaps it is your appetite? Or the company?"

"Or both," Zant came back.

Still holding his fork and knife, Don Rafael gestured as if helpless to figure out his grandson. "What have I done now? I am aware of nothing—"

"Bullshit."

Don Rafael's face darkened dangerously. His knuckles whitened as he gripped his utensils tightly. "I will not tolerate that language at my table." He slammed his fist down on the table, making the silver candelabra jump and Conchita flee from the room. "And especially not in front of my servants. I did not pay a handsome sum to free you from prison just to have you—"

"Just to have me what?" Zant leaned forward, as hot and angry as the old man. "Come back here and *not* kiss your ass? I didn't ask you to get me out, and I won't thank you. The price is too high."

Don Rafael stiffened and sat back, his black eyes glaring daggers at Zant. In the next moment, he took a deep breath and smoothed out his features. Zant knew this look by heart. This was not over, just glossed over. And only for now.

Don Rafael thinned his wide slash of a mouth. "Very well, then. I won't ask you to thank me. It doesn't matter. Because, thanked or not, the result is the same—you are out of prison."

Zant snorted and leaned back against his chair's high back. "I'm out of *one* prison, at any rate."

Don Rafael stared a moment and then very carefully, giving the act his full attention, placed his knife and fork beside his plate, arranging them just so on the table's polished-tile surface. Then he raised his large, white-haired head and turned his swarthy attention on Zant. "Why do you hate me so? You are my blood, the only child of my only child. My heart's desire is whatever is best for you, *mi hijo.* Everything I do is for you."

Zant said nothing, only stared. He'd heard all this before.

Don Rafael's features melted into an entreating mask. "How can you call this a prison?" He made a broad gesture with his thick hand, indicating the elegantly furnished room, but meaning, Zant knew, all of the walled compound that comprised La Casa del Cielo Azul, The House of the Blue Sky. "How can you think of Cielo Azul that way? It will be yours one day soon."

Zant smirked his contempt. He knew too much and suspected even more about Don Rafael to be fooled by his show of hurt. "I don't want it."

Don Rafael narrowed his eyes and jutted his chin out. He spoke in a low and deadly tone that reminded Zant of a hissing snake. "What you want does not matter. You are my blood. What will be yours, will be yours. It can be no other way."

Zant stared levelly at the black-clad old man at the other end of the long table. For long moments, the creaking-squeaking of the breeze-stirred, overhead fans ruled the silence between them. Zant then breathed in deeply and let it out slowly. ''Speaking of blood, why are you having the Lawlesses tracked?''

Don Rafael, in the act of picking up his fork and knife again, stilled and then leaned toward Zant. ''Who says that I am?''

''Rafferty.''

Don Rafael raised an eyebrow, but then lowered his gaze to his plate. He very precisely sliced his knife through his steak's all-but-raw flesh as he asked, ''Where did you see him?''

Zant watched the old man raise the fork-impaled chunk to his mouth. ''Tucson.''

Don Rafael chewed slowly, swallowed, and shook his head. ''I know of no tracking going on. I gave no such orders.''

The old man's lie nearly catapulted Zant to his feet. Exercising great restraint, but tensed like a mountain lion ready to spring, he clutched at his chair's armrests. ''That's not what Rafferty said.''

''Then Rafferty lies.''

''Yeah, he lies . . . in a shallow grave about halfway between here and Tucson.'' Zant shifted in his chair and crossed a black-booted ankle over the opposite knee. ''I know because I put his worthless hide in it.''

Don Rafael closed his thick-fingered hand around his wine goblet, much as if he grasped a delicate, helpless throat. He raised the crystal to his lips, drained its contents, and then set it gingerly on the table. ''I wish you hadn't done that.''

Zant shrugged. ''I didn't have any choice. He insulted me, my father, and my mother—your daughter.''

Don Rafael licked his lips and worked his mouth, as if tasting the last of the wine that clung there. ''I see. Tell me, Zant, why was Rafferty with you?''

Considering his answer as carefully as he would a chess move, and already anticipating his opponent's surprised reaction, Zant replied, ''Because the Lawless woman was with me.''

Don Rafael disappointed him by merely frowning as he leaned back against his chair. ''I see. But where is she now? She was not with you when you rode in last night. Does she, then, perhaps share a grave with Rafferty?''

Zant's hands fisted. His grandfather's words confirmed his

involvement, and yet gave nothing away. Zant'd forgotten how wily the old man was. And how much better he was at this game than he could ever hope to be. Or want to be. "I wouldn't raise my hand against a woman."

Don Rafael grinned in a cold and superior manner. "The day may come when you will, *mi hijo*." He then placed his napkin on the table and stood, easily lifting his still powerful body out of the chair. "If you will excuse me on your second day home, I have business to attend to. I will see you this evening?"

"What choice do I have?"

Don Rafael nodded sagely. "True." He then turned his back on his grandson and left the room.

Alone now, Zant slumped and exhaled heavily. It had always been thus between him and Don Rafael. Always the mistrust, the sparring. So what made him think this time would be any different? What a fool he was to hope that the old man, just once, would—*Forget it, Chapelo. He'll never change, and neither will you.*

Knowing it and accepting it were two different things. Downhearted, Zant stared at the room's arched entryway under which his grandfather had passed only moments ago. Finally shrugging off the old hurts, Zant chided himself for tipping his hand. He'd revealed far more than he'd learned. And he'd just made things worse for Jacey. A lot worse.

Zant ran a hand over his mouth and muttered, "Son of a *bitch*."

CHAPTER SIX

"It ain't no lie, Phelps. Ah'm a-tellin' ya J. C. Lawless hisself is right here in Tucson. Seen 'im with my own eyes, Ah did."

Phelps pushed up the brim of his sweat-stained hat with a sausagelike finger. "Pete, you lyin' old hound dog, when'd you see J. C. Lawless?"

"Last night. Just standin' there all leaned up against the Casa Grande Hotel."

A burst of laughter followed his pronouncement. Phelps waved the crowd of men to silence and leaned over the cantina table toward Pete. "Last night? When you was liquored up and stumblin' home? That's when you seen J. C. Lawless? You sure you didn't see yer dead old mama, too?"

Pete made a strangled noise and jumped up, sending his chair and about ten highly entertained men scooting backward. He shoved his ratty gray combination-suit sleeves up his skinny arms. "Don't you be sayin' nothin' about my mama, Phelps. I done tole you once about that."

Rosie parted the crowd and stepped into the breech. "Now, what is this fussing all about over here?" Looking around the knot of suddenly moon-eyed, docile men, she smiled prettily and patted Pete's bony shoulder before batting her eyelashes at the corpulent Phelps. "Señor Phelps, have you been a bad boy?"

Señor Phelps melted and turned red and got the silliest grin on his heavy-jowled, freckled face. He dragged his hat off his head, revealing thinning reddish-orange hair, and held his tattered hat over his heart. "Oh, no, ma'am. Not atall. We was just kiddin' old Pete here. He says he seen J. C. Lawless hisself right here in Tucson.''

Rosie gasped, feigning surprise. She turned to Pete. ''Señor Pete, you saw him, too?'' She hastily crossed herself. Some of the men, obviously startled by her confession, halfheartedly mimicked her actions before catching themselves and looking self-consciously around.

But Pete nearly crowed as he pointed at Phelps. ''See there? What'd Ah tell ya? Ah bet you won't be callin' Miss Rosie a liar, now will ya?''

Phelps ignored Pete as he turned to Rosie. ''You seen him, too?''

Rosie nodded vigorously. ''*Sí.* Two nights ago.'' She lowered her voice to a conspiratorial whisper. The men leaned in to hear better. ''Right here in our cantina. It was very late, and he sat right over there.'' Employing great drama, she pointed to a sun-drenched table by the window. All heads followed her gesture, and a quiet reverence befell the men as they stared at the sight. ''He ordered a bottle of our finest whiskey. And drank it all himself. He never said another word. But when he left, he gave to me a big tip.''

A feminine snort from over by the bar turned heads that way. Rosie grinned and winked at Jacey, who was dressed like her and working as a barmaid. What harm could it do to remind these men that they too could leave her tips?

''Did you see him, too, Catarina?'' one of the men called out to Jacey.

Jacey nodded and wiped the bar down with more vigor than necessary as she spoke out the side of her mouth, ''I'll give you an amen to that. I saw him up close and personal. Real personal.''

A murmuring buzz traveled around the circle of men. Rosie regained their attention when she added, ''Oh, wait, I am mistaken. He did say something.''

Now Alberto chimed in, walking rapidly over to his daughter as he waved his bar towel like a flag of warning. ''No, no, *mi hija.* I am not so sure Señor Lawless would want us to repeat his words. He is *un malo.* And despite our years of friendship, I would not wish to anger him.''

But the men weren't standing for that. Cries of ''Let her speak'' made the rounds. Alberto feigned surrender and retreated, mumbling about having tried to stop her, but what is a father to do?

The men collectively held their breath and leaned in again over Rosie, like tall branches shading a single delicate flower. Rosie put a hand to her waist and tapped a finger against her lips. "Now, what was it he said? Oh, yes. He said he was looking for—no, not looking for—um, hunting down? Yes, that's it. He said he was hunting down each and every man who rode in his gang."

She then smiled brightly and pretended not to notice the shocked looks and paling faces all around her. A tall man with a bobbing Adam's apple spoke up, but with all the enthusiasm of giving his last confession. "Wal, since Miss Rosie and Miss Catarina seen him, I guess it's all right for me to tell y'all that my boy said he spied J. C. hisself over by the livery stable just yesterday afternoon."

Rosie and the men all stared at this new speaker. But none of them was as surprised as Rosie. Jacey'd been nowhere near the livery stable when she was dressed as J. C. Lawless. And certainly not in the afternoon. But apparently Jacey's plan was working—rumors were spreading like wildfire. And after only three days, people were inventing their own sightings. This was good. She hoped.

Through a break in the crowd of men, she saw Jacey shaking her head, as if she were embarrassed by all the lying going on. Grinning, Rosie raised her eyebrows at her friend and then nodded when Jacey gestured that she was leaving out the back way.

Knowing that dark was descending and aware of Jacey's intentions, Rosie focused again on the men. "You know, señores, I would not be surprised if others of you saw him tonight. He could be anywhere in all of Tucson."

That danged Rosie. For someone who professed to hate lying, she sure took to it like stink on a cow patty. In her room now at the back of the cantina, Jacey began shedding her loose-fitting white *blusa* and brown skirt. Bracing her bottom against the bed's headboard, she brought first one leg and then the other up to untie and kick off her borrowed leather sandals. Left only in her thin chemise and bloomers, she stripped them off, too, tossing them carelessly onto the bed. A grin tugged at her mouth. *Never did see Papa wear one of these even once.*

Naked now, except for her thigh-strapped knife, she unstrapped it and tossed it aside. No sense wearing a weapon she couldn't get to. From the foot of her bed she yanked up a tied bundle of Alberto's clothes. She started with the hot and itchy but more manly red combination suit, grimacing as she pulled it up and over her skin. Well, at least since it was dark, and given Papa's fearsome reputation that kept folks from coming too close, she didn't have to bind her breasts.

Twitching all around until the undergarment felt as good as it was going to, she donned the too-big pants, leather belt, white pullover shirt, and silver-studded vest. She next tied a bandanna around her neck, strapped on Papa's Colt, and sat on the bedside to tug on her wool stockings and boots.

Then, she reached for her saddlebags, and with great reverence, pulled out Papa's silver spurs. She swallowed the lump in her throat, even as her hands lovingly traced the spurs' contours. *Hannah's after the killers, Papa. And I'll find the thieves. I swear to you.*

Firming her features and her resolve, Jacey attached the spurs to her boot heels. That done, she stood up and walked around, feeling comforted by the jangling music that accompanied her steps. Then she retrieved a thong of rawhide from off the bed, clenched it in her teeth, and bent over at the waist. With practiced motions she twisted her mane of hair into a whirlwindlike knot until it curled up on itself. She straightened up to tie the huge bun up high on her head, and then donned her black slouch-brimmed hat, pulling it low over her brow. *There. J. C. Lawless lives. And now, to haunt the streets of Tucson.*

She slipped out of her room and made her way outside to the tiny corral where Knight wickered softly when he smelled her. Stepping up to the fence, she stroked the gelding's soft muzzle when he arched his neck and stretched out to push against her arm. "No, you're not going. But it's working, Knight," she whispered. "My plan's working."

The gelding snorted and nodded his head, as if he agreed. Jacey chuckled softly. "Now this is exactly why you can't go. You'd give me away in a heartbeat. I don't need someone recognizing your ornery hide and giving the lie to everything we've done."

With that, Jacey gave the big horse a final pat and turned away. She skulked along the adobe wall's shadows until she came to the latched gate that would admit her into the alley. Depressing the latch, she stepped through and closed the creaking gate behind her. Looking both ways, she decided to wind her way through Tucson's alleys all the way to the wooden fortress that was Fort Lowell.

Once there, she'd haunt its outside perimeter and let the soldiers add to the wagging tongues with their own J. C. Lawless sighting. She'd have to be more than careful, she warned herself, because these men, unlike the civilians who seemed to revere the Lawless name, just might take a potshot at her. But the risk was worth the effort, she reassured herself.

Because her plan was working, and folks were talking about the return of J. C. Lawless. It seemed everyone had seen him, from wide-eyed young boys, to whispering old women, to lolling drunks. And they all had a different, wilder story to tell about their encounter with the outlaw himself. Jacey shook her head and chuckled as she raised her hat just enough to swipe her sleeve over her sweating forehead. How folks loved to talk.

Resettling her hat and turning into the next mazelike stretch of alley, she figured she didn't have long to wait until word spread to every corner of Tucson and to the far hills. And when that happened, someone would be flushed out. A guilty someone. Yeah, some thieving skunk who had reason to come see how it was that J. C. Lawless was here. And alive.

And when that so-and-so made himself known—Jacey hitched at the heavy Colt holstered against her right hip—she, Jacey Lawless, would be ready. With her steps marked by the jangling spurs strapped at her heels, Jacey heard Hannah's words come back to her. "For J. C. Lawless. For Catherine Lawless. Vengeance."

Zant turned toward the pinging sound and tensed. Staring at the closed beveled-glass French doors which opened onto a narrow balcony ledge outside his bedroom, he tucked his towel more firmly around his waist, picked up his pistol, and edged closer to the curtain-paneled doors.

Cautiously moving aside the sheer material, he looked down onto the night-enshrouded courtyard below. Nothing out of the ordinary. And certainly no one was there. Shaking his head, figuring he must be hearing things, he turned back to the tub he'd just vacated and tossed his gun onto his bed.

Ripping the damp toweling from around his waist, he finished drying off. One nice thing about being at Cielo Azul was the steady baths and shaves. He rubbed the towel over his hair to dry it. Not to mention the haircuts Anna gave him, when she wasn't cooking up his favorite meals and exclaiming over how good it was to have him home. Zant snorted. Home. Hardly.

Ping!

He jerked toward the sound again and frowned. *Dammit.* Was someone playing a game? Yanking his pants off the end of his wide bed, he pulled them on and fastened them as he walked over to the doors. Just as he tugged aside the sheers, he remembered his gun. But before he could turn away for it, he heard the owl's hoot. And froze.

Blue. Recognizing their secret call, perfected in their childhood, Zant quickly unlatched the French doors and stepped onto the narrow, wrought-iron-grilled balcony. Looking down into the dark courtyard, hearing the fountain waters splashing and the crickets chirping, Zant grinned at the sight Blue made standing there and looking up at him. Grasping the balcony's railing, he called out, "It's kind of late for me to sneak out, Blue."

But Blue wasn't in the mood for teasing. Looking all around and then putting a finger to his lips to hush Zant, he removed his hat. Speaking just above a whisper, he hissed, "It's later than you think, *amigo*. I need to talk to you—now."

Zant's abdomen clenched at his friend's serious tone. "I'll be right down."

"Good. Conchita nearly caught me out here a minute ago. I had to duck back behind the fountain. I'll go wait for you in *el campo*."

Zant nodded, picturing the nest of dwellings outside Cielo Azul that abutted the hacienda's adobe walls. The encampment was nothing more than a small city for Don Rafael's servants and for those men who'd sworn their loyalty and their guns to the old man. Like a feudal lord and his vassals. "Go on. I'll find you."

Blue nodded and silently slipped away. Zant stared down

at the flagstone tile on which his friend had stood only a moment ago. He took a deep breath of the night air, inhaling the cool disdain of nature for the problems of man. Zant chuckled. He'd been reading too much while he was here. He needed to get outside more and do something physical, something reckless.

Like what? He pictured Jacey Lawless, remembering how she'd looked on the trail when she awakened him with her touch.

Feeling suddenly too hot for his britches, Zant shook his head, hoping to dispel the image before he could harden from the remembered feel of her breast, the taste of her kiss. . . . He looked down at his crotch. *Too late*. Running a hand through his hair in sudden restless agitation, and warning Jacey to get out of his head, Zant stepped back inside and closed the doors, being careful to lock them.

And that act, locking the doors, more than anything else he could do, sobered him and evaporated his heated thoughts of burying himself deep in Jacey Lawless. He looked at his hands on the cold metal latch. Even here, he didn't know who his enemies were. No—especially here.

Instantly, his Spanish blood resettled, withdrew, leaving him alert but not aroused. In only bare minutes, Zant added a black shirt and boots to his pants. With his Colt stuck in his waistband, he edged out of his room and very carefully toed his way down the terra-cotta-tiled curving stairway. The silence of the large, square main rooms downstairs, as he passed by each richly decorated one, seemed to mock him. Zant clenched his jaw until it hurt. *Cielo Azul could never be home*.

Once outside, he carefully closed the heavy, carved wooden door behind him, and then stood still in the night's cool air for a moment as he looked and listened. No telltale footsteps or coughs of a nearby guard. Good. He quickly turned to his right, edging along the fragrant vine-entangled, porticoed walkways that ran the circumference of the courtyard. The irony of having to sneak about his grandfather's property was not lost on him. But in fact the hacienda was like a brightly colored snake—beautiful but deadly.

Finally Zant found the narrow, heavy wooden gate shouldered into the adobe walls. Feeling like a confined eagle whose cage door had been carelessly left unlocked, Zant opened the gate and stepped through. To bright moonlight and freedom. To wing-spreading, flight-taking, exhilarating freedom. And to Paco Torres's well-armed girth. Zant's thoughts of freedom were rudely interrupted. "At ease, *paisano*. It's just me."

Under his sombrero's wide brim, Paco's broad, reddish-tanned face split into a wide, gleaming smile as he lowered his rifle. "*Buenas noches, jefe.*"

Zant smiled at being called *jefe*. Chief. "*Buenas noches, Paco. ¿Dónde está Blue?*"

Paco turned and pointed in the direction of the corrals. The strong odors of dung and hay, which carried on the night breeze and mixed with distance-muffled snorts and whinnies of the horses, marked it better than did the wood railings which enclosed the area. "*Allí. Con los caballos.*"

There. With the horses. Typical. Blue liked horses almost as much as he liked women. Zant nodded at Paco as he walked past him. "*Muchas gracias, Paco.*"

Paco touched his sombrero's wide brim. "*De nada, jefe.*"

Zant hadn't gone three steps before Paco called out to him again. "*Jefe?*"

Zant turned. "*Sí?*"

With the moonlight full in his face, Paco grimaced, like something was troubling him. To Zant's surprise, the big, simple man spoke in broken, heavily accented English. "It is good for you to be home. I am not the only one who says this, who believes you are our one true *jefe*. Many of the men believe so. Many. You should know this . . . when the time comes."

Frowning, Zant stood rooted to the spot. Touched by the man's words, but more than slightly alarmed at their underlying implication, he soberly met the man's black-eyed gaze. Things must have been pretty bad here for the past five years. "I take your words into my heart, Paco."

Equally sober, Paco nodded. "*Bien.*" With that, he resumed his guard duty, turning his back on Zant and pacing heavily around a corner.

This is turning out to be one strange night. Zant shook his head and started for the corrals. Once there, he stopped and looked around, finally spotting Blue, who was crooning low to his Appaloosa mare and stroking her muzzle. He turned his head at Zant's approach and nodded to him. Again Zant noted Blue's unusual grimness as he came to stand beside him. Zant stretched his arms over the top wooden rail and rested a booted foot on the bottom one.

"What's with Paco?" he then asked without preamble. "He just gave me a speech—in English—about me being *el jefe*."

Blue did him the favor of not acting as if he didn't know what he meant. A shrug accompanied his words. "Dissatisfaction, mostly. You don't know the half of what's been going on around here while you were in prison."

Zant reached out to stroke the Appaloosa's finely arched neck. "So I gathered. Is that what couldn't wait until morning?"

Blue huffed out his breath. The Appaloosa jerked back at the sound. Blue cooed to her until she calmed and stepped back up to be petted. Keeping his gaze focused on the horse, Blue shook his head, speaking as if his words were for the mare. "No. I have to ask you something."

"Ask away, *compadre*."

"It's about the Lawless woman."

Every muscle in Zant's body stiffened. "What about her?"

Blue finally turned to face Zant. "She's a Lawless, Zant. A Lawless. Now, I'm the first one to admit that she's a fine-lookin' woman. But you know what that name means around here. I used to know what it meant to you. But I'm not so sure anymore."

Zant narrowed his eyes at his best friend. "Make your point, Blue."

"I'll make it. First off, I didn't know it was Jacey Lawless who shot you until Rafferty told us. I knew he was tracking her, but I didn't know she was in Tucson. Or what she looked like."

Feeling a sudden throb in his injured arm, Zant sniffed and looked away from Blue, training his gaze out into the fathomless desert night. "I appreciate that. But I haven't heard a question—or your point—in there anywhere."

"I'm getting to it. I saw you and her . . . kissing . . . out in the desert that morning, and—"

"That's not your business, Blue."

Blue pulled back and straightened up, turning to face Zant. "Well, if it ain't, it'll be the first time in our lives. How can you kiss the daughter of the man who killed your father? You've changed, Zant. You've changed a lot."

Zant blinked and went very still. To anyone who knew him, this was a warning sign as obvious as the sound of a rattler's coils. "Prison will do that to a man, Blue."

"So will a woman." Blue's words were at once an accusation and a challenge.

Zant pushed away from the fence and turned to face his angry friend. "Leave it be, Blue. I'm warning you. I have my reasons, that's all I'm telling you." He stared steadily into Blue's eyes, waiting for a sign that he understood not to bring it up again.

Blue eyed Zant a moment and then looked at the ground, shaking his head. Zant exhaled, hating like hell that a Lawless could bring them to such a pass. But still, he prodded Blue further. "I still haven't heard your question."

Blue met his gaze again. This time there was no flaring challenge. Only concern and some remaining anger. "I guess it's not a question, after all. I just thought you'd want to know that Quintana got called into the hacienda this evening after supper. He was inside with the old man about ten minutes. When he came out, he started packing and said he was ordered to Tucson. He's riding out tomorrow."

Zant caught and held his breath. Ramon Quintana made Rafferty look like a schoolboy. Exhaling loudly, his mind already working, Zant remarked, "Quintana, eh? What else did that sadistic bastard have to say?"

Blue clutched at Zant's arm, looking full into his face. "Listen to me, Zant. He said that where Rafferty failed, he would succeed."

Well, I'll be a gap-toothed old mule skinner, if that isn't Jacey Lawless all dressed up and entering the mission church.

Just south of Tucson, Zant reined his roan stallion off to one side as a stream of folks flowed respectfully around and past him on their way to the Sunday service at San Xavier del Bac. Barely acknowledging the few mumbled greetings that came his way, Zant focused instead on the mesquite-wood façade of the starkly white and imposing mission church.

Eyes narrowed, blood aboil, he honed in on one slender female figure whose back was to him, and who was flanked by Rosie and Alberto. She looked no different than the other women around her, what with her loose white blouse, brightly colored skirt and lacy shawl which covered her hair. But in Zant's mind, she stood out like a rosebush among the cactus. He shook his head and chuckled. He'd told her to be gone in two weeks. Well, it'd just been over one, but she didn't give any sign of leaving a minute early.

Stubborn little hellcat. Zant wasn't the least bit happy to find her here. She was daring him, plain and simple, to do something about it. He shifted in his saddle and rubbed a knuckle under his nose. *All right, then, little lady, I'll do something about it.* Because, truth to tell, he didn't figure Tucson was any bigger today for both of them than it'd been over a week ago when he'd told her what-for.

Zant's hand tightened around the reins he held. Lucky for her it wasn't her scrawny neck in his grip. She obviously didn't listen any better than Quintana had. Zant frowned, thinking of the man whose corpse now fed the vultures out in the desert. The *desperado* was good with a whip, but he should've been practicing with a gun all these years.

Zant clenched his jaw with his next thought. It wouldn't be long before Don Rafael realized Quintana wasn't coming back . . . and sent someone else. Someone more ruthless, even more determined to succeed where the others had failed. Someone anxious to curry the old man's favor.

And only he stood between that faceless hired gun and Jacey Lawless. Despite his hat's sheltering brim, Zant squinted in the bright sunlight as he watched her pass through the mission church's sanctified doors. *Does she think being in a church will keep her safe from me?* Just the sight of all that black, silky hair of hers . . . Just the sight of her slender shoulders and back, narrowing to a tiny waist. . . . just the flare of her rounded hips . . . He wanted her with a savagery that shook him.

Zant took a deep breath. Not even holy ground could keep at bay the lurid images of what he wanted to do with her. Nor could it take from his heart the wrenching guilt that it was her—a Lawless, just as Blue said—that made him feel this way.

She'd tormented his days, invaded his dreams, and worried the living hell out of him for the last time, dammit. She'd made him restless, made him fight yet again with Don Rafael, made him nearly have a parting of the ways with Blue. Hell, he'd even killed two men over her already. Men who deserved to die, true enough, but would his luck hold? Could he stop every man that Don Rafael sent after her? Probably not. Don Rafael had more men than Tucson had bullets.

But Zant had another weapon. Jacey herself. Because he'd made up his mind regarding Miss Lawless. He had a plan for her. He'd purge himself of his raging desire for her by possessing her. Until she carried his seed. It was perfect, for two reasons. One, Don Rafael might not be so quick to kill her if she carried his great-grandchild. And two, with her belly full of his bastard child, Zant would send her packing to her father.

He wanted J. C. Lawless to know, through his grandchild, the shame of being a bastard, of having no name, no father. Just imagining the sight she'd make up in No Man's Land, swollen with his child, brought a wolfish grin to Zant's face.

On the heels of that leer, though, came a moment of clarity. His grin bled into a frown. Why should he want to protect a Lawless? And why should the notion of giving the old man an heir be so pleasing to him? Balking at the answers, his foul and gritty mood deepened. He'd spent three fitful nights on the desert floor and three long days seeing her face like a mirage, floating before his eyes. Zant nudged his roan forward, wondering if the walls would cave in on the pious when he strode in and took one of the parishoners out with him.

As he rode closer, the last of the folks trailed in. A brown-robed monk pulled the dark and heavy door closed. A moment later, Zant reined his stallion to a halt, dismounted, and hitched the thoroughbred to a rail. A grin born of pure calculation accompanied his swaggering stride to the sanctuary's closed door. He heard the sound of voices raised in a hymn that swelled to the heavens. But not even the holy music made him falter.

He'd come for the Lawless woman. And leave with her, he would. He put his hand on the wrought-iron rattlesnake that formed the door's latch handle. And tugged it open.

Jacey's first inkling that something was wrong came when the singing began dying down—from the back of the church to the front, like a waving blanket settling to the ground. Finally, only a hush filled the overflowing church. She sent Rosie a questioning look. But she was no help. She shrugged her confusion. They both looked to the priest at the altar.

And turned with him and the rest of the congregation to the open door behind them. Folks to the left and to the right of the aisle strained to see what was going on.

Standing in front of their smooth-worn, wooden pew about halfway to the altar and all the way over on the right side of the whitewashed church, Jacey had all she could do not to hop up onto the pew and see for herself what was going on. It appeared she owed Rosie an apology—because she was definitely liking church. This was mighty interesting. But when the swelling whispers reached her ears, she had all she could do not to duck under the pew and crawl out on her belly.

"Chapelo," they were all whispering. "Chapelo." "Chapelo."

"Oh, my God," she intoned in a breathy whisper of her own, garnering for herself the wide-eyed stares of Alberto on her left and Rosie on her right. "He's here, and he's going to kill me." She then turned to Alberto and cuffed him on his sleeve. "You and your no-guns-in-church. Now look at what's happening. Chapelo's out for blood, and I'm unarmed."

Alberto put his arm around her shoulders and shook his head. "Do not worry so, *querida*. Señor Chapelo would never shoot a woman."

Jacey wanted to believe him. She tried to believe him. But he just wouldn't leave well enough alone.

"At least . . . not on holy ground. I hope." He then frowned and shook his head, as if having to convince himself. "No, he would not do this thing." He looked into Jacey's eyes, a hopeful smile tugging at his mustache. "Perhaps he only comes to church to worship with us."

Jacey pulled back from Alberto and eyed him. "Yeah. That's it. He wants to worship with me."

Just then, Zant's booming voice in the high-raftered, templed structure sounded like the wrath of God. Or perhaps like the devil himself. "I'm looking for Jacey Lawless."

After a second's deathly quiet, the entire congregation erupted into crossing themselves and sending up prayers and supplications for mercy. A few souls fainted dead away. Here and there a baby cried, a small child wailed. As the priest called for calm, Rosie sucked in a breath and grabbed Jacey's arm, very nearly startling her into crying out. Holding on to

Rosie, Jacey abruptly sat down with her and stared blankly at her friend.

The priest's voice boomed out. "Everyone, please, a moment of quiet. If you will be seated. . . ." His voice trailed off as he obviously waited to be obeyed.

Jacey looked up to see the congregation turning toward the priest. Then, like wind-blown tallgrass out on the prairie, the good folks sat down in waves, quieted, and looked to him for guidance. The kindly holy man at the front of the church held his hand out to the belligerent outlaw at the back of the church. "All are welcome here, my son. Will you join us?"

Everyone—including Jacey—turned to the outlaw. Staying hunkered down as best she could behind Alberto and peeking around his narrow shoulder, she swallowed hard at the sight Chapelo made. Grim-faced. Gritty. Dusty and rumpled from the trail. Three days' growth of beard on his face. "I thank you, *padre,* but no. I'm here for Jacey Lawless, like I said."

By the time the congregation had turned again to their spiritual leader, the white-robed priest looked very harrassed. "It seems everyone has seen J. C. Lawless this past week. I assure you, you will not find him here. But what you will find is peace for your troubled soul, my son. Please . . . join us."

"No, I can't do that. I'm sorry for interrupting your service, but I'm here for Jacey Lawless." He pulled his Colt out of its holster, cocked it, and held it up in the air. "When I leave, I'll have a Lawless with me."

Over the congregation's gasps, renewed wailings, and loud prayers, Rosie turned to Jacey. "He is going to give you away. Everyone will know who you are. And then your plan will fail. What are you going to do, Catarina?"

"This." Jacey jerked to her feet, standing up before Rosie or Alberto could stop her. With mounting dread in her heart, she turned to face Chapelo. "Chapelo? Leave these nice folks be. Take me. I'll go with you." She heard her own voice ring to the rafters and roll back down on its own echo.

When the priest protested, when Rosie and Alberto clutched at her, when all heads turned to her, Jacey willed away the hot flush on her cheeks. She stood her ground. So far Chapelo'd only said "Jacey Lawless." Folks would naturally hear "J. C. Lawless." So, if she acted now, if she could get Chapelo out of here, and make the congregation think she'd offered herself as a sacrificial lamb, she just might salvage her plan.

So, her spine rigid, her insides quaking, Jacey faced the man. Even though a sea of faces and more than a few yards separated her from him, she felt pushed up against him, such was his effect on her. Fighting the knocking in her knees, she repeated her offer. ''Well, what's it going to be, Chapelo? It's me or no one. And you're keeping these folks from their prayers.''

CHAPTER SEVEN

Zant riveted his attention on Jacey across the sea of worshipers. Only the random shifting of weight and clearing of throats broke the heavy silence around him. Drawing in a deep breath of the dusty air, scented with the closeness of packed bodies and heavy incense, Zant opened his mouth to speak.

"No. You cannot take this girl." Zant turned to see the hefty holy man striding down the aisle, his robes puffed out behind him, his thick hands held up in supplication. "She is but an innocent child in God's house. And therefore in my keeping. I will not allow this kidnapping in broad daylight of one of the Lord's little lambs."

Zant narrowed his eyes at the man's interference—and at all those words. With a split-second cutting of his gaze back toward Jacey, though, he saw her working her way along the pew, saw folks moving their legs and their kids out of her way. So . . . she was coming to him. Zant grinned and turned back to the priest, who stood in front of him now, thick hands folded against his pudgy waist. "Seems to me, *padre,* that the lady made her own mind up."

The priest stared at Zant and then whipped around to face Jacey. He held a hand up, motioning her to come no closer. "No, my child. You do not have to do this. We will protect you."

Zant wasn't the least bit surprised when Jacey quirked an eyebrow at the priest who stood in front of him . . . and who blocked her way. "Protect me? From the likes of him?"—Zant puffed up when she pointed at him—"I thank you, but

I don't believe that'll be necessary, preacher. I can handle his kind with one hand tied behind my back."

While shocked gasps arose from the priest and his flock, Zant had to bite the inside of his cheek to keep from laughing at her. *Damned little hellcat needs her butt whipped.* But more than that, he wanted to grab her up in his arms, swing her around, and kiss that smart-ass look right off her glaring face.

But not giving away a thing, he evil-eyed the shawl-draped Jacey as she stepped around the priest, grimaced up at him, and then proceeded to exit the church. With his eyebrows meeting over his nose in a fierce frown, Zant turned to stare at her backside. He raised a finger preparatory to voicing his retort, but she sashayed her swinging hips right out the heavy, mesquite-wood door. And allowed it to swing closed behind her.

At a loss now, and aware of all the folks staring at him, Zant found himself seeking out the preacher's brown eyes. The man's perspiration-beaded forehead furrowed into deep, sincere lines as he reached out to clasp Zant's arm in a warm, firm grip. "I will pray for you, my son."

Outside, Jacey waited for the outlaw. She leaned up against the long hitching rail, ignoring the tethered and dozing horses behind her. With her arms crossed under her bosom and her legs crossed at the ankles, she eyed the church's entry. A silent, heartfelt prayer for the preservation of her own hide moved her lips. She figured she needed all the divine help she could get because, when Chapelo stepped into view . . . he'd be loaded for bear.

The front door jerked open. Jacey swallowed hard, refusing to obey her mind's screaming order to run as far and as fast as she could—starting about now. Chapelo swaggered out, looked right and then left, spied her, and stopped. Watching him settle his black hat and then hitch at his gunbelt, Jacey reminded herself to breathe. Keeping her arms crossed, her shawl covering her fingernails digging into her skin, she waited him out.

He started toward her. Unable to look away, she marked his progress, seeing him in terms of brimmed hat, shaded face, broad shoulders that cut down to a trim waist, narrow hips, and long, muscular legs. She kept forgetting how big this Chapelo character was. But for as long as she lived—which by her calculations would be about another two minutes—she'd see him as he was now. Strong. Serious. Grim. And intent on her.

Every stalking stride of his brought him nearer . . . and bigger. Jacey straightened up, her eyes widening. *Oh, Lordy, he's not slowing down.* She held her hand out in warning, but he wrenched her to him, pulling her within an inch of his chest. Off balance, her lacy shawl tangled in his grasp, her hands flattened against his damp and dusty chest, she met his black-eyed gaze.

"Damn you, Jacey Lawless. I haven't thought about anything but—" He cut off his own gruff words as his head slanted down and he claimed her mouth.

Surely this sacrilege on holy ground would bring a jagged spear of lightning straight from heaven. Sure enough, she felt the bolt hit, felt it take her feet out from under her and meld her to the outlaw. The hot feel of his lips on hers, his hands on her arms, his tongue seeking hers, the male-musk and trail-dusty scent of him, his hunger for her . . . all combined to render Jacey as weak as a kitten.

And she didn't like that feeling. The womanly softness of her reaction to this one man felt wrong, seemed disrespectful to who she was, to how she thought of herself. His touch, his kiss chipped away at her control and made a mockery of her blood pact with her sisters. For that, more than anything else, she couldn't forgive him.

Wrenching in his grasp, bucking against him, she finally succeeded in tearing her wet and kiss-swollen lips from his. Breathing hard and holding herself rigid, she glared up into his passion-glazed eyes. "Get your damned hands off me, Chapelo."

Her words only tightened his grip on her. Frowning, as if he didn't quite comprehend, he stared down at her. Breathing just as rapidly and as shallowly as she was, he gazed at her and his expression slowly cleared, slowly hardened. He abruptly released her. Jacey staggered back, knocking against the hitching rail behind her. Several horses knickered and pulled back restively. Swiping a hand across her lips, resettling her shawl, Jacey eyed the outlaw. "What do you want with me?"

"I thought that was evident."

She stiffened. "Don't make me slap your face, Chapelo."

Without warning, he snaked out a hand and grabbed her arm, yanking her back to him. "I didn't think that was your style, Jacey. Too womanish for you. Too tame. But go ahead—try."

Stung by his slur on her femaleness—and surprised by her own reactions, Jacey swung her open-palmed hand up in an angry arc that had his hateful face at its apex.

But Zant easily blocked the blow with his iron-clad grip on her wrist. "I don't think so, honey."

With angry jerks, Jacey tried to free her arm, but Zant held fast . . . and held her gaze with his black-eyed, taunting one. A mocking grin curved up a corner of his mouth, and sent a tremor of fear through her. He could break her in two with that one hand, if he so chose. Effectively stilled by her own fearful thoughts, all she could do now was bravely glare at him. And wait for his next move.

"You're going with me." It was an order, plain and simple.

Jacey hated orders. Of any kind. "Like hell I am."

"Like hell you're not." With that, he let go of her wrist to grab her around her waist and haul her—headfirst like a slab of beef—over his shoulder.

Air whooshed out of her lungs when she smacked bellyfirst against the granite width of his shoulder. With her arms, her head, and her cascade of black hair hanging down the man's back, with her butt even with his profile, with his arms wrapped around the bulk of her petticoats and skirt, with her legs dangling down his front, Jacey stared dizzily and in wide-eyed shock at the bare, sandy ground just behind Chapelo's boot heels. *How dare he, the rotten, no-good*—She blinked and focused on what she was really seeing. Then, her heart nearly stopped.

He was wearing silver spurs.

And they jingled merrily as he started walking, striding easily on his long legs as if her added weight were no more than a flea's. Jacey fisted her hands around his flannel shirt. Belatedly, she began bellowing out her protests and kicking for all she was worth. "If you don't put me down right now, Chapelo, I swear I'll—"

Zant smacked her bottom, just hard enough for her to feel a sting. "Keep quiet. You'll interrupt the church service."

Stunned, humiliated, feeling her Lawless blood rush to her face, Jacey bucked in earnest. "But you're the one—If you don't put me down—"

"You'll what?" He shifted her on his shoulder with as much care and passion as he would a sack of grain. And held on tightly.

"I'll—" *What? What will I do? Think, Jacey. Think.* Then, she saw her answer. Chapelo's Colt revolver. She grinned. Clutching her hair out of her line of vision, she caught sight of the back ends of various horses as Chapelo stalked past them. So he was heading for his horse. She had to hurry. Jacey edged her hand toward his holster.

But just then, she was dumped, empty-handed and teeth rattling, on her sandaled feet. Blinking back the dizzying stars and the blackness that rimmed her vision, she grabbed helplessly at Chapelo's sleeves and stared at the man's shirt button. In the next instant, she was bumped from behind with enough force to knock her into her tormentor. A yelp tore from her as she reflexively looked up at Zant.

He smirked down at her. "Well, that's one horse's opinion."

Jacey frowned at his smiling mouth and then wrenched around—as best she could with Zant gripping her elbows—to see his prissy stallion eyeing her with his ears laid back. Turning back to the horse's equally ill-mannered owner, Jacey jerked an arm free and poked at Chapelo's unyielding chest as she nailed him in place with her words. "I don't know what you've got up your sleeve, Chapelo, but I'll tell you one thing, I don't want any part of it. Or *you.*"

He ducked his head at a daring angle and shifted his weight to his other booted foot. "Is that so? Well, what if I tell you your choices are that you either come with me now—willingly—or we turn right back around and go inside San Xavier and tie the knot. What do you have to say to that?"

Disbelief screwed Jacey's face up. "Tie the knot?"

"Fine. If that's your decision." He grabbed her wrist and began hauling her out from between the horses.

Shock drew her along for several docile paces before Jacey realized what he was about. The mission-church door loomed large. "No!" She dug in, dragging her feet and clawing at his fingers wrapped around her wrist. "No! That's not my decision. It was a question—not an answer. Stop! All right, Chapelo, I'll go with you. I'll go. Do you hear me? I said I'll—"

He stopped and turned to her, never loosening his hold on her. One eyebrow rose as he slanted a questioning look down at her.

"—go," she finished. "I said I'll go. You win."

Now he grinned. "I knew you wouldn't go back inside that church with me."

"I wouldn't go to a dogfight with you, you snake-bellied mud toad."

The snake-bellied mud toad's grin broadened until white,, even teeth gleamed. "Don't get your drawers in a wad, Miss Lawless. I don't want to get hitched to you any more than you do to me. I was bluffing, trying to get you to say you'd come along peaceably."

Stung by his rejection—what was wrong with marrying her?—and even more stung that she'd even think that, Jacey gritted out, "Good thing. Because our getting hitched is not going to happen."

He nodded in agreement. "Furthest thing from my mind."

Jacey eyed him. "Well . . . good thing for you." Even to her own ears, her grumbling answer sounded lame. When he just stood there, looking big and superior . . . and good-lookin' as hell, Jacey fought her female reaction to him by poking her bottom lip out the least bit and waggling her imprisoned arm. "Are you ever going to take your hand off me, Chapelo?"

"For now." With that, he let go of her. Jacey rubbed her sore and reddened wrist as she watched him cross his arms over his chest and take a spread-legged pose. "I swear you've got the biggest chip on your shoulder I ever saw."

Jacey pursed her lips and squinted up at him. "You aiming to knock it off, Chapelo? If so, you'd better bring some help. Because if you ever jerk me over your shoulder again, you'll think a mad dog got ahold of your ass when I turn you every way but loose."

Jacey's threatening glare turned to a look of dismay when Chapelo burst out in a braying-jackass guffaw that unsettled the horses some paces away from them. Finally, tears cresting in his eyes, he bent over to rest his hands on his knees. His shoulders shook with each rumble of laughter that escaped him.

Eyes narrowed, and embarrassed as much as mad, Jacey crossed her arms and frowned all the way down to her sandaled feet. *Damned lunatic outlaw doesn't know a threat when he hears one.*

She watched him straighten up. Still chuckling, he shook his head and then settled his black hat low over his brow. "Who taught you to talk like that? I've never met anybody who was as full of piss and vinegar as you."

Jacey squinted at him. "Maybe you just bring out the best in me."

His black eyes alight, he chuckled yet again. "Then God knows I don't want to see the worst."

"Well, you're gettin' ready to if you don't tell me what this is all about and why it couldn't wait until after church. You scared ten years' growth out of that entire congregation, coming in like you did. I durned near had to tie Rosie and Alberto to the pew to get them to stay put when I came out."

Finally, he sobered . . . some. Like it was new business between them, he stated, "It's about you clearing out of Tucson."

Jacey huffed out a breath as she raised a hand to shade her eyes from the strong sunlight. "Not that again. I already told you I've got business here, and I aim to see it through."

"Is that so?"

"It is so. But what it isn't, is any of your business."

Zant put his long-fingered, square hands to his waist, and leaned toward her. "Well, I say it is. I've already killed two men because of you."

Lowering her hand from her brow, Jacey gave him a sidelong look. "Nobody asked you to, Chapelo." Then, she frowned. "Two?"

"Yeah. Two. Rafferty you know. And the other's Ramon Quintana—a whip-toting son of a bitch who also draws his pay from Don Rafael. Or did." His expression changed to one of . . . could it be? . . . concern when he added, "The hired guns aren't going to stop coming, Jacey. Don Rafael will keep sending them after you."

Even though his words sent a jolt of fear lancing through

her, Jacey eyed the outlaw in front of her. "I can take care of myself."

Zant shook his head, managing to convey impatient disgust with her. "Like hell you can. You don't know these men like I do. And that's why you're coming with me." With that, his long legs carried him right past her.

Jacey turned to watch him, noting the proud width of his shoulders and the way his black hair curled over his collar. A frown of yearning settled on her face, which she quickly blanked when he stopped and turned back to her. "What?"

"You said you'd go with me. And I'm guessing a Lawless's word is good." His seriously squared jaw dared her to go back on her word.

Jacey stared at him, took a deep, slow breath, and watched him shift his weight from one booted foot to the other. She glanced at his spurs, but couldn't get a clear look at them from this angle. When she focused on his face, his black eyes were shaded by his Stetson's brim. But his stare was no less threatening.

"Dammit," she muttered, clutching the ends of Rosie's lace shawl in her fists. Making a disgusted noise, she hitched the fringed fabric around her shoulders and stormed over to him with stiff-legged, stiff-armed strides. Her momentum carried her past him and saw her marching to. . . . ?

She stopped with her back to the outlaw, remembering that she'd come in Alberto's wagon, so Knight was still back at the cantina's corral. And she sure as shooting wasn't walking all the way back to Tucson. *If* that was where they were going. She realized she had no idea where Zant was taking her. Stopping just shy of stomping her sandaled foot on the rough-gravel ground, she pivoted around to face him. And pulled up short. He was right behind her.

"Where were you going, Jacey?" He reached out a hand . . . Jacey flinched . . . but all he did was brush back a curl from her too-warm face. His brows lowered into a frown. "Are you afraid of me?"

His voice, all soft and husky, raised goose bumps over Jacey's skin. Fighting the sudden weakness in her limbs, she blurted out, "No."

"Good. Because I'd never hurt you." He rubbed his knuckles gently down her cheek and then under her chin.

Jacey hated every bit of it. Hated how she wanted to move into his caress, hated how she was dangerously close to purring and rubbing around his legs like some danged tabby cat. But especially she hated how much she wanted to touch him back. How much she wanted to smooth her hands over his face, how much she—Realizing her eyes were closed and her mouth was open, instead of the other way around, Jacey jerked back from Zant's touch and batted his hand away from her. "Stop that, Chapelo."

"For now," was all he said as he grinned and took her arm, hauling her all the way to his roan stallion.

Watching him unhitch and back the tall, rangy stud, Jacey eyed it and its master. "What am I supposed to ride? And where are you taking me—and why?"

Zant glanced at her. "Full of questions, aren't you?" He then brought the prancing horse around to her, holding the reins in one hand and offering the other to her. "Mount up. I'll tell you the whys and wherefores on the way into Tucson."

"You expect me to ride with you?" Jacey started backing up.

Chapelo frowned and scrubbed his hand over his face, finally giving her a long-suffering look. "Just get up here, Jacey, without causing an all-out battle for once, will you? Why does everything have to be so hard with you?"

Raising her Lawless chin one prideful notch, Jacey stepped up to the stallion, ignored Zant's offered hand, and bent her leg so she could put her foot in the stirrup. She had to balance one-legged on tiptoe to barely inch her left foot through. Frustrated by the horse's height, she shoved her tangling skirt up her leg, not caring if she exposed a length of bare thigh to the outlaw. It couldn't be helped, if she had any notion of sitting this animal without help. One hand clutching for the pommel but not quite reaching it, her other gripping the saddle, she hefted her weight up.

Immediately, she felt a hand on her bottom as Zant shoved upward—and dang near catapulted her over the roan's back and onto the ground on the horse's other side. Jacey fell forward over the pommel as her left foot came out of the stirrup. She grabbed two handfuls of reddish mane. The stallion raised his head and danced in a tight circle until Chapelo quieted him with soothing words and stroking hands.

Jacey straightened up and settled herself in the sun-warmed saddle, with her skirt bunched up around her. From her great height atop the restive steed, she stared down at the gunslinger. "The day I need any help mounting a horse, Chapelo, is the day I'll take to my rocking chair. Until then, you back off. You got that?"

Zant grinned up at her, easily slid his booted foot into the stirrup and gracefully hauled his long-legged self up behind her, handling the reins over her head and around her as he scooted up against her back. Perched behind the saddle, he put his arms around her—Jacey stiffened as her feet dangled free—and put his mouth right next to her ear. In a whispering breath that she felt brush her hair, her ear, and her neck, Zant said, "Yeah. I got that."

The ride into Tucson was agony. The outlaw behind her touched her everywhere. Through the scant protection of her loose *blusa*, her skin burned from the heat of his body. His muscled chest pressed against her back, his legs bent into hers, and his arms rested under hers, against her ribs. In easy control of her and the stallion, with the reins entwined through his long fingers, he settled his hands against her belly.

Sucking in a shocked breath at his presumptuous familiarity with her person, Jacey gripped Zant's forearms and stiffened her spine, trying her best to break any contact of her body with his. But that proved impossible. Because the horse's smooth, loping gait threw her against Zant and him against her. Together they rode the horse as if she sat on the outlaw's lap in a rocking chair. It was that easy. And that all-fired difficult.

Just when Jacey was sure she'd slide right off the saddle with wanting the man behind her, just when she was sure she'd never forgive herself for wanting him, he reined in at Alberto's closed and locked-up cantina. With no ceremony or taunting words, he dismounted and, grinning like a pig in slop—to Jacey's way of thinking—held his hands up to her.

Jacey glared and snarled, "Step back, Chapelo. I don't want or need your help."

Zant quirked his mouth into an is-that-so expression and then held his hands up, as if giving up. He stepped back. "Suit yourself."

Satisfied that she'd won that round, Jacey expertly swung

her right leg forward over the roan's neck and made a show of sliding down the big roan's left side. Only to remember that this nag was about two hands taller than Knight. Squawking out a warning that she was falling, Jacey instinctively grabbed for Zant. He jumped forward and caught her under her arms, like he would a baby, and swung her up in an arc. He abruptly set her on her feet. "That was a real smooth dismount, Miss Lawless. Real smooth."

"Shut up, Chapelo." Jacey shoved him back and settled her clothes all around. She then looked up and down the streets. Glancing back at Zant, seeing him making the same sweep of the near-deserted adobe town, Jacey put her hands to her waist. "What do you make of all this quiet?"

Zant met her gaze and shrugged. "I don't. The cantinas are usually open all day and all night. Even Sundays. But it's even stranger that the mission church is as packed as a cattle yard. Most Sundays, so Rosie tells me, the mass is so sparse of folks that you can hear a cricket chirp."

Then his black-eyed stare seemed to sharpen and gleam as he considered Jacey with an up-and-down look. "But I'd be willing to bet a shiny dollar that you have something to do with it. Since trouble seems to be your middle name, girl."

Ignoring the heat that stained her cheeks, Jacey notched her chin up. Realizing he was right, figuring her rumors of J. C. Lawless being in town had everything to do with the crowded church, she elected to brazen it out. "Well, my dollar says the folks around here got religion about the time you got sprung from prison and put in an appearance."

Zant chuckled. "That could be." Then, he became all business. "All right. We're alone and not about to be interrupted. Let's go to your room and—"

Jacey shoved him back a step. "My *room? Since* we're alone? Not on your life."

"Oh, hell, Jacey, I wasn't even thinking that." Still, he cocked his head and grinned at her. "Although that does sound mighty tempting, now that you mention it."

Jacey shoved him again. "That's not going to happen."

"So you say. Gather up your belongings and saddle that black horse of yours. I'm escorting your skinny little butt as far as Apache Pass, just to make sure you keep on riding. You're going home. Today."

Jacey squared off with him in the sunny, dry, deserted street and put her hands to her waist. "Like hell I am."

Zant mimicked her stance. "Like hell you're not."

Like hell she hadn't. Jacey grinned to herself that night as she donned the clothes that would transform her into J. C. Lawless. She peered up at one of the three crucifixes in her room behind Alberto's cantina and smiled. Just one trip to church, however brief, seemed to be helping already. Maybe she'd make it a regular habit. Because here she was still in Tucson, despite that danged Chapelo's determined wish to see her nose pointed toward No Man's Land.

Drawing the red bandanna around her neck and knotting it at her nape, she chuckled, recalling his near-to-purple face when she'd led him back here, only to reach under her pillow, pull out her Colt, and level it at him. She'd told him to get out or get ready to wear lead-filled britches. Being a smart man, he'd left . . . but with a bellowing heap of threats and warnings in his wake. Yes, she'd won that round, but just for safety's sake, she'd locked herself in the small room until Alberto and Rosie returned from church.

And here she'd stayed, with them being lookouts for her and posting regular reports of Chapelo's being in a nasty temper and camped out in the cantina all afternoon. Waiting. And listening to every drunk's report of J. C. Lawless himself being in town. But now it was dark. And Chapelo'd left about thirty minutes ago.

Jacey picked up her black slouch hat and settled it over her thick bun. She looked down at herself. Shirt, vest, pants, boots, Colt. J. C. Lawless. *Time to move out, Papa.* As she unlocked the door to her room, she wondered what tonight's haunting of Tucson's streets would flush out. So far, she'd had no luck with her ruse. Well, except for scaring some folks sober, others back to drinking, and all of them to church. Which was well and good. But what she needed was guilty parties. *Maybe tonight, Papa.*

Jacey brazenly chose a main-street adobe storefront at the other end of Tucson for J. C.'s appearance. Leaning back against it, absorbing its sun-warmed heat, she pulled out cigarette fixin's and began rolling one like Alberto and Emilio had laughingly taught her. With only the moon's brightness for light, Jacey fumbled with the papers and the tobacco pouch and almost chuckled, recalling Rosie's scandalized face during the smoking lessons.

Shaking her head, Jacey decided that girl was probably the most innocent and saintly barmaid in any saloon or cantina anywhere. Probably the *only* innocent and saintly barmaid in any saloon or cantina anywhere.

Finally, after much fumbling and grumbling, Jacey had a serviceable smoke rolled. Pocketing her fixin's, she mouthed the cigarette and bent a knee to rest her booted foot against the wall. Mindful of the few passers-by and their gasps of "It's him," Jacey strove for studied calm as she struck a sulfur match against the store's wall—praying all the while that she didn't set her britches on fire—and lit her tobacco.

Shaking out the fire and flinging the match out in the street, she took a puff and remembered not to inhale, like Alberto'd warned her, lest she choke. Still, under her hat's low brim, Jacey made a face. *Danged nasty things taste awful.* She started to blow her smoke out. But catching a movement to her left, she stiffened—and sucked the acrid cloud into her lungs.

Jacey's eyes widened in direct proportion to her not being able to breathe, even as the innocent source of her fright—a scroungy yellow dog—sauntered by and turned into the alley. A hand to her chest, and dropping the cigarette where she stood, Jacey jerked around and wrenched her hat off as she tore for the alley beside the darkened store. Holding her hat over her face to muffle her gasping coughs, she bent over and coughed and teared up and danged near lost her supper before the fit eased up some.

As the storm subsided, and bracing her hands on her knees, she edged backward with mincing steps until her bottom braced against the rough wall behind her. Bent over, her hat dangling from her fingers, she stared unseeingly at the dark ground, concentrating as she was only on breathing. In and out. In and out. Realizing it was getting easier, she pulled herself upright and rested her head against the store's side, at once grateful for the wall's unyielding strength. Still weak, still shaken, she didn't bother to investigate the source of a scraping sound farther down the alley, dismissing it with a frown, thinking, *That danged dog again.*

Instead, she resolutely fumbled in her shirt pocket for the tobacco pouch, drew it out, and flung it to the ground. *Damned weed nearly killed me. And could've gotten me killed if that'd been anything but a dog.*

Telling herself she was over her fright, disavowing her pounding heart and aching lungs, Jacey drew her hat back on, making sure to settle it low on her brow. Then she poked and tugged at her clothes and holster, making sure everything was still intact. Deeming herself fit for presentation, she turned back toward the head of the alley.

After only two steps in that direction, though, the darkness behind her came alive. And appeared to want her dead. Grabbed around the neck, her hat knocked off, her feet barely touching the ground, she grunted when she was hauled up against a big, hard body. Only gurgling sounds came from her throat as she clawed at the muscled arm that choked off her air. But to no avail. The hard-as-steel, imprisoning arm pressed relentlessly against her throat. With her mouth open, but unable to suck in enough air to scream, Jacey realized she was being dragged farther back into the alley.

A terrifyingly calm thought voiced itself in her head. *So this is how it will end.* Faces from her past, faces from home, Mama, Papa, her sisters, Biddy, the ranch . . . all flashed through her mind. *No!*

Jacey renewed her struggling, kicking efforts to free herself. But she stiffened when a cold steel blade with a very sharp point pricked at her jugular vein. Then a voice, no less cold and steely, no less sharp and deadly, growled, "I've waited a long time to get my hands on you, J. C. Lawless. And now, it looks like that time is here. Out in the street, you murdering bastard, and get ready to slap leather."

Chapter Eight

It appeared her plan had worked. A little too well, perhaps. Because she'd certainly flushed someone out. And it was Zant Chapelo.

As she was dragged toward the street and the light of the moon, Jacey's heart sank with the sure knowledge that the second he realized it was her and not her father, he'd slit her throat for sure. In a blinding flash of memory she saw Rosie drawing her finger across her throat on that first day when she'd met her. In this very alley. And Rosie'd been talking about this very man.

At that moment, Jacey was let go and shoved forward into the hard and gravelly moonlit street. Her arms windmilling, her feet stumbling, she finally slid to a halt and jerked around. Barely aware of the squat, close-set adobes that pressed around them, she sighted on Chapelo. Hands behind his back, he sheathed his knife at his waist. He then adopted a spread-legged stance, his hands held loosely at his sides.

Jacey heard the running feet and the slamming doors as folks made for cover. But she didn't dare look away from the outlaw's itchy gun hand. He rubbed his thumb back and forth across his fingertips and then splayed his long fingers as if they ached. Finally, he fisted his hand and slowly opened it, allowing it once again to hang loose and ready.

Jacey swallowed. Here was the gunfight she'd been itching for. Or so she'd thought until now. Quaking with fright, she prepared her thudding heart to meet her Maker. Drawing herself up to her full height, she adopted the outlaw's stance, and stilled into a waiting attitude.

But gasped when her hair came undone from its twisting bun, fell loose, and spilled all around her shoulders and over her chest.

Zant poked his head forward, as if he couldn't believe what he was seeing. "*What the hell?* Jacey Lawless, is that you?"

Run. If only she could. But the man's steadily advancing strides rooted her to the spot. The closer he came, the wider Jacey's eyes got. Suddenly she was aware of the weight of her clothes, the rocklike heaviness of Papa's Colt, and the too-big bagginess of Alberto's pants. And the foolishness of her plan.

Then, he was right in front of her and peering down into her face with a fierce scowl. Jacey, reluctant and bold in the same breath, met his gaze. She managed to croak out, "Howdy, Chapelo."

He shook his head and notched his Stetson up with his knuckle. "Well, I'll be a no-good . . . rotten . . . son of a mule-headed jackass." His voice was a slow drawl that didn't fool Jacey. He was mad. Then his expression changed and his voice tightened, taking on a higher-pitched urgency. "Why didn't you say something? Do you know I came this close"—he held his thumb and index finger about a hairbreadth apart and right in her face—"from shooting you right through the heart?"

Jacey did the only thing she could. She balled her fist up and punched him in the stomach. And knew instantly she'd made another mistake. Hitting him was like punching a blacksmith's anvil.

No more fazed than if she'd made a face at him, he put his hands to his waist. "What the hell did you do that for?"

Jacey waved her sore hand in the air. "Because you were going to shoot my father."

"Your father—Like hell. I was going to shoot *you*." Then his eyes narrowed. "And here I thought he'd come to fetch you home. But he's not here at all, is he? You—in this man's getup—you're the J. C. Lawless everyone's been talking about since I got back from Sonora, aren't you?"

Licking her lips, and repeating over and over that she was *not* afraid, Jacey bolstered her courage. "That's right, gunslinger. It's me."

"You ornery brat. Now, this is just about all I'm going to take from you." He gripped her arm and walked her resisting body out of the middle of the street, over to the storefront.

Once there, he turned her to face him. "Does your father even know you're here and pretending to be him? Because I can't picture him—"

Jacey wrenched her arm from his grasp. In her rising anger and grief, her eyes and voice filled with tears. "My father can't know. He was murdered. So was my mother. Last month. Cut down in their own—"

"You're telling me the *real* J. C. Lawless is dead?"

"I am."

"Then you're here to . . . what? Hunt down his killers? By yourself?"

Jacey shook her head. "No. The murderers are back East. I—"

"Back East? How do you know that?"

"Because my sister's there now, flushin' them out."

Zant shook his head. "None of this makes any sense. And it still doesn't explain you bein' here."

Jacey huffed out a breath. "I came here because of the salt rubbed into my wound. I don't have all the details yet, but some lowlife scum stole something of value to me. Just *stole* it from me."

Zant's scowl pinched a vertical line between his eyebrows. "Stole what?"

"Stole a family portrait of my great-grandmother."

"A portrait?"

"Yeah. About the same time as the murders."

"Dammit, Jacey, you're telling me you're here—risking gettin' yourself killed—because of a *picture*?"

Jacey stiffened dangerously. "It's not *just* a picture. It's my only keepsake from my mother. Something she wanted *me* to have, you understand? But now it's gone. And, yeah, I came here to get it back. And to kill the flea-bitten rat responsible."

Still frowning, still absorbing, he rubbed a hand over his jaw. "What makes you think this keepsake was stolen, or that the . . . rat's here?"

Without preamble, Jacey reached inside her man's shirt and pulled out the broken spur on her silver chain. She held it up to him in the moon's light. "This little memento he left behind, along with a broken piece of the portrait's frame. Recognize it?"

Zant fingered it, turning it this way and that. Then, in a

whispering rush, he let go of the spur-pendant and breathed, "Jesus Christ."

As Jacey tucked her necklace back inside her outfit, she fussed, "It's a little late for praying, outlaw."

He eyed her through a squint, and acting like he hated to say the words, he offered, "I'm sorry for your loss. But I can't say I'm sorry that J. C. Lawless is dead. *Damn.* It appears it's a little late for other things besides praying."

Stiff with anger at his callous words about her father, Jacey pushed back, as if afraid she'd fall through a gap widening between them. The outlaw's bald statement left her breathless for moments on end. Moments that gave Chapelo a chance to continue.

"I had a chance in Santa Fe, but I was a raw kid then. And I've sat in a stinking prison for five years thinking about nothing else but killing J. C. Lawless for shooting my father when I was two years old. I intended to head there first thing after celebrating my freedom here. But then you happened along. And now it seems I'm to be denied my eye-for-an-eye."

A surge of hatred for this man's calculating heart set Jacey's features into a snarl. "So sorry to have to bring you the news, Chapelo. I know how disappointed you must be."

Now the outlaw looked her up and down. In a dark and deadly way. "I am. But for reasons other than you think. Reasons that have to do with you."

"Me? Well, I suppose to you one dead Lawless is as good as another." She stepped back, no longer afraid of facing him with Papa's Colt. "Make your move, Chapelo."

"Cut it out, Jacey. I'm not going to shoot you. If I did, I'd just be denying myself another chance at setting things even between our families."

Not ready to back down yet, but not willing either to shoot a man in cold blood, Jacey spat out, "You'd best explain yourself."

Chapelo hitched his Stetson up another notch. "All right. I rode back here from Sonora with a plan in mind. You just ruined it. But it might still work. Yeah, I think it will." He looked her up and down. "Yeah, I'm going to feel a whole lot better when your belly's swollen with my bastard."

"*Your what?* You got it all wrong, outlaw." Jacey's hand strayed to her Colt.

Apparently not the least bit threatened by her, Chapelo advanced on her. "The boy will be yours to raise for three years—the age I was when my mother died brokenhearted over the loss of my father. When he's three, I'll find you . . . and I'll take him from you. Only then will a Lawless know the pain and humiliation that my mother endured, alone and unmarried, bearing a bastard son. Only then will her suffering be avenged. And only then . . . will yours begin."

Her mouth dry, her heart pounding, Jacey stood her ground. That was the coldest, most calculating speech she'd ever heard. She sensed the pain underlying his words. But she just didn't care. Swallowing the thick saliva clogging her throat, she put a hand up to stop him. "You may as well go for your gun right now. Because none of what you just said is going to happen."

"Like hell it isn't." He stood about one pace away and stared at her as if she were something nasty on a cantina floor. As if he'd never kissed her, had never laughed because of her, had never killed two men to protect her.

Afraid for herself, knowing him to be fully capable of doing exactly what he said, Jacey watched him settling his Stetson low on his brow—and seized the moment to catch him off guard. Slapping leather in two blinks of an eye, she had her Colt out . . . cocked . . . and jammed right between his eyes. "Like hell it is, Chapelo. Now, give me a reason to pull the trigger. Please."

Zant sighted down the line of the gun to look into her eyes. In the pale darkness, all Jacey could see of his eyes was the silvery gleam of reflected moonglow. "Pull it."

She nearly jumped when he spoke. Her fear and anger fled, along with her tough stance. She shifted her weight and blinked. "What?"

"Pull the trigger, you spineless little Lawless shit. There. Is that enough of a reason?"

Insulted now and close to giving him his due, Jacey nevertheless began to sweat. "You *want* me to kill you? You're . . . you're bluffin', right?"

Despite the gun to his head, he shook it. "I don't bluff. Do you?"

Jacey swallowed. He was calling her hand, seeing if she was indeed bluffing. She was. She didn't really want to shoot him, only make him take back his threats. She'd never expected him to dare her to kill him. But now, if she didn't, he'd never keep his distance. What could she do?

Then . . . her way out flashed into her mind. Relief cascaded over her like a waterfall. She uncocked and lowered the Colt. "Don't think I wouldn't shoot you, Chapelo. But this time, I'm going to spare your life. Because you did the same for me a few minutes ago. The way I figure it, we're even now."

Chapelo showed his legendary nerves of steel when he chuckled as she reholstered her weapon. "Yeah, we're even."

Something in his voice made Jacey look up at him.

"But *only* on that score."

Zant had all the tossing-turning night to think about . . . her. And what to do about her. And how he was going to do it. If he had any hope of getting her out of Tucson alive and on her way back home before the winter snows came to the mountains, then he had to act now. Because if she stayed here through winter, her time would be too near for her to travel, come spring. And if she stayed here until the baby was born, then—

"Dammit!" Cussing at his tangling sheets and thoughts, he got up from his mussed and jumbled bed at La Casa Grande Hotel. Naked, he walked to the washstand and cleaned himself up. Toweling off, he padded over to the window and pulled the curtain back just enough to stare down at the street, streaked as it was with dawn's pinkening shades. Just as busy as it was during the afternoon. Except with a different sort of folk. The men on the streets now were as likely to use a gun or a knife on you, as they were to put an arm around your shoulder and offer you a drink. His kind of men. Hell . . . him.

He allowed the curtain to swing closed. Tossing the towel aside, he turned and began hitching on his combination suit. *So why should I care if Jacey Lawless is safe? Why should I continue to involve myself in her affairs?* He jerked on his tan denims and then sat down to pull on his wool stockings and then his boots. But his own question stilled his hands. He looked at the room's closed door, as if it were arguing with him. *Why do I involve myself? Because I can't abide Don Rafael getting his hands on her. Pure and simple. That's the reason. The only reason.* He yanked his boots on, stood, stomped his feet to square the fit, and reached for his chambray shirt.

Well, that *was* his only reason. Except for his own plans for her. And, hell, she had to be alive to carry a child. Thinking of the process involved to get her that way, Zant went as hard as a gun barrel. *Damned thing had a mind of its own.* He took several deep and calming breaths before jerking his shirt over his head and tucking it into his waistband. Working the buttons that began at mid-chest, Zant walked over to his gunbelt, folded his shirt's sleeves twice to leave the combination suit's ribbed cuffs exposed, and then strapped on the tooled-leather holster, securing it low on his right hip and tying the leather thongs around his thigh.

Going to the bed, he pulled his Colt from under the pillows. Holstering it, he grabbed up his Stetson and canvas duster. *Time to pay Miss Lawless a visit.*

Protected from the dawn's cool air by her covers, and lying on her side, her back to the room, Jacey snapped awake to a gray and pink light spilling into her room. And to a big hand being clamped over her mouth. Her body jerked in fearful response as her scream echoed in her head, trapped as it was in her throat. Stiff with fear, her heart pounding and the hair standing up on her arms, she clawed at the viselike hand that all but prevented her from breathing.

Into her ear, someone whispered, "Shh, Jacey. It's me. Zant."

For a stunned moment, not sure she'd just heard that, she stared at the long shadows on the adobe wall she faced. Then her fear-startled senses cleared. *Chapelo? In my room?* His hand still in place, she turned onto her back. *Yep.* Did he think she'd feel better . . . *safer* because it was *him*?

Instantly angered, Jacey gripped his hand and bit down hard on the padded flesh of his palm. His yelp of surprise and pain as he jerked his injured hand away from her mouth . . . now, that made her feel better.

"You bit my gun hand. What'd you do that for? I told you it was me." As his yelled words echoed and died, he massaged his wound and glared at her, his eyebrows meeting over his nose. "You damn near broke the skin."

Jacey fought off her covers as if she wrestled a living thing and then shot to her feet, standing in the middle of her bed. Mindful of her night attire and her tangle of black hair falling all around her, but never one to hide behind a coy, maidenly demeanor, she pointed an accusing finger at her attacker. "You deserve that and more, Chapelo. How'd you get in here? Better yet, what are you doing in here? Who let you in? And . . . and how dare you?"

Glaring for all he was worth, still rubbing his hand, and looking her up and down, he answered smoothly enough. "I let myself in."

She cut her gaze to the window. Woven curtain now open, but window still locked from the inside. She twisted to the door. Closed and also locked from the inside. She faced Zant. "How?"

A timid knock on the door from the hallway cut off whatever the outlaw'd been about to say. "Catarina, are you safe? I thought I heard voices. I—"

Chapelo found his voice. "Go on back to bed, Alberto. Everything's fine."

In the ensuing and heavy silence, on both sides of the door, Jacey looked at the man in her room. His forbidding expression dared her to say that she was anything but fine.

"Forgive me, Señor Chapelo, but I must hear this from Catarina."

Jacey smirked and raised an eyebrow. At Zant. And at Alberto's courage. Here was help. Still, she eyed the gunman and called out, "It's okay, Alberto. Go on back to bed."

After another moment of silence, Alberto said, "Forgive me, Catarina, but I do not think your father would—"

Jacey spoke in unison with Zant. "Go back to bed, Alberto."

Silence. Then, in long-suffering tones, "*Bien, bien. Pero el desperado—Señor Chapelo—esta in mi casa . . . en la noche . . . con la hija de Señor Lawless. Ay-yi-yi. Dios mio. Mi corazón no está . . .*" His grumbling voice trailed away with his footsteps.

Jacey had no idea what Alberto was saying, but she'd bet she'd hear all about it come breakfasttime. Right now, she had to deal with Señor Chapelo. Who'd taken a seat in the room's only chair. He crossed an ankle over his opposite knee, removed his Stetson, and ran a hand through his black hair.

Jacey stayed planted on the bed. "What are you doing here?"

"I couldn't sleep."

Jacey made a disbelieving noise at the back of her throat. "Well, I sure as hell could. And was." She huffed out her breath and then quirked her lips in disgust. "Since when do you seek *me* out when you can't sleep?"

"Since you became the cause of my restless nights." His black eyes warmed. His lids drooped seductively. His voice was a low, husky drawl that climbed over her skin, shivering her.

Oh, Lordy. Jacey barely stopped herself from backing up and clutching at the wall. Or from calling Alberto back. To disguise her virginal qualms and to steady her knocking knees, she put her hands to her waist and cocked her head. "What do you want?"

"It's not a matter of what I want. It's what you need."

That got her Lawless up. "If I come down off this bed, it's going to be so I can slap your face."

Chapelo had the nerve to chuckle and shake his head. He even scratched it and then stretched mightily. Like a cat readying for a nap. A wildcat. Who hadn't eaten in days. And now had his next meal in sight. And knew it wasn't going anywhere.

"You're not sleeping here, I can tell you that much."

"Sleep here? Hell, I don't intend to. And you won't be, either. For a while."

Suspicious but also intrigued, Jacey flopped down to sit cross-legged, Indian style, on her bed. She tamed her ballooning gown around her legs. "Why won't I? And don't start again about me leaving Tucson."

"You are leaving Tucson. With me. Today. But you're not going home. Just yet."

Jacey cocked her head to one side. "Has this got something to do with that crazy plan of yours? Because if it does, I'm not—"

"No. Not that. Not directly. You and I are going to catch a thief. One with a lot more explaining to do than just accounting for one keepsake."

"Such as?"

"Such as why your father killed mine. Such as what he'd need this picture of yours for. Such as why he was there on the day your folks were murdered, and yet you say someone back East did it. Things like that."

Jacey considered his words and what could be behind them. "Besides that part about your father and mine, what's your stake in all this? Why do you care? You hate my father. So why would you help me?"

"Damned if you don't ask a whole week's worth of questions at once. I care because I think I know who's behind it all. And why. I've been thinking about this all night. And now, come dawn, I'm saddled up and ready to go find out where the trail leads."

Even though she burned with curiosity to know his conclusions about who and why, Jacey stuck to her convictions. "I'm not riding with you. I don't want to be around a man who could say the things you said to me earlier."

Chapelo got that gunfighter look on his face. "You are going with me. Have you forgotten about your shadows, courtesy of Don Rafael? Now, like I said before, we can do this the easy way. Or the hard way. Your choice."

Jacey clamped down on her bottom lip. She hadn't forgotten about the trackers. But, dang it, she really didn't want to be around Chapelo day and night. She was scared more by what she'd allow him than what he'd take. "No way. I'm not going anywhere with you. I can handle this myself. I already know Rooster McGinty lived here, but he's dead from a fever. And I know all five of the remaining men's names."

"Do you know *where* to look? Do you have the time—what with winter coming on—to wander the desert looking for them, and all the while looking over your shoulder for the next surprise from my grandfather?"

Defeated, she sighed. "Let me guess. You know where every one of them is, and you're not about to draw me a map, are you?"

"Right."

"Damn you."

"Ahh, Señor Chapelo, I see you won *la guerra*."

Zant chuckled, keeping his voice as low as the cantina owner's. "It wasn't much of a war, Alberto. I just reasoned with her."

"Ah, *sí*. Reasoned. More like threatened, eh?"

Zant nodded. "More like threatened."

Alberto chuckled, but then turned serious. "Señor Chapelo, you do not intend to hurt our Catarina, do you?"

Slouched against the thick adobe doorjamb to Jacey's room, and completely occupying the narrow space, Zant folded his arms over his chest. He didn't answer right away, choosing instead to watch Jacey. With Rosie's help, she was gathering up her few belongings. Since Alberto was standing behind him, Zant finally looked back at the anxious face of the bartender. "You ever known me to hurt a woman, Alberto?"

"Oh, no, no. But this one"—Alberto nudged his chin toward Jacey, who was down on her knees and pulling her saddlebags from under the bed—"she is different to you, no?"

Zant stared at Jacey's split-skirted bottom and grinned. "*Sí.* She's different. But if I was going to hurt her—even kill her—I'd've done it last night when I thought she was J. C. Lawless."

From the corner of his eye, Zant saw Alberto cross himself. A fatalistic grin claimed his features. But it faded with Alberto's next words. "You mistake my words. I mean in her heart. You are not going to hurt her heart, are you?"

Zant grunted, ignoring the heavy thump of his own heart. "You really think she has a heart to get hurt, Alberto?"

"*Sí.* She has a very big heart . . . with a heavy burden. I would not like to see her in more pain."

Zant swiveled enough to exchange a serious stare with the fatherly bartender. Something tangible, like a subtle warning, stood in Alberto's eyes. Zant honored it and said, "I'll take care of her."

"*Bien.* But tell me," Alberto began, again drawing Zant's assessing gaze from Jacey's backside. "Where are you . . . taking her?"

"Well, she's bound and determined to find the Lawless Gang, and the man, or men, who stole a picture from her. And I know where the old gang has scattered to, so I'm going along for the ride."

"Ahh, *la pictura*. She told me of this last night." Alberto twisted his mustache and added, "You are going for much more than a simple ride, are you not, Señor Chapelo?"

Zant felt a muscle jump in his jaw. How much had Jacey told him? "Yeah. A hell of a lot more."

"Bien."

Zant didn't know what was so good about it, but at least Alberto wasn't asking any more questions. He straightened up when Jacey closed her saddlebags and turned to stare at him, her black eyes rounded and wary. He squinted at her, just to keep that bit of fear in her. "You ready now?"

"Yeah, but I've got one more thing to do." She turned to Alberto. "You got anything around these parts that resembles mail delivery?"

Alberto shrugged. "*Mas o menos*. More or less."

Jacey firmed her lips together and appeared to think about something. "Could you hire someone you trust—I'll pay you back—and have him take that journal and those letters to my sister in No Man's Land? Here. I wrote down the directions."

Alberto took the scrap of paper from her, but shook his head. "No money from you. But I will do this thing for you and for your papa. I would be honored."

Zant watched Jacey nod her agreement and put a hand on Alberto's sleeve. "I owe you so much, Alberto."

Alberto put his hand over Jacey's. "You owe me nothing. Just stay alive."

Moved more than he cared to admit, Zant repeated, "That's a real touching scene, but are you ready now?"

Jacey glared up at him. "As I'll ever be, Chapelo."

Squinting right back at her, Zant strode into the room, took her bags, slung them over his shoulder, clutched her elbow, and said, "Then, let's ride."

Chapter Nine

A hard day of riding saw them heading steadily south, following the Santa Cruz River, and then turning more easterly across desert plateaus and dry gullies. Late that afternoon, Zant finally reined in a short distance from a warped-clapboard shack built against the stone base of a rocky abutment.

Mounted on Knight, Jacey turned a dubious eye on the falling-down corral and the gaping, half-rotted door of the one-room cabin. "This is it? This is where Tully Johnson lives?"

She watched Zant shift his weight in his saddle and notch his Stetson up. "Yep. He did five years ago, anyway. Looks empty now."

Jacey squinted at him. "You're one heck of a guide, Chapelo, what with your five-year-old information. I could've gotten this all wrong by myself."

Zant spared her a glare before calling out, "Hello in the cabin. Is anybody about? We're looking for Tully Johnson."

Silence. A Gila woodpecker ceased drilling a dead juniper to stare at them and then fly away. Watching the bird take wing, they both started, along with their mounts, when a woman's voice called out from the cabin door. "Who's lookin'?"

Jacey reined Knight hard and stared at the dirty, stringy-haired woman whose skeletal nakedness was more or less covered by a too-big faded blue daydress which had seen better days. Jacey exchanged a look with Zant, whose expression seemed to mirror her first impression.

He then turned to the woman and said, "Afternoon, ma'am.

Name's Chapelo. And this is Jacey Lawless. We're looking for—"

"I heard ya. Tully ain't around." With that, the woman spat and stepped back inside the cabin. From the dark interior, she yelled, "I don't want no truck with a Lawless, much less a Chapelo. They ain't never done nothin' for me. Now, git." A steel rifle barrel poked out to glint in the sunshine and back up her sentiments.

"Son of a bitch," Zant muttered, his inflection suggesting this was the last thing he needed. He turned to Jacey, keeping his voice low. "Let's see if money makes her any friendlier." He then called out, "We'll pay you for your time, ma'am. We just need to talk to Tully."

"Pay me? What do I need money for? An' I done tole you—you cain't speak with Tully. Cain't nobody speak with 'im. 'Cepting the devil. Tully's been dead nigh onto three years or more."

Jacey edged Knight over to Zant's roan and whispered, "This could be a trick. He might be hiding inside."

Zant turned a long-suffering look on her. "I think he's dead, Jacey. And it's a particular habit of mine never to call a person pointing a rifle at me a liar. But go ahead—call her bluff."

Thus challenged, Jacey turned toward the cabin. "How'd he die, ma'am?"

"I shot 'im, that's how. You aimin' to be next, lady?"

Jacey's eyes widened. "No, ma'am. Sorry to've bothered you." As she turned Knight away from the cabin, Zant followed suit, but his chuckle only heated her face up more. "If you're so all-fired smart, Chapelo, where's Tully's grave?" she hissed.

Zant nudged his roan into a canter before answering. "She shot him, Jacey. You think she went to the trouble of giving him a proper Christian burial? Hell, she probably dragged him out and let the vultures eat him."

"Skinny as she is, she should've eaten him herself."

Zant's eyebrows shot up. "Remind me not to let you get too hungry."

Jacey didn't dignify that with a response. Instead, she asked, "Where to next?"

"Well, I plan on riding back to the Santa Cruz, making

camp for the night by its waters, and eating some of that good food Rosie packed. You coming?"

You coming? As if she had a choice, what with him having the food and the close-held knowledge of where the other four men in the Lawless Gang were. Jacey fussed around their small campfire, laying out her bedroll. *Why don't you call her bluff?* Danged near got her shot, was what he did.

Looking up, she searched out the source of her fuming. The big outlaw, sipping his coffee from a tin cup, stood quietly still with his back to her at the river's shore. With the blood-crimsons and bruised-blues of the setting sun in front of him, he stood as if framed in a picture.

Jacey's scowl slowly softened into a frown of longing. She couldn't look away from him. A great sadness swept over her, a sense of loss. Loss of a part of herself. When she could no longer deny it, she admitted that she wanted nothing more than to go to him, wrap her arms around him, and lay her cheek on his warm back. She should hate that feeling. But didn't. She put a hand over her mouth, as if trying to hold back a sudden queasiness. *Why him?*

Just then, Chapelo shifted his weight, drawing the seat of his denims tight over his buttocks. She swept her gaze over the man's broad back, down to his tapering hips and long legs. And knew. *He's got that lost part of me.* She shook her head against the sharp prick of awareness and the sinking feeling that told her she cared more than she should, and in all the wrong ways, for the Stetson-wearing, smart-mouthed, swaggering quick draw.

Look at you, a voice in her head taunted. *You can't even stay mad at him, not even when he's provoked you and threatened you and darn near gotten you killed—or killed you himself.* But that was just one side of him, she argued. All the other sides of him showed he felt the same about her. He'd kissed her, followed her, protected her, killed for her. And now, he was here with her, putting himself in danger just to make sure she didn't run into any herself.

Jacey admitted she'd never been one to think about fate and great celestial designs. And she never saw herself as a pawn in a game of destiny. Not before now, anyway. Because all she could think was . . . why this man? Why was he the one who stirred her fires? His last name alone made him as forbidden to her as the fruit of the Tree of Knowledge had been to Adam and Eve. And look what happened there.

Shaking her head, refusing to give up any more of herself to him, Jacey steeled her heart, seeking to explain his behavior in other ways. Could he be here with her, and pretending to have . . . strong feelings for her, just to make sure she *didn't* find the keepsake and discover the truth? It could be that he was. And what about that danged plan of his to get her with child? Maybe that too was his real reason for being here with her.

Squatting down, she picked up a handful of gravelly sand, which she allowed to run through her fingers. All right, so she'd guard her heart from his charm. Jacey let out the breath she hadn't realized she was holding. And almost burst into tears. *See there?* the voice chided. *He's changing you.* Jacey jumped up. She had to get away from him. An inch away from running to Knight and jumping on him and clearing out, she clamped down hard on her back teeth. *Just calm down. You can't go anywhere at night. You're safe enough with Chapelo, for the time being.*

But what about when she got closer to the truth? What then? What if he was the one she sought? Working her lips, biting at them, Jacey aimed a suspicious look at the gunslinger's back. *I've got to keep my eye on him, and at the same time, keep him away from me. And, yes, me away from him. Lordy, what am I going to do?*

At that moment, Zant turned away from the river and called out to her, "You know what you should do?"

Jacey caught her breath. And let it out. He couldn't read minds. "No, outlaw," she called back, "what should I do?"

Without replying, he walked toward her, his muscled legs carrying him effortlessly up the sloping embankment. When he stood right in front of her, towering over her, looking down at her, Jacey realized she was breathless. She looked up, trying to see his eyes under that black hat of his. And caught herself returning his easy grin before she could think to guard against his charm. Instantly sobering, she fussed, "Well? What should I do?"

"For one thing, you should stop calling me outlaw and Chapelo and gunslinger. My name's Zant. And two"—he pointed with his coffee cup to a point behind Jacey—"you should train some manners into that horse of yours."

"My horse?" Jacey turned to see Knight's ears laid back against his head as he showed his big teeth to Zant's fine-boned roan stallion. She chuckled. "Knight doesn't think much of that prissy ride of yours."

"Prissy? You think Sangre is prissy?"

"Sangre? What's that mean?"

"Blood."

"You named that animal Blood?" She turned back to stare consideringly at the now-snorting, nostril-flared stallion as he responded to Knight's bad manners. "Well, maybe old blood. He's kinda rusty or coppery-colored. But nothing like reddish-orangy new blood."

She watched as Chapelo pinched his features into a prunish old-man grimace. She'd insulted him. He tossed his empty mug onto the ground by the campfire and stalked over to his stallion. For once, Jacey's chuckling followed *his* red-faced retreat. Just maybe her own smart-mouthed, swaggering attitude—so much like his, come to think of it—would be the very thing that kept him at a distance.

She watched as the outla—no, Zant—as Zant untied Old Blood from his place next to Knight and restrung the stud's lead rope to a piñon tree farther away. As he stomped back over to her, Jacey asked, "Is that all you wanted to tell me—about my horse not having any manners?"

"Hell, no, but what *is* wrong with that nag of yours?"

Jacey shrugged. "He's been in a bad mood ever since I castrated him."

A shocked and guttural sound came out of Zant's open mouth. "*You* gelded that animal yourself?"

"Well, I had some help, holding him down and all. But, yeah, I did the honors. And with that same knife of mine I showed you on the way to Sonora. It's still strapped to my leg. You wanna see it again?" Loving the look on Zant's face as he shook his head no, a look that said he was just shy of crossing his hands in front of his own crotch, Jacey grinned up at him. "Now, what else were you going to tell me I should do?"

Zant began backing up. "Nothing. Not a damned thing." He turned, grabbed up his bedroll, and took it with him to lay it and himself close to his stallion. And far away from her.

Boots off, holster wrapped in its belt and lying beside her, Jacey climbed into her own bedroll . . . and grinned until she fell asleep.

But she wasn't grinning the next morning when she woke up. Lying on her side, she pricked her ears for the sounds of movement. Any movement. Nothing. Still, some sixth sense told her things were amiss. Never again would she tease Hannah about her *feeling* things. Because this feeling was consuming her. Taking a chance, she pushed her blanket down to her waist and sat up abruptly. She braced herself with her arms behind her and pivoted to face the far piñon tree. No Zant, no Old Blood.

He's left me out here. Jacey swept her gaze over to where, *please, God,* Knight should be . . . and slumped. He was still there, tied where she'd left him and dozing contentedly. So, Zant had left of his own free and sneaking will, the lop-eared polecat. Because if there'd been a struggle or stir of any kind, Knight would've raised a ruckus that would make a flock of nervous chickens proud.

Still, heeding Papa's oft-repeated words of not taking strange surroundings for granted, Jacey looked all around her, listening to the dead quiet of the sandy desert basin. The giant saguaros stood with their thick, thorny arms raised, as if gunmen confronted them. The chuckling waters of the Santa Cruz competed with Jacey's pounding heart. She slid her hand under her blanket, located her holstered Colt, and drew it out. She hid it in a fold of her blanket. *Come on, you. I'm ready.*

Just then, Knight snapped to, raising his head and whinnying as he peered over his shoulder. Following his lead, Jacey looked to the bend in the river, but whoever was coming remained blocked from view by high bluffs. *Great.* Realizing she was a wide-open target, Jacey jerked free of her bedroll and sprinted, gun in hand, to a scrubby creosote bush. As if it offered any cover. But it was the best she could do, in the time she had. Raising her Colt, steadying her aim with her other forearm propping her gunhand, she waited.

Damned if that ornery outlaw didn't ride around the bend on that prissy stallion of his. Jacey let out her breath and lowered her Colt . . . before she could use it on him for scaring her. She stood up, arms at her sides, and waited.

He reined in front of her. Eyed her. Eyed her gun. Eyed the creosote bush. "Morning, Jacey. You expecting trouble?"

Jacey's temper flared, but she bit the inside of her cheek until tears stood in her eyes. She refused to let him goad her, just so he could tease her. "Not until you rode up."

The big man chuckled as he dismounted. "You think I'm trouble?"

Did he have to stand so close and grin down at her? Jacey pinched up her mouth. "No. I know you are." Then because her danged curiosity wouldn't quit nagging her, she blurted out, "Where have you been?"

"Were you scared?"

Jacey took in a deep, calming breath and let it out. "A day's ride from Tucson? Hardly. Now, I asked you—where have you been?"

"Did you miss me?"

That did it. Jacey screamed out all her red-faced anger and frustration. Birds flew up into the air. Critters scuttled through the underbrush. Horses whinnied. The Santa Cruz stopped flowing for a startled second.

But Zant? He laughed and pulled her to him to smack a brotherly kiss on her damp forehead. "I'll take that as a yes."

Jacey wrenched away from him, went to her bedroll to toss her Colt on it, and then stalked off toward the heavy cover of oaks and scrubby bushes under a near bluff.

Zant was right behind her, following her step for step. "Where you headed?"

Not slowing down, Jacey called back over her shoulder. "I've got to relieve myself, outlaw. And I don't need any help from you."

The crunching of his boots said he still kept pace with her stiff-legged strides. "Okay."

"I'd like my privacy. Go away." Jacey stopped, selected a likely spot and stepped behind it. Turning around, her hands on her skirt's closure, she came face to face with the outlaw.

He was still grinning. "What?"

His feigned look of pure, wide-eyed innocence didn't fool her. "I said I need to relieve myself. And I don't need any help from you. So, get."

"Don't you want to know where I've been?"

"No." If he didn't walk away soon, she'd be dancing in place, so urgent was her need.

And he knew it. The son of a rattler grinned, stood spread-legged, and crossed his arms over his chest. "I'm betting I can outwait you."

Jacey crossed her legs. "I'm betting I can get a clean hit in your chest with my frog sticker."

"Not before you wet your pants . . . skirt."

He didn't think she'd do it. He didn't think she'd drop her skirt and wet with him standing right there. Fine. She'd show him. "Suit yourself."

Jacey undid her skirt and began lowering it along with her drawers. Zant abruptly turned his back to her. Jacey squatted. And grinned. Even from the back, he looked uncomfortable. But he didn't walk away. She knew he wouldn't. Not now. Not if his very life depended on it. It was her turn to make the most of his discomfort. "You make a mighty big target . . . from this angle."

He cleared his throat and shifted his weight. "Just . . . take care of your business. I'll do the talking. I got up early and rode back to Tully's cabin, just in case that woman *was* bluffing, like you said. I watched the place for a while, hoping to catch them off guard. But I never did see him. She wasn't bluffing."

Her business done, Jacey stood and rearranged her clothing. *So he had taken her concern about Tully seriously.* Out loud she said, "Hmm. Too bad you didn't scare up some bacon and eggs while you were out there." She stepped around him and headed casually back to the campsite. "Because I'm starving."

This time, his footfalls didn't sound behind hers until she was halfway back to her cold breakfast, and the ashes of last night's fire.

Later that afternoon, and more than a few miles south of last night's campsite, Zant reined in at the well-kept fence line surrounding Buckeye Davis's property. The man had made a good life for himself and his huge family along the Santa Cruz River. Some cattle. Some horses. A few hardscrabble crops. But all of it, including the various cabins spread about the place, were neat and orderly. Just like Buckeye. Who looked well fed and contented with his lot in life as he approached on horseback.

"I couldn't believe my eyes when I looked up from that broke wagon wheel and seen you, boy. I told Arturo—you remember my oldest boy?—that it looked like you." Grinning, chuckling, the older man looked Zant up and down. "And it is. I said to him, 'Arturo, I'll be a ring-tailed coyote if it ain't Kid Chapelo's boy all growed up.' How long's it been, son?" The big, sunburned, smiling old man held out a hamlike hand to Zant.

Grinning, Zant reached over the fence to shake it. "More than five years." He then turned to Jacey and back to Buckeye. "Buckeye, I brought some real royalty with me this time. Meet Jacey Lawless."

The man's eyes widened as he looked Jacey up and down. "Lord above, who'd've thought? A Chapelo and a Lawless riding together again. Why, I plum feel me a need to bend my knee to you, sweet thing. So, you're little Jacey? Your pap talked about you all the time. Always said you was just like him. Yep, the apple of his eye. How is your old pap? He still full of piss and vinegar?"

Zant watched Jacey's face. Her chin went up a notch. She stilled in her saddle. Zant quickly spoke up for her. "Buckeye, we're here because of some trouble."

Buckeye sobered, splitting his gaze from Zant to Jacey, evidently assessing her grim quietness, and then finally refocusing on him. "Let's take it inside, then. I'll get the gate. And don't mind all the kids underfoot. They'll move out the way afore you trample 'em. Now, y'all plan on staying for supper. Maria and the girls are cooking up a heap of fresh beef."

Within a few minutes, they were in the main adobe cabin, introductions were made all around, Zant found himself hugged by Maria and her brood of daughters and grandkids, and then he, Jacey, and Buckeye settled at the smooth-cut and sturdy wooden trestle table. With cool drinks of water in front of them, with the kids shooed back to their chores, with Maria, an ample and pleasant Mexican woman, overseeing the cooking, Zant briefly told their story. At the end of it, he shrugged. "And that's what brought us to your door, Buckeye."

At turns sad, incredulous, angry, and disbelieving while Zant spoke, Buckeye now sat up straight, clamping his big hands on his knees. "Now, you young'uns don't think I had anything to do with any of those goings-on, do you?"

For the first time since they'd arrived, Jacey spoke up. "I didn't know until I met you, Mr. Davis. But now I can see you didn't."

"I thank you for that, little lady. And it's right sorry I am about yer ma and yer pap. I loved him like a brother." He smacked a huge fist onto the table. "Damn, I wish I could help you. But I don't have no doin's with the gang no more. I'm a law-abidin' man. Got this here family to feed."

"I understand. But maybe you *can* help, Buckeye. I'm a little rusty concerning the whereabouts of the rest of the gang because I've been in a Mexican prison for five years, so—"

"You what?" Buckeye bellowed out his laughter. He reared back and called out to Maria, "You hear that, Mama? The Kid's kid's been in prison."

Occupied with making tortillas, Maria turned and grinned broadly. "*Sí, sí.*" Zant felt his face heat up. He dared a glance at Jacey. Bright-eyed with held-back laughter, she quirked up a corner of her mouth. Glad to see her smiling again, even if it was at his expense, Zant shrugged his shoulders and grinned back at her. She shook her head and turned to Buckeye as he recovered and spoke again.

"I swear if this don't beat all. Now, how can I help?"

Before Zant could say a word, Jacey jumped in. "Were you there the day my father and Zant's . . . got into it?"

"Hell, sweet thing, which time?"

Grim now, Zant merely stared at Jacey when she cut her gaze to him and then looked back to Buckeye. "The last time."

He sobered and shook his head. "No. I'd already quit the gang by then. And I'm not sorry I had. Would've hated to see J. C. and the Kid go at it with guns."

Zant tamped down his own emotion to ask, "Do you know, or have you heard, *what* caused them to come to a final stand-off?"

Buckeye firmed his lips together as he looked off to a point out the open front door of his good-sized home. A group of dark-skinned, laughing children ran back and forth outside. But when he shook his head, Zant's hopes fell. "No, not directly. But I did hear tell it was over a baby." Now he looked right into Zant's eyes. "That baby was mostly likely you, son."

"Me?" A cold chill swept over Zant. Next to him, Jacey's tense quietness spoke more than anything she could've said.

Buckeye frowned and worked his mouth, as if he were having trouble coming up with the right words. His blue eyes held a hint of sympathy when he finally spoke. "I'm figurin' you know how your pap left your ma and you to fend for yerselves? You mayhaps was too young to remember that he also . . . well, he used his fists on her. Ya see, J. C. wasn't having no part of a man who'd act like that. He already had a wife and two little girls of his own. Already knew what it was to be a pa."

Dim, distant memories, all of them ugly, flooded Zant. A hand gently squeezed his forearm. He looked over to Jacey. She was unsmiling, but her soft, luminous eyes spoke for her. He looked down at her small hand on his arm. He'd been around her long enough to know that expressions of sympathy from her were few and far between. Which made her simple gesture all the more wrenching. He abruptly stood up. "Excuse me."

Only quietness followed him out the door. With long strides, Zant walked a good ways from the cabin, from the laughing kids, from the pleasant and loving family here. He'd never known this kind of family devotion in his whole life. Only Don Rafael's bullish and manipulative variety. Within a stride or two of the boundary fence, Zant stopped, bent a knee, put his hands to his waist, and stood with his head hung down. Staring blindly at the ground, his mouth worked around the erupting emotion that threatened to send him to his knees.

He stood like that for a long time. How long, he didn't know. He looked up only when Jacey silently walked past him and stopped at the fence. Keeping her back to him, she rested her forearms on the split-rail fence and looked out over the vast desert on the other side of the Davis property. She stared silently, as if something of great interest were happening in the far mountains. "You heard some mighty rough things back there, Chapelo."

Zant eyed her slender back, her long black braid, and her booted foot up on the fence's bottom rail. And felt instantly better for her lack of gushing sentimentalism. Had she come out here and put her arms around him and cried and carried on, he'd have been so humiliated—because he would have given in to the same things—that he could never again look her in the face.

Instead, this way, he regained his control and shook it off. "Wasn't anything I haven't heard before."

"That doesn't make it any easier, I suppose." She was silent another moment and then said, "Buckeye and his family are nice people."

Zant nearly grinned at her offhand attempt to cheer him up. "Yeah, they are. He kept up with me all my growing-up years. He started coming to see me and my mother after . . . my father died. He'd always bring me a little present and leave my mother some money to get by on."

Jacey turned around to face him for the first time. "Money? I thought Don Rafael was rich."

"He was, still is. But he wouldn't help her or allow her to live with him after she gave birth to me—a bastard. Hell, the only reason the old son of a bitch took me in when she died was because he finally accepted that I'd be his only heir."

Jacey shook her head. "It's hard to believe someone could be that cruel to his own flesh and blood." She looked down and then up at him again. "How old were you . . . when she died?"

"Three years old, almost four."

"No more'n a baby." She got quiet again, stared at him. When he didn't offer anything further, she became matter-of-fact. "I came out here to fetch you for supper. Maria wants us to stay the night, too. Leastwise, I think she does. I can't understand her Mexican. Or her English."

Zant wanted to hug her for making him laugh. "Then we'd better get going. With all those mouths to feed, we won't get anything but bones and gristle if we're late."

Jacey pulled away from the fence and sauntered toward him. "Even that sounds pretty good right now. I never did get my bacon and eggs this morning."

As she sashayed by him, Zant turned with her, matching his stride to hers. Restored now, grateful, but not knowing how to thank her for what she'd just done for him, he put his arm around her shoulders and held her close to his side.

She didn't move away. Not then, and not all the way to the house.

"Guess I was right, huh?" Jacey chuckled in a self-deprecating way as she looked over at Zant.

Freshly bathed and in clean clothes, as was she, he sat his roan like a nobleman on parade. "Yeah, I guess so. Maria did want us to stay overnight."

"What'd you make of all the shuffling around of kids and grandkids last night to find places for us to sleep?"

"You mean her putting me up in one house and you in the farthest one away from me? I'd say Maria was making sure your virtue stayed intact."

Jacey gave a less-than-delicate snort. "If I stayed around her long enough, there'd be no danger of me losing it, what with all the food she stuffed into me. I'd be as big as a heifer, and about as pretty, inside of a month. I still may not want to eat for another week."

"Good. Then I'll keep all these vittles she gave us for myself."

"Just try it, outlaw."

At total ease with him for the first time, Jacey laughed right along with him. Since yesterday afternoon, since she'd come out to the fence, he was different with her. She was different with him. Almost brotherly and sisterly. Almost as if they liked and respected each other. As if they could have been good friends, if all this other stuff wasn't between them.

But friendly wasn't exactly what she felt when she looked at him, when she found she had to increasingly look down from his steady gaze. It seemed he couldn't look at her, either, without that certain light flaring in his eyes. In self-defense, Jacey tugged her slouch hat down low over her brow and rode along beside him in a silence she chose to call companionable.

But they hadn't gone half a desert-heated mile over endless sand and gravel and around tumbled outcroppings of huge boulders, before a sudden thought broke the quiet between them. She looked over at the big outlaw to her left and said, "It could be a girl, you know."

He met her gaze with a frown already tugging his mouth down. "What? What could be a girl?"

"Your baby. The one you think I'm going to carry. You kept calling it your son. It could be a girl."

She watched several emotions play over his face before he conceded, "All right. It could be a girl."

"That wouldn't change anything for you?"

He stared as if afraid to look away, as if he thought she'd go for his jugular if he did. "No."

Jacey nodded, looked down, fiddled with Knight's reins, and then tilted her chin up at a questioning angle. "Then, what about your spurs?"

Zant blinked. Sniffed. Swiped his hand under his nose. And frowned. "Jacey, what the hell are you talking about? Do we need to find some shade and get you some water, girl?"

Jacey scowled. "It's not the heat. And I just had a drink from my canteen. I know what I'm asking. I said, what about your spurs?"

"And I'm asking you—what about them?"

She looked down to his stirrup and stared at his boot heel. Large-roweled silver spurs. He'd been wearing them since the night he'd thought he had his hands on Papa. "Where'd you get 'em? And why?"

"In Nogales. Before I came back to Tucson. And because I felt it was time to get my own pair. Why—you want some now?"

"No. I have my father's." Through with questioning him, Jacey fell silent again.

But still the man's gaze stayed riveted on her. Heat that had nothing to do with the shimmering desert bloomed on Jacey's cheeks. She frowned and looked over at him. "What're you starin' at?"

He didn't answer her, except to finally look away and glare at the far mountains. She thought she heard him say, under his breath, "Beats the hell out of me."

"Beats the hell out of me," Zant muttered. *Why'd she go and bring up the baby?* Yesterday at Buckeye's, when she'd questioned him out at the fence about his mother, was the only time he'd even thought about his plan since they'd left Tucson two days ago.

Well, at least now she knew why he felt the way he did—about a lot of things. But was being with her causing him to lose his edge, softening him toward the Lawlesses? Maybe making him think twice about such a cruel plot as his? *Cruel plot?* Zant frowned. Since when had he thought of his intentions as a cruel plot? Far from it. They were just. They were warranted. He stole a quick glance at his companion. Damn her for being so little and ornery and painfully desirable.

But, no. Hell, no. It wasn't her wearing him down. It was this desert. It had a way of doing that to a man. Made you think about nothing but your next patch of shade, your next drink of water. Made you wary of rattlers and Gila monsters and scorpions. And not just with regard to yourself. You'd best have a care for your mount, lest you find yourself afoot and as good as dead out here. Plenty of bleached bones about to testify to that.

Having thus sidetracked his thoughts to the daily concerns of survival, Zant turned to Jacey. "Come tomorrow, about noon, if we keep heading west, we'll be at Two-finger McCormack's place."

With her dark eyes shaded by her hat's floppy brim, she looked over at him and grinned. Knowing why, he grinned right back. She then chuckled and shook her head. "Papa's best stories were about Two-finger. He said bad luck chased that old outlaw like coyotes do field mice."

"Yeah. I heard the same. Heard he got the name Two-finger because he blew the other three off his hand while cleaning his own gun."

Jacey went wide-eyed and leaned over her pommel, giving in to her hilarity. To Zant, the musical sound was like tiny tinkly bells. But the desert citizens apparently had different opinions. Lizards dived into rock crevices. Furry creatures scurried under yuccas. Two wrens took wing. But Zant's chest swelled with sudden high spirits. He wanted more than anything else to hear more of her unrestrained laughter. So he quipped, "I wonder what he looks like after so many years. You think he's got a three-legged horse and maybe only one eye by now?"

Grinning ear to ear, Jacey sat up, stared wide-eyed at him, and gurgled out, "You think there'll be enough left of him to recognize?"

Zant pretended to consider that. "Well, maybe if he's lost an arm or a couple legs, we can just roll him into a corner and search his place, see if he has your keepsake."

Jacey held a hand against her belly as she laughed with him. Her words came with gasping gaps between them. "Yeah . . . and he wouldn't be . . . able to shoot at us . . . like that old woman back at . . . Tully's aimed to do."

A score more far-fetched predictions and storied remembrances of Two-finger McCormack accompanied them west, toward their next encounter. And toward the gentle, starry . . . waiting night.

Chapter Ten

That warm and windless evening, as the sun set, they made camp alongside a deep, muddy pool that offered the only wetness they'd seen all day. Tracks of various animals and birds encircled it, attesting to its being the only water for miles around. Brackish, warm, a pool in an otherwise dry rill, the liquid was wet and life-giving and therefore welcome.

Squatting at the water's edge, Jacey hurriedly filled the small coffeepot and their canteens by dragging them across the surface while Zant held the neighing, restless horses at bay. As likely as not, those two'd drink the mudhole dry once they got at it.

Done, Jacey capped the second canteen, came to her feet and turned around. "All right. Bring 'em over before they start buckin' and bitin'."

She stepped back as Zant moved in with the now frantic animals. For once, as they lowered their heads and drank, there was no all-out war between the two horses about being side by side. Well, Jacey figured, they were tired and thirsty. But also, maybe they'd come to an agreement that since necessity had thrown them together, they should make the best of it. Maybe they realized that to fight each other now, out here, meant neither one of them would survive. Jacey shook her head, bridling her unguarded thoughts. She was still talking about the horses, wasn't she?

She looked away from the animals to the man. And suspended thought in favor of just watching the play of heavy muscle under his sweat-stained shirt as he stretched and rocked from side to side, as if loosening cramped muscles.

If she wanted . . . if she dared . . . she could reach out and touch him. He was that close. Gripping instead the canteens and the coffeepot with two-handed determination, Jacey spoke the next thought that came to her head. "Tired of the saddle, huh?" *Oh, that's great, Jacey. Just let the man know you've been standing here leering at him.*

Both sets of reins threaded through his fingers, Zant turned sideways toward her, looking surprised that she was still standing there. He then grinned and stretched mightily. "I'll say. A few more days of this and my new name will be Flat Butt."

Not from where she was standing. Her eyes widening at the splayed-out, masculine sight he made, Jacey found herself incapable of laughing with him. She desperately groped for a canteen cap and finally found one. She fumbled it open and gulped a mouthful of nasty-tasting water. She grimaced, swiped a hand over her wet lips, and offered the open canteen to him. "Me, too," she offered.

"You too what?" He took the canteen—his long fingers covering her smaller ones for one brief, electric second—put it to his mouth, and drank deeply. Jacey braced her suddenly wobbly knees. He handed the canteen back to her and swiped his forearm across his lips and dripping chin. He then turned back to the horses, checking to see that they didn't take in too much water. He smoothed a hand over his stallion's red coat, stroking, patting.

But it was Jacey who shivered. "Um, my butt's flat, too."

He turned back to her, frowning. "What?"

Heat seared her cheeks and neck. "Nothing." She beat a new path up the shallow incline. Her ranting insults to herself marked each stiff-legged stride. *Stupid, crazy, big-mouthed, asinine, lovestruck—* She stopped. Lovestruck? No. She jerked around to Zant. He'd squatted on his haunches and was sluicing water over his neck and through his hair. His denims stretched tightly over his far-from-flat butt and his steely thighs. Oh, yes. Lovestruck. The realization tore out of her in a loud, distressed curse. "No, dammit!"

Instantly, Zant and Knight and Old Blood straightened up and turned their heads and dripping muzzles to stare at her. "You okay?" Zant called out. He combed his fingers through his thick black hair.

"No." She heard the pout in her voice and covered it by squawking, "I mean yes."

"Then what were you yelling about?"

"I wasn't."

Zant stared at her and then exchanged a look with the two horses. He shrugged his broad shoulders. They arched their necks and shivered their manes all about.

Jacey turned on her boot heel, stalking to the much-used campsite they'd claimed for the night. To one side of the trampled brush and the blackened ring of stones encircling a gray-ash-filled center, she set down the coffeepot and canteens. Tossing her thick braid back over her shoulder, she busied herself with gathering wood for a campfire, which was about all she could do until Zant brought the horses over. Still saddled, they carried the food, utensils, coffee, and bedrolls on them.

With the wood crooked in her arms, and squatting to dump her load, Jacey gave a start when long shadows fell over her and stretched out on the sandy earth before her. She jerked around. Zant and his two four-legged companions were plodding up to her. Still feeling defenseless in the face of his powerful maleness—at once so foreign and so inviting to her—she stood up and held her hand out. "Took you long enough. Give me Knight's reins."

He separated them from his stallion's and held them out to her, his face mirroring a quizzical yet assessing look. "You sure you're okay?"

"Never better, outlaw." She snatched at the reins.

He pulled them back. "No. Something's eating at you. Whenever you call me outlaw or gunslinger, I'm anywhere but on your good side."

She'd die before she'd tell him what was wrong. "Why should that bother you? Do you care if I'm sore at you . . . I mean, really care?"

His level stare unnerved Jacey as much as his gunfighter's stance. But she stood her ground, held her breath, waited for him to speak. He shook his head. "No. I don't guess I do."

Jacey's heart plummeted. She just wanted to take her horse and get the heck away from him, if only for a few minutes. "Then just give me the reins."

He held them out to her, allowed her to grip them, and then

refused to let go. Jacey looked up into his scowling face. "I lied," he said. "I do want to know what the hell's wrong with you. When we went to the watering hole a few minutes ago, we were getting along just fine. Now you're a spitting alley cat. How come?"

Jacey wanted to turn and run. But where to? Out here, alone with him in unfamiliar and deserted and desolate country, she was completely at his mercy. So, she drew in a deep breath through her pinched nostrils and tugged at the reins. But with no better luck than she had the first time. "All right. Fine. I'll tell you what's wrong."

"Well?"

"Well," she repeated with emphasis, "I'm . . . hungry, is all. I haven't had a bite since breakfast."

He frowned, but then his face cleared. He even grinned. "Then I must be looking pretty good to you about now."

Jacey sucked in a dry breath and began choking. *Could he read her mind?* "What?"

He grinned and pounded her—unnecessarily hard, in her opinion—on the back. "Tully's woman. You said she should have eaten him herself. And I said I'd have to make sure you didn't get too hungry. What'd you think I—Wait a minute. Why, Jacey Lawless"—the ornery sidewinder chuckled in a purely mocking way—"*am* I starting to look good to you? Is that what's wrong with you?"

"Hogwash."

He stared at her a moment and then threw his head back and laughed. With her bottom lip poked out far enough for her to trip over it, Jacey snatched Knight's reins from him and practically dragged the animal away to unsaddle and hobble him for the night.

Zant's mocking words chased after her. "Hogwash, huh? We'll see, Jacey Lawless. We'll see."

All was done. The horses were unsaddled, brushed down, hobbled, and left to graze among the tough grasses. The fire burned brightly in the cool and starlit night. Jacey's stomach was full of Maria's tortillas and beef and beans and a slice of mock-apple pie. She reclined in her bedroll. Zant did the same in his—across the fire from her. And he'd better stay there, if he knew what was good for him.

But apparently he didn't. Her stomach muscles clenched, Jacey watched him roll easily to his feet in a smooth display of coordination and grace. Well, give the devil his due. He *was* something. Bending over, grabbing his boots by the mule-ear straps, he tugged them on and started in her direction. As he approached, Jacey gripped her blanket and spoke in a low, threatening voice. "I'm not asleep, so tread carefully, outlaw."

"Settle down, Ornery. I'm just going to relieve myself."

Looking straight ahead at the fire, refusing to admit her blunder, Jacey muttered, "Well . . . see that you do."

He chuckled and stepped around her. Lying on her side, facing the fire, she listened to the grainy shifting of the sand under his boots as he moved farther and farther away. Jacey grinned. Why couldn't she stay mad at him? She never had any trouble staying mad at anyone else she knew. Even Hannah and Glory and Biddy. Why, if anyone put her in a snit, she'd stay there for days, making everyone around her miserable, until Papa would—

"Jacey?"

Alert to the eerie, hissing sound, Jacey tensed. When the sound didn't repeat after several moments, she dismissed it as a bird and resettled in her thoughts, recalling Papa getting tired of her grumpiness and tanning her seat if she—

"Jacey?"

Frowning, Jacy turned over and sat up. There it was again. She looked out into the night, in the direction Zant had gone. If that rotten mud toad thought she was going to help him with relieving himself, then he could. . . . No, he wouldn't do that. So, the sound—no more than a rustling of scrawny branches—had to be her imagination.

Flopping back down, she again took up her fond memories of life at home. Papa'd tan her seat if she so much as raised her voice to Mama. Well, she learned early on not to do that. Which meant her sisters were fair game. They were never any match for—

"Jacey?"

Jacey sat up. That was no wind and no bird. It was Zant. If this was his idea of a joke—"What do you want, Chapelo? You think you can scare me with your whispering?"

Jacey picked up his note of urgency and, yes, the fear in

his voice. Was he bluffing her? And if not, what made him think she wanted to see anything that could scare *him*? "What are you up to? I'm not about to come out there to look at your—"

"Quiet." His voice was no more than a squeak. "Bring . . . your gun. Now."

Still not convinced, but nevertheless dropping her voice to just above a whisper, she called out, "Why?"

"There's a—" He bit off his words.

Jacey came to her knees. Was that the sound of rattles she heard? She gave the night her full attention. The dry rasp of a rattler's warning carried to her. Sweat instantly dewed her lip and seemed to pool under her arms. "Oh, my God." She said it as a prayer. She swallowed and bent to search out her Colt. "I heard it. I'm on my way."

"Jacey?"

She stood up, wiped her sweating palm on her skirt, and cocked her gun. "Yeah?"

"Knight's . . . hobbling this way. If he . . . senses the snake, then. . . ."

Jacey exhaled audibly. "Then he'll raise hell, and you'll be a dead man."

After a long moment of silence, she heard Zant's hissed, "Thanks."

Jacey grinned, despite the seriousness of the situation. Then, feeling as ready as she'd ever be, she stepped off her sleeping bag and away from the reassuring glow of the campfire light.

Plunged now into the relatively pitch-black night, she blinked until her eyes adjusted somewhat to the covering darkness. But having no idea which cactus or bush or rocky outcropping he'd chosen, she could only place one booted foot cautiously in front of the other. No sense stepping on the snake. And that was another thing—it'd be nice to know where the danged rattler was in relation to Zant. And to her.

What she did know, though, was the critter would be none too pleased with her approach. In fact, it'd be pretty riled about now. Instinct would have to guide her. Suddenly, Jacey was shoved forward from behind. That push was too solid to be instinct. Stumbling, tripping, fighting to keep her feet, she barely got her hand over her mouth before she cried out. The renewed alarm of *big* rattles being shaken—very close by—

greeted her flat-footed halt. The sharply in-drawn breath she heard had to be Zant's.

Behind Jacey, Knight whuffed and blew and nudged her again. Her heart in her throat, she turned, but was barely able to discern the black gelding from the surrounding night. Reaching out, groping, she located him and rubbed her hand over him. He faced her head-on. With no choice and hating it, she thumped his tender muzzle and hissed, "Git."

Startled, the horse reared his head and stepped back as best he could with hobbled feet. But his retreating footfalls, as he headed back in the direction of the campfire, were a welcome sound.

Jacey closed her eyes in a moment of prayerful thanks. And then traded her gun from one hand to the other, so she could wipe each damp palm down her skirt. The snake rattled again and stirred. She froze. It was on her left. Sounded like it was about waist-high to her. Which meant, if its coils started on the ground, it was about fifty feet long. Or much smaller if coiled on the sun-warmed boulders next to her. Jacey prayed it was lying atop a boulder. Okay. Waist high to her. Which put it about . . . crotch high to Zant, who had to be on the other side of the boulder, since she hadn't knocked into him yet.

Crotch high. *Lordy*. Now she understood why he hadn't just stomped it or backed off. If he got bit, it'd be on his—Jacey made an awful face. That would hurt. Poor Zant was in a very delicate predicament. And one she had to get him out of. In a hurry. No telling how long the snake would remain patient with them. So, living up to her reckless reputation, Jacey made a deliberate feint, hoping to make the snake rattle again—but hopefully not strike—so she could better pinpoint it. The snake cooperated by shaking its rattles.

Good. About two arm-lengths away. But who was it facing? Her or Zant? Suddenly afraid to the point of irritation, Jacey fumed. Could this be any trickier? If she knew its tail was to her, then she'd just grab it and sling it, like she did back home when she came across the varmints. Danged things were always underfoot up in No Man's Land.

Suddenly Jacey realized she hadn't heard a sound from Zant in a while. Had he already been bitten? Was he even now lying on the ground and writhing? No, if the rattler'd bitten him, he'd be making a bunch of noise and the snake would've slithered away. Usually. Sometimes, they just kept biting, depending on how threatened they felt. *Jacey, why are you spooking yourself with these thoughts? Just shoot the danged thing. Zant's expecting it. He'll get out of the way.*

Jacey raised her cocked gun, held her arm out level and steady, yelled, "Now, Zant!" and began firing. Bullets pinged off rock, striking bright flashes of fire, but a few hit something, made no noise. Jacey prayed she'd hit the snake, and not Zant. But figuring Zant'd probably prefer a quick death by bullet over a lingering, painful one like the rattler would deliver, she fired until her Colt was empty. When she finally lowered her arm, all about her was as calm and quiet as Christmas Eve night.

Until the air was split with the most beautiful sound she'd ever heard. "Son of a bitch!" Zant screeched from the other side of the boulder. "You trying to kill me? That damned rattler *and* his blown-off head flew off that rock and hit me in the chest. I must've flung that monster all the way to California. And now my hands are shaking so bad I can't get my pants buttoned."

Grinning in relief, glad he couldn't see her trembling chin in the dark, Jacey called out, "Hey, Chapelo! Aren't you even going to thank me?"

"Thank you?" He sounded closer, like he was stepping around the boulder. "For what? You damn near shot my . . . *head* off. Bullets whizzing by, I'm trying to jump out of the way and get down. Scared the *hell* out of me." He then pushed past her, still buttoning his denims, and reverted to rapid, angry Spanish as he tromped back to the campfire.

To his back, Jacey called out, "I did warn you, remember?" He didn't bother with a response. She grinned again. *Big baby. Wasn't nothing but a little old snake.* Shaking her head, Jacey trudged back to the welcome glow of their fire. A sidelong glance across the flames showed her Zant seated on his bedroll and tugging his boots off. He didn't even look up at her approach. Quirking her mouth, Jacey sat on her own blankets and busied herself with reloading her Colt, plucking bullets out of their confining loops on her gunbelt and expertly poking them into the empty chambers.

The next thing she knew, the campfire's light was blocked and the outlaw's stocking feet were standing in front of her.

She eyed them a minute before walking her gaze up the long drink of water that was Zant. Looking into his darkness-shaded face, detecting only the gleam of his black eyes, she remained quiet, waiting for him.

"I'm sorry I yelled at you, Jacey. And . . . thank you."

Her throat working, Jacey looked down at her gun in her lap, quietly telling it, "It was nothing. You'd do the same for me."

"Yes, I would." He squatted in front of her and tilted her chin up until she had to look into his eyes. "And, Jacey, what you did was far from nothing. It was everything—to me. And I know you didn't have to save my hide. You could have done nothing and been rid of me once and for all."

Jacey ignored the wrenching heartache at just the thought of him dead and spoke with all the spit and vinegar she knew he'd expect from her. "The thought crossed my mind. But that snake didn't have anything to do with . . . what's between me and you. I don't run from any fight. And I don't take the easy way out, Chapelo. So, when the time comes, you can be sure we'll be on even footing. And it'll be only my hand and yours that sees this through to the end."

He quirked a grin and said, "You could win a fight against your weight in wildcats, couldn't you?" He let go of her chin, his black-eyed gaze making a slow sweep of her face, as if he were trying to find a chink in her armor, a soft spot, an opening. Apparently not finding one, he stretched to a stand, stared down at her, said, "Thanks, anyway. I owe you one." And walked away.

Jacey finished reloading her Colt, her task made all the harder for her shaking hands and the tears blurring her eyes.

The next day, about lunchtime, Zant and Jacey found themselves pinned down behind a single boulder outside Two-finger McCormack's old place. And exchanging gunfire with Two-finger. As luck would have it, Angel Peterson, one of the meaner sorts from the old Lawless Gang, was inside with him and firing away.

In a lull, which Zant used to duck down and reload—Jacey did the same—he shoved bullets into the chambers and spoke rapidly. "Mean old sons of bitches. They need a whipping more than they need anything else." With his back to the rock and his knees drawn up, he labored over his task.

Done first with her reloading, Jacey rubbed against his side as she raised up enough to peek over the boulder's rounded top. "Well, I'll be a—Zant, look at this."

He looked up. "Look at what? What're they doing?"

"Just look."

His gun fully loaded again, Zant popped the cylinder back into place, spun it, and cocked it. Turning around, he edged himself up the rough-sided boulder, noting Jacey's look of disbelief, and looked toward the cabin. A once-white combination suit, with the left arm and right leg cut short, hung over the end of a long stick and waved back and forth out the window. He turned to Jacey. "I'd say those drawers belong to Two-finger. You think it's a truce flag?"

Jacey chuckled and said, "That's what I'm guessing—on both counts."

"It could be a trick."

"It could. What do you make of it?"

Zant considered that. Rubbing a hand over his growth of beard, he decided it was a truce flag and not a trick. Because his and Jacey's heads were poked up over the boulder and no one had taken a shot at them. He turned again to Jacey. "Stay low. Let's see what they do. Make them make the next move."

Jacey nodded her agreement, and they both turned to look at the waving drawers. They didn't have long to wait. From inside the cabin came a sharp-edged voice. "Who are you out there?"

Zant notched his Stetson up in disgust and called back, "You'd know, you old coot, if you hadn't started shooting the minute we rode up. You're just damned lucky you didn't hit our horses before we yee-hawed them away."

"Don't fret, stranger. They'll come back. Now, I'm not goin' ta ask ya again." But then he did anyway. "Who are you?"

"I'm Zant Chapelo—the Kid's son. And the lady is Jacey Lawless."

After a moment of silence: "J. C. never was no lady. You're lyin'."

Zant bonked his forehead down on the warm, solid rock and closed his eyes. From that position, he asked Jacey, "Would you please explain your name to them?"

To his right, Jacey huffed out a loud breath and then called out. "I'm Jacey. J-A-C-E-Y. J. C.'s second daughter. I was named after him."

Zant raised his head at the hushed but frantic whisperings carrying to them from inside the cabin. Then, a different, rasping voice called out, "All right. We believe you—even though Angel says he never thought he'd live long enough to see a Chapelo and a Lawless riding together all peaceable like. But bein' who you are don't change nothin'. What you two want?"

Zant figured he'd call riding with Jacey anything but peaceable, but he kept that to himself and said, "We just want to talk to you."

Both old men answered. "About what?" Then, Two-finger, the raspy-voiced one, added, "We don't know nothin' about what it is you want."

Zant turned to exchange a look with Jacey. Just in time to catch her waistband as she went over the rock. "Get down, dammit." He shoved her onto her bottom in the sand.

She came up clawing and hissing. "They know something. Why else would they have said that?"

Zant clamped his hand on her shoulder, holding her down as he got right into her face and hissed, "So they can draw you out and shoot you. Now, stay put, and let's *see* if they know anything. You got that?"

She nodded, but every rigid line in her body said she didn't like it. Zant raised up enough to see the cabin. "What do you think it is we want?"

"You're here about the money. We ain't got none of it."

Zant frowned and looked down at Jacey. She shrugged her shoulders. He turned to the cabin. "What money are you talking about?"

Silence. Then came Angel's voice. "If'n you don't know, we ain't about to tell ya. You think we're simpleminded?"

Zant bit back his honest opinion and lied, "Far from it, old-timer. But we're not here about anything to do with money. We're here about J. C. Lawless himself."

"Wal, he ain't here."

That did it. Zant lost control and screeched like an owl. "I know that, you old fart." Then, taking a deep, calming breath, he jerked his Stetson off, barely suppressing his urge to bite it and crumple it. His still raised voice sailed across the distance. "J. C. and his wife have been killed. And we're—"

"We didn't do it. Go away."

Near to bellowing again in frustrated rage, Zant slid down the boulder to sit next to Jacey on the hot sand. "Tell me one thing. How in the living hell was the Lawless Gang ever anything to fear?"

He watched as suppressed humor lit up her delicate face. "I guess they were different when they were younger. They're all old men now. My father and yours were the youngest ones, remember?"

"I do. But if this is all I have to look forward to—being some crazy old outlaw coot without a pot to piss in or a window to throw it out of—then I'm beginning to think I should've let that snake do his worst last night."

Jacey grinned, showing white, even teeth. "Sorry I saved you."

"Yeah, thanks for the favor." He then crammed his Stetson back on, rested his elbows on his bent knees, and said, "I'm about ready to do just what Angel says and go away. Five more minutes of this, and I'll shoot 'em both for being so stupid."

Jacey chuckled. "I think they're kind of funny. Look what they've done to you. You're red-faced and cussin' and spittin' thorns."

Closer to laughing with her than he cared to admit, Zant feigned being put out with her. "Is that so? Since you're the one who thinks they're so all-fired amusing, why don't you try reasoning with them, missy?"

She raised her arched eyebrows at him. "I think I will." And she did just that. Pushing her bottom off the sand, she turned and edged up the boulder. Her first words, though, were for Zant. "The flag is gone." She then turned to call out, "Hey, you inside? We just want some information. I've got a piece of spur to show you and some questions to ask. That's all. I swear it—on my Lawless name."

Her words and her oath were met with silence, which slowly became a sustained, suddenly suspicious, and too quiet silence. Frowning, Zant joined Jacey in peeking over the boulder. "I don't like the looks of this."

Jacey eyed him. "Me, neither. What do you think they're doing?"

"Well, either they're reloading. Or they fell asleep. Or they went out a back way."

"I figured along the same lines."

Zant eyed the cabin, taking in the jutting foothills behind it, the thick covering of oaks and junipers and the creosote bushes that nestled the ramshackle abode. No movement from anywhere. He picked up a good-sized rock and chunked it at the squatty old house. Jacey ducked behind their boulder with him. But, nothing. No response. He turned to her again. "I guess you already figured, too, that one of us has to go out there and search the cabin."

"One of us? You're the one who doesn't want to end up an old coot. I say you go."

"Thanks."

"Just tryin' to oblige, Chapelo. I'll cover you."

Zant yanked his Stetson low over his eyes and nodded. "Just try not to shoot me."

He made a movement to dart around the covering rock, but froze with Jacey's retort. "Try not to give me a reason to."

He looked back over his shoulder at her. Her grin and that sparkle in those damned black eyes of hers said she'd do it, too. "Before this is all over, Jacey Lawless, I'm going to put you over my knee."

She held her gun up parallel with herself and cocked it. "Now those are the words of a man intent on giving a woman reason enough to shoot him."

Zant grunted his opinion of that and then slouched around the side of the boulder. No man and no bullets challenged him. Thus emboldened, he skittered to the cabin's edge, looked back to see Jacey with her Colt trained on the open window, and then edged his way over to it. He jerked around to quickly peek inside, gain an impression, and then jump back to the cover of the outside wall. He thought about what he'd seen. Dirt. Rough furniture. Unmade beds. Dried-up remains of countless meals and scattered clothes everywhere.

Otherwise, it was empty. Of Angel and Two-finger, at any rate. On the dirty floor was the makeshift flag. He signaled the all-clear to Jacey and then went to the closed door. When she joined him, staying behind him as he indicated for her to do, he opened the door and burst inside, his gun leveled at anything that might move. But nothing did. He relaxed his stance but didn't reholster his Colt.

At his side now, Jacey grimaced. "Those two stinkers. Just as we thought—gone."

Notching his Stetson up, Zant took a good look around. "Yep. Right out this back door, I'd say." He kicked clothes and tin plates aside as he strode to the crude, gaping-open doorway. He looked out, training his gaze on the upward slope of a steep foothill. "Look here, Jacey."

Stepping close to him, she peered between the doorjamb and his shoulder. She looked in the direction he pointed and chuckled. "I'm guessing that cloud of dust tells its own story."

Watching the obvious signs of a full retreat up the cactus-studded hill, Zant reholstered his gun and crossed his arms over his chest. He looked down at Jacey, finding himself once again captivated by her fragile size, which made her enormous fighting spirit a never-ending surprise. "Well, there went numbers three and four of the five remaining Lawless gang desperadoes. You think we should go after them?"

Jacey shook her head. "No. I don't think they know a thing beyond what goes on right here under their own noses." She then turned to look around the rumpled room. "And maybe not even that."

Zant scanned the room with her—anything to keep from staring openly, longingly at her—and then started for the front door. "Come on. Let's go locate our horses and clear out. Wouldn't want those two old Jaspers to die from the heat while they wait up in the hills for us to leave."

"Dammit, Jacey, we've been hunting for two hours. Just how far do you think that nag of yours shied?"

"What's wrong, Chapelo? Am I too heavy for your prissy stallion?"

"He's not prissy."

"And Knight's not a nag."

"If he doesn't turn up soon on his own, he'll be vulture bait when I'm through with him. And quit squirming. You're about to knock me off the back of my own horse."

"How can I be squirming? I'm sitting in the saddle. Now

head this burro of yours over by that stand of mesquite trees. And move your hand, outlaw, before I slice it off and hand it back to you."

"Oh, hell, my hand's not even touching your—"

"Over there! Did you see that?"

"See what?"

"I think I saw a flash of black moving around in those mesquites. Maybe Knight got his reins tangled in a branch. Turn this animal."

"I am. At least Sangre had the sense to wait close by."

"Sense? The only reason this swaybacked mule was close by was because he was standing on his own reins and didn't have enough sense to lift his hoof."

"It's a trick I taught him."

"Oh, for crying out loud. You taught him to tromp on his own reins and thereby take a chance at throwing himself and breaking his own neck? I'm not sure he has the sense to do that."

"Sangre is a blooded stallion with Arabian lines. He's not a donkey or a mule or a dumb animal."

"Then maybe it's you I'm thinking of."

"How'd you like to walk until we find that gelding of yours?"

"Fine. It's too hot up here anyway what with your big-boned self all mashed up against my back. And move your arm."

"Ouch, dammit. You want down? Then, get—Don't jump. You'll . . . fall on your butt. Like you just did. You okay?"

"I'm fine. I like walking. I was walking before I was riding. Suits me fine."

"Get the hell back up here. You can't walk in this heat. I mean it—*now*."

"You can't tell me what to do, Chapelo."

"I can. And I do all the time."

"Yeah, and I don't do it."

"The hell you—Fine. Suit yourself."

"I always do. And back off some. That Arabian of yours is blowing his hot breath on me."

"Whoa, Sangre. Hey, wildcat? Joe Buford's place is another two-day ride—or five-to seven-day's walk—northwest of here. You intend to walk it the whole way?"

"I will if I have to. But I intend to find Knight way before that. You can always go on ahead, if I'm holding you up."

"If I had any sense I would. Now get back up here with me."

"Not until you apologize."

"Look out for that scorpion."

"I see him. There. Now he's dead. And you better hope that's Knight in those mesquites. He's got my bedroll and most of the food. How'd you like to go to sleep tonight with your belly grumbling and having to share your bedroll with me?"

"You offering? Because if you are, I'll abandon this search for that ornery black critter of yours right here and now."

"Shut up, Chapelo. That was no offer. It was a threat."

"Yeah? How about I get you to make good on it?"

"I'm not sleeping with you—no how and no way."

"Maybe not tonight."

"Maybe not ever."

"That's a mighty long time, Miss Jacey."

"Not near long enough, Mister Zant."

"We'll see."

"Yes, we will. And I'll be the winner."

"I doubt it. Now, what am I supposed to be apologizing for?"

"I forgot. Oh, for saying Knight's a nag."

"All right. I'm sorry your horse is a nag."

"Is that supposed to be funny? I'll tell you one thing, I can't wait to get to Buford's place. Because after that, I won't have to put up with your bossy ways anymore. I'll be heading back to Tucson. And you can go to hell."

"I probably will. But it appears to me you're betting heavy on Buford knowing something that the other ones didn't."

"Call it a hunch. He knows. It's always the last one who knows."

"How do you figure that?"

"Because you quit looking when you find the one with the answers. Leastwise, smart folks do."

"Ahh. Well, would the smart folks—particularly the one on foot and sweating like a washerwoman—maybe want a drink of some nice, cool water?"

"Nope. I'm fine, thank you."

"Yeah, you're fine, all right. I swear I never met someone

with so much spit and—Hey, come back here. Where you running off to?''

"To get Knight. It's him—just like I said, outlaw. I was right about where he'd be, and I'll be right about Joe Buford's knowing. You just wait and see.''

Chapter Eleven

She was right. And they were just barely in time. Joe Buford was dying.

Jacey went quietly to sit in the bedside chair that his wife, a sad-faced, weary old woman, directed her to. The finely stitched and stuffed seat cushion retained a warmth that told her Alma Buford had been sitting here herself. For a long while.

Unsure how to proceed, Jacey pivoted to look over her shoulder to Zant's quietly serious expression. With a nod of his head, he encouraged her to speak. Jacey turned again to look down at the poor sight that was Joe. He lay thin and wasting, but clean and neat, on a bed obviously kept fresh with loving hands. His eyes were closed.

Jacey turned to Alma, a rounded little woman with a gray bun atop her head and a white apron over her neatly patched skirt. "I don't want to disturb him. Is he asleep?"

Alma nodded. "Most likely. He sleeps a lot nowadays. Seems like livin' just wears him out. But go ahead—wake him up and talk to him. It won't hurt him none. I 'spect he'll soon enough be restin' a long, long time."

With a heavy heart and sympathy clouding her eyes, Jacey smiled at Alma. The old woman's chin began to quiver. She turned away. "I 'spect you'uns would like a bite to eat. I'll see to it while you're talkin'. Just don't wear him out too much, if'n you can help it."

"We won't," Jacey assured her. "But please don't fuss on our account. You don't have to—"

"I'd like to, if'n you don't mind. We . . . me and Joe . . .

we don't see too many folks. No one much to talk to, 'ceptin' each other." With that, she turned away, walked to a tall cupboard, and began quietly pulling dishes out.

Jacey looked from the older woman's solid form to Zant. He hovered just inside the doorway, his Stetson respectfully removed and held in front of him. He now came to stand beside her. He put a hand on her shoulder and squeezed gently. Jacey momentarily covered his hand with hers and then turned back to Joe. Reluctant to cause the balding old man any undue suffering, she stuck her hand out and took his. His warm skin was sallow, dry, and felt paper-thin. "Mr. Buford? Can you hear me?"

Thin, veined eyelids opened to reveal brown eyes, the whites of which swam in yellow. Joe blinked a time or two and ran his tongue over cracking lips. Then he looked squarely at Jacey and up at Zant. "I knew you'd come," he rasped out. "You both look . . . like your daddies."

Not sure he was lucid, Jacey turned in confusion to Zant. He swallowed and said, "He knows who we are. Ask him, Jacey. It's what you came for."

Jacey nodded and turned again to Joe. "Mr. Buford, I need to—"

"Call me Joe. Everyone does."

Jacey managed a smile for him. "Okay, Joe. We need to know about our fathers."

The sick old man closed his eyes. "I know," came his whispery voice. His eyelids fluttered open. He blinked and shifted his long, thin legs under his covers. "It ain't pretty . . . what I have to say."

Her heart thumping, Jacey quickly assured him, "We know. We've been told some of it."

"Good," Joe mouthed. Then, "Your daddy's dead, ain't he? That's why you're here."

A deep breath caught in her chest. "How'd you know?" Her voice was no more than the whisper that was Joe's.

"Right now . . . I'm closer . . . to him than I am you. And I know."

Exhaling shuddering breaths, smelling the meat Alma was frying, and hearing Zant shift his weight behind her, Jacey asked, "What do you know?"

"I know why . . . your daddy killed his." He looked up at

Zant. "Sit down, young fella. Sit. On the bed. It's okay. I want . . . I want you to listen good."

Zant sat and said, "Yes, sir."

"Good." Joe then launched into his story, telling it like he'd been rehearsing for years what he would say when this day came. "It was years ago. We was all younger then, full of mischief. J. C. was . . . was our leader. Didn't nobody question his say-so. Best of our lot, he was. The Kid was the only one . . . on the outs with J. C. Only one. See, boy, your daddy didn't . . . take care of you and your mama . . . like J. C. thought he should. J. C. was already a daddy twice over. And he wanted . . . out of the outlaw life. We all felt the same. 'Cepting the Kid."

Joe stopped talking when Alma came over to tilt his skeletal head up and give him a drink. "Here, old man, take you some of this." Joe's hands, big knuckled, long fingered, and shaky, cupped his wife's as he drank in little sips and swallowed with obvious difficulty. When he indicated he'd had his fill, Alma handed the cup to Jacey. "Give him some every now and then."

Jacey looked at the cup's contents. It wasn't water, but a milky liquid. "What is it?"

"Something an old Navajo woman showed me how to prepare. Just give it to him every now and then. Little sips, now." Alma rubbed her hand tenderly over Joe's balding pate and then walked across the adobe to the tiny kitchen area. Rich aromas now wafted throughout the warm, close space.

After a moment, after a deep and sudden breath, as if he'd given in to his fate, Joe turned his head on his pillow to stare unblinkingly at Jacey. For one alarmed moment she thought he was dead, but he breathed again and picked up his tale. "That day . . . the Kid took off from the hideout . . . in a fierce mood. He was pretty riled up at our talk of disbanding. Said he'd . . . show us how a real outlaw acted. A hot-blooded Spaniard, that one. That afternoon, he came back to brag about . . . how he'd already begun his life as a . . . lone desperado. Said we was all a bunch of . . . cowards. J. C. listened to about all he was goin' to. Stepped up to the Kid . . . and told him to explain hisself."

Jacey tensed. Here it was. She just barely stopped her impulse to cover her ears. Beside her, on her left, Zant sat up straighter on the bed. Jacey gripped the cup of medicine in her lap so fiercely her knuckles turned white.

"Plain awful . . . what the Kid had done. Plain awful. J. C. was fit to be tied. So was the rest of us."

Zant broke in, his voice soft and hoarse. "What'd the Kid do, Joe?"

Jacey wanted more than anything to turn to Zant and hold his hand through this next part. But her own dread at what Joe had to say kept her rigid in her chair.

Joe stared at Zant for a moment. "Hard words for me . . . to this day. What he done ain't no . . . reflection on the man you are, son. You . . . remember that. Seems the Kid had robbed and . . . killed a young family. They was all alone and making their way . . . by wagon to Californy. He caught 'em in . . . Apache Pass and killed 'em. Took their few valuables. Left 'em for dead. 'Ceptin' the baby girl."

"Baby girl?" A dawning suspicion rooted in Jacey's heart. "What baby girl, Joe? What was her name?"

Joe turned his jaundiced gaze to Jacey. "Don't know. Never did hear." He then resumed his tale. "J. C. done what any of us . . . would've done in his place. Our gang . . . never picked on hard-workin' folks. Never killed no one who didn't deserve it. Just robbed trains or banks. And only a few of those. Never was as bad as we thought we was."

Another grimace, or smile, contorted Joe's features. " 'Ceptin' for the Kid. Always was a bad sort. Only tolerated him 'cause . . . to cut him out meant we'd have to . . . dodge his tryin' to kill us . . . in revenge. J. C. figured he could . . . control the Kid better . . . if'n he knew where he was."

"What happened then, Joe?" Jacey prompted, suddenly anxious to have the story completed, wanting as much to spare Joe as to get to the end of this painful chapter in all their lives.

No more than a wrinkle under his covers, Joe slowly edged his big hands together until they met in his lap. He folded them together. "J. C. got into . . . a fight with the Kid. They went at it pretty heavy. The Kid just kept makin' it worse. Bragged 'bout leavin' that girl-baby . . . out in Apache Pass. Alone and squallin'. J. C.'d finally heard all he wanted to, I s'pose, and before any of us seen it comin' . . . he called the Kid out."

Zant pushed to his feet, diverting Jacey's attention to himself. He put his Stetson back on and crossed to the open doorway. He stood looking out at the desert landscape. Taking in his rigid stance, his broad back, and his intense quiet, Jacey frowned her of sympathy. She made a movement to get up but, turning in her chair, caught Alma staring at her.

The old woman shook her head, her expression seeming to say there was nothing anyone could do to spare Zant the next few minutes. Jacey sagged in her chair and turned back to Joe, only to realize he'd kept on talking.

"... an' I believe this was just what ... the Kid'd been wantin' all along. A piece of J. C. Shoulda knowed better. J. C. was the ... fastest gun out West ... in his day. Never seen quicker. Before you could say ... pass the potatoes, the Kid went down. Still managed to clear leather ... and take a shot at J. C. as he fell. He missed, but J. C. finished him off with a second bullet."

"Son of a *bitch,*" Zant said from the doorway. He stepped outside and closed the door behind him. Jacey stood up.

"Leave him be. He's a man now. Got to get through this on his own."

Jacey stared at Alma through a waterfall of standing tears. "But he—I can't—"

The gray-haired woman wiped her hands on her apron. "Yes you can. If you love him, you can."

How did she know? Then Jacey heard her own thought. She hadn't denied to herself that she loved him. She'd only wondered how Alma knew. Could it be? Was her love written on her face? Could Zant see it? Jacey sat down heavily, staring straight ahead. But when Joe raised his feeble, shaking hand, she sprang to and gave him a few halting sips from the cup she held.

"Thank you, girl." He laid his head back against his many pillows, swallowed, and closed his eyes. After a moment, he opened his eyes, looked right at Jacey, and said, "You're the baby, aren't you? You're Jacey."

Jacey automatically shook her head. "No. I'm the middle girl. Glory's the baby."

Joe held her gaze. "Glory." He said the name as if praising the Lord. "Is that ... what your mama named her?"

Not as confused as she should be, and fearing why that was so, Jacey nodded. "Yeah. Glory. Glory Bea. Mama said 'Another girl. Well, glory be.' And the name stuck."

Joe smiled with a radiance not of this world. "I like that. But you *are* the youngest Lawless. You know that, don't you?"

Jacey looked down, turning the cup around and around in her lap. "I think so, Joe."

Joe then went on with his story as if he and Jacey'd never had their quiet little conversation. "After . . . shootin' the Kid, your daddy mounted up and . . . lit out. Thought he wasn't comin' back. But he did. Had that baby girl with him. She was real quiet like . . . like she knowed she was okay now. Or maybe . . . she was just all cried out. But anyways, J. C. stopped back by the hideout—it wasn't more'n a few miles from Apache Pass—and told us all . . . to go on home. It was over."

Just then, the door opened. Her heart racing, Jacey pivoted to see Zant standing there. Wordlessly, he took off his Stetson, held her gaze, his own expression unreadable, and came to sit at the end of the bed again. Jacey continued to stare at him, and him at her, until Joe spoke.

"We done buried the Kid and . . . and said some words over him. Then J. C. dismounted, handed me the baby—purtiest . . . little thing I ever saw—and went by hisself to the grave. He took his hat off . . . and knelt on one knee by the Kid's . . . resting place. And spoke in a low voice over him a few minutes.

"Then he got up, put his hat back on . . . took the baby from me . . . and said he was going to . . . the squaws at a close-by village . . . and see what they could tell him about feeding . . . the young'un on his way home. He said he was going by Tucson way one last time, too. And then home. Tucked that . . . baby up in his arm and shook our hands. Said our good-byes . . . and he mounted and rode off. Never did see no more of him. No, never did."

Jacey took a deep breath. And heard Zant do the same thing. Then, Joe added, "Finest man . . . I ever met, J. C. Lawless was. The finest. Man of honor and principle . . . for all his outlaw ways. Had a code, he did . . . and held every one of us to it . . . whilst we rode with him. Never did hurt me none to know him. No, never did."

Jacey couldn't look away from Joe Buford, not even when

he closed his eyes and turned his head to the rough adobe wall. In her heart, she felt a certain kinship with him. Almost as if they'd gone through the same things together. In a way they had, she supposed. So very saddened by it all, she turned to look at Zant. His head was down, his gaze on his hands as he restlessly turned his Stetson around and around by its stiff brim.

Perhaps feeling her gaze on him, he looked up. His black eyes reflected the torment in his soul. "My father was a rotten son of a bitch."

Tears for Zant, for his father and hers, for his mother and hers, threatened to track down Jacey's cheeks. She blinked them back. But had no words for him.

After lunch, after thanking Joe, after chatting with Alma, Jacey and Zant mounted up.

"Where're you'uns headed from here?" Alma shaded her eyes from the sun and squinted up at Jacey atop Knight.

Jacey started to answer, but then closed her mouth. She realized she was at the end of the trail with still no clues about the silver spur and the portrait of Ardis. She looked to Zant, whose Stetson-shaded eyes kept their secrets, and then she turned back to Alma. "I don't rightly know. I guess back to Tucson."

"Tucson? I'd think you'd head for Mexico."

Creaking saddle leather next to her told Jacey that Zant was paying close attention. As was she. "Why Mexico, Alma?"

"Because that's where them other three men was from."

"What three men? When?" Zant's sharp tone drew Jacey's and Alma's attention.

Alma shrugged. "Oh, less than two months ago, I suppose. They came around—big, ugly, mean-lookin' men—wantin' to ask questions of Joe."

Almost afraid to hear the answer, Jacey asked, "And did they?"

"No. I wouldn't let 'em inside, wouldn't let 'em bother Joe. He was havin' one of his spells then. Still haven't told him about them three. Seems they wanted to get real mean with me about not lettin' 'em in. But right over atop that ridge there"—she pointed to a sharp jut of rock not thirty yards away—"some of them Apache showed themselves. Stayed real quiet and still, but them men didn't want no truck with 'em. They left peaceable enough."

Happy that Alma and Joe hadn't been hurt, but still frustrated to be so close and yet so far, Jacey plied her further. "Alma, this could be important. Did the men ever say what they wanted?"

"Oh, yes. I let 'em ask me their questions." She wiped her hands on her apron and swiped its tail end over her brow. "They wanted to know where your daddy had settled. I told 'em all I knowed was up in No Man's Land somewheres. And they showed me one of them silver spurs that the Lawless Gang wore. I recognized it right off. One of 'em—a man with almost no color to his eyes—said it was the Kid's. Well, that was curious enough. But I b'lieve the most curious thing they kept concernin' themselves with was that baby girl Joe just told you about. Said they was lookin' for her special."

Afraid she was going to be ill, Jacey put a hand to her stomach. She turned to Zant, hearing the panic in her own voice. "They didn't want me at all. It's Glory. They're after Glory, Zant. Oh, my God, they're after Glory."

As he stared at her, Zant's expression became predatory, vengeful. "Don Rafael." With sharp movements, he turned his horse to the southeast and put his spurs to it. The stallion responded with a burst of speed that left Jacey fighting the grunting Knight for control and left Alma choking on the dust.

Alma coughed and signaled to Jacey. "Go after him, girl. Go."

Had Knight not been as swift and powerful as he was, Jacey might never have caught up to Zant. But, hot on his dust-raising trail, she nearly rode Knight right over him late that afternoon as the gelding blazed around a turn in a rocky slope shouldering a sluggish river. Who would've thought the outlaw'd be bent over, his butt to them, and occupied with picking up good-sized rocks? With only inches to spare, Jacey and Knight thundered by Zant.

At the last possible second, he straightened up, turned, and froze. Wide-eyed and mouth agape, he dropped the rocks and dove out of the way. His momentum sent him rolling and cussing over the rocky shore and into the muddy water. At the water's edge, and splashed by Zant's antics, Old Blood was startled and reared, pawing the air and bellowing his rage.

By the time Jacey reined in Knight and turned him around, Zant was up, dripping, and making for her. Flecks of blood marked his face and hands where he'd rolled over the unforgiving rocks. Swallowing hard, Jacey figured that running him down had done nothing to improve his mood, judging by his red-faced, evil-eyed expression.

Pointing stiff-armed at her, his every step a calculated one, he glared at her. "Get down off that damned nag. I'm going to whip your butt, just like I promised."

Using her legs to control Knight, Jacey backed him up. Zant kept coming. "Back off, Chapelo. I didn't mean no harm. I didn't even know you were there."

Zant never slowed down. "Get down. Or I'll pull you down."

Jacey made Knight sidestep when the outlaw lunged at her. "I mean it. Back off. I said I was sorry."

"Not as sorry as you're going to be, Jacey Lawless." He lunged again for her, trying to capture her by her waist.

Knight snorted and lowered his head, using it as a battering ram as he charged Zant. Jacey reined in the stiff-legged gelding at the last second. "He'll do it, too, outlaw. Leave me be. I'm warning you."

"Get down off that devil right now. We've got some talking to do."

Still edging Knight back, Jacey called out, "Talk? You don't want to talk. You want to fight. What's eating at you, Chapelo?"

As if her words were a solid barrier, Zant stopped short, his arms at his sides. Breathing hard, he stared at her. He swiped his wet sleeve across his brow. Then he bent forward from the waist to rest his hands on his bent knees. His head hung between his shoulders. "I'm sorry, Jacey. I'm just so damned sorry. First my father. And now Don Rafael."

Hurting for him and for herself, Jacey reined Knight to a stand and dismounted, all the while keeping her troubled gaze on Zant. Almost absently, and out of sheer habit, she looped and tied the reins' ends loosely over her saddle's pommel, allowing enough length for her horse to stretch his neck down to drink. She then hit Knight on his rump. The winded gelding needed no further provocation to head for the water.

After Knight passed in front of her, Jacey hesitated only a second before walking over to Zant. Stopping beside him, close enough to touch him, she watched the water dripping off him onto the desert ground. His breathing was labored. She put her hand out to touch him, but then withdrew it. She opened her mouth two or three times to say something, but each time changed her mind about what she wanted to say. And so, said nothing.

After a moment or two of quiet, marked only by a hawk crying out overhead and the scamper of a big lizard fleeing from one bush to another, Zant straightened up. He didn't look at her, but directed his gaze to the razor-edged cliff of the rocky slope about fifty yards from the water. "Shooting him would be too good for the old son of a bitch."

Jacey sucked in her bottom lip, bit at it, and then let out her breath. "You mean Don Rafael?"

Soaking wet, still staring upward, and putting his hands to his waist, Zant nodded. "Yeah. I had no idea, Jacey. You have to believe me."

Jacey nodded, drinking in his strong-jawed profile. "I do."

As if he hadn't heard her, he went on. "I was in prison for five years. I didn't have any idea. But now, a lot of things are coming clear and clean. A lot of things at Cielo Azul. I couldn't figure out what the men were talking about, about me being the true *jefe*. But now? I think I understand."

"What's a 'hef-eh'?"

Zant turned to Jacey, eyeing her as if he'd really been talking to the cliff and she'd just popped up here next to him. "It means 'chief'. Or 'boss'."

Jacey nodded. "Oh." Then, looking around her, remembering what she'd seen him doing when she came around the bend, she looked up at him. "What were you doing with all those rocks just now? And why'd you take out so fast from the Buford place? Were you trying to lose me?"

"No. I just lost my temper. Got too mad at Don Rafael to sit still any longer." Zant then quirked up a corner of his mouth. And darned if his expression didn't turn . . . well, sheepish. Jacey frowned up at him, trying to ignore the damp lock of black hair that fell over his forehead, giving him a wicked yet playful look. "The rocks . . . I was throwing 'em."

"Throwing 'em? At what?"

He chuckled to himself, and then raised his hand as if to tug at his Stetson. Only, it wasn't on his head. He looked around and then turned toward the water. Jacey followed his long-legged strides, stopping a ways from the shore's edge. But Zant didn't. Already wet, he stopped long enough to tug his boots off and throw them at the water's edge. He then waded in about knee-deep and caught his Stetson as it floated by. From the middle of the current, he called out, "I was throwing them at anything that moved. And some things that didn't."

Watching him slog back out, shaking his hat and reshaping the black felt as best he could, Jacey persisted. "Why?"

He waited until he'd walked up the incline to where she stood before he answered her. "Because I was mad. Still am." With that, he put his dripping hat on his head and undid his gunbelt. Examining his Colt, he shook his head and frowned. "Damned gun is soaked through. I'll have to spend the evening cleaning it." He then looked over at her. "Get my boots, will you?"

Involved in their conversation, and eyeing his every movement, Jacey obediently fetched them, dropping them at his feet when he indicated she should do so. Zant tossed his gunbelt down atop them. Jacey brushed her hands together and dried them on her skirt. "Who're you mad at—besides me? Don Rafael?"

Zant nodded as he began unbuttoning his chambray shirt. "Yep."

Her gaze locking on his moving hands as they opened his shirt, Jacey finally remembered to ask, "What are you going to do about him?"

Zant tugged the sodden shirt over his head, turned it right side out, and headed farther inland. "Bring that stuff there."

Suddenly put out with his ordering her around, Jacey made no move to obey as she watched his retreating back. He stopped in front of a thorny bush that fronted a nearly horizontal slab of outthrust rock. Marking the angle of the sun, he placed his shirt on the bush so it could catch the day's last warming rays.

He then turned as if expecting her to be right behind him. Jacey watched him as he spotted her at the water's edge. She put her hands to her waist, and waited. Zant shook his head.

"Please? Please bring them here. Is that better?"

Well, some. Jacey scooped up the dripping items and trod heavily to the man. "Here." She dumped them in his waiting arms.

"Thanks." He slung his gunbelt over his shoulder, removed his Stetson to set it atop the bush, and then upended his boots, shaking out the last drops of water. He positioned them on the ground, at the base of the bush and angled up on the toes to catch the sun inside them. Only then did he stand up and resume their discussion. "What'd you ask me a minute ago?"

Jacey had to think about it. "Oh, yeah. I asked you what you were going to do about Don Rafael."

"Ahh. Don Rafael. Maybe kill him, if I have to."

"Kill him? Your own grandfather? Zant, you can't do that."

He began opening the button-fly front of his denims. His combination-suit-covered chest and biceps bulged with his hands' motions. "Why can't I?"

As if just realizing the man was undressing in front of her, when he began skinning the heavy denim fabric over his hips, Jacey backed up and looked down to study her boots. The fire on her cheeks could heat up the surrounding desert. "Because you wouldn't be . . . any better than he is, if you did."

"Who says I am anyway?"

His words brought her head up. But his state of undress caught her reply in her throat. His denims were now laid out next to his shirt and hat. His gunbelt still rode his shoulder. And he, himself, stood before her in his soaked white underdrawers. The wet fabric, stretching from his neck to his ankles, left nothing underneath to the imagination. Nothing. Drawing in a shocked breath, she spun around. "Put some danged clothes on, Chapelo."

"I intend to," he drawled to her back. "But first I've got to get out of these wet ones. And it's your fault they're wet. Once I peel off my drawers, I'll go get my dry clothes out of my saddlebags."

Jacey spun to her right, heading for the man's stallion. "I'll go get them. You . . . stay right here. And cover yourself or something."

His chuckle followed her a few steps before he called out, "Think you can get Sangre to let you that close to him?"

Over her shoulder, Jacey called back, ''Either he'll let me, or Old Blood will run with blood.''

The words were barely out of her mouth before she was tackled around the waist by a big, warm, and wet somebody, and carried under his arm like a sack of flour toward the water. Her slouch hat went one way, her Colt another, her long braid swung wildly in her face . . . and she went sputtering into the water with that danged war-whooping Chapelo.

Screaming, fighting, kicking, cussing, Jacey nevertheless ended up being tossed like a carcass into the deepest part of the muddy river. Skidding along the slippery rocks on her bottom, she grabbed for handholds, found none, and sat hard on her backside. The sluggish current was still strong enough to nearly roll her over and dunk her.

Maddened beyond rage, Jacey fumbled for and finally found a toehold—and her sheathed knife. Gripping it in her fist, she rose up out of the water like an avenging goddess and looked everywhere for Chapelo. Or tried to. Water streamed into her eyes. She coughed hoarsely. Cussed loudly. Made screeching, enraged sounds and called out for his blood. ''Where are you, Chapelo? Show yourself, you big coward! I dare you!''

She was again grabbed from behind and pushed down in the water. Squawking like a wet hen, she snarled and tried to turn around in the now churning current. But couldn't. Cursing at her heavy, water-filled boots, she stumbled to a stand and—had her knife wrenched out of her hand and sent flying onto the shore. It hit with a metallic clunk among the rocks. Her lips pulled back over her teeth in a snarl, she launched herself at the big target that was the laughing Chapelo.

The big skunk handled her easily. He held her wrists and . . . that was about all he had to do. She was too weighted down with wet clothes and brimming boots to do much more than scream at him. ''What the hell did you do that for, you mangy coyote? Let me go. I mean it! Right now.''

''Or you'll what?''

Locked in his grip, as tight and effective as handcuffs, Jacey seethed and glared and tried to come up with an appropriately dire threat. ''Or I'll . . . skin you alive. *And* your horse. That's what.''

''Ewww, please don't. I'm really scared now.''

Jacey froze for a moment, staring up into his mocking face.

"What in the living hell has gotten into you, Chapelo? Why'd you dunk me like that? What if I couldn't swim? What then?"

"The water's only knee-deep. You couldn't drown."

Jacey looked down at the water. Knee-deep to him. Mid-thigh to her. And back up at him. "You didn't tell me the why of it."

"I thought you needed a little cooling down."

"Me? You're the one who was hot and mad."

"Yeah. And you're the one who was just hot."

"What?"

"I saw the way you were looking at me."

"What?" Was that the only word left to her, she had to wonder.

He let go of her wrists. "Go ahead, deny it. You want me."

"*Want* you?" Jacey lowered her arms and put her hands to her waist, carrying on their conversation as if they stood in a drawing room and not in the middle of a muddy river out in the godforsaken desert of the Arizona Territory. "You think I want you? Hell, maybe the sheriffs in four states want you. But not me."

The sun glinted off his smiling face, brightening his black eyes and white teeth. Even his growth of beard shone bluish along his jaw. The big, muscled outlaw dared to reach out and gently knuckle her nose. "Liar."

Jacey glared up at him. "Kiss my ass, Chapelo."

A grin of pure evil, one that would surely delight Satan's soul, spread across his face, even crinkling the skin at the corners of his eyes. Right there in the water, he began unbuttoning his combination suit. "Sweetheart, you read my mind."

CHAPTER TWELVE

Jacey began backing upriver. Not only did she have to face him down, her hands outstretched as if to ward him off, but she had to fight the current, which wanted to push her into him. "Don't even think it, Zant."

"Oh, so now it's Zant?" His angled chin and slanting eyes made him pretty scary. And unpredictable. But her choices were either to watch his face . . . or stare at his muscled chest and the crisp sprinkling of hairs revealed there by his partially unbuttoned combination-suit.

Jacey swallowed—about a pint of muddy river—and brazened it out. "Zant. Chapelo. Outlaw. Gunslinger. Take your pick."

"How about lover?"

"Never."

"Never's a long time, Jacey."

"Not long enough, outlaw." How come the danged current didn't seem to bother his big-bodied self? He walked—barefooted—through the water as if he were tramping booted through wooded undergrowth.

Aware that he was gaining on her inch by inch, and knowing that all he had to do was reach out to take hold of her, aware that he was toying with her in a purely seductive way, Jacey tensed and her teeth began to chatter. She clamped down on her back teeth until she could control her clacking jaw and cried out, "Knock it off, Zant. I'm soaking wet and freezing."

His black-eyed, ornery gaze slipped to her chest and then flicked back up to her face. "I know. You'll be warm enough soon."

Knowing and yet not knowing what that meant, but realizing her female instincts were alive and screaming—for him—Jacey feinted right and then left. She wanted with all her might to put some distance between them. If she could just get him out of this water, maybe he'd calm down and quit—Zant abruptly snaked out his right hand and grasped her arm. She gasped and drew her arms up in a defensive posture.

"Quick. But not quick enough, Jacey. Come here."

"No." She wriggled in his grasp, but to no avail.

Despite her sodden, sagging clothes and drooping boots, Zant easily lifted her in his arms and carried her to the shore. Despite the warmth of the day, the warmth of the water, and the heat of Zant's body, Jacey shivered as her skin bumped with gooseflesh. "What . . . ?" She flicked her tongue over her lips and tried again. "What are you going to do?"

Setting her on her squishy feet, he said, "Nothing." Then as he walked away, he called back over his shoulder. "Now we're even."

Watching his departing back, avoiding looking below his waist, Jacey stood frozen on the rocks, hugging herself. *Now we're even? What the heck does that mean?*

That evening, sitting on his side of the campfire, Zant eyed Jacey on her side. Seated with her legs bent to one side, her head angled away from him, and with her now dry hair thrown forward over her shoulder, she was braiding her black and silky waterfall. Zant swiped his hand in agitation down his mouth and chin, fuming about how she had no idea what the sight did to him. But even before he knew he was going to say it, he heard himself at the same time she did. "Leave it down. Don't braid it."

Her fingers stopped. She looked up at him. The leaping flames between them, separating them, threatening to burn them if they got too close, lit and shadowed her doe eyes and unsmiling mouth. "Why?"

Zant swallowed. *Because all that black silk flowing through my fingers would*—He shrugged. "No special reason."

She cocked her head at an angle and arched her brows. "You okay, Zant?"

Zant. She'd been calling him that since this afternoon. Since he'd damned near lost control and ripped her clothes off her to—"Yeah. And you?"

She shrugged, lowering her hands from her half-braided hair. With every movement of hers, the loose braid began to unravel . . . right along with Zant's control. "I'm fine. No worse for having been dunked a couple times."

Zant started to chuckle, bit it back, and looked down at his bedroll. He stayed like that until the urge to laugh passed. When he looked up, he saw that apparently she'd never looked away from him. His heart leaped, but he said, calmly enough, "Tell me what you think about what Joe and Alma said."

Jacey huffed out her breath, as if it were painful to do so, and drew herself up on her bent legs, resting her hands lightly on her skirt-covered thighs. "Which part?"

"Any of it." *I just want to watch you talk. I just want to look at you.*

As if she weren't quite aware she was doing it—although Zant was . . . to the point of painful discomfort—Jacey repeatedly ran her fingers through the length of her hair, further unbraiding it and combing the shiny, dark fall all at the same time. "I guess the part I'm most upset about is finding out that Glory's not—" Her fingers stilled. She closed her eyes and shook her head. "I can't even say it. It might be the truth, but I can't accept Glory as anything but blood kin. As anything but my baby sister."

Zant watched her, saying nothing. This was hers to deal with. It didn't involve him. Finally, she opened her eyes and gazed into the fire. "Glory's not my real sister," she intoned, as if the fire had hypnotized her into the admission.

Once again, Zant spoke before he realized his thoughts had found voice. "Only if you say she's not."

Jacey's head snapped up. The assessing light in her eyes danced along with the fire's flames. "You mean, only if I don't tell her?"

He'd suspected she was thinking along those lines. "No. But that's one way. Probably not the best way. But I was thinking she's not your sister—in your heart, where it counts—*only* if you start thinking that way."

Jacey's changing expression, to one of frank surprise, riled Zant. Did she think he wasn't capable of understanding such things? Hell, did she think he didn't have a heart? He admitted that he'd not given her much of a reason to think otherwise. But the painful truth was, if he wasn't careful to stay away from one Jacey Lawless, he wouldn't have a heart left to call his own. Mad at her for making him feel that way about her, Zant snapped, "If you didn't want my opinion, you shouldn't have asked for it."

She held a hand out, as if to calm him. "No, that's not what I was thinking. I was thinking you're right. You are, you know. It's what's in my heart that counts. But that won't be any comfort to Glory. When she finds out she's not a Lawless. Whew." Jacey shook her head as if already seeing the scene Glory'd cause.

His ruffled feathers resettling, Zant asked, "Why? What will she do?"

Jacey focused on him. "She'll fall apart, that's what. She'll come to realize she's been orphaned twice in her nineteen years."

Anger turned to guilt as Zant picked up a small stone and tossed it back down. "Yeah. And both times by a Chapelo."

Jacey sucked her breath in sharply. Zant looked up to see her getting to her feet and walking around the fire . . . to him. His heart picked up its pace. He shifted his stretched-out legs on his bedroll, moving aside, making room for her . . . if she wanted it. She did. She lowered herself beside him and said, "You don't know that . . ." Zant eyed her, challenged her to say differently about his family's guilt, begged her to believe better of him.

"You don't know that second part's true, Zant."

Zant made a disgusted noise and crossed his legs at the ankles. He supported his weight on his bent elbow. "The hell I don't. My father killed her real parents. And I'm betting Don Rafael had something to do with your folks' being dead."

Jacey shook her head and put her hand on his knee. The warm shock of her touch traveled up his thigh. "No, he didn't. Hannah's letter said Mama's family—"

With only a crunching of his belly muscles, Zant sat up, capturing her hand where it lay on his knee. "Listen to me, Jacey. Don Rafael is guilty as hell."

Jacey stared at him. Her mouth opened and closed. Her chin quivered. Her black eyes filled with tears.

"Dammit." Zant grabbed her to him, drawing her full-out

to lie next to him. He held her tight within the circle of his arms. So little. So warm. Her black-silk hair tangled in his hands. Never had anyone ever felt so right. Zant rested his cheek on her head. He'd never comforted anybody before in his life. No one had ever turned to him like this. And he'd never drawn comfort from anyone. So, he had no words for her.

Her cheek against his chest, her hands fisted atop his heart, her shoulders heaving, she shook her head and blubbered into his shirt, "I'm sorry, Zant. I don't cry. Usually I—But I don't have anybody to—"

"Shh, you've got me." Zant stilled at the sound of his own voice. Those tender words, never spoken before by him, surprised him as much as they seemed to soothe Jacey's wounded-bird heart. She opened her fists to clutch handfuls of his shirt. Zant rode out the storm with her. He lay there, holding her, a vessel for her fear, her sadness, her torment. And wondered if he'd found someone who could ease his heart from a lifetime of hurt.

Jacey finally stilled and raised her head. Zant peered down at her. Her tears had spiked her long lashes into star-points. He brushed her hair out of her tear-dampened face. Never before had she been so beautiful to him as she was at this moment. His heart pounded with his need for her. And then stopped between beats when he heard the three words she whispered to him. "Love me, Zant."

Zant pulled back, the better to look into her face. "What did you say?"

Jacey's head jerked with each shuddering breath she took. But she never looked away from him. Never hesitated. "Love me."

Zant went limp, leaning his head back and closing his eyes. "Don't say that, Jacey. Just . . . don't."

She shifted in his arms. He looked down at her when she pulled herself up on an elbow. "Don't you want me?"

Just the words, *those words* coming out of *her* mouth, being said by *her*—this one woman of all women—in the velvet softness of a starry desert night, left him breathless. He took a deep breath and huffed it out raggedly. "I want you more than I should, Jacey. More than I have a right to. But I'm not sure you understand what you're asking. Do you?"

She eyed him levelly. "Yes."

Zant stared at her, believed her, and withdrew his arm from around her so he could lie flat on his back. He closed his eyes and listened to his heart thudding and felt his blood pumping. If she said it one more time, if she spoke those words again, he'd be lost.

Jacey fell across his chest, her hands gripping his torso as best she could, her black hair covering him like a blanket, her cheek pressed to his heart. "Please, Zant. I need you."

Zant opened his eyes, stared at the stars, and stroked her hair. Why in the hell was he hesitating like this? He'd never made another woman beg him to make love to her. Hell, he'd been more than eager. But with her, with Jacey? It wouldn't be simply a physical act with her. Because he cared, damn it. Damn her. He cared. And caring took away his edge, left him wide open. To what? Hurt? As if he hadn't known that before. But not this way. Not like this.

And suddenly Zant knew. He loved her. It was the worst thing he'd ever admitted to himself in his whole life. Her—Jacey Lawless. And he loved her. She could either uplift him or destroy him. Her. One tiny little spitfire with a Colt and a temper. He grinned but it quickly faded. He had the same power over her, didn't he? He could either uplift her or destroy her, too. And knowing himself as he did, he'd destroy her. Like he had everything else in his life.

Zant felt her sweet little body move against him. Felt himself harden. Couldn't he just quit thinking and make love to her? He thought about it for a moment, considered doing just that. Her words said she wasn't asking for anything but this one night of loving. She said she needed him. One night only? Why, then, couldn't he just give her this night?

Zant, you're a rotten son of a bitch for even thinking that. Making love to her tonight would only make things worse, come the morning. Because it would only make things worse between them. With his body voting one way, his heart another, and his head still another, Zant broke his silence. "No, Jacey. I can't. We can't. It'd be for all the wrong reasons. You're upset tonight. You just want the . . . closeness. I can understand that. But what you're really asking—"

"Is for you to make love to me. I know what I'm asking."

"No you don't." He had to make her understand. Any way

he could. Gripping her arms, he pulled her off his chest as he sat up. He then cupped her chin in his hand and looked right into her eyes. "Don't think I'm being noble. Don't think I have some dignified reason not to do exactly what you want, Jacey. Because I don't. I'd love to oblige you. Believe me, I would. But I won't. Not you. Not like this."

Jacey's expression hardened. She jerked her head, releasing her chin from his hold. "Yeah? Then how about like this, outlaw?"

Before he knew what she was about, Jacey rose to her feet and, staring him right in the eye, began undressing. A muttered curse escaped Zant as he hung his head and searched his soul for a last shred of self-control. If he had any sense, he chided himself, he'd turn her Lawless butt over his knee and spank the sass right out of her. But he knew he wouldn't be mad anymore if he got her in that position. Especially if she was naked. He looked up. She was damned near naked already.

He couldn't look away. In the moonlight, in the firelight, her bare skin shone pearly where it wasn't tanned. She was every bit as little and slender as he knew she'd be. She tossed her hair back and lifted her blouse over her head. Zant's breath came in shuddering gusts. Her dainty undergarment was unexpected. The lacy, ribboned thing did little to cover her high, rounded breasts. And Zant remembered how those breasts felt in his hand.

His breathing quickened as she slipped the delicate fabric over her head. Her full breasts arched with her movement. The firelight caught and reflected the silver chain around her neck and its spur pendant. There it was. The best reason in the world not to touch her. He started to stop her, but froze when her nipples hardened into little buds within their dusky-rose circlets.

Rational thought fled Zant. He burned now, as primitively and as dangerously as the campfire in the black night. He could only watch . . . and feel. Feel himself harden again, feel his heart thudding, his blood rushing like a torrent through his body. And feel his soul crying out for Jacey. He fisted his hands against the wrenching urge to grab her and throw her down and under him, and shove himself—

No. His pounding heart beat painfully. No. Any other woman and he would have. Any other woman who played with him like this, who tormented him with her nakedness, who stood just out of his reach. . . . Yes, any other woman would get the rough treatment she was begging for. But not Jacey. She was innocent. Untouched. Womanly, yes. But so damned achingly still a child. A brave and wounded little bird who needed . . . love—something she couldn't even name. Something he wasn't sure he had in him to give her.

How will you ever know if you don't try? Zant nearly jerked around to see who was behind him before he realized the words had come from his heart. It begged to love someone. Before it was too late. Still watching Jacey, still enchanted with her innocent sensuality, Zant took a deep breath and sat up straighter. All right, by God—his hand fisted tighter with his declaration—he'd try. But, he swore to himself, if he did only one thing right, one thing pure, in his whole stinking life, then this act . . . with her . . . would be it.

Zant's promise to himself almost fled before he finished pledging it, when Jacey undid her split skirt and slid it, along with her bloomers, down her sleek, slender hips and stepped out of the pooling garments, carelessly toeing them aside. Zant's gaze was riveted on the dark and curly-crisp hair that covered her womanhood. Then he saw her knife, still sheathed, its case circling her slim but rounded thigh. Her last defense. He looked up into her eyes.

Wordlessly, Jacey bent her right knee and leaned over. With the silver spur bobbing between her full breasts, she unfastened the beaded sheath and dropped it onto the sandy ground between her and the fire. Zant met her solemn gaze. Jacey then lifted the silver chain over her head, freed it from her hair, and sent it the way of her knife. Zant understood. There would be nothing between them this night. Not the past. Not the future.

Her simple act humbled him and terrified him like nothing else could. Did he have it in him to accept this sacred trust? He stared at her, searched his own soul. And knew he had to try. His chest expanded with this new and powerful resolve. He was wanted. Needed. A guttural noise escaped him. He felt a primitive energy seize him, an urge beyond time that told him to claim this woman. Giving himself over to this new emotion, allowing it to flood his senses, Zant watched Jacey again with hot and hungry eyes.

* * *

Jacey stood proud and defiant, and trembling inside, as she looked down on Zant. It was a reckless thing she'd done, just jumping up and shedding her clothes like this. Gooseflesh puckered her exposed skin in the cool night air, despite the fire's crackling warmth. Every virginal nerve in her body screamed at her to cover her nakedness. But her modesty surrendered to her fighting spirit. She was going to do this, go through with it, because it was what she wanted. With him. And only him. Right here. Right now.

But still, her quaking heart warned that if he didn't make a move in the next few seconds. . . .

Zant came to his feet, stood before her. He touched her nowhere. But his gaze traveled over her, memorizing her every line, her every curve, her every hollow. Jacey breathed through her partially opened lips as she looked up at Zant's strong, unshaven face. Dear God, she loved him. How could she ever forgive herself?

He reached a hand out to her. Jacey's thoughts and breath hung suspended in midair as his fingertips touched her flesh. He caressed her cheek. His touch was hesitant, as if he expected her to fade into the night like a spirit. His face a storybook picture of wonder, he smoothed his long fingers along her jaw, down her neck, hesitating there to feel her swallow and draw a shuddering breath.

Jacey's knees nearly buckled, but she stood her ground, even when he skimmed his hand down the center of her chest, between her breasts. No man had ever—Her muscles contracted when he flattened his hand over her belly and smoothed his fingers around in slow, sensuous circles. A sound, a moan she'd never uttered before in her life, tore from the back of her throat.

As if that sound was what he'd been waiting for, Zant grabbed her to him, spanning her waist with his large hands, holding her tightly, roughly, whispering her name as his nipping kisses followed the still tingling path his hand had just blazed. "So damned small. So tiny. I'm afraid I'll break you."

Jacey shook her head in denial. She clutched his thick hair as his head dipped down. Unmercifully, he nipped at her collarbone and slid his moist kisses across her chest. With every movement, his rough beard rasped across her skin, abrading it, marking her as his own. When his lips closed around the tender flesh of a nipple, Jacey cried out hoarsely. She never knew—Her back arched, her knees buckled.

Zant raised his head. Jacey opened her eyes. His black eyes burned with an intensity that frightened her. His voice was low, husky, animal. "This changes nothing."

A thrill of fright raced across Jacey's numbed consciousness. She shook her head, felt the curling ends of her long hair brush feather-light over her bottom. "No. It changes everything."

With a growl, Zant half lifted her, half carried her, lowering her and himself to his bedroll. Lying beside her, supported on his bent elbow, he again smoothed his hand over her body, like a blind man memorizing her shape, her texture. Only this time his touch wasn't so much tender as urgent, demanding. Laid out before him like she was, Jacey knew her first moment of fear, of womanly vulnerability, when he slipped his hand down to her . . . there.

His touch was hot but petal-soft, wanting but yielding, giving yet taking. Jacey gasped and thrashed about, trying to pull his hand away. But she was no match for his strength. She'd known that all along. But never as she knew it now. She wanted to turn on her side, draw her knees up, and cross her arms over her breasts. She wanted him to stop. She was on fire, burning. Couldn't he see that? Couldn't he feel the slick clutching of her inner muscles?

When a cry of protest spilled out of her, Zant removed his questing fingers from her and pushed himself to his feet. Jacey looked up helplessly at him. Was he even now going to turn her away? No. With lightning-quick movements, the man shed his clothes like a molting snake in a deadly hurry. Not in all her girlish imaginings had Jacey ever thought this moment between a man and a woman could be funny. But Zant's fumbling fingers and flying clothes—some of them landing dangerously close to the leaping flames of the campfire—were rib-tickling.

She grinned and put a hand over her mouth. But her hilarity lived a brief life. Her gaze dipped. She sobered, felt her eyes widen. Down went her hand. *Oh, my God.* Her courage fled. Her desire cooled. That couldn't—He wouldn't—No. It was so . . . big. She tried to swallow her fear, but the painful lump in her throat seemed to be stuck there.

It reminded her that for all her yapping about the cattle drives Papa took her on and about having bedded amongst men and lived with them for months at a time, she hadn't seen a single one naked. Not because of any lack of curiosity on her part. But because of Papa. He would've killed any man who dared—She looked up at Zant's strong and handsome face. Her heart beat irregularly with the realization that Papa would've killed him—a Chapelo—for sure. *Long* before he ever got anywhere close to skinning out of his clothes around her.

That thought, and the wrenching ache in her heart over just the idea of Zant being hurt or killed, overrode her guilt, her family loyalty, and even her fear of what was to come. Traitor she may be, betrayer of her blood oath with her sisters, yes. *But, dear God, forgive me, I want him.* Sure she was forsaking her soul, but equally sure she could protect him with her embrace, Jacey raised her arms to the man she loved.

And he came to her. With her name a whisper on his lips, he lowered his warm and heavily muscled, smooth-skinned, sculpted body down onto her. He settled himself between her spread legs, covered her against the night, and held his full weight off her by resting on his elbows. Jacey reveled in this man's scents and textures. So foreign, so new, so right and tantalizing was the feel of him atop her.

She breathed in deeply. Clean and rugged, smoky and seductive. That's how he smelled. That was his musk. Desire and awareness pooled in Jacey's core, setting off a thrumming in her womb like that of a plucked guitar string. Closing her eyes, a smile on her face, she slipped her arms under his and flattened her splayed hands over the rigid muscles of his back.

She held him tightly. His hands cupped her head, drew her up to him, drew her up to his kiss. His lips, firm and moist, slanted across hers, rubbed them lightly, sharpened her tingling response, until Jacey cried out and drew his head down to hers. Zant kissed her with a savage yet tender ferocity that stole Jacey's breath. She opened her mouth. His tongue found hers and claimed it.

Jousting, thrusting in and out, he bade her fight back, follow his lead. With his heated breath steaming out of his nostrils like a dragon breathing fire over her, exciting her, Jacey matched him stroke for stroke, plunge for retreat, until he was the one to break their kiss. Breathing hard, he looked down into her face. She looked up at his heavy-lidded expression. So this was passion. She wanted more of it.

She raised her head again for his kiss. Zant fed her hunger with his questing tongue, and then began a slow descent down her body, down to her breasts, kissing and swirling his tongue around each dusky peak until Jacey pushed against his shoulders, wanting him away from her sensitive nipples.

He looked up and grinned at her. "Lower? Is that what you want?"

Breathing hard, alive with sensual sensations, Jacey opened her eyes to look into his passion-warmed face. "I don't know. I don't know what I want. I just . . . want, Zant. Help me."

His grin widened to a purely evil one. His black eyes reflected the snap of the fire's flames. "Yes, ma'am. Always happy to oblige."

He slipped down even lower on her. Jacey's breath caught at the back of her throat. Just his kisses on her belly, between her navel and her womanhood, quivered her insides, made her draw her knees up, made her . . . need. And Zant gave. He dipped down and drew her legs up over his shoulders, cupped her buttocks . . . and lifted her to his mouth.

At the first swirl of his tongue, the first ripple of pleasure, a ragged sound tore out of Jacey. She clutched at his bedroll, at the desert sand, at his hair. She tried to sit up, only to fall back limply. She tried to call out his name. No words would come. She tossed in earnest now, feeling her world, her entire being, centering on what he was doing to her. The sensations rippling through her bordered on the painful, they were so intense. Never in her life had she ever—She wanted him to stop, wanted him to go on forever until she melted in a pool of purely physical sensations.

As if he knew, as if he had always known, Zant continued his relentless assault. Swirling, sucking, kiss after kiss, of the sort they'd shared with their mouths only moments ago, brought Jacey to the edge, to the height of her sanity. Every muscle tensed. She arched her head, her mouth a grimace of pleasureful pain.

Just when she thought she'd die, when she thought she

couldn't experience more, the tightening coils deep inside her sprang to life, spreading throughout her, releasing in spasmodic jerks that robbed her of dimension and time, that dried her mouth, warmed her cheeks, and curled her toes. Reduced to a creature of one floating sensation, of one greedy pleasure, she rode out the waves, she made helpless noises, wanted more, could stand no more. Only when she cried out Zant's name did he take mercy on her and stop.

Spent, weak, drained, she lay spread-eagle and helpless as Zant pulled himself up and over her. Zant kissed her. He smelled of a musk, her musk, she tasted it, he shared the saltiness with her. "This is what you taste like, Jacey," he whispered.

He then raised himself up, positioned himself between her spread legs, and began a slow penetration that told Jacey, like no words ever could, that the sensations, the pleasures were only just beginning. She opened her eyes, saw him watching her face. "Put your legs around my hips. This first time will hurt some. Maybe burn a little. I'll go easy."

Jacey shook her head. "No. Not easy. I want it all."

Zant shook his head right back at her. "No. Trust me, Jacey. It has to be slow this first time." He then looked at her, his eyebrows fairly meeting over his nose. "This is your first time, right?"

His question heated up her cheeks and made her turn her head. She nodded and bit at her bottom lip. "It's my first."

Zant leaned over her to kiss her forehead. "I'll go easy."

She nodded, trusting him. Zant slid a little more into her. He kissed her, whispered in her ear, telling her how beautiful she was, how much he wanted her, until his words, his touch, his actions spun a misty web that saw her raising her hips to his reflexively. Zant pushed into her.

The burning sting, the sharp pain. Jacey clutched at Zant's shoulders, wrapped her arms around his neck, laid her forehead against the expanse of his shoulder. And gasped in tiny breaths. Zant soothed her, kissed her, moved his hips against hers, tested her slick readiness. The pain became a memory with each gentle thrust of his. He moved again. Jacey arched into him, some instinct showing her the way, urging her to feel.

Within a few thrusts, she was meeting him stroke for stroke.

She clung to him, as if letting go of him would plunge her into a deep pit. She arched into him, felt the coiling begin again, breathed in and out with lusting need, and drove into him with a ferocity matching his. Jacey looked up, saw his straining muscles, his rigid arms, his grimace of intense pleasure. She pulled him down more fully atop her and held him, scratching at his back, not able to stop herself. His husky gruntings and sounds of need mingled with hers. She wanted—

The dam burst. Her body clutched at him, pulling at him, holding him inside her. He gasped and went rigid over her, as if frozen in the moment. Jacey moved her hands to his rock-hard biceps, gripped him clawlike, and took over the thrusting rhythm, helping her body pleasure him.

Zant cried out and collapsed atop her. "Enough. You'll kill me," came his ragged words into her ear. He gathered her to him, held her tightly. Jacey smiled, reveling in the sound of his heartbeat, the slick wetness of their bodies, their panting breath. So this was what it was like to love. This was what Mama'd been talking about when she told her girls about the loving pleasures of the marriage bed.

Marriage bed. What marriage? Jacey stiffened.

Zant immediately raised up on an elbow, brushed a strand of her hair out of her face, and smiled down at her. "What's wrong?"

Jacey turned her head away from him. "Nothing."

Zant tugged her chin back around until she had to look up into his eyes. "Like hell. Now, what's wrong? Are you sorry we did this?"

"It's a little late for sorry." Especially when he was still inside her and she was under him, naked.

He nodded and chuckled. "You are sorry. I tried to stop you."

Jacey frowned up at him. "I'm not sorry. And don't tell me how I feel."

He grinned like a devil. "Why not? I *know* how you feel." He dipped his head down to kiss her neck and breathe in deeply of her scent. "You feel wonderful."

Jacey smacked at his shoulder. "Get off me, Chapelo."

He reared back, still inside her, still weighing her down, and laughed. "That's not what you called me a minute ago."

Stung to the point of heated cheeks and sudden tears, Jacey shoved in earnest. "Get off me."

"Yes, ma'am." Looking her right in the eye, making his point, Zant slid out of her. And then off her. He stood up and held a hand out to her.

Jacey looked up the solid, naked length of him to his face and then to his outstretched hand. And took it. Zant pulled her easily to her feet. To her chagrin, Jacey realized she was sore, wet, and could barely stand on her own. Not to mention embarrassed to be naked in front of him, even after what they'd just shared. Zant smiled, as if he understood, and pulled her to him. He held her against his broad chest and said nothing.

Jacey wrapped her arms around him, flattening her palms against his muscled back. She closed her eyes and breathed in the man-musk scent of him, absorbed the feel of her cheek against his chest, her woman's body against his hard, male one. If only they could stay this way forever. *But you can't.* Her eyes opened with the warning taunt from her conscience. She stared into the vastness of the desert night, seeing the world from the shelter of Zant's strong arms, listening to his heart beating under her ear. The voice was right. This was but a moment in time for them. And not forever.

Saddened, angry, she pushed away from him and stepped back. Looking up into his night-and fire-shadowed face, at his black eyes and slanting half-smile, Jacey spoke before she lost her courage. "This right here, what happened between us? It doesn't change a thing, Zant."

Zant nodded, as if he agreed. His black eyes looked clear through her, to her heart, her soul. "Yes it does. This right here, what happened between us, changes everything. For both of us. Forever."

Jacey shook her head, afraid now as the enormity of what she'd caused to happen sank in. She took a step back, felt the flames behind her heat up her legs. Or maybe it was the judgmental fires of Hell. Either way, she burned. He was a Chapelo. She was a Lawless. And nothing could change that.

"No," she cried out. But even she didn't believe it.

CHAPTER THIRTEEN

Zant was right, Jacey mused. Everything was changed. Not so you could tell by looking. But everything was changed inside, where it counted. How could their shared intimacy have caused them to fuss so afterward? For days afterward. Zant acted like he wished she wasn't riding with him to Don Rafael's. Well, she wasn't exactly happy about it, either.

But it seemed the closer they got to this Cielo Azul, this Blue Sky place—as he'd translated it—the more they picked at each other. Why was that? Maybe like her, he didn't know how to think of her, how to treat her . . . what to call her. Before two nights ago, their relationship was clear-cut. He'd been the outlaw, somewhat of a stranger, not really her enemy, and not her trusted friend, either.

But now? He was also her lover. She looked over at him sitting his saddle with masculine ease. She had a lover. Zant Chapelo. If Papa wasn't spinning in his grave right this minute, then she'd be a dog-eared coyote.

Jacey sighed. What had she done? Why him? She stared hard at him, trying to see in his remote posture the same man who'd held her tenderly, whose hands had awakened her body, whose—Jacey made a noise to cut off her thoughts of the man. Zant turned to stare at her. Shaded by his Stetson, his black eyes squinted questioningly at her.

Jacey ducked her chin to look down at her pommel. Just one look from him now, and she was undone. *That* was the problem. She now saw him as an M-A-N. And she now knew what that word meant to a woman. His big, muscled body, that black hair, those smoldering eyes, his way of looking at her, the sound of his voice, the way he moved his hands, all combined to make her fidget in her saddle. And brought a possessive smile to her face.

Which she wiped away with her hand. Damn him. If only it could be as easy to scrub him out of her mind. But every motion of his, whether he was squatting down in his denims, eating by the campfire, currying his stallion, shaving his beard, or washing in a stream, now seemed less than innocent. Instead, his every action seemed a calculated display for her, like a stallion made for a mare in season. Preening, prancing, showing off his strength, his . . . maleness. And, Lord above, it was working.

"Things aren't going to be so easy for us once we reach Cielo Azul."

Jacey started at the sound of his voice and looked over at him. His mouth was no more than a straight line. But hers quirked up mockingly. "Easy? When's anything been easy for us?"

A smile tugged at the corners of his mouth as he notched his Stetson up and shifted his weight in his saddle. "Once we get there, you'll think that everything that's come before was a church picnic. Since we'll be there in less than two days, I've come up with a plan."

Jacey stared at the big outlaw, stared at the way his hand splayed atop his thigh. "You've got to have a plan to get into your own home?"

"Only because you'll be with me. But it's not my home. It's my grandfather's."

"Then where do you call home?"

He shrugged. "I guess I don't."

"You count yourself a drifter, then?"

He got that look on his face, like he was going to shoot someone. "No."

"Everybody's got to be somewhere, Chapelo. Got to belong somewhere."

He tugged his Stetson down and looked straight ahead. "Maybe."

Jacey gave herself up to the rhythmic sway of Knight's easy gait. After a moment, she said, "What's this plan of yours?"

He rubbed a finger under his nose, stretched forward in his

saddle, and kept his gaze on the southeastern horizon. "When we ride in, you'll be my prisoner."

Jacey reined Knight to a standstill. She watched as Zant's stallion continued on ahead of her. She saw Zant turn his head to where she'd been a moment ago on his left and heard him say, "And I don't want any argu—" He stared at the empty space and then jerked this way and that. "What the hell? Where—" He finally looked back, found her, turned Old Blood and reined in his big roan. "What are you doing back there?"

Jacey called out, "Your prisoner? Is that what you said?"

"Yeah."

"Why?"

"It's for your own good."

"You tell me how, and I'll judge for myself, outlaw."

He shook his head and nudged his stallion into walking back to her. He reined in beside her, Old Blood's head to Knight's tail. "If Don Rafael thinks I'm coming home—" He frowned, daring her to say something.

Jacey understood—he'd called Cielo Azul home after having just denied it. She said nothing, gave nothing away with her poker face.

"Thinks I'm coming home for good, and you're with me as my peace offering, then I stand a chance of keeping your skinny butt alive long enough to figure out what he's up to."

Jacey took a moment to assess his words and what they said about him . . . and what he felt for her. "Why *are* you concerning yourself with keeping my skinny butt alive, Chapelo?"

That got him. His eyes narrowed. "That's my business."

Jacey stared hard at him, but finally let it go. For now. "All right. It's your business. But answer this. Why don't you just ask him right out what he's up to? You afraid of him?"

Zant sucked in a deep breath, held it, and let it out slowly. "Don't push me, Jacey. I'm not afraid of him, but of what he's capable of doing. And I did ask him point-blank why he was having you three tracked."

Three? You three? Jacey eyed him in a sidelong glance. *What three?*

Zant went on, as if he hadn't heard himself, as if he didn't notice the change in her expression. "But he denied that he was behind it. He's lying, he's up to no good, and he's not about to tell me or anyone else what that is. If you hope to save yourself and your sisters, you'll have to meet him on his own ground. And on my terms. It's the only way."

Your sisters? His words froze Jacey in her saddle. A sick feeling roiled through her belly. *Hannah. Glory.* "Zant, I didn't think about that back at Buford's place. Three men paid them a call. You killed one—Rafferty. Where are the other two? Are they still tracking my sisters, or did they go back to Cielo Azul?"

Zant notched his Stetson up and looked mighty grim. "They didn't go back to Cielo Azul, Jacey. Not according to Blue."

"Blue?" Jacey's mind raced back to her first day in Tucson and then forward to that night in the desert when Zant killed Rafferty. The blond-headed, smiling Blue'd been there then. Her building anger tugged her mouth down. "How long have you known that those men are still tracking my sisters?"

When Zant didn't say anything, Jacey's belly flip-flopped, her heart thudded. Her voice husky with betrayal, she repeated, "I asked you a question. How long have you known?"

As grim now as death, the outlaw backed his stallion two paces and gripped Knight's bridle. Only then did he speak up. "Since about a week after you got here."

Jacey gulped for air. In a sick sweat, she could only stare at the big man for several seconds. Her words, when she could form them, were a whisper. "I've been here nearly a month, and you didn't tell me?"

Exploding with equal amounts of anger at him and fear for her sisters, Jacey gripped Knight's belly with her legs and jerked his reins, wanting to turn him, wanting to ride for home to warn her sisters. But all the black gelding could do was dance in place and rear his head. Zant's roan stallion reacted with a snorting sidestep of his own. But neither animal could do more, because Zant's grip on both horses was firm.

"Damn you, Chapelo. Let go of my horse." Thwarted, frustrated, held in check, Jacey gritted her teeth and glared. She'd not give him the satisfaction of fighting his hold on Knight. She knew, and he knew, that his grip was ironclad. She was no match for his strength. "Hannah and Glory—especially Glory—could be dead by now, you son of a bitch."

A muscle jumped in Zant's jaw. He spoke through gritted teeth. "They're not."

"How can you know that?"

"Because you're not."

"What kind of an answer is that? The only reason I'm not dead is because you killed Rafferty." She then spoke in measured tones, giving each of her next words equal weight. "Now . . . let go of my horse. I aim to ride for home."

Zant shook his head. "Your enemy isn't in No Man's Land, Jacey. He's in Sonora. Listen to me. You're not dead and your sisters aren't dead because—and *only* because—Don Rafael hasn't ordered it yet."

Jacey leaned forward in her saddle, got in the outlaw's face. "And what if he has by now? We've been out in this stinking hellhole of a desert for a week and a half hunting down sick or dead or crazy old men, asking them about a keepsake portrait, for crying out loud. And all the while, you've known this about *my sisters*? Anything could've happened by now. Anything."

Jacey met the outlaw's grim stare, matched him breath for breath. She wanted only to ride for home. That's where she belonged . . . not here, no matter what he said. She never should've left Glory alone. Glory's the one they wanted. And Hannah was in Boston—who'd watch out for her? All their lives, Jacey knew, she'd been the tough one, her sisters' protector and defender. They looked to her, to her daring. Without her, they were alone.

Zant leaned toward her, close enough for her to see herself reflected in his black eyes. "What if he's given new orders? There wouldn't be a damned thing you could do about it. You're too far away to help your sisters. Even if you'd left the minute I knew about it, you'd still be a week behind and too late. Your sisters will have to take care of themselves. If they're anything like you, they can."

Jacey heard but dismissed his praise of her, so intent was she on making her point. "Maybe Hannah can take care of herself. But not Glory. She's the baby. She doesn't have the first idea how to—"

"Oh, hell, Jacey." Zant pulled back and shook his head. "Glory's got to be near twenty years old. She's not a baby. And she was raised by the same parents you were. Are you going to tell me that if someone threatens her, she'll just lie down and die without a fight?''

Jacey turned her head away from him. Focusing on the shimmering heat ripples dancing above the desert floor, she weighed his words. Grudgingly, she admitted that he was right. Glory would fight . . . *if* she got a chance, *if* she saw the trouble coming. Calming some, but still hating the fact that he'd kept this from her, she turned back to him.

He appeared to sense her inclination to cooperate, because he relaxed and released Knight's reins. ''That's better. Now, our only chance for all three of you is to''—he looked away from her—''to stop Don Rafael.''

Stop Don Rafael. A clamminess swept over Jacey, raising the hair on her arms. She knew what those words meant. There was only one way to stop a man like Don Rafael. And that was to kill him. Anger and betrayal bled from her. For once in her life, she looked outside herself. She considered what those words meant to Zant and the enormity of what he was prepared to do for her. She watched his troubled profile, his narrowed eyes, his working throat.

Like the spark that becomes the flame, awareness built in Jacey, until it burst forth fully ablaze. The dignity, the horror of sacrificing one's self . . . one's heart . . . for the sake of another. . . . She closed her eyes, shook her head. It was too awful. The price was too high. Would she do the same thing for him, if their situations were reversed? Could she kill Papa for Zant? Jacey hung her head in shame. No. And if *he* killed Papa, no matter how much he might deserve it? Why, she'd hate him to her dying day. Just like Zant would hate her if he killed his grandfather for her. Just like he would hate her if she killed Don Rafael.

Tears clogged her throat. She couldn't allow him to kill his own kin. Which meant there was no other way . . . she'd have to do it herself, if it came to it. And she'd have to bear, for all her days, his hatred of her for what she'd done. Only in that way could she save him. Barely recognizing this new selflessness for what it was, Jacey swallowed and stiffened her spine. ''You don't have to be the one to do this.''

Still without looking at her, he answered. ''It's me or you. So, yes, I do have to be the one to do this.''

In sudden desperation, knowing in her heart that from this

point forward she was losing him . . . no matter what happened . . . she found herself trying to stop destiny, trying to stop what she'd set in motion. And that meant defending Don Rafael. "Why does he have to be . . . stopped? We don't even know what he's guilty of, Zant."

Zant turned to her, a burning light already shining in his eyes. "Didn't you hear what Alma Buford said? Those men who paid her a visit had *my* father's spurs with them. *Spurs,* Jacey. Not a broken piece of one. That places them in your house. Before the murders."

Her heart lurched at the memory. But still she pleaded her and Don Rafael's case. "Maybe it does. But *only* if the piece around my neck came from your father's spurs."

Zant's face turned dusky with his rising voice. "You know it's my father's. You know it. And why in the hell are you defending Don Rafael? He's set two men on you that I know of. And probably there's another one hunting you this minute. Blue says my grandfather sent his hired guns after your sisters, too. Do you think it's so he can invite you all to a party? Hell, no. How guilty does he have to be, Jacey?"

Breathing hard now, staring at her, his eyes a steely-black, he pounded home his points. "I may not know yet why he's having you three tracked, but one thing I do know—it's for no good reason. Sooner or later, he'll make another mistake. I intend to be there when he does."

Truly scared by his intensity, Jacey could barely take a breath. "Another mistake?"

"His first was threatening you."

Her mouth went dry. Frightened for him, for herself, she shook her head. "No. You can't do this. Not for any reason that has anything to do with me, Zant. I won't be your excuse to rid yourself of the old man."

"I don't need an excuse. He's given me plenty of reasons."

"Then why haven't you had it out with him before now?"

"I was a kid. Then I was in prison. Until now, until you, it was enough to be everything he hated."

Jacey's heart flopped around in her chest. "Look, all I came to Tucson for was to find the unfortunate so-and-so who took my keepsake. I'll find out who did it and why, get it back, and go home. I didn't come out here looking for murderers.

They're back East. That's where the clues lead. Not to Mexico. Not to Don Rafael."

Zant stared hard at her. "You don't still believe that, do you, Jacey? That all the murderers are back East?"

Taking no time to reflect on what she believed anymore, half afraid of what she'd find, Jacey let her voice echo his for quiet challenge. "I believe what I believe. When the time comes, if the truth shows Don Rafael to be responsible, he'll die by my hand. Not yours."

Zant chuckled, but it had nothing to do with humor. "No. The old man is mine when reckoning time comes. There's too much between us . . . things way beyond murder. No, Jacey. He's mine."

A huge scream began building in her lungs. "If you kill him, Zant, you'll be as good as dead, too. He's your blood kin. And family—no matter how rotten—means everything. I won't let you do this."

Zant's expression hardened into unforgiving stone. "You can't stop me." With that, he wheeled his horse and urged him into an all-out gallop, heading south. To Sonora, Mexico.

Jacey watched him a moment. And knew she had to go after him. "Damn you," she yelled, cursing him to the cloudless blue sky overhead.

Two long, dusty days later, as the sun cast late-afternoon shadows over the land, Zant reined Sangre at the crest of a hill that overlooked La Casa del Cielo Azul. He raised his Stetson to swipe a sleeve across his sweating brow. Squinting at the bright sun, and keeping his eyes on the walled hacienda in the valley below, he intoned, "There it is. Home sweet home."

"It's big."

Zant firmed his lips, nodding his head. "It is that."

"Nice gardens and tilled fields, too."

"Yep."

"Lots of people down there."

"Yep." He resettled his hat low over his eyes.

"You think they've seen us yet?"

"Yep."

"Is this how you're going to talk the whole time we're here?"

He turned to look at her. "Nope."

"Good."

Zant fought the grin that tugged at his mouth. Little spitfire. The more scared she was, the mouthier she got. He turned his gaze back to the valley, sparingly dotted with mesquite trees and occasional yuccas beyond the crops and gardens outside the adobe walls.

Two riders turned out of the compound's front gate, galloping hell-for-leather in their direction. Zant split his attention between them and the activity inside the adobe walls. Running. Scurrying. Pointing up at them. Preparing. For trouble. Seemed that Trouble was all that came calling here. And this time was no different. Zant shifted in his saddle and nodded toward the two riders approaching them. "Here comes our welcoming party."

"You recognize 'em?"

"Yep. Blue and Paco. That's good news."

"Yeah? How so?"

"They're on my side."

"Your side? Against what?"

"Not what. Who. Don Rafael."

"These sides you're talking about, I'm guessing they don't have anything to do with me, do they?"

"No. There were sides here long before you came along."

"Sides for what?"

"A revolution. A takeover." Zant frowned. When had he come to that conclusion?

Jacey echoed his words. "A takeover? In all of Mexico, or just here?"

"Just here." And suddenly, he knew it was true.

"Great. Wish you wouldn't leave out little details like that in the future."

Zant grinned at her drollness. "I'll try to warn you of any bloody coups coming up. Okay, they're almost here. Remember, you're my captive—even in front of them. No one else but you and me will know differently until it's necessary for me to tell them. So try to act like a captive."

"I don't think that'll be a problem, outlaw."

Zant chuckled and looked over at her. That thick braid lying over her shoulder was the biggest thing about her. Except for the scowl on her face.

"What're you laughing at? Since I'm your prisoner, shouldn't I be tied up or something?"

He shook his head. "Nope. I don't work that way. If you tried to get away, I'd just shoot you before you got out of reach. They know that."

Jacey made a choking noise. "Now see there? That's one of those little details I was telling you about."

In a sudden burst of high spirits, brought about by her smart-mouthed bravado, Zant swept his Stetson off and bowed over his stallion's neck. "You have my most sincere apologies for not informing you, Señorita Lawless."

"I'm your captive, Chapelo. Try to act like it. Put your hat back on and look fierce or something."

Still chuckling, Zant plunked his Stetson on his head and waved at Blue and Paco. He let out a familiar whistle that they would recognize and laughed when they whooped in return and raised their hands in recognition. He turned to grin at Jacey. "They love me here."

"Somebody's got to." She spoke through gritted teeth as she looped her hands in the reins, pulling them taut and keeping her gelding's head up, so he couldn't buck. The black was not pleased with all the whistling and whooping going on around him.

Zant turned to Blue and Paco when they reined in beside him with a thundering of hooves and rising dust that further unnerved Jacey's gelding. Born to such displays, Sangre merely raised his noble head and eyed the other, lesser horses.

"I thought that was you, you old son of a gun." Blue clapped Zant on the back and leaned over to shake his offered hand.

"None other." Zant then turned to Paco, nudging the big man on his hamlike shoulder. *"¿Eh, compadre, como estás?"*

Paco ducked his head, showing respect and causing his sombrero's oversized brim to flop up and down on his big head as he nodded. *"Muy bien, jefe. Muy bien."*

Zant didn't even flinch when called chief this time. *"Bien."* He then turned to Jacey to translate. "Paco says he's fine."

Jacey huffed out a disrespectful noise. "Well, isn't that just wonderful? Like I give a rat's—"

"*Basta!* You will show respect to me and my men. Or you will suffer the consequences, Señorita Lawless." His face stiff with disapproval, Zant adopted the icy manners and steely tones of a Spanish don. Jacey went wide-eyed and silent. She'd never seen this side of him, he knew, the powerful young lord of the manor, used to giving orders, brooking no arguments, a man whose every wish and whim were carried out.

Zant turned to Paco and Blue. They looked like they wanted no part of him, either. Apparently they too had gotten his message that the prodigal son had returned home. Not that he'd intended to behave like a little lord, but if this was the tone that worked with her and them, then so be it. Because he couldn't afford for her or Blue—Paco would never dare—not to take him seriously in front of the other men.

But especially Jacey. His doubts about being able to control her caused him to meet her unwavering gaze. She had no idea of the dangers she faced, or of the ones she posed—for him, for herself, and for those men loyal to him. Because if she gave him reason to punish her, he would have to do it. To spare her would be to appear weak. And to show weakness, especially for a woman, would cost him the men's respect. And that could lead to bloodshed.

Knowing his silence wouldn't be interrupted, Zant looked down on what was really a small city below. The compound's high walls undulated across the rolling hills as if they were a natural outcropping. He then concentrated on the villa mellowing in the sun, its adobe colors blending with the desert, its many flowering vines in the courtyard providing surprising dots of color in a land essentially brown.

His Spanish family built Cielo Azul hundreds of years ago. He loved it. It was his home, his birthright. Don Rafael was right about that much. It was to this land that he belonged.

But would the fierce fighting men here accept him as their leader? And was their leader what he wanted to become? He searched his heart. Yes. That was exactly what he intended to be. Perhaps he had all along. With that revelation came a newfound sense of his place in the world. Then so be it.

As the mantle of leadership draped itself around his shoulders, Zant turned to Jacey and eased back in his saddle. "Everything you see spread out here before you belongs to me. As do you. Do we understand each other, señorita?"

"We do." Jacey glared at him, but she did duck her chin,

mimicking Paco's respectful pose of a moment ago. Zant knew, without a doubt, that with her it was a pose and nothing more.

"*Bueno.*" He then turned to Blue and Paco, and spoke in Spanish for Paco's sake. "*La Señorita Lawless está mi prisionera.*"

Paco nodded and narrowed his eyes at Jacey. With barely suppressed humor, Zant watched her narrow her eyes in return. Interesting. Perhaps he'd assign Paco as her guard. But all humor fled when Blue found his tongue. "What in the hell are you talking about—your prisoner?"

Zant eyed his oldest friend, knowing that Blue, because of his special closeness to him, might be as difficult to control as Jacey. "Things have changed, Blue. I'm home for good. Don Rafael wanted Jacey Lawless. Well, here she is. Call her my peace offering."

Wide-eyed, Blue looked from him to Jacey and back. "You brought her here as a . . . a peace offering? For Don Rafael? You're just going to turn her over to him . . . after killing Rafferty and Quintana for trying to do the same thing? Are you *loco, mi amigo?*"

"*Basta.*" Zant purposely hissed the same warning to Blue as he had Jacey. He needed to make it clear that he would allow no insolence from anyone, not even his lifelong friend. Not if he hoped to unseat Don Rafael. To do that, he had to take control right now, right here . . . before they rode under the gated archway of La Casa del Cielo Azul. "Understand, Blue, that I have changed. There'll be no more running away. I've come home to take my place here. The old man is just that—an old man. He will die soon. And this"—he swept his hand out over the valley—"will be mine."

Blue shook his head, looking at Zant as if he'd never seen him before. "I never thought I'd live to see the day when you'd say those words."

"Me, neither, Blue." And he truly meant that. "But I've grown up some in the past few weeks." His gaze slipped to Jacey. He saw her sit up tall in her saddle. "I'm ready to do what's right."

Blue's expression changed, and he looked hopeful. "Do what's right? Do you mean what I think you—"

Zant raised a hand. "*Mañana.* Tomorrow. Now we go greet

Don Rafael and present him my gift." He turned to Jacey. "You will keep quiet and do as I say. Or your life will not be worth living."

Don Rafael Calderon watched his grandson and the woman ride under the arched gateway of Cielo Azul. Paco and Blue flanked them. Standing at the hacienda's sheltered entrance, all but lost in the lowering sun's shadows, he turned to Miguel Sereda. "My grandson returns. Yet again."

Miguel, a slight, whipcord-thin man, nodded. "*Sí.* He always does."

Don Rafael looked out over the width of the central courtyard, smiling, watching Zant lean over from his saddle to clasp hands and accept the loud homecoming greetings from the men. "Look at him. This time will be different."

To his left, Victor DosSantos spoke up. "Why do you say that, *mi jefe*?"

Without turning to the big, simple, and lethal *pistolero,* the old man's smile broadened. "Look at the way he sits his horse, Victor. See how my men flock to him, how they pay him respect? Zant is a man now. And he comes home for good this time. I have waited many years for this day."

"You must be very proud."

Raising his eyebrows, Don Rafael turned to Victor. "Proud? *Sí.* Everything I do, I do for him. But I wonder, does he understand that? Does he truly return my love for him? Or will he kill me someday?"

Miguel spoke up, capturing Don Rafael's attention. "Just let him try. I who have been more loyal to you than your own grandson, I who have been here all these years, when he was not, I will shoot him for you, should he try."

Don Rafael's face darkened with his rising anger. He focused his harshest glare on the young man. "Zant has been in prison, or he would have been here. He is out now, and he is here. It is enough. I will not tell you again, Miguel. Stay out of his way. My grandson is mine to deal with. Not yours. Do you understand?"

The contemptuous light in the man's eyes only dimmed as he came to attention and ducked his chin. "*Sí, mi jefe.* As always."

Don Rafael assessed the man. Miguel Sereda was a useful

man, a cunning and ambitious right-hand man. He'd done distasteful things that needed to be done. He'd helped extend the Calderon power over half of Sonora state. All that was true. And yes, he had once spoken with Miguel about succeeding him here. But only if Zant did not return to claim his inheritance. Now his grandson was home for good. He could feel it in his bones. And Miguel would have to accept that . . . or die.

Victor's question pulled Don Rafael out of his thoughts. "Do you know this woman with him, *jefe*?"

Don Rafael raked his gaze over the dark-haired girl sitting her black horse as if she reigned here. "No. But it does not appear she wishes to be here, does it? A mystery, no? Come, let us greet my grandson. Perhaps he will tell us who he brings with him. And why."

With that, and followed by Sereda and DosSantos, Don Rafael ambled his large body down the three wide, tiled steps, walked into the sun, and raised his hands and a laughing, ringing cheer in greeting to the arriving party.

The men clustered around Zant immediately quieted and parted, clearing a path for him that led directly to his watching, waiting grandson. Passing through the hushed gauntlet of his men, men he could barely trust, but men he controlled with fear and threats, Don Rafael concentrated on the barely concealed wariness etched in his beloved grandson's face.

It had always been thus between them. Zant was hard now, a seasoned killer, an unfeeling fighter. Don Rafael's chest swelled with pride. He'd formed Zant into everything he had ever hoped he could be. Buoyed by such thoughts, he greeted his grandson with a warmth born of cunning manipulation. "*¡Mi nieto!* You are home. I greet you and your lovely guest with open arms. Come, give your poor old grandfather a hug. Show him how much you love him."

CHAPTER FOURTEEN

Come dusk that evening, Jacey still stormed around her elegantly furnished, second-story prison of a large bedroom. She again tried the door. Pumping the wrought-iron latch to no avail, she heard that huge Paco outside the door call out some Spanish warning to her.

Jacey thought up several curses she could fling at him, but what good would that do? The big Mexican didn't speak English. So why waste her breath? Flinging her sweat-stained slouch hat onto the lace counterpane of the four-poster bed, Jacey darted across the room to the glass-paned double doors.

She jerked them open and stepped onto the narrow balcony. Grasping the wrought-iron railing, she peered down. Too far to jump without hurting herself. Not to mention she'd land in a heap of prickly-looking bushes and low-growing cactus. But even if she managed to get out of the house, could she get away? She assessed the central plaza that stretched to the adobe walls. Not one blamed place to hide. Nothing but a circular tract of sand around a flagpole. And the adobe walls were crawling with armed men.

Damn that Chapelo. If he was here right now, I'd—Jacey swung around at the sound of a metallic click that signaled the door being unlocked. She stepped back into the room, put her hand to her holster, and huffed out her breath at its being empty. All she could do was await her fate.

The door swung inward, revealing that damned Chapelo. Jacey's breath caught at the back of her throat. He was all cleaned up and dressed in tight-fitting black pants that flared over his boots. A waist-length, silver-trimmed black jacket topped a crisp white shirt. A red sash circled his waist and trailed halfway to his knee. The little lord was clean-shaven, his hair cut, and he looked the very image of sensual, dark, and handsome Spanish nobility.

Something purely feminine fluttered deep inside her. She squelched that little betraying emotion. The man was too pretty for her tastes. And he also had the spit-and-vinegar gall right now to ignore her and smile and joke with Paco. In Spanish. They were making fun of her. She just knew it. Why else would they laugh and both turn to her?

Jacey raised her chin and glared. Zant sobered some, kept his gaze on her but spoke again to Paco. The big man nodded and ducked out of the room, closing the door behind him. Jacey burned as Zant's gaze swept over her. Before she could stop herself, she clutched at her riding skirt, and hated the way he had of making her feel small.

She blurted out her feelings in a bleat that disturbed the stillness of the finest room she'd ever been in. "I changed my mind, Chapelo. I don't want to be your prisoner or your peace offering to Don Rafael. I don't like the way he looks at me, like I'm his next meal. And I hate being cooped up in here. This place is crawling with armed, mean-looking men. Anything could happen. And I don't have a way to defend myself. That buffalo you set outside my door took my gun and practically threw me in here."

Zant chuckled, put his hands to his waist. "He took your gun on my orders. He told me you were . . . less than gracious about handing it over. But you still have your knife, don't you?"

So Paco'd been tattling? She'd remember that. Out loud, she carried on her ranting. "I've got my knife. Paco'd be dead if he'd tried to lift my skirt to get to it. But what good does that do me? I've never seen the blade yet that could beat a bullet to its target."

Zant just smiled, as if enjoying the entertainment. The little lord then pointed to her. "You're not dressed for our evening meal with Don Rafael. Why not? Conchita also tells me you were uncooperative."

Jacey's cheeks burned. That danged little maid. She'd come in here earlier, all chattery—in Spanish—and ordering men about as they brought in her bath. Jacey recalled herself standing cool and quiet, her arms crossed over her chest and glaring them all out of the room. It'd seemed brave and defiant then. But now, with Zant standing here? Well. . . . "I'm not taking my evening meal with you and Don Rafael. I've already met him, thank you, and I don't need to see more. With the tensions between you two, I could find myself in the line of fire and end up with a fork sticking out of my chest. I'll play your prisoner, if I have to, but I won't put myself on parade."

"First of all, you do have to play my prisoner. Because my grandfather is thrilled with my little gift to him, almost as much as he is with my being home for good. So it's especially important now, Jacey, that you act the part." Zant then stared at her, squared his wide shoulders, and stood with his black-booted feet apart. "And yes, you will put yourself on parade."

Jacey's bottom lip poked out. "No I won't."

"Don't try me, Jacey."

"What're you going to do about it? You can't make me take a bath if I don't—"

"Yes I can." With that, he whipped off his jacket, threw it on her bed, unknotted his sash—

"What are you doing?" Jacey began backing up.

—and flung it atop his jacket. He then rolled his sleeves up and put his hands to the silver catch of his string tie, sliding it down far enough to loop it over his head. "I'm making you take a bath, since you won't do it on your own." He threw the tie on her bed.

Jacey whipped around to the far side of the bed and held on to one of the posts. "Like hell you are. I'm not getting in that water. It'll be cold by now."

Zant shrugged, striding slowly toward her, his spurs jingling. "You should have thought of that earlier."

"Get out of here, Chapelo. I'll take my bath by myself."

"I don't think you will."

"I will." Jacey held a hand out to him, wanting him to stop advancing on her. "You have my word."

He shook his head and grabbed for her. Jacey jumped onto the bed and rolled across it. When she came to her feet on the other side, Zant stood in front of her. Startled, she cried out when he grabbed her arms. "Your word means nothing here, Señorita Lawless. You are my prisoner. And now, it's bathtime."

Jacey gritted her teeth and jerked in his grip. He only tightened his hold. She kicked at his shin. He sidestepped and spun her around, gripping her about the waist, hauling her up against his chest, with her feet off the floor. Her kicking now resulted only in her boots flying off her feet and hitting the thin-paneled, black-laquered screen that hid the tub from the room's view. The partition toppled onto the tub's rim and slid gracelessly to the floor, landing with a wooden clunk and clatter.

Jacey stilled with Zant at the unexpected noise and stared at the exposed tub. There it was. Zant headed for it. Jacey scratched, hit, kicked, cussed, twisted, jerked, stiffened. But Zant held her firm, all the while marching her steadily, fully clothed, over to the water-filled tub. Once at its rim, he cheerily announced, "In you go."

Jacey screamed as he dunked her bottomfirst into the cold water and let go. Waves of water spilled over her, over him, over the rim. A gasping breath announced her reaction to the water's cold. Blinking, sputtering, she stood straight up in the tub, and tried to climb out. But Zant was quicker. With his hand atop her head and whistling a happy tune, he plunged her back down until her head was under water. He held her there. Cheeks puffed out from holding her breath, Jacey clawed at the tub's rims. Zant let her up.

Gasping for air, her sopping braid weighing her down, her wet clothes dragging on her limbs, she stood up and pitched a full-blown Lawless temper tantrum. Sluicing water at him, stomping even more out over the sides, calling him every name she could think of, Jacey howled out her hot-faced anger. But she didn't try again to get out, even though Zant, every bit as soaked as her, merely stood back from the tub, his arms folded over his broad chest, and watched her. Drops of water dripped off his chin and elbows and even more pooled at his feet.

When she paused in her name-calling to catch her breath and wipe sodden strings of her undone hair out of her face, she cast a wary eye on her tormentor. He bent over to retrieve a bar of soap and a thick towel, which he first swiped across his face and then flung over his shoulder. Stepping around the felled partition, he plunked the fragrant bar into her hand.

"Think you can take it from here, señorita? Or do I need to stay and help?"

Jacey seethed, gritted her teeth, and gave in. "I can take it from here," she said, her teeth chattering, now feeling the effects of the cold water. Hugging herself with her arms wrapped around her waist, she waited for him to leave.

"Good." He bent over again and stood the partition upright, placing it just so around the tub and the wet floor. He stayed on the far side of it, but the room's candlelit lamps silhouetted him against the thin panels. Jacey watched his every action, bracing herself for him to step around her scant protection. But he didn't. He thunked the towel atop one of the lacquered panels, and said, "I'll send in Conchita. She'll help you dress, and you will let her. I'll be back in thirty minutes. You'd better be ready."

Thirty minutes later, her hair still wet but braided and coiled around her head—by that Conchita maid—into a coronet heavy enough to give her a headache, Jacey slid onto the red velvet padded seat of the tall-backed chair held out so graciously for her by Zant.

Her silver chain with its spur-rowel pendant around her neck, and dressed in a too big red silk dress that showed more flesh . . . in her opinion . . . than she'd exposed for her bath, Jacey nodded to her host, seated at one end of the long table. Looking like a big, white-haired lion in a black suit, he smiled and ducked his head in acknowledgment. She then anxiously sought out Zant.

He was taking a seat at the other end of the long dining room table from her. Yes, she was still mad at him, but she was glad he was here. While the two men talked in Spanish, in polite enough tones, Jacey took a quick inventory of her surroundings—with an eye to possible escape routes, should the evening meal turn violent. She didn't have much faith that this buried-hatchet truce between Zant and Don Rafael would last too long.

Looking around, she missed no detail of the staggeringly beautiful room. Each piece of polished furniture, each silver bowl and candelabra, each tall, shiny ceramic vase, all screamed of untold wealth and hundreds of years of history. And made her feel surrounded. Which of course, she was.

Because in every corner of the room, neat and starched and quiet servants stood at the ready. Jacey hoped they were servants.

As she fiddled with her white linen napkin, she stole a surreptitious glance under the sweep of her lashes at each of her fellow diners. At one end of the long table, Don Rafael was now conferring sternly with a thin, young Mexican male. Apparently the poor kid had brought in the wrong wine for the soup course. At the other end, Zant slouched back in his chair, twirling the stem of his empty wineglass and staring at Don Rafael.

Her belly tense, her palms sweating, Jacey looked down at her lap while she considered her situation. A man at each end of the table. Her in the middle. She needed a weapon. The silverware to either side of her steaming bowl of soup caught her eye. Forget the spoons. They were useless. But the forks, all three of them, sported sharp tines. On the other side of her plate were a couple of knives, one with a serrated cutting edge.

She made her decision. When the bloodletting began, she'd definitely go for the biggest fork. She could then duck under the table—she scissored her slippered feet under the table, making sure it was open space under there. It was. And then she could—

The sound of a heavy slap followed by a wounded-animal cry tore Jacey out of her thoughts. She jerked toward the sound, heard Zant's chair scrape back on her other side, but couldn't look away from the poor boy lying in a crying heap at Don Rafael's feet. Her mouth open, her hand to her bosom, Jacey realized *The old bastard slapped that servant.* Hard. Over wine?

She was stunned into inaction, but apparently Zant wasn't. When he began yelling, she snapped her attention back to him.

"What the hell did you do that for? He's just a kid."

Jacey saw the veins standing out in Zant's forehead, saw the outraged anger shining from his eyes. She turned to Don Rafael. Chills of fear crept over her skin at the calm but slightly surprised expression on that one's heavy, craggy face. "Oh, come now, Zant. He's a servant, and nothing more. His job is to know the wines. He didn't. And he wanted to argue with me. He paid for his mistake."

He then snapped his fingers at the huddling boy, whose nose

was bleeding. He said a few harsh words in Spanish and the boy pulled himself up, holding his nose and crying, and walked as rapidly as his shaking legs could carry him. Jacey stared after the boy until she felt Don Rafael's gaze on her. She spared him only a glimpse before quietly staring down at her soup. She heard Zant reseat himself. She also heard his angry breathing.

"I hope you found your room to your liking, Señorita Lawless."

Jacey came close to jumping out of her dress—right through the drooping bodice, which she gracelessly tugged up again. Feeling no need to be civil at this point, she stared at him and sneered, "Actually, I found my room when Paco flung me into it after—"

A loud coughing from Zant's end of the table cut off her words. Her lips puckered, Jacey silently watched while another young boy poured what she prayed was the correct wine. Jacey lifted her goblet to her lips, and sipped delicateley before starting over. "My room is fine." Under her breath, she muttered, "And soaked."

"Ah, *muy bien.* We always strive at Cielo Azul to ensure our guests' comfort."

Jacey raised an eyebrow at the terrifying old man. He was almost as big as that Paco fella, but had all that white hair and fine clothes and . . . nice manners. Still, none of that disguised the pure evil of him. Even if Zant had never told her a thing about Don Rafael, even if she hadn't witnessed what she just had, she would have known him for what he was. A cruel, heartless man who'd stop at nothing to get what he wanted. And apparently, he wanted his grandson here. And her, too. And her sisters.

Scared, wanting to run and cower, Jacey reverted to her habitual defense—a smart-mouthed attack. "A guest, am I? Do you always lock your guests in their rooms?"

Don Rafael stopped in the act of buttering a crusty roll and looked up. His unexpected hearty laugh rang out in the room. But from the husky, threatening noises Zant was making, Jacey figured he was pretty sorry that he'd seated her out of his reach. Not for all the gold in California would she look at him.

Don Rafael sobered to a winning smile and shook his head. "Señorita Lawless, you are a treasure, indeed. I did not lock you in your room. My grandson did. His belief is that it is necessary for *our* protection . . . from you, he tells me. And from what I see, he may be right. But I assure you that—in my heart, at least—you are not a prisoner here. I would hardly outfit a prisoner in such finery and invite her to dine with me, now would I?"

Not quite brave enough to call him a liar, Jacey shook her head. "No, I don't suppose you would. But that's another thing, Mr. Calderon. Where'd this fancy dress come from? It doesn't fit me, so whose is it? Some former dinner guest's, maybe?" She held up a handful of skirt for emphasis.

Don Rafael hooted out again and smacked a big hand on the table, clattering his silverware. "No, no, my dear, that dress and the many others you have no doubt discovered in your room have never graced another woman. They were made for you alone, in anticipation of your . . . visit. Of course, you will inform Conchita of any alterations you may require." He then focused on Zant. "She is everything you told me she was. And more."

Jacey's heart all but stopped. In anticipation of her visit? Why, she'd known only a few days ago herself that she'd be coming here. Even if Don Rafael had somehow found out then, there wouldn't have been enough time to put together all the fancy clothes up in her room. As if that wasn't enough to chew on, she had to worry about exactly what it was that Zant might have told Don Rafael about her. Slowly she turned her head to glare at her warden.

His hair still damp from her splashing him, but changed now into dry clothes almost identical to the ones he'd had on earlier, the little lord merely glanced at her before focusing on his grandfather. "I knew you would be delighted, Grandfather. That is why I brought her here."

Jacey's heart now quit beating altogether. Was this the same man who only moments ago had come to his feet in anger? Was he over it so soon? That poker face of his gave nothing away. Probably came in handy, him being a gunfighter. But now? His cool calm and relaxed pose were unnerving.

Jacey swallowed and bit at her bottom lip. If she didn't know better, she'd never guess he was just pretending. He was pretending, wasn't he? Or had he manipulated her into some evil plot known only to him and his grandfather? Suddenly, that made perfect sense to her. They were blood kin. And she was a Lawless.

Feeling feverishly ill, Jacey gulped and raised her napkin to her sweating lip. "May I have some water, please? I don't feel well."

Don Rafael made a small gesture. Still another Mexican boy dressed in white stepped forward and filled her glass. He stepped back into the shadows. Jacey raised the glass to her lips and sipped. How was she going to get out of this place alive? These men were bigger, stronger, maybe smarter than her, and definitely more wicked than her. If her fears about Zant were true, then she may as well leave this dress on to be buried in. Because her funeral would come soon.

As she sipped and worried, and realized her hand was shaking, she heard her name being called softly from her left. She put the water glass down and turned to Zant. He looked at her and then cut his gaze to Don Rafael. Jacey followed his cue. The don was conferring in low tones with a large-girthed woman. His gestures indicated something to do with the meal.

Praying this old lady didn't end up in a crying heap in the next moment or so, Jacey turned back to Zant. His expression instantly softened, and a gentle smile reached from his mouth to his steadily warming dark eyes. He gave her a slow wink. And the moment was over. His expression reverted to that of the cool, solemn nobleman who hid his thoughts and feelings.

He might be cool and calm, but Jacey came darned near to bursting into tears, so deep was her relief. He *was* just pretending. She took a deep, openmouthed breath, and looked down at her lap. When had she fisted her hands there?

"Are you feeling better, Señorita Lawless?"

Equal to his challenge now, knowing Zant was on her side, Jacey raised her head and met the old man's concerned expression. "Yes. Never better."

Don Rafael inclined his head. "Wonderful. Then perhaps you are ready for the next course, since the soup was not to your liking?"

Jacey looked down at her soup bowl. It was untouched. She'd forgotten to eat. She caught and held the don's gaze. "I'm ready." And she meant that.

* * *

Jacey declared the villa's moonlit courtyard to be pretty enough. She'd never seen such a tangle of green vines and big flowers, none of which she could name. They smelled nice, though. With her slippered foot she toed the glazed-tile walkway under her. Stepping gingerly over the slippery tiles, she tugged aside a drooping vine that hung from the latticed roof. The covering ran the circumference of the courtyard and sheltered four wrought-iron benches.

Standing in front of a bench, Jacey put her hands to her waist and decided that what she liked best was the centrally situated fountain. Ornamented with the same blue tiles as the walkway, the good-sized fountain's water splashed gently over its three tiers. Competing with the water's music was the warm breeze, the hoot of an owl, the meow of a passing cat. But Jacey stared longingly at the fountain. Because at its edge stood Zant.

Seating herself, her hands in her lap and still dressed in her red silk dress, Jacey stared at Zant's back. He had one foot up on the tiled rim of the fountain and leaned forward with his crossed arms resting on his knee. He stared into the night, his head raised to look above the high adobe walls to the mountains beyond. From outside those walls, Jacey could hear the soft whinny of a horse, the quiet words of some passing conversation, the spur-jingling steps of one of many posted guards.

But that was outside the walls. Inside all was peaceful calm. Well, she admitted, except for inside herself. She stared at Zant's backside and shook her head. The man's erect posture stretched his coat and pants tight over the muscled expanse of his finely formed body. She was lost. It was that simple. Caught like this, in repose, he exuded a leashed power, and something else she couldn't give words to. But he'd changed somehow. . . .

She didn't have the words to name it. But he'd changed somehow in just the several hours they'd been here. When she'd caught him off guard at supper, when he didn't know he was being watched, she'd seen the worry lines, the tenseness. Somewhat like his pose now. As if he were deep in thought, and not even aware of his surroundings.

But it was even more than that. She struggled to settle it in her mind. He looked like . . . like he'd just accepted some heavy burden he didn't want. Like the troubles of the world were settling themselves on his shoulders. She looked at those broad shoulders. Were they strong enough to carry the burden?

Just then, Zant turned and found her in the dark alcove. "I'm sorry you had to witness that scene at supper, Jacey."

"Me, too. But not half as sorry as that boy, I'd bet."

Zant grunted. "Poor kid."

"Does that sort of thing happen a lot here, Zant?"

He nodded. "Yeah, and not just to the servants."

Jacey frowned. Did he mean himself? Had he been treated that same way when he was a boy? Not daring to ask, she changed the subject. "You didn't eat much."

Zant's unexpected grin gleamed in the moon's light. "Maybe I didn't like the soup, either."

Jacey grinned back at him, forgiving him for her forced bath earlier. In the ensuing quiet between them, she sobered and brought up her concerns. "I'm not so sure we should be toying with your grandfather, Zant. He reminds me of a snake. Not his looks, but his behavior." When he didn't move or say anything, she added, "You mind me saying so?"

Zant shrugged. "Why should I?"

"Well, he is your grandfather."

A chuckling snort preceded his words. "Through no fault of my own."

"I guess not." Jacey stood up, ruslting the silken material of her dress. She smoothed her hand down the skirt as she went to stand next to him. "What will happen next?"

Zant looked down at her briefly, impersonally, before refocusing on the near mountains. "I can't say exactly. But he appears to believe me when I say I'm here to stay and ready to knuckle under and be the lord and heir."

There it was. What was different about him. "Good. That was your plan. But, Zant"—Jacey paused, spoke more softly—"you really are, aren't you? Going to stay, I mean."

He made a self-deprecating noise and then nodded. "Yeah. And no one's more surprised about that than me." His look of passionate intensity, when he turned to her, startled Jacey. "You saw what happened in there. I've been standing here thinking . . . and I can't let it go on any longer. This is my home, Jacey. I can't just walk away while it's being torn apart.

It's all I have. And the majority of the men here are good. I owe them.''

For some reason, his words saddened Jacey, made her feel she'd just lost him. But had she ever really had him? ''I guess you do.''

He nodded. ''I do. I learned some things after we got here that don't sit right with me. It looks like I'm going to have to buck the old man—sooner than I thought. And harder than I want.'' He was silent for a moment before adding, ''I just hope I'm still standing when the dust settles.''

Jacey hugged her arms around her waist, suddenly chilled. Whether by the cooling air or by his words, she couldn't say. Maybe both. A second shiver wriggled over her.

A movement to her left signaled Zant peeling off his jacket. He draped its warm heaviness across her shoulders. His hand then smoothed around her back to rest on her shoulder.

Jacey closed her eyes with her next exhalation. All she wanted to do was lay her head on his shoulder. Fighting her weakness for him, she forced her mind to stick to the subject. ''Zant, what *is* going on here? Earlier, I saw you talking to a group of your men outside these walls. What were you talking about?''

For a moment there was only silence. Then Zant removed his arm from around her. He focused on the fountain's water. ''You don't miss anything, do you?''

Jacey stared at the surrounding black humps that in the daytime were mountains. ''Not when the only thing I have to do in my locked room is look out the window.'' After a moment, she quietly added, ''If I can see you, so can someone else.''

''I was just thinking the same thing.''

Getting anything out of this man was like trying to pull cactus stickers out of a donkey's behind. Jacey firmed her lips. ''You haven't answered me.''

He looked over at her. She turned her face up to him. He was smiling. His white teeth gleamed in the moonlight. ''I'm gathering my forces.''

''For what?''

''For the right moment.''

''This 'right moment' doesn't have anything to do with me, does it?''

''Maybe. Maybe not.''

Now he was really beginning to irritate her. "Well, when this 'right moment' of yours comes along, will you try to remember that I'm locked upstairs in that room and please not leave me there to starve to death?"

His black-eyed gaze warmed as he made a slow sweep of her face. "I could never forget you, Jacey."

Suddenly shy, she looked down. "Zant, what's going to happen to me? I'm not saying I want you to, but I'm beginning to see why you'd want to kill that old man. There's something missing in him."

"Like a heart?" Zant tugged her chin up until she met his gaze. "Only I have the key to your room. No one else. You're safe. My room is just around the corner from yours. And Paco will be right outside your door, day and night."

Jacey stared up into his handsome face. Moonlight and darkness chiseled his features into slanting angles. "Don't think I'm scared for myself, Chapelo. I just want to be prepared when the trouble comes."

Zant chuckled. "The trouble is here. It rode into Cielo Azul on a black gelding." With no warning, he then dipped his head down to kiss her lips.

Jacey's knees buckled at the sharp, stinging contact of his mouth with hers. She grabbed for his shirt, holding on as he gripped her arms and held her immobile. His tongue begged entry. Jacey granted it. Her breathing changed with the ritual, rhythmic plundering of her mouth. Low in her belly, the coiling began. She was liquid in his arms. She was surrendering.

Zant broke the kiss. He pulled back. Jacey opened her eyes, whispering, "What's wrong?"

"We can't do this."

Before she could stop the words, they were out. "You started it."

Zant chuckled. "I know. I just meant we can't do this here. In the open. Too many eyes, as you reminded me. And you're supposed to be my prisoner, remember?"

Jacey looked down to study her gown's hem. "I remember." She was his prisoner in ways he'd never know.

After a moment's quiet, Zant's breath left him in a slow hiss. He gripped her arm and turned her away from the moonlit fountain. "Come on. We'd better go inside."

Once they were out of the moonlight and hidden from curious eyes by a tangle of vines dripping from the latticed portico above them, Jacey stopped and looked up at Zant. "I don't want to be alone tonight."

His grip tightened on her arm. "You won't be."

As Zant waited for the household to settle in for the night before he could go to Jacey, he paced his room and kicked his own mental butt. What the hell had he been thinking to bring her here? She was just one tiny little woman. Smart as a whip. Heart of a wildcat. That was her. But what made him think he could keep her safe?

She was as liable as anyone here to start a ruckus and get herself killed. Keeping her locked in that room was no solution, he knew. Nor did he figure she'd stay put for long. Hell, he wouldn't put it past her to tie all her bedsheets together and climb down them, just to prove to him that she could. And then what?

One hand to his waist, he swiped his other through his hair. He should have known how bad things would be here. But, damn, he'd been in prison for five years, had come home for only a week, and then had left. Again. How *could* he know? Well, he just should've. Because bringing her here was one big mistake. Her nearness, his feelings for her, his responsibility for her life, all made him hesitate, made him weigh every step, every decision. Such caution could see him and her and about half the men here dead.

It'd be one hell of a sight easier to take control from Don Rafael if he just didn't give a hoot about Jacey Lawless. But he did. She was a fire burning away at the middle of his soul. Just to look at her was to want her. He could've taken her right there by the fountain in that damned red silk dress—

See there? She'd already distracted him. He should be concentrating on stopping Don Rafael's plan to raid surrounding villas and begin a bloody battle amongst the dons in northern Mexico. Zant reflected that he had only days to win over men who hadn't seen him in five years, men who'd seen him behave in every manner except a responsible one, men who had no reason to trust him. Here war was, nipping at their heels, both inside the walls and out. And he'd brought Jacey into the middle of it.

And that was another thing. When and how was he supposed to help her find answers to the questions that'd brought her here in the first place? Just trying to probe into the Lawless murders and the theft of her keepsake could bring everything to a head before he was certain of how much, if any, support he had. Damn!

He stopped his pacing and found himself facing the door to his room. His gaze cut to the key to her room, where it lay innocently on the stand beside his bed. Jacey. Zant took three long-legged strides, picked up the key, and opened the door. Maybe if he put out one raging fire, he could concentrate on the others.

Chapter Fifteen

"I can take it from here, Conchita. No. Stop it." *What was that Spanish word Zant used?* When it came to her, Jacey shouted it at the short, round woman. "*¡Basta!*"

It worked. Conchita, looking offended, slung the white bed gown over her shoulder, put her hands to her ample waist, and then proceeded to cuss Jacey out . . . as near as she could tell. Because all she understood was "no" and the red-faced woman's headshaking and her pointing at the knife strapped around Jacey's thigh.

Standing there naked, the red silk dress and all its underpinnings pooled beside her on the floor, Jacey squinted and grimaced, trying to catch any of the older woman's rapid-fire chatter. She couldn't. If it was the last thing she did, it would be learning enough Spanish to get this little demon to leave her be.

But for now, and deciding she'd listened to about all she was going to, Jacey fisted her hands at her waist and leaned over toward the maid. "Cuss all you want, sister, but I can dress and undress myself. Now back off."

Conchita didn't. Moving as fast as she talked, the determined bundle of short woman, no higher than Jacey's shoulder, forced the nightgown over Jacey's head and all but tugged her arms through the long sleeves. Then she pulled it down to her charge's ankles, straightened up, gave a triumphant nod of her head and eyed Jacey in an all-out dare. Then . . . she picked up the hairbrush.

Jacey eyed the brush . . . thought of all the pain Conchita'd put her through braiding her wet hair earlier . . . and turned to the locked door. "Paco!"

Instantly the door was unlocked. Jacey turned smugly back to Conchita. "Now we'll see just who gets tossed out of here."

"What's going on?"

That voice did not belong to Paco. Jacey froze and stared at Conchita. The maid grinned evilly at her, looking around Jacey, and began counting off her complaints on her fingers. Jacey spun to face Zant, her movement swirling her gown out around her legs. But he ignored her, listening instead to the maid.

Jacey cut her gaze to the man-mountain behind him that was Paco. He stood framed in the doorway, his broad face impassive. No help from that quarter. She turned back to Conchita and listened uncomprehendingly to the charges against her. Zant nodded and kept saying, "*Sí, sí. Ahh. No. Sí.*"

Then he apparently said something to end Conchita's heartfelt tirade because she snapped her lips shut and went wide-eyed. Then her whole demeanor changed, as did her tone of voice. She looked and sounded like she was apologizing. Or pleading. But Zant remained adamant, and held his hand out. The maid backed up, holding the brush close to her chest, and shaking her head no.

Jacey'd seen enough. Was he going to beat the poor old thing? She stepped between Zant and Conchita, turning to face Zant with her arm held out to shield the old woman. "Now hold on right there, mister. Don't you be talking to her like that and threatening her. I can yell at her all I want—she's my maid. But don't you come in here and practically put her in tears just because—"

"Jacey." He spat her name in the same tone of voice he'd used with that *basta* word.

Feeling Conchita tugging on her arm, as if she were trying to see around her, Jacey used her body to further block the Mexican lady from her angry master, and fired back, "What?"

"I asked her for the brush. I told her *I'd* brush out your hair, and she could go on to bed. She's not too happy with the thought of me being in here alone with you."

"Oh." Jacey blinked a couple times. Then, pointing behind

herself to indicate the unusually quiet maid, "So she was defending me against you?"

He nodded. "Yeah, but only after she cursed you and your stubborn ways to three kinds of hell and back."

Jacey grinned. "She said all that?"

Zant rubbed his hand over his mouth and chin. "She did. She thinks you need a good whipping and a lot of time in church to straighten you out."

Jacey turned around to Conchita. "You said all that about me?"

Conchita smiled and nodded. "*Sí, señorita.*"

Jacey turned to Zant. "Does she know what she just agreed with?"

"No," he assured her.

"Oh." Jacey looked him up and down, taking in his own state of undress. Loose white shirt, black pants, and boots. That was all. She then turned to Conchita, holding her hand out. "Give me the brush, sister."

Conchita's black eyebrows met over her nose. She held the silver-backed brush with both hands. "No."

Jacey turned back to Zant. "Your turn."

"Dammit." His expression mirroring his maid's, Zant stalked over to her. Then, a long string of official-sounding Spanish from him earned him the brush, if grudgingly.

Conchita swept by Jacey and Zant with all the grace a short, round little maid with an apron on could muster. She even turned her nose up at Paco. Before leaving, she turned around and shook a finger at both of them, letting loose with her parting opinions. Her sermon ended with her crossing herself. Paco did likewise and then closed the door after them both.

They were alone. Jacey turned to Zant. "Let me guess. She thinks we'll burn in hell, and then she said she'd pray for us, right?"

Zant chuckled. "You wouldn't have to speak Spanish to get that one."

Jacey smiled, but then the smile fled from her face with her next thought. "Zant, what if she . . . tells? I mean, that you're in here with me?"

He shook his head. "She won't. For one thing, she's terrified of my grandfather and probably couldn't get up enough nerve to tell him his chair's on fire. And two, she practically raised me. And still thinks she can mother me. We can trust her.''

Blue, and then Paco, and now Conchita. He'd said he was gathering his forces. ''Good.'' Jacey smiled and then felt that strange shyness that came over her when Zant was near. Lowering her gaze to the floor, she spied her dinner attire, drawers and all, in plain sight. Her eyes widened and a fierce heat traveled up her cheeks.

Apparently Zant's gaze had followed hers, because he nonchalantly stuck his booted toe out and nudged the entire outfit under the bed. ''That better?''

Mortified, Jacey spun away from him. The man had already seen her naked. Why should his seeing her drawers embarrass her? All she knew was that it did. Then, with only the scuffing sound of his boots on the wood floor to tell of his approach, she felt Zant's hands in her hair.

His touch was gentle, probing, as his long fingers moved through her coiled braid, removing hairpins when he encountered them. She didn't move, didn't protest. She couldn't. Every nerve ending in her body raised the gooseflesh on her arms. His touch, his nearness, his clean, musky scent. If he didn't stop soon, she'd swoon. And never forgive herself. Or him.

Zant's hands, one still holding the brush, left her hair to grip her shoulders. Still behind her, he guided her to the low stool in front of the lady's vanity against the far wall. ''Sit here so I can get to you easier.''

Jacey sat down and stared at his reflection in the oval mirror in front of her. He was frowning, staring at her coroneted hair, and moving his head from side to side, as if trying to decide how best to attack this problem. He stood like he was getting ready to go into battle. Legs spread, feet apart, shoulders squared. A giggle, probably the first one she'd ever produced in her whole life, escaped her.

Zant quirked a raised eyebrow at her, put his hands on her shoulders, and bent down to put his face next to hers, the better to see her in the mirror. ''What's so funny?''

''You. You're standing like you're about to charge into an Indian war party. It's just hair.''

He grinned and straightened up. ''Yeah, but there's enough here to braid Sangre a new saddle blanket. What's holding this mess up on your head, anyway? I thought I got all the pins.'' To prove his point, he dug through his shirt's pocket, pulled out a tangle of pins, and reached around her to lay them on the vanity.

Jacey eyed the pins and then looked at him in the mirror. ''Mess? Don't let Conchita hear you say that about her handiwork.''

''I'm not worried,'' he said absently as he again eyed her hair and poked and prodded the coils as if they belonged to a sleeping snake. With the suddenness of a snake's strike, her long braid snapped loose and swung down her back. Zant made a noise and jumped back.

Jacey broke out into chuckling guffaws and shook her head. Zant warned her with a squint-eyed expression and stepped back up to her, gripping her cheeks firmly with his hands and turning her head straight forward. ''Sit still.''

''I was.''

''Don't look at me like that.''

Jacey obediently sobered, but only by drawing her lips in over her teeth and clamping them there. In the mirror, she watched Zant's increasing absorption with his task and the look of wonder that came over his face as he unbraided her hair bit by bit. His touch was silken, mesmerizing. Jacey released her lips from her teeths' grip and said, ''You've never done this before, have you?''

He glanced briefly at her in the mirror. ''No. Am I hurting you?''

''No,'' came Jacey's soft reply, but she was thinking of all the ways he could hurt her forever. Just by turning away from her one day soon, when all the trouble here came to a head. She took a deep breath and exhaled it slowly, her shoulders slumping with her sense of loss.

''You sleepy?'' Zant caught her reflected gaze again.

''No. You?''

''No.''

And that was all they said as he lost himself in her long black hair. Dry now, but kinked and crimped from being braided when wet, the tight curls wrapped themselves around his fingers when his free hand followed his brushing hand. He stroked her tresses and coaxed the tangles out, his face in the mirror showing his every expression, his every emotion.

Clearly, he marveled at the sheer length and thickness and shine of her mane. He drew each stroke of the brush out to its fullest. They laughed together when her hair crackled and stood out straight, following the brush as if anxious over being separated from it. Jacey was the one to break the sensual silence between them. "I think you've about brushed it off my head."

"Let's see." Zant reached around her, his chest rubbing against her shoulder, and placed the silver brush next to the hairpins. He then straightened up, put his warm hands on her shoulders, and stared at her a long time. Jacey watched him in the mirror. His expression changed, became dark and penetrating, singular and compelling.

She knew what was about to happen . . . again. They'd never really talked about that first time out in the desert, never really said much, except to say that their . . . being together like that had changed everything and nothing. Jacey wondered what this time would mean. Nothing? Everything? Then she realized it didn't really matter. Because she wanted him with all her body and soul. Without breaking the eye contact between them, she reached a hand up to caress and cover his.

Zant read her gesture perfectly. He turned her to him and, taking her hands, pulled her to her feet. Walking backward, drawing her with him, he unerringly found the four-poster bed and stopped. "Jacey," he whispered, "I've wanted you so damned much. I'm on fire, girl. What have you done to me?"

His words slipped over her skin, thrilling her and sparking that needle-sharp throbbing between her legs. "I think," she tried to answer, but then hesitated and smiled and started over, "I think I've made you love me."

A heated smile curved his mouth. He smoothed his hands over her shoulders, down her arms. His black eyes smoldered with desire as he stared into her upturned face. "I think you're right. What are we going to do about it?"

"This." The word was a hiss. She boldly rose up on tiptoes and drew his head down to hers, claiming his mouth in a hot kiss that weakened her knees and saw her clinging to him.

A hoarse sound from Zant melted into her mouth as his tongue began its plundering raid. Kissing her, demanding more, he grabbed her to him and wrapped his powerful arms around her, holding her tight enough to cut off her air. She didn't complain. No matter how close he held her, no matter how tightly, it couldn't be close enough for her. Even if she could curl up in his heart and stay there forever, warm and safe, it wouldn't be close enough.

Jacey pulled back from their kiss, gasping for air, breathing hard, and holding on to the tensed muscles in his arms, her small hand no more than a child's against the sheer size of his biceps. She tugged at his shirt, wanting it off him, wanting the feel of his skin against hers. Zant obligingly ripped his shirt off over his head, tossed it away, and then helped Jacey tug her gown over her head. It too disappeared the way of his forgotten shirt.

He then quickly, heatedly, looked her up and down, his finely shaped, sensual hands following his eyes, caressing her, stroking her. He went to one knee and unfastened her knife sheath from around her thigh, setting it carefully on the wooden floor.

Still kneeling before her, he pulled her to him, his cheek against her quivering belly, his hands cupping her buttocks. Jacey was undone. Her mouth slacked open, her eyes closed. And then she felt his warm, moist kisses trailing across her stomach, her navel, and lower, down to the black and curling hair that sheltered her woman's core. Jacey's knees weakened, she clutched at Zant's thick hair and heard little mewling, whimpering sounds coming from her mouth.

Zant held her tighter . . . and tongued aside the crisp hairs at her vee until he found her pulsing desire. He flicked it, circled it, coaxed it into a rage of want. Jacey's mewling sounds became gasps, her muscles tensed. She heard herself saying his name over and over. He pushed up to his feet and allowed her to roam her hands over his hard-muscled chest while he unfastened his pants.

Jacey surprised herself and him by taking over the task of undressing him. She opened the last of the silver buttons and began sliding his pants over his hips. She grinned at her sensual power over him when he began making those same noises she'd made only moments ago.

Zant stopped her hands, took a deep breath, and mouthed, "Let me." He sat on the side of the bed to remove his boots and heavy stockings, and finish divesting himself of his britches. Then, naked, proud, he stood before her, his own desire evident as it jutted between them. Jacey looked from it to his face. And stepped into his embrace.

As he held her close, she roamed her hands over his back. She then pulled back enough to explore his flat brown nipples, his crisp chest hair. With her fingers, she traced the narrow band of black hair that bisected his torso and pointed down like an arrow to below his navel. Just as her hand would have closed around him, a growl escaped Zant as he abruptly picked her up and laid her on the bed behind them.

As he crawled onto the four-poster with her, his crouching posture like that of a panther stalking its prey, he warned, "Don't play with fire, girl."

Feeling wicked, laid out in a decadent position, Jacey rose up on her elbows and teased, "Why not? I know how to put it out."

Zant froze for a second. Then he slowly raised one of his eyebrows and his grin became pure, seductive evil. "Do you?"

"Try me."

Zant's other eyebrow joined its mate, and he pounced on her. Jacey squeaked and grinned, making a feint for the other side of the bed. She never made it. He was atop her before she could move away. In a fevered rush, he kissed her mouth, her jaw, her neck, and moved down to her breasts, claiming one nipple and then the other. Swept along with his storm of passion, all she could do was arch into him and wriggle beneath him. Zant slipped lower on her, kissing his way ever downward.

When he dipped even lower, Jacey cried out, her legs jerked spasmodically, and her body prepared a place for him in her loving saddle. Zant slid back up her. "I'm sorry, Jacey, but if I wait another second, I'll explode. I've got to have you now. I've wanted this, I've wanted you every damn day since—"

Jacey cut his words off with her finger against his lips. "Shh. Me, too." She smiled up at him, her hands now on his desire-dusky cheeks. She watched him search her eyes, her mouth. She pulled him down to her. Zant needed no further nudging. In one swift move, he ensheathed himself in her. Jacey's cry against his bigness inside her slick tightness was muffled by his kiss. But she instinctually matched his stroking, plunging pace, working in rhythmic time with him. She wrapped her legs around his waist, locking her ankles together. Her arms went around his neck.

But Zant pulled himself up, enough to look into her eyes, enough to arch over her and gauge her reaction to each and every long, suddenly slowed stroke. Jacey's mouth opened but no words came out. She moved with him, unable to separate sensation from thought, pleasure from need. She became aware that he was whispering to her in Spanish, uttering phrases of such tenderness and passion that they needed no translation. She listened with her soul as he made of her name an endearment. As he made of her body a temple, and offered up his own in loving worship.

With a staggering suddenness, though, the sensual loving gave way to the purely physical coiling and tightness that forced Jacey's mouth into a grimace of greedy want. She picked up her pace. Zant matched it. He pulled himself up on his arms, then his hands. He sat back on his haunches, pulling Jacey up with him, until she straddled his hips. He then gave the pacing, the stroking over to her. He bent her back just enough to get to her breasts, which he kissed and sucked and circled with his tongue, all the time holding her close with his flattened hands on her back.

As her raging desire peaked, when the coiling tremors exploded into hot spasms, she gasped out raggedly and went tense, clinging to Zant as if only he could keep her from falling over a cliff. His hands slid down to cup her buttocks as he took up the stroking that made Jacey throw her head back, open her mouth, and gasp . . . and gasp . . . and gasp in animal need and satisfaction.

At that moment, with her inner muscles clutching hotly at him, Zant went over that cliff with her. He went rigid as his seed pumped into her. He drooped forward until his forehead rested heavily against her shoulder.

How long they sat there, lost in their loving climax, clinging together in a slick and loving sweat, Jacey couldn't say. But her breathing was almost back to normal when Zant finally lifted her off him and fell limply with her onto the bed's now mussed lace counterpane. Jacey lay on her back, spread-eagled next to him. His pose matched hers. Smiling, satiated, her hair a damp and tangled mass all around her, she closed her eyes and ran her tongue over her lips. What could be more wonderful than this?

Several moments later, she had her answer when Zant moved, and then again lay across her. Jacey opened her eyes, smiled up at him, and wrapped her arms around his neck.

"What does *basta* mean?"

Zant looked up from his breakfast plate. Jacey sat on his immediate right, having pulled her heavy chair there. Her soulful black eyes stared unwaveringly at him. But it was her almost childlike appearance, what with her scrubbed and glowing skin and her hair pulled back simply at her nape and held there with a tied ribbon, that tugged at his heart.

Dressed as she was in a loose white *camisa* and brightly patterned skirt, she could be mistaken for a Spanish beauty. Unless she opened her mouth. But was this young girl really the sensuous woman he'd held in his arms half the night before going quietly back to his own room?

"Well?" she repeated. "Why are you looking at me like that? Is *basta* a bad word?"

He shook his head and chuckled. "As if that would stop you from using it. But no, it's not a bad word. It means 'enough.' "

"Enough, huh?" She took a big bite out of her butter-and-jam-slathered hunk of toast and chewed. And watched him. Silently.

Even though she stared at him as if a hen perched on his head, Zant picked his fork up and took a bite of his now cooling eggs. Chewing and swallowing under her sustained gaze, he finally clattered the heavy silverware onto his plate. "What now?"

"I want you to teach me Spanish."

Immediately, about fifty reasons why he shouldn't, and only three why he should, occurred to him. "Teach you Spanish? Why?"

"So I can hold my own here. So I can know what's going on around me. So I can know if what I'm hearing is important."

Zant blinked in surprise. She'd just named all three of his reasons. Still, he hesitated. "That makes sense. But I'm not sure I'll have time to teach you. Or if you'll be here long enough for lessons to do you any good. Because the Spanish you need to learn is more than a few simple words like 'cat' and 'dog.' "

She leaned over the table toward him. "Try me, Zant. I'm a quick study. Especially when my life might be at stake. And remember, you owe me. I saved your . . . you know . . . from that rattler. Or have you already forgotten?"

"Forgotten?" Zant raised an eyebrow at that. "I still have nightmares." Then, thinking through her proposal, he rested his elbow on his chair's polished-wood arm, looked outside through the open double doors to the flowering gardens of the courtyard, and rubbed his hand over his mouth and chin. Finally, he turned again to her, and said, "All right."

Jacey's face lit up. "All right?"

"Yes. I'll teach you Spanish."

"Good. But since I'm a prisoner here, your lessons will have to be up in my locked room. You'll have to sit in there all day with me, even when it's hot and boring, and you won't be able to get out to do anything, not even see to your own horse."

Zant grinned at her underhanded—and effective—scheming. "I see now what you're up to. All right, you don't have to stay in your room today. Don Rafael's gone to a neighboring villa to . . . um, look over a promising stallion, and he won't be back until late tonight. So I guess it's okay for you to get some sun on your face."

Jacey's broad grin brightened the room like no sun could.

Zant held up a cautioning hand. "Not so fast. You have to stay right with me all day. You can see I'm wearing a gun, and that should tell you something. I don't want you out of my sight."

Her grin dimmed. "You think there could be trouble?"

"Hell, yes." He stood up, tossing his napkin next to his unfinished breakfast. "But you'd be the one causing it." He held his hand out to her.

Eager, and suspiciously unoffended, she scraped her chair back and stood, taking his hand and following him outside through the courtyard.

The very minute Zant was surrounded by a knot of his men, including Blue and Paco, Jacey slipped away from him. She shouldered her way through the heavily armed men. They absently stepped aside as they listened to every Spanish word coming out of Zant's mouth. Once out of their midst in the wide-open welcoming plaza that circled the central flagpole, she kept her head down and hustled away with stiff-legged strides.

With every step, she expected to hear Zant bellowing her name. But luck was with her. She wasn't called back. Jacey looked up to get her bearings. Off to her right were the double-wide mesquite-wood gates that she'd ridden through yesterday. Only desert lay beyond it. Directly in front of her sat the villa itself with all its windows and watching eyes.

Making up her mind, Jacey veered left, making for the shadows at the base of the adobe walls. There was a mighty interesting gate tucked away in those walls that she meant to investigate. She'd noticed it yesterday when she and Zant had reined in above Cielo Azul. From up there it'd looked to her like it opened onto the corrals and that cluster of low adobes where probably the hired guns and the servants lived. She didn't know exactly what she hoped to find out there, but she told herself she was going to check on Knight.

Let Zant and his men burn up the daylight with all their pointing at the hills and putting their heads together and nodding and discussing things in Spanish. Not her. She had a horse to find. And maybe even some answers.

It was clear to her now, after an hour of following him around inside the compound's walls, with him pointing things out and naming them—she now knew that "cat" was *gato* and dog was *perro*—that Zant was right. He didn't have time to teach her. It seemed that everyone on the place needed an answer from him or demanded his time or wanted to greet him, if they hadn't seen him yesterday.

At first the interruptions had irritated her, but then she'd recognized this opportunity for what it was. She wasn't locked up inside, Zant wasn't paying the least bit of attention to her, Don Rafael was gone, and Paco wasn't dogging her steps. But Jacey's mood slipped with her next thought. Yep, she was free, but she didn't know the first Spanish word that was the least bit helpful to her. Still, she figured she could find Knight easily enough. He was a horse. He'd be in the corral.

If she didn't find him right off, at least she knew *caballo* was Spanish for horse. She'd just ask. But if some sombrero-wearing Jasper strung together about two hundred words to answer her, then she'd be lost. Her thoughts carrying her to the gate she wanted, Jacey grabbed for its latch and looked both ways and behind her. Alone. Good. She opened it, slipped through, and then closed the gate behind her.

She turned around and gasped. No wonder it wasn't locked. It was guarded. Jacey smiled up at the somber, sombreroed man on a rangy mustang right in front of her. He held the longest rifle she'd ever seen, its butt resting against his thigh and its steel barrel pointing skyward. He gripped the metal barrel extremely close to the firing mechanism. And stared down at her.

"Um, *caballo*?" Jacey ventured.

"*Sí.*"

"Um, *where* is my *caballo*? Not yours." She pointed to his horse. "I know this one is yours. I mean *my caballo*." She thumped her chest with her fingers.

The guard shook his head. "*No es su caballo.*" He pointed to his horse. "*Esto es mi caballo. Su caballo esta in el corral.*" He turned in his saddle, using his rifle to point back over his shoulder.

All those *caballos* in one breath. Jacey's head was swimming, but she did think she'd heard the word "corral." She nodded and tried again. "Where is this corral?"

He shrugged dramatically and shook his head. "*Lo siento, señorita, pero no hablo ingles.*"

How could he not know where the corral was? Where in the heck did he think he'd gotten his own horse from this morning? Starting past him, intent on winding her way through the clustered adobes that ringed this side of the compound, Jacey raised a hand in parting and said, "Thanks, anyway."

The man moved his horse between her and some staring, dark-skinned women and their children. A dog or two barked at her. Jacey looked up at him, shading her eyes with her raised hand. "What now, Jasper?"

"*Usted, señorita.*" He pointed at her with his rifle. And then shook his head while intoning his next words, giving them a sinister sound. "*Señor Chapelo.*" Now he pointed the gun at the ground. "*No aqui.*" He pointed at her again. "*Usted. Señor Chapelo. No aqui.*"

Jacey thought she understood his gestures, if not his words. Señor Chapelo didn't want her out here. Well, too bad. She looked up at Jasper and grinned and nodded. "Señor Chapelo said it was okay."

Again she started off on her own. Again Jasper stuck his brown horse between her and her business. Jacey's Lawless temper flared to its boiling point. She frowned up at the man and raised her pointing finger at him as she opened her mouth. She sure hoped he understood loud, angry English.

Behind her, cutting her off before she could utter a word, came a deep, well-modulated male voice. Speaking English. "Perhaps I can be of some assistance, señorita?"

Sharp surprise spun Jacey around. A slender, dark-skinned man, well dressed and handsome, not too tall, bowed gracefully to her. Caught off guard by his formality, Jacey ducked her chin in acknowledgment. "You speak English?" was her smiled greeting.

"Yes, Señorita Lawless, I do."

Jacey frowned the slightest bit. "You know who I am?"

The gentleman smiled, showing white, even teeth. "Indeed. No woman as beautiful as you would escape my notice. But even so, you are the honored guest of Don Rafael Calderon, are you not?"

Jacey shook her head. "No." And then caught herself. "I mean, yes. Who are you?"

"Ahh, where are my manners? Allow me to introduce myself." He made another low, sweeping bow. "I am Miguel Sereda. And I am at your service."

Chapter Sixteen

"Pleased to meet you, Mr. Sereda. Since you're at my service, would you please tell Jasper here that I'm just trying to find my horse?"

He inclined his head to her as if he conferred with royalty and then turned to the mounted guard. After a couple of exchanges of rapid Spanish with the man, Miguel Sereda turned back to her. "Enrique says your horse is in the corral."

Still peeved at Enrique, Jacey made a face at Mr. Sereda. "I know that. The problem is, he won't let me past to go to the corral."

"That is because Señor Chapelo has left orders that you are not to be over here. Or in fact, anywhere outside of the villa . . . unless you are with him. Surely you knew this?"

Jacey felt her face heat up, but Mr. Sereda grinned and turned to Enrique, shooting off a dozen or so brusque words that saw the guard's expression turn belligerent. But he nevertheless backed up his horse, allowing a passage for Jacey, much to her pleased surprise. Mr. Sereda then turned to her and took her elbow. His grip was warm, but almost painfully tight. "Come, señorita. I will take you to your horse."

Jacey's first alarmed instinct was to pull her arm free, but that seemed rude and unnecessary, under the circumstances. Because it was broad daylight, she reasoned, several people milled around, and he was only doing what she'd asked of him. And if she needed it, her knife was strapped to her thigh. So, she allowed him to guide her. But a vague unease still pricked at the back of her conscience, troubling her. Giving in to it, Jacey eyed her escort. "You don't seem to be too concerned about disobeying Mr. Chapelo's orders."

At her side, Miguel smiled. "Neither do you, señorita."

He'd kill her, that's what he'd do. He'd find her, make sure she was all right, and then? He'd kill her. It was that simple. He should have known better than to give in to those black doe's eyes of hers at breakfast and allow her out of her room. But he had. When would he learn?

Alone, reluctant to enlist help in finding her, since he'd have to admit she'd slipped away from him, Zant stalked angrily through the courtyard, hoping she'd come here to sit and enjoy the fountain. Hands to his waist, he stopped and looked around. Jacey Lawless sit around and enjoy a fountain and flowers? Hardly. The fragrant enclosure's emptiness testified to the truth of that. He shook his head, as if trying to dispel the taunting voice there that whispered he was more worried than mad.

Think, Zant, think. What'd she say at breakfast? She'd said she wanted him to teach her Spanish. And then she'd said she didn't want to stay in her room. Because . . . ? It was hot and boring and she couldn't—Dammit, that was it. She couldn't see to her horse. Relief flooded through him. She'd gone to check on her horse. Zant huffed out his breath and turned to make his way to the courtyard's vine-bedecked ornamental gate.

The gate. Not this one, but the heavy one that opened into the camp where the corrals were. A frown marred his features and slowed his steps, until he was standing in place. *Who had let her through that gate?* He'd asked Blue last night to make sure all the men understood that if she was seen anywhere on the grounds by herself, or with anyone but him, then she was to be brought to him . . . unharmed. Anyone disobeying that order would be fired. Or worse.

Zant searched his mind to remember who was on duty this morning. The "who" was important, because the man would either be loyal to him or to Don Rafael. With no middle ground. Joyous homecomings and public reconciliations aside, Cielo Azul was an armed camp of divided loyalties.

"Señor Chapelo? Un momento, por favor?"

His hand to his gun, Zant spun around and found the speaker. The *guardia* named Enrique stood outside the low courtyard gate, his sombrero in his hands. The middle-aged man quickly swiped a thick, stubby hand through his sweat-matted black hair and straightened his clothing. Zant smiled at this nervous show of respect as he strode over to the man. But who, Zant wondered, was this simple man loyal to? Him or Don Rafael? In Spanish he asked, "What is it, Enrique?"

Answering in Spanish, Enrique told his story. "The young lady, the señorita, only minutes ago, she came through the gate to the houses outside."

Zant's heart skipped a beat. Just as he'd suspected. "Was she alone?"

"Yes, sir. I stopped her, as Mr. Blue instructed last night, but she insisted on seeing her horse. I tried to tell her—but she does not understand Spanish—that you did not want her out there. With my horse, I blocked her way. Twice. But Mr. Sereda came upon us and ordered me to allow her to pass. I told him my orders were from you. He said to hell with your orders, that he took orders from no one but Don Rafael Calderon himself."

Miguel Sereda. A muscle in Zant's jaw jumped. "What happened next?"

Enrique looked down and twisted his sombrero in his hands. "I am sorry to say that I yielded to him. I did not know what to do." He looked up, indecision and confusion mirrored in his dark eyes. "What are we to do? Mr. Sereda speaks for Don Rafael. And you have only been home these two days. No one knows what to do." Looking hopeful, he added, "But I did follow them—"

"Them?"

"Mr. Sereda and Miss Lawless. He took her to the corral as she requested. They are there now with that black beast of hers." Enrique became quiet and then bowed his head. "I have disobeyed you, my chief. And now I will gather my family and my things and be gone from here."

My chief. Zant stared hard at the man. Enrique was most likely loyal to him. He needed all the men he could get. But he also had to be able to trust them, to know every one of them would obey his orders without question, without being swayed, such as Enrique had been. This was his fault. He hadn't made his intentions clear enough yet. Well, he could take care of that right now. So, unsmiling, he put his hand on the man's arm. "Don't leave. Return to your post. Stay there and remain watchful."

Enrique let out a long breath. "Thank you, Mr. Chapelo."

Zant acknowledged the man's gratitude with a nod and then pushed open the ornamental gate, walked past the guard, and headed for the mesquite gate in the adobe walls. After a pace or two, he turned and called out Enrique's name. The short, heavyset man looked up. "Tell the men I am truly home to stay. Tell them they can trust me. And Enrique, if you disobey an order of mine again, I'll kill you myself. Tell the men I also said this. Do you understand?"

Wide-eyed, Enrique stiffened. "I will tell them. And I swear to you on my mother's grave that it won't happen again. I will take my own life first."

"It'd go a lot easier on you if you did." Zant then turned and sprinted the few remaining yards to the gate. Once there, he shouldered through it and zigzagged his way around the curving, narrow streets of the small adobe city.

At his approach, silence fell over the many women hanging out wash or gossiping or bathing small children. Older boys stopped their rough games, stepping aside for him to pass. A few of the bolder ones called out smiling greetings to him, addressing him as *jefe*. Zant acknowledged them, but only with a nod or a raised hand. His attention was distracted by the hooting and laughing voices coming from the close-by corrals.

Sidestepping a yellow dog that darted in front of him, Zant turned the next corner and stopped. A quick once-over of the area revealed only the men whose job it was to tend the horses. Ranged around the corral's wooden fence, they whooped and cheered a *caballero* breaking a wildly bucking mustang. Knowing Jacey as he did, Zant eyed the cowboy atop the bronco. No, it wasn't her. Then, hands to his waist, his mouth firmed into a grim line, he made a second sweep, this time picking out individual faces.

Jacey's and Sereda's weren't in the crowd. Not that he'd expected them to be. Because Sereda wouldn't remain in the open with her. He knew these *caballeros* knew of Zant's orders regarding her. One or more of them would have come to him, just as Enrique had. That thought narrowed Zant's eyes. Enrique had come to him . . . just as Sereda knew he would. *That son of a bitch.*

Sereda wanted Zant to know he had Jacey. Because . . . ? He wanted Zant to do something rash, prove she was much more to him than just a prisoner. And thereby . . . ? Give Don Rafael an edge in this game of nerves and rebellion they were all playing.

Zant clamped his jaw against the urge to bellow out a string of curses that could change the weather. Sereda was smart. This horse-breaking was the perfect distraction for him to spirit Jacey away. He'd kill that oily bastard if he'd so much as—

Zant turned on his heel, proceeded around the corral, staying at the mens' backs, and entered the horse barn. He breathed in the scents of hay, leather tack, and manure without a second thought. At the other end of the open barn doors, Zant stepped into the sunlight and spotted Sangre, proud, fierce, and aloof in his own corral. The gleaming roan stallion raised his head, stared at Zant, and went back to his feeding.

Zant could remember not so long ago when he'd been just like his horse. Hadn't needed anyone. Hadn't let anyone close to him. Had lived his life for himself. But now? Jacey's sweet little ornery face popped into his head. He'd find her, make sure she was okay, and then he'd kill her. And after that? He'd throw himself in the same hole with her because life wouldn't be worth living without her. Dammit.

Winding his way through the workaday commotion coming from the various shops that made Cielo Azul self-sufficent, Zant heard the sound of Jacey's voice. From somewhere around the next corner, she was laughing and chattering. Not a care in the world. Quickening his steps, he rounded the long barracks that housed the unmarried men. And stopped short, putting his hands to his waist.

There she was. Riding bareback and without so much as a halter or bridle on her gelding. Holding on to a long lock of black mane, she pranced the big horse around the enclosed circle of his corral. And there, leaning against the outer railing, thoroughly enjoying the display, was Miguel Sereda. His hungry, leering gaze was fastened on her. He followed her every skirt-hitched-up-to-her-thighs move.

Zant focused on Jacey. She appeared oblivious to any and all as she, with the unspoken, unseen gestures of a true equestrienne, effortlessly worked her mount through various gaits and commands. That long black hair of hers bounced along with her breasts. He'd seen enough. A mixture of fear for her, anger at her, and jealousy over her stiffened Zant. His hand instinctively reached for the Colt holstered at his hip.

Drawing his gun, he held it up in the air and fired. The sharp report spun the armed Miguel his way, jarred the gelding out of his canter, and threw Jacey forward over the black's neck. From all sides came the sounds of running feet and shouting voices. Within seconds the suddenly silent crush of men loosely circled them, staying well back from the arena . . . out of fear, respect, or perhaps just desire to keep out of the line of fire.

Seeing Paco and Blue among the men, Zant felt safe enough to make a show of holstering his Colt, of purposely daring anyone to draw on him. But his speed was legendary. And perhaps the recent deaths—at his unmerciful hands—of Rafferty and Ramon Quintana were still fresh in the mens' minds. Whatever their reasons, there were no takers.

A smile of triumph tweaked a corner of his mouth, but Zant kept his gunfighter's gaze on Miguel. From the corner of his eye, he could see Jacey, still atop her motionless gelding, but silent and watchful. Just like the crowd of men. Just like Miguel.

Zant curved a grin at the man, daring him. Did his grandfather's right-hand man wish to reveal by deed or word what shone so plainly on his sneering face? The hate. The ambition. The conniving intelligence. With a gunfighter's unerring instinct, Zant sensed the thickening of the air, felt the approach of this critical moment between them. He blanked his own face of all emotion . . . and waited. The moment arrived. And then passed. Zant relaxed his stance. Miguel would not challenge him. Not this day.

Still, Zant did not look away, in case Miguel waited only for him to be distracted before going for his gun. Which he knew was more the *pistolero*'s style. Eyeing his enemy, Zant broke the heavy silence by calling out to Jacey. "Get down off that horse and come here."

When she immediately dismounted by sliding down the black's sleek left side and started his way, Zant's only visible response was to twitch his nose against the sweat beaded under it. But inside, he was slumping in relief. With her, it could've gone either way. No one knew that better than him.

Only when Jacey was safely at his side did Zant speak again, this time in Spanish. He directed his words to Miguel, but knew that what he said would be marked by all the men present. They would then spread his message to those who weren't witnesses to this first of many showdowns. "I'll tell you the same thing, Sereda, that I just told Enrique. Disobey *any* order of mine again—no matter what it is or who it pertains to, and I'll kill you myself. Is that clear?"

Miguel's swarthy jaw clenched, but then, with seemingly no effort at all, his entire demeanor changed. He dropped his aggressive pose and relaxed his expression. His grinning face now radiated conciliation. But Zant wasn't fooled, not even when Sereda bowed to him. "You have my sincere apology. I meant no harm, Don Chapelo. The lady requested to see her horse. I merely accommodated her wish."

"Neither you nor anybody else will accommodate the lady in any way. With any wish—or anything else." He swept the crowd with his gaze. "Understand?"

Nodding heads, mutters of *"Sí,"* and darting gazes met his words. Sereda turned and walked away, his bearing stiff and erect as he pushed his way through the gathered men. Zant marked his retreat and then, trying to gauge the impact of his words on the men, sought Blue's eyes. His blond friend winked and smiled. Zant nodded his acknowledgment and then looked to Paco. The big man glared threateningly at every man around him.

Covering an amused grin by swiping his hand roughly over his lips, Zant then looked to the side, looking for Jacey. She was gone.

Jacey stalked stiff-legged back through the squatting adobes. She didn't have to speak Spanish to know what had just happened. That damned Zant Chapelo had called out Mr. Sereda on her account and had done so in front of all his men. Like two stallions with one mare. Well, he was just lucky she'd accepted the seriousness of the moment and had kept her mouth shut and gone to him. But nobody treated her like some danged victory scalp he could hang from his belt, as if she were his to—

A hand clamped around her arm, stopping her with staggering unexpectedness. As she was spun around, her tied-back hair swung over her shoulder and around her neck. Startled, fearful, Jacey fisted her hand and came around swinging. But Zant easily caught her wrist and glared down at her. A second glance showed her that Paco impassively flanked his *jefe*.

Jacey sucked in a deep breath flavored with raised dust. "Zant!"

"That's Don Chapelo to you, missy." He began dragging her along beside him. Paco dogged their every step.

Her bottom lip stuck out, Jacey jerked at her imprisoned arm and fought him every step of the crowd-lined way. Eyeing her audience, seeing all the women staring at her, Jacey hissed, "What do you think you're doing?"

Not even doing her the courtesy of looking at her, and ignoring the women to both sides of them, Zant gritted out, "I don't *think* I'm doing anything. I *know* I'm taking you back to your room. You've proven you can't be trusted."

"Like hell. You let me go right this minute, or I'll—"

He stopped. This time he did look at her. Suddenly she wished he wouldn't. Because his granite-hard, unyielding expression was the same one he'd leveled on Mr. Sereda. "Or you'll what, Jacey?"

She had no idea. Sudden inspiration told her to change the subject. "Look here, *Don* Chapelo, you're taking this all wrong. All that Sereda fellow did was take me to my horse."

"He did a hell of a lot more than that, Jacey. And so did you. Miguel Sereda is a vicious, back-stabbing snake who happens to be Don Rafael's right-hand man. And by disobeying my orders with regard to you, by forcing Enrique to let you pass, he all but challenged my right to lead here. That's what he did."

"Well, I didn't know all that, did I?"

Zant glared at her. "What do you have to know? Didn't I tell you before we arrived here what was at stake? Grow up, for God's sake. Quit bucking me at every turn. I'm not trying to boss you or own you. I'm trying to keep you alive, me alive, and this whole damned place from exploding around us. I thought you were smarter than this, Jacey. I trusted you to keep your word. And what happens? I nearly had to kill a man, just to make a point with all the other men."

Feeling about two inches tall, Jacey looked down at her

leather sandals. "I'm sorry, Zant. You're right. I shouldn't have done it." She then sought his eyes, hoping to see forgiveness there. There was none. "I said I was sorry."

"That doesn't undo what you've done. You lied to me, you sneaked off, you said God-only-knows-what to Sereda—"

Forget guilt and forgiveness. Now her Lawless back was up. "I didn't tell him anything . . . about anything. And you're to blame for a lot of this, you know."

Her words hung in the air between them. Oops. The moment . . . and time . . . and the entire Earth . . . stood still. Jacey's blood congealed in her veins. Her eyes widened as her heart picked up speed. Were the man not holding on to her wrist, she would have run away like a scared rabbit.

Zant's expression went from darkly challenging . . . to bright red . . . to deep purple. Veins stood out at his temples. Daggers flew from his eyes. His jaw hardened into stone. Had fire shot from his flared nostrils and smoke from his ears, had his Stetson flown straight up in the air under its own power, she could not have been more frightened.

Once or twice, the man opened his mouth. But no words, or even sounds, issued forth. The corded tendons in his neck popped up under his skin with his efforts at . . . control? He raised his free hand to point at her, but still no words issued forth.

Jacey stood as still as a cactus, barely daring to breathe. Suddenly Zant made a jerky move. Jacey braced herself for whatever was coming. Zant gave her over to Paco, whose hammy paw closed around her same wrist. Zant then turned on his heel and stomped off.

Jacey and Paco, along with the myriad of women and kids gathered around them, watched the young lord's departing back. When he rounded a corner and disappeared from view, Jacey looked up at Paco, drawing his sombrero-shaded attention down to her. "Whew, Paco, I think I made him mad."

This time, language was no barrier. Paco nodded. "*Sí.*"

Right back where she'd started. Jacey paced her locked room. Damn the man. She'd apologized. What more could she do? Why couldn't he get it through that thick skull of his that she wasn't bucking him? It was already past the middle of November. If the mountain passes to home got snowed under, then she couldn't get back before next spring. She had to get her answers, find her keepsake, kill the thief, and go home. It all seemed pretty straightforward to her. Why wasn't it clear to him?

Defeated, Jacey groaned and flung herself facedown onto her bed. With her arms and legs flopped out limply, she lay there not thinking, just breathing, her eyes open, her senses absorbing, her fingers fiddling with her long hair. Stirred gently by a breeze wafting through the open balcony doors, warm air caressed her skin. Men's voices called out lazily. A horse neighed. A child laughed. Chirping birds and a barking dog added their voices to the afternoon's lullabye. Despite her anger and her concerns, Jacey closed her eyes.

When she jerked awake, rolling to sit up on the bed's side, the room was shadowed in dusk. Every sense alert, she sat still. What had awakened her? She looked around the room. Nothing had been moved or had changed. And she was alone. She listened a moment and heard the heavy shifting of Paco's boots outside in the hall. Everything was as it should be. Wasn't it?

A sudden stinging pain in her cheek made her jump and forced a cry from her. Her hand went to the already-swelling bump there and rubbed. She looked around herself on the bed. There on the lace counterpane lay a rounded pebble. She picked it up, examining it as if it could tell her where it had come from. She bent over the bed's side to examine the floor. Found another one.

Straightening up and frowning, she stared at the open double doors to the balcony. And waited. Sure enough, another pebble sailed through. This one Jacey easily dodged, following its arc until it landed on the throw rug at her feet. Completely intrigued now, she jumped up and skittered to the French doors, stepping outside only far enough to see who was down there.

Jacey's jaw dropped. She stepped boldly into view, steadied herself with her hands on the wrought-iron railing, and leaned over, calling out in the loudest whisper she dared. "Blue! What are you doing? Someone will see you."

The blond, good-looking man smiled and, keeping his voice as low as Jacey's, called up to her. "No they won't. There's no window under your room. And these bushes hide me from the guards on the walls."

Jacey squinted through the gathering darkness as she looked around the open central plaza. He was right. She called down, "What do you want?"

He shrugged. "Just wanted to know how they're treating you in there."

Jacey chuckled. "Awful, that's how. I'm locked in this room here except for meals—"

"And horseback riding."

Jacey pitched his own pebble right back down on his head, completely missing him. He shook a finger up at her, as if scolding her. Grinning, she again whispered. "They make me wear fancy dresses. And at dinner I have to sit at a long table between them, like I'm a target."

He nodded. "You are." He then looked furtively around him. When he raised his face to her again, gone was the chuckling humor and friendly banter. A sense of urgency was now evident in his features. "Don Rafael and his men just rode in, Jacey. He's back early. Now, look, we didn't expect this. But it can't be helped. You'll have to eat with him alone tonight."

Confused, the least bit alarmed, Jacey frowned. "Alone? Where's Zant?"

"He's . . . not here. And I'm ridin' out to meet him right now. I'll tell him what's happened when I catch up to him. But before I leave I wanted you to know that Zant didn't plan it this way—for you to be alone here with Don Rafael. He thought you'd be safe enough."

Jacey swallowed. "You're not making me feel any better, Blue."

Before he could answer, the thudding hooves of fast-approaching horses disturbed the night. Blue faded into the villa's shadows, and Jacey stepped back inside her room. Peeking out, she saw about five or six mounted men ride by and then leave the compound through the main gates, which had been tugged open for them by the sentries.

When the horses' hoofbeats receded into the distance, and after the gates were closed, Jacey stepped back out to see Blue standing where she'd left him. "Those riders have anything to do with you?"

He grinned. "Let's just say I'm supposed to be ridin' with

'em right now. I've got to go. You just . . . well, just watch your step and your words tonight with the old man. I figured if I warned you, you could take care of yourself."

"I will. Does Don Rafael know Zant's not here, or will I have the honor of telling him?"

"He knows. I told him myself. I said Zant's visiting the cantinas and the señoritas in Santa Cruz. That's the nearest town to here."

Caught off guard by the scorpion sting of jealousy that pricked her, Jacey blurted out, "But he's not really there, is he?"

Grinning, Blue said, "No. But I'll tell him you asked."

"Don't you dare. But tell him. . . ." She took a deep breath. "Just tell him . . . I said to be careful."

Blue's expression warmed. He winked up at her. "I'll tell him, sweetheart. For all the good it'll do. Like you, he doesn't seem to know the meanin' of the word 'careful.' "

Crunching bootsteps followed by silence told Jacey that those were Blue's parting words. Digesting his words, she stood there a minute, looking out over the compound, which seemed to hunker down with the night. She noted the armed men walking the wood bracings built high into the adobe walls.

Her mouth turned down into a frown. It seemed Don Rafael kept enough men about the place to call them an army. She looked at the big main gates. Locked, secure, heavy, forbidding. Why all the safeguards? Why all the guards? Why were they looking out into the hills and the desert beyond? Were they expecting an attack by some other army? And if so, what were they doing inside these walls that called for such an attack?

Jacey put a hand to her fluttering stomach. What had her own search for justice landed her in the middle of? Glory's words came back to haunt her. Something about her riding off to what could be her own death, instead of some sorry old outlaw's. *Baby sister, you couldn't have been more right.*

Then, feeling threatened and cornered, Jacey firmed her lips into a tight smile that reflected her calculating thoughts. Whereas only minutes ago, the idea of a meal alone with Don Rafael was unsettling, now she looked forward to it. Maybe she could learn something from him to help Zant's cause here.

But more importantly, she hoped to find out something of interest to her own mission. Because all roads on her trail ended here. With Don Rafael. And tonight, she had him all to herself.

"Ahhh, Señorita Lawless, here you are at last. And such a vision in that lovely gown. You are truly worth the wait. Come. Manuel has built us a nice fire. Join me here by it, won't you?"

Jacey eyed the fireplace. It was big enough to roast a whole beef in. She then eyed Don Rafael, who held his hand out to her. Would he fling her into the fire? Her smiling face not reflecting her wary thoughts, Jacey held up her midnight-blue taffeta skirt and tromped into the very formal, very large. . . . She looked around. *What would you call this thing? A town-meeting hall?*

Barely hiding her distaste at his touch, she took her black-clad, white-haired host's proffered hand and allowed him to seat her. He led her to a high-backed, padded chair, which proved to be completely uncomfortable when she sat down. Wary as a cornered wolverine, Jacey perched on the edge of her seat and again eyed that roasting oven he called a fireplace. Too close. With both hands, she clutched the chair under its padded seat, half stood, and inelegantly scooted it a few scraping paces away.

When she righted herself and her chair, she looked up to see Don Rafael staring at her, amazement and censure warring for a place on his long, aristocratic face. But Jacey refused to be intimidated into a blush of embarrassment. Too bad, if he didn't like it. She then noted that the overstuffed leather chair onto which Mr. Calderon finally lowered himself looked much more comfortable. Did he intend for her to be uncomfortable? Why?

With the roaring firepit of Hell between them, she lifted the wineglass off the tray held out to her by a servant. She eyed the black-eyed, brown-skinned man bowing in front of her. That was another thing that bothered her. Other than Conchita, not a one of the servants did anything to distinguish themselves from the others. Was that from training? Or fear and unhappinesss? Or was it a calculated silence? If so, to hide what? And from whom?

Pretending interest in the cavernous room's many furnishings, Jacey looked all around, sipped at her wine, sweated from the fire, and warned herself to keep a cool head. Because once her suspicions were aroused, she saw a monster under every bed, a threat in every look, a hidden meaning in every gesture. And tended to act without thinking. Just as she had this morning.

Feeling the old man's stare on her, she finally looked across to Don Rafael. Sure enough, he was boldly observing her over the top of his wineglass. He didn't look away or down or say a darned thing when she just as blatantly looked him in the eye. Somewhat unsettled and wondering what to do next, she opened her mind to Papa's voice and words of caution.

He'd laughed . . . she could hear him now, could feel his big, rough hand tousling her hair . . . and said, of his three girls, he figured Jacey'd be the one to purposely walk into some old bear's den and challenge him on his own ground. *Look where I am, Papa.* A grin of fond remembrance stole over her lips.

She drank it down with her next sip of wine and watched Don Rafael set his drained glass onto a low table next to him. He then sat back and, resting his elbows on his chair's arms, tented his long, thick fingers and considered her. His arch smile gave her the unsettling feeling that he was reading her thoughts and smiling right along with her.

Feeling her bravado slip, Jacey quickly recited Papa's advice to herself. He'd said that if you wanted to be the last one standing, then watch everyone and everything going on around you—and do it *before* the shooting started. Because it was too late when the bullets were flying. Trust no one. And know where everyone in the room is. Watch your own back. He'd even teased her . . . *And make sure your gun's loaded, Jacey.* It is, Papa. I just don't know where it is.

"You're deep in thought, Señorita Lawless."

Jacey started at the sound of Don Rafael's eloquent voice. Her wine sloshed dangerously about in its glass. Holding it out away from her, she looked over at him. Before she could censor her mouth, she blurted out the first thing that came into her head. "You asking me or telling me?"

His burst of laughter reacted on Jacey's nerves the same way an arrow shot at her by an angry Apache would. That did it. She reached over to her left and put the wineglass down onto a low table that exactly matched the one next to Don Rafael. She'd be wearing more of the red stuff than she could drink of it, if she held on to her full glass any longer.

"You are a delight, señorita. No wonder my grandson finds you so enchanting."

Alarm raced along Jacey's nerve endings, alerting her. She now heard Blue's words of a couple of hours ago. *Watch your step and your words.* "Who says he finds me enchanting?"

Smiling now, showing strong white teeth that Jacey figured could tear apart a small animal . . . or a small woman, he nodded his white-haired head at her. "Why, I do. And he does, of course."

Staring at him, smiling just enough for politeness' sake, Jacey remained absolutely silent . . . by biting the inside of her cheek until it hurt.

Apparently seeing he was getting nowhere with that line of questioning, Don Rafael switched tactics, went for her jugular. Almost literally. "I find your necklace to be of particular interest. I noticed it last night at supper, also. What is that unusual pendant? Does it have some special meaning to you?"

Holding his penetrating gaze, Jacey automatically sought and fingered the silver rowel dangling from the chain around her neck. "Yes, it does." *And well you know it.* "It's a rowel from a silver spur. Only the men of the Lawless gang wore this particular type."

He nodded. "I see. Then perhaps that is from . . . your father's spurs?"

So he wanted to play cat and mouse? Her gaze unwavering, Jacey simply replied, "No."

He raised a bushy white eyebrow and allowed himself the barest of smiles. "Tell me, Señorita Lawless, what really brings you to Cielo Azul?"

Up to her elbows in the poker game of her life, Jacey considered her answer. And decided to stick with what she knew best—hedging and sass. "What brings me here? Why, your grandson and my horse, as near as I can recall. Remember me? I was the one yesterday with her hands tied to the pommel. Which, like locking me in my room, was some of your grandson's handiwork. Because he finds me so enchanting."

Don Rafael's eyes narrowed, but otherwise he showed no

sign of anger or impatience. "Ahh, yes. Now I remember. That was you, wasn't it?"

Knowing he didn't expect an answer to that, Jacey looked around the room, crowded as it was with huge paintings in dark, swirling colors of grand-looking Spanish men and women. Calderon ancestors, no doubt. Grandmother Ardis's tiny little portrait would be all but lost here. Which wasn't very far from how Jacey felt. "This is some spread you've got here, Mr. Calderon."

He nodded his head in acknowledgment, apparently choosing to accept her words as a compliment. "Yes. Generations of my family have built upon this land over the past three hundred years. One day, it will all be my grandson's."

Jacey riveted her attention on the frightening old man. Those last words of his sounded like a threat. She didn't say a word. And the silence stretched out between them.

Finally, the old don shrugged in a very smooth, aristocratic manner. "I understand, señorita, that I have you to thank for Zant's . . . capitulation?"

Jacey had a glimmering of a notion about what that word meant. Frowning, giving nothing away, she asked, "How so?"

Her opponent leaned forward in his seat, as if readying himself to spring for her. His voice vibrated with warning. "You tell me, Señorita . . . *Lawless*."

Jacey narrowed her eyes and sat forward in her own chair. "Look, Mr. *Calderon*, you and I both know I'm being held here against my will. And for some reason that has to do with *you* sending hired guns after me and my sisters. It seems funny to me that your guns showed up on the same day my folks were killed. So let's cut through the horsecrap and say what we mean."

Well, that hadn't taken long. So much for heeding Blue's words of caution. And Papa's.

Don Rafael matched her glare for glare and then abruptly sat back in his chair. His big hands clutched clawlike at the leather-padded armrests. "As you wish, Miss Lawless. But I'm afraid you'll find you never should've opened that particular door."

At that moment, a loud and fearful babbling in Spanish out in the terra-cotta-tiled foyer, accompanied by the sounds of a breakable something hitting the floor and shattering, grabbed the two combatants' attention. Jacey came to her feet, as did Don Rafael. She turned with him to face the room's square portal. Wide-eyed, her heart pounding, her hands clutching at her full skirt, she started when a frantic Manuel ran past, his face a mask of terror. He didn't bother to slow down long enough to explain.

The little man had no more than passed from view before the mesquite-wood front door banged open with the force of a lightning bolt and struck the thick wall behind it. Terrified, Jacey drew in a deep breath and held it. A second of absolute silence passed. Then the boot-scuffing and spur-jangling sounds of someone's purposeful and unerring approach, each long stride bringing him closer and closer, assaulted Jacey's already overwrought nerves. Whoever this was, he wasn't bringing good news. Not with a walk like that.

He turned the corner and stopped, standing framed in the entry. Jacey's heart flopped over in her chest. *Zant*. Tall, powerful, exuding danger, he stood with his booted feet apart, his arms held loosely at his sides. A sudden wind gust blowing down the hallway, allowed in by the open front door, billowed his black duster, like raven's wings, around him. The ankle-length coat then settled obediently over his denim-covered legs. From under the forbidding brim on his equally black Stetson, he focused his gleaming eyes on her. She could only blink at him. His gaze then slipped to Don Rafael. And back to her.

Jacey felt herself shrivel under his intense scrutiny. His square-jawed, handsome face, bronzed by sun and wind, only accentuated his deep frown. He stood immobile in his gunfighter's pose. The unbuttoned front of his duster allowed a glimpse of the firepower holstered at his hip and tied to his muscled thigh. Firepower he wouldn't hesitate to use.

He finally opened his mouth to speak. In a voice husky with warning, he gritted out, ''Am I in time for supper?''

Chapter Seventeen

W*as he in time for supper!* Maybe she hadn't heard him right. But apparently she had because Don Rafael became suddenly animated, raising his hand in fond and laughing greeting to his grandson.

"Zant! You're back so soon? Were the señoritas in Santa Cruz not to your liking?"

Is everyone but me plumb loco?

"Can't say that they were." As he stepped farther into the room, Zant shed his duster and threw it casually onto a nearby horsehair sofa. Next he untied his holster's leather thong from around his thigh, unbuckled his gunbelt, and sent his weapon the way of his duster. His Stetson followed. He then ran a hand through his unruly black hair as he acknowledged Jacey's watching presence with only a passing glance that she couldn't read.

He turned and spoke to his grandfather. "We didn't expect you home so early this evening, Don Rafael."

"Apparently not," the don acknowledged archly, looking from Zant to Jacey and back. "But you're just in time. Miss Lawless and I were having a lively conversation about what brings her here."

Zant jerked his head around to her so fast Jacey figured he'd have a neckache come tomorrow. "Were you now?"

She swallowed, tried to smile . . . couldn't hold it . . . gave up. "Yes, we were. We were just getting ready to cut through the horsecrap."

"The horse—What?"

Don Rafael jumped in. "The, uh, horsecrap, as Miss Lawless so delicately phrased it. She tells me her parents have been killed. And she seems to think I have men tracking her and her sisters. I was about to assure her that she is mistaken."

Looking her right in the eye, his expression unyielding, Zant spoke levelly. "As I can also assure her. Let me remind you, Miss Lawless, that you are a guest in this house. My house. My grandfather's house. We will not take it kindly should you accuse either of us of plots or treachery against you and your family. Do you understand?"

Stung, embarrassed, angry, even though she knew full well the true warning behind Zant's words, Jacey just could not see herself sitting down to a meal with these two right now. Holding her skirt up out of her way, she started across the room. "I understand. And I'm hoping you two gentlemen will excuse me if I just don't feel like breaking bread with you this evening."

Stopping even with Zant, she looked up at him. "Providing guests are allowed a tray up in their rooms, could you please see that one's sent to me?"

Not giving him time to answer, and hoping *her* message sank in, Jacey stepped around him and left the room, in much the same temper as Zant had entered it. When she'd stomped her way to the foyer, she gingerly stepped around the shards of a pottery vase littering the tiles, and then slammed, with all her might, the wide-open front door.

Only slightly mollified by that bit of violence, she attacked the stairs. Damn all these winding, curving steps. She'd be huffing and puffing by the time she got to the top, what with this danged corset and such binding her. Sure enough, when she reached the landing, she had to hold on to the ornately carved, polished-wood newel post a moment. She fanned her face with her hand until she caught her breath.

Then, frowning all the way to her toes, she set off again. Down the shadowed and quiet hallway that would take her to her room. Approaching her door, she saw Paco standing in front of it. As impassive as ever. He turned at her approach. If he was surprised to see her back so soon, it never showed on his face. Neither did any other emotion. Ever. And that really irritated her, too.

Stopping in front of her giant guard, Jacey craned her neck

back to look into his face. "You're just as bad as the rest of them. Get the hell out of my way."

Paco apparently knew what was being asked of him. He nodded, replied, "*Sí, señorita,*" and opened the door, holding the knob as she swept past him. Once she was inside and turned to face him, he wordlessly closed the door behind himself. And locked it.

Jacey gritted her teeth and scrunched her taffeta skirt in her fists. She made a screeching noise at the door. Could she not get a fight from anyone here? She needed to . . . needed to—she looked around the room—needed to throw something. Or break something. She sighted on the four-poster bed. Or choke something. Letting go of her abused skirt, she made claws of her hands and advanced on the post nearest to her. The wooden furniture never saw her coming. Jacey grabbed and choked the life out of it.

Jerking herself around more than she did the stalwart post, she took out all her pent-up rage on it. Her curled hair bounced around her shoulders, her arm muscles cramped, her face hurt from her taut grimace. She kicked at the footboard, too late remembering she had on sissy slippers and not her boots.

Yelping in pain, she loosed her victim/post and hopped one-footed around to the bed's side. Throwing herself on it, she pulled and yanked and tugged the yards of skirt up around her thighs so she could get at her throbbing toes . . . and froze when she saw what was on the bed with her, just beyond her feet.

A silver spur with one rowel missing.

Her anger fled, chased away by the swell of shock and triumph that tumbled over her in hot waves. She stared at the spur, but couldn't bring herself to reach for it. Not yet. Slowly, movement returned to her limbs. She let go of her skirt, absently tugged the dress's cap sleeves back up onto her shoulders, and looked around her room, as if the armoire or bureau or vanity had an explanation for her.

Who could've been in here during the less than thirty minutes that she'd been downstairs? A broad, swarthy face popped into her mind. Paco! Whoever came in would have to go through him first. Not touching the spur, not sure yet if it was placed here as a threat or a helpful clue, Jacey scooted off the bed and fled for the door. She rapped on it, calling out,

"Paco? Paco? Open this door! I have to talk to you. Open up—"

Paco opened the door with a suddenness that threw Jacey into the wall behind her. Obviously he'd unlocked it during her tirade. Stepping into the room, the huge Mexican looked right and left, not seeing her. Jacey closed the door behind him. Paco jerked around, his pistol in his hand. The noisy end of the weapon pointed to her heart.

Wide-eyed with alarm, Jacey threw her hands up. And waited in a cold sweat for him to realize it was her. He finally did and relaxed, reholstering his gun. Much to Jacey's relief. Crossing his massive arms over his barrel chest, standing with his booted feet apart, Paco raised an eyebrow at her. *"Sí, señorita. ¿Qué pasa?"*

Jacey bit at her lip and worked her mouth, trying to think of how to phrase her question in simple words and gestures. "Um . . . Paco—nice big man I wish could understand English. Uh, who"—she hooted like an owl—"*who* has been in"—she stabbed her finger at the floor—"*in* my room?" She whirled that same finger in broad circles to indicate the room at large.

Through it all, Paco frowned at her, followed her gestures, and finally commented, *"¿Qué?"*

Jacey straightened up, her arms at her side. "Kay? Who's Kay?"

Paco shrugged his shoulders. *"No entiendo, señorita."*

Jacey just shook her head. "Boy, me neither . . . whatever you said." Then inspiration struck her. She held her hands up to Paco. "Wait. I'll show you." With that she pattered to the bed, reached across it, and grabbed up the spur, abandoning her earlier reluctance to touch it. She turned and held it up to him, pointing at it with her left hand. "This. Who brought it in here?"

Paco looked from her to the spur and back to her. *"¿Qué?"*

Jacey gritted her teeth. "Well, then, just who the hell is Kay?"

The room's door began slowly opening. Paco put a finger to his lips and noiselessly drew his gun. Jacey didn't move or breathe. The door pushed open. Zant stood framed in the door opening, a covered tray in one hand, his Colt revolver in the other. Armed and ready, he and Paco faced each other, trading surprised looks. Jacey slumped in relief and ran to Zant, tugging on his gun arm in her excitement.

"Look, Zant, look what was on my bed. Paco says someone named Kay put it there." She held the spur about two inches from his face. "Who's Kay?"

His eyes all but crossing, Zant pulled his head back, like a turtle retreating into its shell. "Whoa, Jacey. Wait a minute. Let me . . ." He reholstered his gun and held the tray out to Paco, who promptly relieved him of the burden. The big guard stepped back, holding the tray in one hand, his gun in his other.

"Zant, listen to me." Jacey spoke slowly and distinctly, as if he were a slightly slow child. "This spur was on my bed. This is *the* spur, Zant. Look—one rowel is missing." She held the spur up to the pendant on her chain, fitting them together. The rowel's jagged edges fit the spur perfectly. She exhaled sharply and stared at Zant. "I knew it. This is the one. Now, who's Kay?"

Zant stared more at the spur in her hand than he did her. He frowned and lifted his gaze to her face. "I don't know any Kay."

Jacey firmed her lips in frustration. "Paco does. Ask him."

Jacey turned to Paco with Zant, and listened as he strung together a bunch of Spanish words. Paco nodded, set the tray on top of the bureau, shook his head, and said one or two words back. They both then turned to Jacey. Her gaze flitted from one male face to the other. "So? Who's Kay?"

"Nobody. He said *'qué,'* Q-U-E. It's Spanish for 'what.' "

Jacey slumped. She thunked the all-important spur into Zant's hands as if it were no more than a used hanky. "Then who did put it here?"

Zant turned the spur of contention over and over in his hands, his expression hardening. "This is my father's." He then looked up at Jacey. "Paco says no one but you has been in here."

"Not even Conchita?"

"Not since she was in here earlier helping you bathe and dress."

Jacey's mind raced with further possibilities. "Couldn't someone have thrown a rope over the balcony railing and climbed up and put the spur in here and then climbed back down without Paco ever knowing?''

''Probably. But climb up the balcony on a rope? With all the guards out there, I'd think one of them would have noticed something.'' Even as he spoke, Zant paced over to the balcony doors and tested them. He turned back to her. ''They're locked. From the inside.''

Then that meant . . . A sudden fright sent Jacey skittering away from the bed. Safely across the room from it, she turned and spoke to Zant in whispers as she pointed at the four-poster. ''Maybe someone's still in here.''

Zant frowned at the innocent-looking bed. He then laid the spur on the bureau next to Jacey's covered supper tray. Drawing his gun, and using due caution, he approached it from the far side. He signaled for Paco to go quietly to the near side.

Across the room, Jacey watched wide-eyed and dry-mouthed. She licked at her lips, feeling the tension coil in her belly when Zant, through signals, indicated to Paco that on his finger-raised count of three, they were going to jerk the floor-length coverings up. Paco nodded his understanding.

When they were in place, Zant began his count. On three, they jerked the covers up, yelled in Spanish, and poked their guns under the bed. Starting at the sudden noise, even though she knew it was coming, Jacey drew back.

To her utter surprise, a screeching child shot out from the end of the bed, scrambled to his feet, and in a flash of white—before Paco could get to his lumbering feet, before Zant could do more than pop up from his side of the bed, before Jacey could register what exactly was happening—he flew past her and out the open door. His running footsteps receded down the hallway.

Jacey's astonishment opened her mouth and widened her eyes. She pointed to the doorway and stared at Zant. ''That was a boy. A little boy.''

Impatiently, Zant holstered his revolver and hurried around to the door. ''I saw him. Dammit, Jacey, why didn't you grab him?''

''Grab him? How could I? He took out of here like a whirling dust devil.''

Zant gave her a look and then peered out into the hallway, listening. A cry of surprise sounded from downstairs. But at the same time, the front door slammed. For the third time that evening.

Zant headed for the closed balcony doors. As he passed Paco, he issued some terse orders in Spanish. Paco nodded and left the room. Zant opened the double doors, stepped outside and peered right and left. He then grasped the railing and called out, "Jacey, look at this."

She was right behind him. He pointed to a knotted length of rope that was tied to the wrought iron and dropped over the side. "It appears you were right—at least partly. However that kid got in, he intended to leave this way." Using a hand-over-hand grip, he hauled in the rope, allowing it to coil on the balcony's floor. "Long enough to reach the ground."

Jacey stared at the rope and shook her head slowly. Who could be behind all this? With Zant, she then looked and listened to the sounds carried on the air. "Can you see anyone?"

He shook his head, jutting his chin toward the armed men patrolling the high adobe walls, which were lit at intervals with flaring torches. "Just them. And they won't see anything, either. Trust me."

With that, Zant ran a hand through his hair and turned back into the room. He began looking into drawers and opening armoire doors. "I'm sorry I jumped on you. I was closer to him than you were. If I couldn't grab him, how could you?"

Jacey silently acknowledged his apology as she watched him turning things over and pacing about the room. "What are you looking for?"

He stopped in the middle of the room and put his hands to his waist. "Hell, I don't know. Clues, I guess. Did you get a good look at the kid?"

Jacey shook her head. "No. Not a good one. All I know is he was dressed in white, he's Mexican, scared to death, and about eight or nine years old. You didn't recognize him?"

Zant's grimace forced dimples into his cheeks. "No. I've been gone five years. I hardly know any of the men around here anymore, much less their kids. You think you could recognize him if you saw him again?"

Jacey shrugged. "I don't know. I'd like to try, though. I still don't know whether to be scared by the spur showing up, or relieved. Someone is either helping me or threatening me. Either way, I'd like to know who it is."

She paused, taking a deep breath, reluctant to voice her next thought. But seeing no help for it, she plunged ahead. "Zant, I've thought of something else. Maybe you have, too. I'm thinking if the spur is here, then so's my great-grandmother's portrait. My keepsake." Feeling the hot tears prick at the backs of her eyes, Jacey spoke around the gathering tightness in her chest. "I'm sorry for what that means."

His black-eyed gaze settled on her with a dark intensity. The quiet between them took on a life of its own. Zant finally looked down, shaking his head. When he again looked at her, no emotion shone from his eyes, or showed on his face. "No need to be sorry. It's why you're here. You've never said otherwise."

Her palms slick with sweat, Jacey clutched at handfuls of her skirt. "I know. But I hate the fact that it's true. After everything I've gone through to get here, after all my smart words and bullheadedness . . . But especially now, feeling the way I do . . . about you, I hate it, Zant. I'd give anything for it to be anyone but your grandfather. Anything."

"I know you would. So would I." With those words, some ragged emotion settled on his features, created lines in his face that she'd never seen before.

Then, that heavy quiet descended again. Staring at him, seeing him as a lonely little boy, his mother and father dead, a little three-year-old in Don Rafael's care, Jacey wanted only to crumple to the floor in a heap and cry until she felt nothing, cry until her burden was lifted from her heart.

But Zant's next words forestalled, perhaps purposely, any but practical considerations. "If that kid can get in here, then so can someone else. Obviously, this room isn't as safe as I thought. We're going to have to do something else."

His brisk manner told Jacey there'd be no more discussion of their heart-wrenching predicament. To do otherwise would paralyze them. So, responding to his cue, she asked, "What do you want to do?"

He appeared to let out his breath as he shook his head. "I don't know. Maybe put you in my room. Or stick you in my pocket."

Was he teasing her? Frowning, not quite sure, Jacey sent him a sidelong glance. "Those are my only two choices?"

Zant surprised her by grinning. "Yeah. Pick one."

Jacey put her hands to her waist. "Put me in your room?"

He nodded. "Good choice. Because little as you are, I don't think you'd fit in my pocket." He advanced on her and grabbed her wrist. "Come on."

As he pulled her toward the door, Jacey grabbed up the all-important spur from off the bureau, and then dug her heels in. But given her satin slippers' soft leather soles and the polished-wood floor, all she did was slide along behind him as she protested. "That was a question, not a decision. Zant, you can't put me in your room. What would you tell Don Rafael?"

Out in the hallway now, he stopped and turned to her, meeting her gaze, but not releasing his hold on her. "He expects this, Jacey. He's already asked me how come I haven't . . . sampled your delights, as he put it. The Calderons are a hot-blooded lot. Don Rafael included."

When Zant's sustained stare told her he was waiting for her to catch on, Jacey frowned in thought, going over his words. When she got his message, her breath caught in her chest and her eyes flew open wide. "You don't mean—You do, don't you?"

"I do. The old son of a bitch has his eye on you."

Jacey stiffened. Fear and outrage and disgust battled inside her. But Lawless temper won out. Jutting her chin out, she jerked ahead of Zant, now pulling him along behind her as she made for his room. "All right, I'm staying in your room. But some things are going to change around here. One, I'm not wearing any more of these fancy gowns. Get me some decent clothes. And two, I want my gun back. Now. Tonight. And three, you and I are going to make that old man think we're a couple of rabbits hell-bent on producing him a great-grandchild. You got that? Any questions?"

From behind her, all she heard was the sound of Zant's boots striking against the floor and the jingling of his spurs. Then he chuckled and said, "I got it. And I have no questions, ma'am. I fully understand my duties."

Zant woke up the next morning and, grinning, shook his head at the ceiling above his bed. Apparently one of his duties was to hold an exhausted Jacey all night as she cuddled against his side and snored gently. She had an arm thrown across him and her hand around his neck. Her hair fanned across her bare shoulder and over his bare chest. Bare, yes. But innocently so.

The rabbits had been anything but productive last night. She'd been too shy and embarrassed about actually sleeping with him for Zant to do anything but hold her and reassure her that sleeping next to a man wouldn't kill her.

But it was killing him just to lie next to her like this. Like some damned gentleman. He looked down the long stretch of himself to his hardness, which poked up against their covering sheet. He exhaled a breath savage with need. *Get it out of your head, Chapelo. Think of something else. Think about how this is a first for you, too. You've never slept all night with a woman without first—*

Zant found he couldn't even think the crude word, not if it were applied to Jacey. That wasn't what he did with her. It was lovemaking, pure and simple. Not so simple, but certainly pure. He smiled at the ceiling again. *Next thing I know, I'll be married and sitting in a church pew every Sunday. A decent man.*

He looked down at the sweet face reposing on his shoulder. Was she turning him into a decent man? Was it because of her that he was here trying to do the right thing—for the first time in his life? He considered that a moment, deciding it was only partly true. He then thought of the coming showdown between Don Rafael and Jacey. In his mind, Jacey would win . . . and walk away. Forever. Zant blinked and let out a deep breath. *Face it, Zant. Say it.*

All right, he acknowledged, she'd walk away. And he'd have to let her. There could be no other way. Because, God forgive him, after everything, even after all the heartbreak and treachery, he loved his grandfather. Loved him. How could that be? But he also acknowledged that there'd be no way he'd ever let Don Rafael harm Jacey. He'd kill the old man himself before he'd let that happen.

Zant tried to picture that scene, that showdown, but his mind shied away from it. *Dammit.* All right, think about afterward. Afterward, what would be left between them—him and Jacey? Nothing. There were some things that just couldn't be forgiven. Or forgotten.

Zant fisted his hand around the sheet, picturing his life here alone. No Don Rafael. No Jacey. Would there be anything left to make his life worth living? Only yesterday his answer to himself had been no. But surprisingly, this morning, his answer was yes. There was something here that was good and right at Cielo Azul. He had plans for his home—honest, decent plans that involved horse-breeding and cattle.

So, there it was. His life was here. And Jacey's wasn't. She'd brought him back home, but now it was Cielo Azul and its people, not Jacey, that wouldn't allow him to run anymore.

Zant shook his head at these uncustomarily deep thoughts of his. He looked down at the girl who lay against his side. She was the only thing in his life, aside from his decision to fight for Cielo Azul, that had ever felt right. He wondered if, after the next few days, either one would be left. Hell, would he himself even be alive? With a certain sense of futility, Zant chuckled at himself and tenderly kissed Jacey's forehead.

She frowned and mumbled in her sleep, tossing over onto her back and then turning yet again to present her back to him. She tugged her knees up almost to her chest, which put her bedgown-covered bottom warmly against his hip.

Zant rolled his eyes. His thoughts had momentarily killed his desire. But it reared its lusting head anew under the sheet. *Oh, for crying out loud*. How much more of this torture was he supposed to bear?

Just then, Jacey stiffened. Zant stared at the back of her head. With a jerk and a twist, and a swirling of long black hair, she was sitting up next to him, completely awake and wide-eyed, staring at the foot of the bed. Zant folded his fingers together behind his head, using them as a headrest against his pillows. And waited. With another twist of wariness, she faced him, stared at him, didn't seem to comprehend exactly what he . . . what she was doing here.

Zant grinned at her. "You're in my room. My bed. Remember? And nothing happened."

Jacey let her breath out and flopped over onto his chest, her cheek against his heart, her arms around his ribs. "Oh, thank God."

Zant's grin fled as he stared at the top of her head. She was here for now. She was his for now. Not forever, but for now. He brought an arm down to caress her hair. "Well, thanking God wasn't exactly my thought."

She turned her head until she could look up into his eyes.

Planting her chin on his bare skin, she arched a black-winged eyebrow. "I'll bet."

Then, with a suddenness that took his breath, she bent her head and pulled herself up just enough to run her tongue around his flat brown nipple. When he stiffened and gasped, she looked up at him again. "Was this more what you were thinking?"

Did Señor Zant and that little hellion Miss Lawless think that no one was aware of what they were doing? And them not even married. Conchita shook her head at such a scandal. *And then their lying abed until half the morning was gone had made her run late with her chores and her eavesdropping.*

Downstairs finally, after having seen Señor Zant and Señorita Lawless dressed, fed, and out the door, Conchita pretended to be dusting the already gleaming hallway table. Pushed up against the wall as it was, and across from Don Rafael's office, this table was never dusty. Because from here, she could hear everything said inside.

Even now the muted sounds of raised voices and angry words came clearly to her. She listened as the old man himself ranted and raved at Miguel Sereda, that snake, and Victor DosSantos. She shook her head. *Ahh, Victor, how did you ever find yourself a* pistolero *to such a one as the don?*

Occasionally casting a wary glimpse up and down the hallway, making sure she remained undetected, Conchita cocked her head to hear better. Knowing she couldn't trust the simpleminded Victor to accurately or even completely report to her all the details of his meeting with Don Rafael, she was forced to be a spy.

She suspended thought in favor of listening when her employer's already raised voice became a bellow aimed at the two men inside with him. "No, Victor, I am not happy in the least. Why is it I don't know exactly what is going on under my own nose—in my own villa, Miguel? What do I pay you for, if not to carry out my orders and to keep me informed?"

"My chief, I do follow your every order. And I tell you everything. Even now, I have a full report from the men about last night's raid on Villa Delarosa. I met with them first thing this morning. And have I not brought Victor here with me to tell you of our first blow against the other dons of Sonora?"

Conchita smirked at Señor Sereda's desperate, almost whining words. She flicked her feather duster over an intricately patterned Mayan vase that graced the long narrow table. *Señor Sereda has not been his usual mean self since Señor Zant faced him down in front of the men yesterday.*

"I am not speaking of the raid. Do you not hear me? I am speaking of what goes on *inside* the walls of Cielo Azul. Inside." A loud thud told Conchita he'd pounded his fist on his desktop. Most likely. "All around me, there are scurrying feet, like little mice. There are whisperings and secrets. There are nightly meetings. What do you know of this?"

Victor spoke up, and Conchita cringed. There was no telling what would come out of that one's mouth. "Our first raid at Villa Delarosa was successful. We killed many of their men and lost none of ours. When we rode off, the fire we set lit up the night sky. And they never knew who we were."

When silence followed this memorized speech, Conchita knew why and sighed. His words had nothing to do with what Don Rafael was talking about. The old man's voice, when next he spoke, reeked of false patience.

"Victor, I am happy that you had such a wonderful time last night, raiding and burning. Truly, I am. But I am talking about what is going on *here*"—another pounding ensued—"under my very nose. If you and Miguel cannot sniff it out, then neither of you will *have* a nose, do you understand me? Your rotting carcasses will feed the vultures."

Conchita stiffened and put her hand to her mouth. She'd never heard Don Rafael speak to Miguel Sereda like that. Victor, yes. But not Señor Sereda. She grinned. He would be livid.

Just then Manuel, Don Rafael's personal servant and the only one he truly trusted, rounded a corner from the dining room and came down the hall. Conchita stared at him, her dusting all but forgotten. This one's loyalty she wasn't sure of. No one was.

Smiling but wary, Conchita silently greeted him. Manuel acknowledged her with a nod, cut his gaze to the raised voices coming from behind the closed office door, and then looked again at her. His expression never changed. He didn't slow down or challenge her. He continued on to the foyer. Conchita raised her eyes heavenward in a silent prayer.

Which was interrupted by the lowering of the voices in the office. She scooted across the narrow hall, giving her undivided dusting attention to a life-sized painting of some ancient Calderon, whom she dismissed with a flip of the tied-together feathers in her hand, as she leaned toward the door.

"There will be no need to make war on my neighbors, if I am dead. And let me remind you, Miguel, you have already had one opportunity to rid me of the thorn in my side. And you failed me. Should I die, you will have no power here, my friend. No say at all. All you have, I have given you. You are my creation. But should that change, should I die, you will die with me. Why? Because my grandson hates you. He will kill you. So, you better make sure I stay healthy."

"As always, Don Rafael, that is my life's work and my heart's wish. I will not fail you again."

Conchita rolled her eyes. It was a wonder that the sugary words which rolled off that one's tongue did not attract flies. When she heard Victor ask to speak, she brushed and dusted the proudly painted Calderon's crotch with singular and nervous intensity. *No, Victor, say nothing. Please.*

"What is it, Victor?"

"I for one do not believe the rumors that your own grandson plots against you and wants you dead."

Conchita nearly fainted. She clutched at the picture's heavy frame, her knuckles white around its gold-leafed edges as it swung askew with her added weight.

After a moment of quiet came Don Rafael's voice. "Rumors? What rumors? Miguel, do you hear this simpleminded idiot? He knows more than you do." Apparently done with Miguel, he now addressed Victor. "What have you heard that makes you think I was speaking of my grandson, Victor? I was referring to that little Lawless bitch. It is she who wants me dead. Not my grandson. Everything I do, every bit of power and control I gain in Sonora, I gain for him. Because he is home now to take over his rightful place here. Am I wrong to believe this?"

"No, Don Rafael," Victor's dull voice assured. "I remember now. It *is* that little Lawless bitch who wants you dead. Because you killed her father."

Conchita gave up and just slid down the wall to sit on the floor with her stubby legs straight out in front of her. Victor vas digging his own grave. All he needed was the shovel.

Silence, once more, followed the poor *pistolero's* bald pro-
ouncement. When Don Rafael next spoke, his voice was a
leadly hiss. "I killed no one, Victor. Do you hear me? No
one. I never gave orders for Señor Lawless to be killed.
Never."

Victor immediately added, "And yet, he is dead. And his
daughter is here. She now has the Kid's spur, too. All of it."

Still seated on the floor out in the hall, Conchita stared
traight ahead, wide-eyed. Only her flattened palms on the cool
loor to either side of her kept her from slipping onto her side
and dying right there. *How could Victor know that already?*
Then, it came to her, bringing with it a heartsick fear that
beaded her lined forehead. She closed her eyes and bit at her
bottom lip.

That little stinker Esteban must have slipped out this morn-
ng to meet Victor—the boy's favorite person in the whole
world—when the men in the raiding party rode in. The two
had no doubt exchanged tales of their courageous exploits
from the night before.

Conchita's heart pounded so loud she wasn't sure she would
be able to hear what was said next. She then realized she didn't
need to hear anything else because she knew what was com-
ng. Poor simple Victor. He'd get them all killed.

Struggling to her feet, hoping and praying that Victor did
not give away her little grandson before she could hide him,
Conchita bustled down the hallway, through the dining room,
and out the courtyard doors.

She had to find Señor Zant right away and warn him.

Chapter Eighteen

Peering into every little brown-skinned boy's face, Jacey wandered through the outcropping of sunbaked adobes behind Cielo Azul. Zant and Paco flanked her. Whenever they approached, a path opened for them, the folks moved aside, quieted. A few women nodded to Jacey, some even spoke, and, most surprising, a group of old men each touched two fingers to their foreheads in a sort of salute. Not sure what was expected of her, she smiled at each of them and nodded her head in return.

The shy greetings and casual acceptance of her gave Jacey a pleasant sense of well-being, one she hadn't felt since before her parents' deaths. As she walked, she breathed deeply of the invigorating morning air, thinking that in every cluttered corner of this tangled neighborhood, life went on. Her reason for being here at Cielo Azul might be a matter of life or death, but only for her. And no matter the outcome, these folks would be here to carry on.

Their lives couldn't be easy, living as they did under the constant threat of Don Rafael's whims and cruelty. But somehow she knew they'd persist in spite of him. Because they shared the strong ties of family. They had children to feed and raise, loved ones to worry about, and loved ones who'd see them through. Yes, family was everything.

Giving in to this rare and reflective mood of hers, Jacey tried to get a feel for what made this struggling existence outside Cielo Azul's walls seem so much more desirable than the tense high living that went on inside the villa. Looking around herself, moving among these proud, hardworking people, she observed the morning's chores being done and heard the women's laughing conversations in Spanish. These people belonged here. That was it.

And by accepting her, at least outwardly, they made her feel as if she belonged here, too. Smiling at the chortling babies most of the young women carried, winking at the shy toddlers clinging to their mothers' skirts, laughing with the carefree children shooting past, intent on their games, Jacey was surprised by a sudden sense of melancholy, of homesickness, that swept over her. A huge lump of emotion lodged in her throat.

A frown replaced her smile of a moment ago. Was she going to cry? What was this all about? But she knew. All the sights and sounds here, all the cheerfulness, all the simplicity of life, made her long for the good times before Mama and Papa had been killed. They'd been a real family then. A happy family.

In her mind, Jacey saw her home. The ranch house, the barn, the corrals, the meadows and the cattle. But mostly she saw the people, her loved ones. There was Mama and Biddy laughing and talking as they hung out the laundry. She saw them cooking and canning. Saw them shooing chickens from the verandah by flapping their aprons at them. Yes, they'd laughed and lived and loved. But now it was gone.

Not ever again would she have Papa's strong arms to run to and make her feel safe, to protect her, to encourage her in her wildness, much to Mama's consternation. Jacey sniffed, and knew she had to face it. She was an adult now. On her own. Responsible for her own life, her own happiness. Just like her sisters were. Thank God they still had each other and Biddy. But it wasn't the same. She wondered if her sisters felt this way, too.

She wondered if she herself would ever feel again the joy of living, the sheer high-spiritedness of being young and safe and loved. Or would it all end here?

Realizing she couldn't lay claim to the bigger happinesses right now, Jacey settled for the small ones. Like her outfit. For the first time in the three days she'd been here, she felt herself again. Her leather vest, along with her split riding skirt and blouse, had shown up, clean and pressed and folded, outside Zant's room this morning. She almost blushed again to think that maybe someone had placed her clothes there while she and Zant were . . . in bed and making a certain amount of noise.

Jacey's mind flitted away from that scene. Still, she marveled how, in the short time she'd been . . . without her virginity . . . she'd become a free-thinking woman. A smile curved her lips. And certainly one to appreciate a fine-looking man. Suddenly aware of Zant's closeness, of his tanned and muscled body that gave definition to his denims and cotton shirt, of his long-fingered hands and what he could do with them, Jacey had to take a big, openmouthed breath. Now, he was certainly a happiness she could lay claim to in the here and now. She let that same breath out.

Instantly, Zant was at her elbow. "What's wrong? Did you see him?"

With a start, Jacey realized that while she'd been drifting in thought, she'd probably passed about twenty young boys without so much as a glimpse at them. She turned away from the male-musk scent of Zant, from the crisp black chest hairs that peeked above his shirt's opening, and lied. "No, I thought it was him, but it's not."

"How do you know it's not? You said you didn't get a good look at him."

Any attraction she was feeling for him at that moment poofed into nothingness with his irritable words. She turned her face up to him. "Look, do you want me to do this, or not? I told you before that if you have something else to do, go ahead and do it. I believe I'm safe enough with Paco at my side and my own Colt strapped on. Besides, after your performance at the horse corral yesterday with Mr. Sereda, your men don't want anything to do with me. I believe they'll step around me like I'm a coiled rattler."

To her surprise—and the morning seemed full of them—Zant laughed outright. "Yes, ma'am, I'll leave you to your task. I need to talk to Blue and some of the other men, anyway. Look, I'm going to be gone for a while today. Away from Cielo Azul, I mean. Think you can stay out of trouble?"

Insulted, Jacey's Lawless temper flared. "I won't go looking for any, if that's what you mean. But I won't run from trouble, either. If it presents itself, well, I'll just have to deal with it, won't I?"

Zant's mouth twisted with exasperation. "Dammit, Jacey,

for once just—Forget it. You wouldn't listen, anyway." He grimaced and ran a hand over his mouth before going on. "You think you can make Paco understand when—if—you find the kid?"

"I think I can manage. I'll point and holler and jump up and down. Think that'll work?"

Glaring now, Zant warned, "There's no need for the sass, Jacey."

She looked him up and down. "I believe there's always a need."

"Fine. Have it your way." He then turned to Paco, spoke some Spanish, and walked away.

With Paco, Jacey watched Zant's long-legged strides carry him away from them. She looked up at her sombreroed guard. "You think I made him mad again?"

Paco nodded. *"Sí, señorita."*

For someone who didn't speak English, he sure did seem to understand everything she said. Jacey narrowed her eyes at him. "You sure you don't speak my lingo, Paco?"

The big man stared at her. He didn't nod, or shake his head, or say a word. He just stared.

Jacey decided to test him. Hands to her waist, she smiled as sweetly as she knew how and intoned, "You big, ugly Mexican son of a bitch, that stupid old hat of yours makes you look like a giant walking mushroom."

Paco remained impassive. *"Sí, señorita."*

Jacey huffed out a breath and spun on her heel. "Well, let's keep looking. The day's not getting any longer."

"Sí, señorita."

She shook her head and kept walking and looking. There must be a hundred boys in this camp. How was she ever going to find the one she'd only sort of seen? Well, at least she wasn't locked up in that stuffy room. That was one good thing—

"Mujer."

Now what? she stopped and focused on Paco. "Moo-hair? Now what does that mean?"

"Sí. Mujer." He pointed to a woman and repeated, *"Mujer."* He then pointed to an adobe. *"Casa."*

Jacey looked at the house and then back at the woman that Paco'd pointed to a moment ago. *What the*—And then she realized what he was doing. And felt really bad for having insulted him. Her guilt trembled her tentative smile. "Paco, are you trying to teach me Spanish?"

"Sí, señorita." His expression never changed. He pointed a thick finger at three little boys who ran by. *"Niños."*

"Neen-yos," Jacey dutifully repeated. Adding, "I'm sorry I called you a name and made fun of your hat, Paco. I was just . . . testing you. I didn't mean it."

"Sí, señorita," he answered. He then pointed to a broken-down buckboard wagon. *"Carreta."*

"I should've been there last night with you, Blue."

Zant watched his friend shrug and shift his weight in his saddle. "I don't know as it would've gone any different if you had. Besides"—his grin teased his solemn friend—"you had other things on your mind. Never saw a man retrace his steps like you did when I told you Don Rafael was home."

Zant laughed. "I wasn't a minute too early, either. Jacey'd just told him that they needed to cut through the horsecrap and say what they mean."

Blue's bleat of laughter bent him over his pommel. His Appaloosa mare did a sidestepping dance, which he easily controlled. "She said 'horsecrap' to the old man?"

Zant chuckled and shook his head at his blond friend. "That she did. What the hell am I going to do with her, Blue?"

"Hell, I think you ought to marry her. She's your match, sure enough."

Zant grunted. "Well, my match is back there looking for that kid who was under her bed. I can't figure out how he got in or who gave him my father's spur. I know it sure as hell wasn't the old man. If he meant to hurt Jacey with that spur, he'd hand it to her himself. That's his style." The weight of his concerns gave Zant pause. After a moment, he went on. "Damn, Blue, this is a mess. What do you think he's done to Jacey's family?"

Blue shrugged, wouldn't look at him. "All I can tell you is what you already know. He's hated J. C. Lawless since the day your mother took her own life over his killing of the Kid."

Hearing his past summed up in one sentence like that didn't affect Zant as much as did Blue's tone of voice and his not looking at him. "You know something else you're not telling me, Blue?"

Blue looked up, his eyes widened. "Hell, no. I'm not about to keep anything from you. I was just thinkin' . . . well, fearin' is more like it . . . what all this means for *you, compadre.* With Don Rafael, I mean, and aside from Jacey's reasons for being here."

Zant searched for the right words. "Every day it's looking more and more like I'm going to have to kill him. I could never control him, Blue, even if I just walked in and said I'm in charge. He's got some idea that he and I'll overthrow all the other dons in Sonora and rule some big kingdom here. He's intent on war and nothing will stop him. It's insane."

Zant drew a deep breath, let it out, and went on. "We're too different to live side by side. We don't want the same things out of life. But Blue, how can I kill my own grandfather? Or let someone else do it, either?"

Blue shook his head and looked down at his own hands. "I don't know as you can, *amigo.*"

After that, Zant gave himself up to the swaying motion of Sangre's gait over the uneven and sandy ground. The day was blessedly cool, but his mind was full, his heart heavy. He feared that with every step, with every decision, he was rushing himself and those he loved toward some inevitable cliff. And when they got to it, they would all go over. No one would survive.

A few minutes later, Blue broke the silence between them. "What're you goin' to say when we get to Villa Delarosa, Zant?"

"I'm going to tell Don Alizondo what's going on. And what I plan to do about it. I hope to convince him to sit tight and not retaliate."

Blue snorted his opinion of that. "Good luck. That old man and his five sons ought to be up in arms and marchin' this way at the head of an army of *pistoleros*—as we speak."

Zant notched his Stetson up and nodded. "I suspect they would be, if they knew who'd raided and burned their villa last night."

"Yeah, it was dark, and we had our faces covered. Still, the fire we set didn't burn much but an old outbuildin'. And no one was killed. I told Victor to tell Don Rafael otherwise. Hope that slow-headed son of a gun remembers and gets his words right. And doesn't add anything."

Zant nodded his agreement. "It could've been a lot worse last night, Blue, if I hadn't been able to convince Don Rafael not to use his hired guns on the raid. I told him they'd be recognized at Villa Delarosa. He finally accepted that and decided to go with some rank-and-file workers."

Zant looked inward for a moment, recalling that scene yesterday afternoon. He then went on. "And I don't mind telling you I'm damned thankful you were outside when he sent Sereda to ask for volunteers. I couldn't come up with an excuse to get away from the old man."

Blue shrugged. "There was no luck to it. Manuel sneaked out to the bunkhouse and alerted me. So I spread the word to men I know are loyal to you. And we raised our hands first."

Zant reined in Sangre and stared in disbelief at Blue. "Manuel? The Manuel I know—my grandfather's personal servant?"

Blue grinned. "Yep. One and the same. Seems Don Rafael made the mistake about a year ago of having Ramon Quintana use his whip on Manuel's cousin's son, Pablo. Over a stolen horse. Cut the kid to ribbons. Nearly killed him. Pablo wasn't more'n about fifteen. And family's family, you know."

Thinking, no, he didn't know, that he'd never had a family, Zant shook his head as he looked off in the cactus-dotted and rocky-hilled distance. "Quintana was a heartless bastard. I'm glad I killed him." He then sought Blue's gaze. "*Did* the boy steal the horse?"

Blue nodded. "Yep. But just so's he could sneak away and ride to Villa Delarosa to see a girl he was sweet on. He brought the horse back that evenin', no worse for wear."

Zant absorbed that and let out a breath heavy with the terrible weight of his grandfather's many transgressions. "Where's Pablo now?"

Blue grinned. "At Don Alizondo's. Some of the men took him there later that night. We told Don Rafael he'd died. The boy healed and married his sweetheart. I hear he's a pretty good broncobuster."

Zant's burden lifted a little from his heart. "Good. When we get there, point Pablo out to me. I'd like to have a few words with him."

"All right." Then, without being prompted, Blue added, "That incident was the last straw for most of the men who aren't hired guns, Zant. That was the turnin' point. They've been waitin' ever since for you to come home, for you to make it better. Out here like this—with nowhere else to go, with all the other dons havin' all the people they need—you're their only hope. They look to you to lead them in havin' better lives."

Blue's speech stunned Zant. Everything he said was true enough. Hadn't he thought the same things, hadn't he already taken some steps in that direction? But to hear it all spoken aloud . . . it made him feel, well, tied down. He cast a grim eye over the landscape. Hell, he was still on Calderon land. But this idea of being a don was still foreign to him, still not second nature.

It wasn't too late for him to just ride away. He'd done nothing so far that reeked of finality. With that thought came the realization that maybe he'd done so on purpose. Maybe it was because he doubted himself, wasn't sure of himself. Hell, he was still stumbling through his days. He still questioned every decision he made, every order he gave. Dammit, it was just too soon to hear the rest of his life laid out for him.

Zant looked over at Blue, saw the expectancy in his friend's clear-eyed and solemn gaze. Zant looked away, looked to the north. There lay freedom and independence. But the way he was headed right now? If he went on to Villa Delarosa, he was as good as declaring himself to be everything Blue said he was. A leader. A don. Responsible for all the lives in his hands. He looked at his hands. All they'd known was fighting and gunplay. Was his head any better, any cooler and wiser, than his gunhand? Could he do this?

If he did, then never again could he worry only about himself or make a decision without considering its effect on more than two hundred lives. He looked again to the north, to the Arizona Territory. A strong desire seized him to urge Sangre into a gallop that would see him far away from Cielo Azul. Then, feeling Blue still watching him, knowing he awaited his reaction to his words—in effect, his decision—Zant realized this was it.

He could turn and run. Or he could stand and fight. Which would it be? He took a deep breath, and looking forward, in the direction of Villa Delarosa, he said, "How many men you figure we can count on when things come to a head?"

Blue exhaled loudly, dramatically, drawing Zant's suddenly bemused gaze his way. Blue smiled grimly, proudly at Zant, and then shrugged, as if nothing important had just happened. "About half, as of today. Some of the other half want you to take over, but are too afraid of Don Rafael, should you lose. They could go either way. And still others, along with all those hired guns, are Don Rafael's men. And will remain so."

Blue was quiet for a moment. Zant thought he was done, but then his friend added, "You can't wait much longer to act, Zant. Not more than a few days, a week at most. Last night's raid was only the first of many. Too many more of those, and someone *will* get killed. And then, no one will be able to stop the fightin'." Blue turned in his saddle to look Zant fully in the face. "The time is here. It's now or never."

Blue's words pushed Zant's new resolve heavily against his heart. "Dammit, Blue, why didn't you tell me any of this before? Why not that first time when I was here after getting out of jail?"

Blue's sincere blue eyes hardened and forgave in the same expression. "I did try. I did mention it to you that night I had you come out to the corral. Remember? That was the same night Paco surprised you with his English and called you *jefe*."

Zant thought back. The memory flooded him. "Damned if you didn't. And I just let it pass. What the hell was wrong with me?"

Blue made a dismissive noise. "Don't be so hard on yourself. You just weren't ready to hear it. You were still too restless to settle down, too mad at the world. Not that I blame you. If someone had framed me and got me thrown in jail, I'd find the—"

"That's exactly what I intend to do, when all this is over. If I'm still alive. Someone will talk or brag. And when I know who, I'm going to kill him."

Blue nodded his agreement, but then gave Zant a speculative look and frowned, acting as if he weren't at all sure if he should say what was on his mind. Zant saved him his doubts. "Spit it out."

Blue's eyes widened, but then he settled his features into respectful lines. "All right, I will. I'm just . . . well, I'm just glad that you're here *now*. That's all that counts. And I'm glad you've . . . grown into the man you are. I was afraid you'd never realize your responsibility to your home. And to your people."

My home. My people. An overwhelming emotion seized Zant's heart. His throat working, he quickly turned his head and blinked his eyes at the desert landscape. Without looking back at his friend, and hating the husky tone in his own voice, he asked, "What makes you so sure I can do this, Blue? What if I can't? What if I'm not ready . . . or able?"

"You are."

Blue's quiet words made Zant turn to face him. But seeing the serious, proud, almost worshipful look now on his friend's face, and fearing what he was preparing to do, Zant tightened his hand around the reins, clamped down on his back teeth, and fought to stay dry-eyed. He then gritted out, "Don't do this, Blue. I'm not ready for this. Not from you."

"You are ready." His eyes filling with moisture, Blue fisted his right hand over his heart, held it there, and looked Zant right in the eye. "My life is yours . . . *mi jefe.*"

Back at Cielo Azul, standing in front of her daughter's adobe, Conchita was frantic. No one was here. Most probably Blanca had little Teresa and Pedro with her while she helped the other women with the villa's laundry. Not knowing if something horrible was already happening to her firstborn grandson, Conchita decided there was no time to look for Blanca. Besides, she would only be hysterical and no help at all in finding Esteban. Especially when Conchita told her what she'd had him do last night.

So, hands on her mouth, her rapidly graying black hair slowly loosening itself from its bun, she looked right and left. Where could Esteban be? He wasn't at home. He wasn't with his friends. He didn't come when she called him. When she found him, when she knew he was okay, she would hug him and then turn him over her knee. How could he scare her, an old woman, like this?

And, she asked herself, *why am I standing here like simple-minded Victor? Oh, Victor, you idiot!* Conchita trundled off again, her short legs pumping as fast as her heart. She made another circuit of the adobe camp. At the end of it, again standing in front of her daughter's house, she had to admit that Esteban was nowhere to be found. Holding her hands again to her plump face, she swayed from side to side and singsonged, "Ay-yi-yi-yi-yi," as she tried to decide what to do next.

Señor Zant? Gone. And Señor Blue was with him. Those two had picked a terrible time to leave. Then, there was no help for it. She'd have to find Señorita Lawless and tell her. But the first problem to be overcome was the little gringa's not speaking Spanish. Another face popped into her head. Paco! Señorita Lawless was with Paco. He knew some English. He wouldn't want to use it, not in front of the señorita, because Señor Zant had told him not to, but she would make him. This was an emergency.

The boy did not exist. Giving up, hot and thirsty, but richer in Spanish words, Jacey flopped down on one of a group of chairs that, at home, would have been kindling by now. But here, close to the big horse barn, somebody'd left them leaned up against an equally rickety old shed. All around her busy men carried on with their work, essentially ignoring her and her guard.

Breathing in the maturing scents of manure, hay, and horse, Jacey used her forearm to shield her eyes from the midday sun. Squinting up at Paco, she spoke over the neighing and hammering and laughing coming from inside the barn. "Are you as tired and thirsty as I am?"

"Sí, señorita."

"You know, Paco, I'm beginning to think that *niño* doesn't exist. I need to rest a bit. Why don't you pull up a *silla* and sit here with me?"

"Sí, señorita." But he stood in place, unmoving.

Jacey sniffed and quirked her mouth, thinking she'd give anything if Rosie were here with her to translate this infernal language. Still peering up at Paco, she added, "How about some *agua*, then? I know—*'Sí, señorita.'* Just go find us a drink, please."

"Sí, señorita." Her big guard turned away, apparently and surprisingly going in search of water. And leaving her here alone. Had he and she reached a higher level of trust? Just then, Paco turned and faced her again. Squinting and grimacing in a way that warned he wouldn't be disobeyed, he pointed to the ground and said, "Stay here."

Jacey nodded fatalistically. "Sure, I'll stay here. Where else am I going to—" She froze, her mouth still open to form "go." She seemed capable of moving only her eyes in their sockets. She swiveled her gaze up to Paco's reddening face. And recovered her power of speech. "Did I just hear you say something in English?"

He blanked his expression. *"No, señorita."*

"Aha! You just gave the right answer." Jacey jumped up, shaking her finger in his face. "Why, you old faker. You do speak English." She remembered all the terrible things she'd said to him in the past few days. She withdrew her accusing finger and lowered her arm to her side. "Oh. You speak English."

"Un poco." He held his thumb and index finger up about an inch apart.

Jacey cocked her head questioningly. "What's that mean . . . 'a little'?"

Paco smiled broadly at her. "*Sí.* A little."

Jacey put her hands to her waist. "Well, I'll be damned, Paco."

Paco nodded and pointed to himself. "*Y yo tambien.* And I too will be damned, *señorita*."

Jacey laughed out loud at this suddenly lively guard of hers. Just then, Paco went grim and yanked his gun out of its holster. Jacey's jaw dropped.

"¡Cuidado, señorita! ¡Venga aquí!" Paco fanned the air with his big paw of a hand, as if urging her to come to him.

"What?" But then she knew what. Someone grabbed her arm, she cried out, and was spun around. She drew back in shocked surprise. "Conchita! What's wrong?" She then grabbed the red-faced, out-of-breath woman's arms to steady her.

The short, heavyset maid sucked in air, held on to Jacey, and spat out Spanish faster than Zant could draw his gun. She was clearly scared to death about something, but Jacey felt helpless to understand her. She finally remembered Paco. "Come here, Paco. Tell me what she's saying."

Paco stepped up, his gun holstered, and spoke with Conchita. He listened, nodded, looked around, turned mighty grim, and shook his head. Jacey became nearly as frantic as her maid. She let go of Conchita to tug on Paco's sleeve. "What'd she say?"

Conchita quieted, looking in supplication and hope up at Paco. Jacey frowned, scared of what could be happening, what with Zant and Blue gone. But whatever it was, she was on her own with it. She bit down on her bottom lip when Paco began speaking to her in very hesitant and broken English phrases. "Conchita . . . *¿que dice?* . . . um, say her *nieto,* her grandson Esteban, is . . . gone. She looked and looked. But he is nowhere."

Jacey slumped in relief. "Everybody's somewhere, Paco." A missing boy. That wasn't too terrible. She could handle that. After all, wasn't she herself . . . sudden suspicion caused her eyes to narrow at Conchita . . . looking for a missing boy, too? She directed her gaze back to Paco. "What else did she say? Why would she come to me with this, and why wouldn't she have the whole camp helping her look?"

Paco exchanged a look with Conchita, who suddenly looked down at the ground. Jacey put her hands to her waist and waited. Paco shifted his considerable weight and began. "*Porque* Esteban is, um, in . . . troubles plenty. With Don Rafael. Conchita say Esteban gave to you the, um, *espuela*"—he lifted his booted foot and pointed to his spur—"and now Don Rafael will know. She also say Victor is an idiot."

Jacey had no idea who Victor was or why he was an idiot. Nor did she care. Her shock at learning Conchita's grandson had placed the spur on her bed was so great that all she could do was stare straight ahead. Her hands fisted over her heart, she tried to think her way through all this. She then turned to Conchita, knowing the woman spoke no English, but still feeling a need to put her questions to the source. "Let me get this straight. Your grandson gave me the spur?" She pulled it out of her pocket and pointed to it. A wide-eyed Conchita nodded. Jacey repocketed it. "Where'd he get it?"

Without prompting, Paco translated her words for Conchita. She gave a short answer. Paco turned to Jacey. "She say he got it from her."

Numb now, Jacey nodded her head. "And where'd she get it?"

Paco put the question to the maid and listened to her answer. "Don Rafael's *oficina.*"

Jacey recognized that word without a translation. "His office. Ask her if there was anything else in there. Like a small picture."

Paco'd done no more than nod before a deep and cultured voice behind them answered Jacey's question. "Yes, there is. Would you care to see it?"

With Paco and Conchita, Jacey spun around. There stood Don Rafael. Flanking him was the sly, grinning Miguel Sereda and some big *pistolero* whose mouth slacked open and who stared at them dully. At least their guns weren't drawn.

Still, Jacey's mouth dried, her insides cringed. She was aware of Conchita grabbing her arm and all but whispering, "*Dios mio, señorita. Esteban.*" Jacey's knees threatened to buckle at Conchita's words. But still she kept her unwavering gaze on the old man. And the third person with him.

Don Rafael's hand was clamped firmly on the shoulder of a boy, a very scared and shaking boy, of about nine years old.

Jacey finally found her voice. "Let him go, let them all go"—she indicated Paco and Conchita—"and I'll come with you."

Don Rafael chuckled and shook a finger at her. "You make me laugh, as always, señorita. But you forget you are a guest here. Therefore you do not give the orders. I do. And my first order is for you and Paco to unbuckle your gunbelts and toss them away from you." He repeated his order in Spanish for Paco and then waited silently as they both complied.

His next words were in English. "That is good. Very good. Now, unfortunately, I cannot allow Esteban to go. Or Paco and Conchita. They have proven they are not to be trusted, and so, they must be punished." He snapped his fingers. "Miguel, Victor."

The two men stepped around Don Rafael. Victor picked up the two discarded gunbelts while Miguel took Esteban from his boss. The men then drew their guns and waved them at Conchita and Paco. Those two stepped away from Jacey and stood in a knot with Esteban. The boy began sobbing and clutched at his grandmother. She took him in her arms and stared wide-eyed and frightened at Jacey.

Frustrated and foiled, Jacey turned her glare on Zant's grandfather. "Harm any one of them, and you'll pay, Mr. Calderon. I swear you will. As long as I'm alive, I'll—"

"Uh-uh, señorita." He wagged a finger at her. "I would think by now you would realize you cannot make threats of vengeance that you have no hope of carrying out. It is very reckless of you to do so."

Having thus warned her, all trace of humor left his face. "Now, so far I have been patient. But no more. You will come with me now, or Miguel will, regretfully, have to shoot Conchita—in front of the boy. The choice is yours."

Chapter Nineteen

The night was cool, the sky clear, the moon full. Stars winked down from the black canopy of the heavens. But no soft wind stirred. No owl hooted. No coyote yowled. The ragged pinnacles of the surrounding mountains peered over the high adobe walls of Cielo Azul. Nesting against those same walls, the small adobe houses of the camp, with its all-but-deserted streets, seemed to crouch in silence. And wait.

Inside the villa itself, in the bedroom where Paco'd previously guarded her, Jacey sat alone and scared on the four-poster bed. With nothing but worries to occupy her time, she stared at the locked door. She could hear, out in the hall, every movement of her new guard, a most unsociable man with one eye and a knife-scarred face. And a big gun. Relieved of her own gun that afternoon by Miguel Sereda, and escorted here by her unfailingly pleasant host, she'd spent the afternoon by herself. Locked up. And praying for Zant's return. Where could he be?

Too, she could only wonder what had become of Paco, Conchita, and Esteban. Were they even still alive? Her heart thumping leadenly, Jacey closed her eyes and sent her prayer heavenward. *Please, God, let them be alive. And send Zant home in a hurry. I could really use him right now. But please don't let him get hurt. I couldn't stand that. But if he doesn't make it back here in time, then, God, find some way to let him know how much I loved him. Amen. Oh, and my sisters, too. And Biddy. Tell them too that I loved them. Amen again.*

Opening her eyes, blinking against the sudden wetness and blurring of her vision, Jacey looked down at herself and grimaced, fisting her hand around the delicate material of her skirt. Those danged maids. She shook her head at the events that had taken place earlier at sundown, in this very room. Three maids, none of whom she knew, had entered. Six big men had followed them, hauling up the bathtub and buckets of hot water.

Seeing what was about to happen, she'd thrown enough of a tantrum to gain for herself the few moments of privacy it took her to undress herself behind the screen—and to hide her knife inside one of her boots.

But after that, the chattering women had been all over her like cows on clover. They'd proceeded to bathe her and rub scented oils on her skin. They'd then stuffed her into a score of underclothes, which they topped off with what was, she had to admit, the prettiest and fanciest dress she'd ever seen.

Once they'd poked and stuffed and hooked her into the purple-reddish gown, they'd sat her down, settled a combing jacket over her shoulders, and then begun torturing her hair. After a vigorous, eye-watering brushing, the three hens had settled on a style that wrenched all her black hair up in a ponytail knot that allowed a heap of curls to hang free over her shoulders.

She'd reached the end of her rope when they fetched about twenty yards of ribbon and began trying to tie bows all through the curls. Silliest thing she'd ever heard of. Jacey grinned wickedly. She'd let them know exactly what she thought of such folderol. Those three witches had run screaming from the room when she'd begun yelling and shoving them. Enough was enough!

Except for when it came to this gown. She yanked now at the scandalously low, scalloped bodice. But to no avail. There just was no material to spare. She gave up, flopping her hands onto her lap. Her barely covered bosom rose and fell with each agitated breath. Jacey watched her mounded flesh and wondered why she'd been trussed up as fancy as a fir tree at Christmas. Were killings around here formal affairs? Or did that Don Rafael have other plans for her? Plans that had nothing to do with a sit-down supper . . . and more to do with the pleasure of her, uh, company?

Zant's words from last night, about Don Rafael having his eye on her, came back to haunt Jacey. She put a hand over the stuttering beat of her heart and tried to take a deep breath around the sudden constriction in her chest. But the corset and gown were too tight for any but the shallowest of breaths. Still, she jutted out her chin and narrowed her eyes, vowing she'd die first before she'd allow Don Rafael to put a hand on her. She'd die, or he would.

As if Fate meant to give her a chance to find out which ending was her destiny, the key turned in the lock. Jacey sat stock-still and stared. The door swung inward. *I swear, Zant, I'll stay alive. I'll do whatever it takes. I won't die. I love you. Please hear me. And please hurry. I need you.* Old One-eye stood there, grinning like he'd heard her prayers and laughed at them.

Gathering courage from fisting her hand over the hidden sheath strapped again to her thigh, Jacey raised her head. "What do you want, you ugly lizard?"

Old One-eye, who obviously spoke no English, remained grinning. *"Venga, señorita."* He crooked a finger at her in a come-here motion.

Raising an eyebrow, Jacey remained seated, her hands folded tightly in her lap. "Kiss my gelding's ass."

One-eye nodded. *"Sí. Venga."*

"I'll *venga,* all right," she muttered. Jacey forced herself to stand up. Walking over to One-eye, as if stepping onto a scaffolding that sported a noose in her neck size, she said, "Lead the way, you mother's nightmare. There's nothing that can happen to me that'll be any worse than you look."

Again, no response from her guard. He turned and preceded her down the long hallway. A few steps behind him, Jacey began her litany of courage. *I love you, Zant. I love you. I love you. Please hurry home. Please be in time.*

Zant reined in Sangre atop a hill that overlooked Cielo Azul. "You feel that, Blue?"

Blue pulled back on his Appaloosa mare's reins and shook his head. "Feel what—the cool air? Nice, ain't it?"

"Not the air." Zant gave himself over to the gut-deep unease that gripped him. "Something else."

"Like what?" Blue's movements in his saddle creaked the well-worn leather.

"It's too quiet. Down in the compound. Listen."

Zant watched as Blue did just that. Then, frowning, his blue-eyed friend turned to him. "Damned if you're not right. What do you make of it?"

Zant drew in a deep breath, letting it out in a low whistle. "Trouble, that's what. Something's happened while we've been gone. I can feel it. *Damn.* We put out one fire at Villa Delarosa, only to have a bigger one crop up at home."

Blue was quiet for a minute, but then spoke his mind. "Assuming you're right, and I think you are, what d'you want to do?"

Zant shrugged. "I'm not sure. All I've got is a hunch, and that's not much to go on. Hell, I could be completely wrong. It could just be a quiet night."

Blue looked askance at him. "You don't believe that for a minute, do you?"

Grim, Zant shook his head. "No, I don't." What he didn't give voice to was his worst fear, that this trouble had something to do with Jacey.

Blue exhaled sharply. "You think it could be all over, and we're just riding into the tag end of it?"

Zant gazed down on the quiet of Cielo Azul. "No. Could be they've done their dirty work, and now they're in place and waiting. For me. I must be the missing piece. Otherwise, there'd be celebrating going on down there."

It wasn't much, but it was his only hope that Jacey might still be alive. If she was the carrot being used to lure him in, then they'd need her alive. Maybe if he kept thinking, *She's alive, she's alive,* the thought would make it true. God help them if it wasn't.

Zant felt Blue staring at him and met his friend's eyes. When Blue reached a hand out and squeezed Zant's arm, he looked down at it. Blue's quiet words sounded loud in the night's calm. "She's okay, Zant. They wouldn't dare hurt her."

Zant clenched his jaw until it hurt. "I hope you're right."

Blue drew his hand back and considered the silent compound below. His tone, when he spoke, was the impersonal one of a general scanning a battlefield for its strengths and weaknesses. "There's hardly a guard posted. Not even a dog out in the arena. Only a few lights shining. And those are in the villa." He straightened up, looking at Zant. "So how d'you want to handle it?"

Zant urged Sangre into a walk. Blue did the same with his mare. After a few paces, Zant told him, "We go in nice and easy. Gun drawn and stuck in your waistband. Fold your duster around it to hide it. And proceed right through the front gates."

From his right came Blue's softly spoken answer. "I'm with you, *jefe*. But don't you think we ought to go in the back way, by the camp's gate?"

Looking straight ahead as he pulled his duster back and drew his Colt, Zant shook his head. "Nope. That's exactly what they'd expect. I won't sneak into my own home. If they're going to kill me, they're going to have to do it out in the open, by God."

It was worse than he'd thought. But better than he'd feared. No one challenged him and Blue at Cielo Azul's main entrance. The heavy mesquite-wood gates swung open at their slow approach. Inside, there was no bloody scene to greet them. No bodies littered the ground. But not one of the guards looked him or Blue in the eye or greeted them.

They didn't have to, because Zant recognized the men. They were some of his own. And they never operated the gates. Where then were Don Rafael's men? Ranged around the central arena and hidden, their rifles trained on him and Blue?

Zant's men's tight expressions sent him the only message he needed. Don Rafael was still firmly in control. After exchanging a look with Blue outside the villa's front door, Zant dismounted and handed him Sangre's reins. Zant watched him go, knowing Blue'd make directly for the bunkhouses and find out what was going on. He'd then handle things outside the villa—and would watch Zant's back when the time came.

Just then, the front door opened, flooding Zant in light. He tensed, his hand on the Colt stuck in his waistband. But he relaxed when he saw Manuel standing there. The man's expression was grim as an undertaker's, but he bowed Zant in, closed the door behind him, and spoke quietly. "Supper has been held for you, Señor Chapelo. Don Rafael and the Señorita Lawless await you in the salon."

Zant nearly slumped against the wall. *Jacey's alive.* Keeping his relief to himself, he merely nodded and removed his Stetson. As if the gesture helped him think, he ran a hand through his hair and cast his gaze down the hall to the salon. He then turned to the silent, waiting Manuel and grabbed the Mexican man's arm. Pulling him closer, he whispered, "What the hell has happened here, Manuel?"

Manuel's dark eyes held the same look the gatemen's had. He looked all around the foyer, as if hidden ears listened. He then spoke rapidly. "I am not at liberty to say, señor. Just, please, hurry and change."

Zant considered the servant a moment, then let go of him and sighted down the long hall to the open arch of the salon. He didn't need to change clothes for what he had to do. He took a step in that direction, but Manuel's hand on his arm stopped him. This had never happened before. He looked down at the short man.

"Please, señor. Go upstairs and change."

Zant gritted his teeth in impatience and frowned. "Why in the hell is what I wear so important?"

Manuel's expression reflected a desperate urgency. "It is not your attire so much, señor, as it is what awaits you in your room. You must go there first. I can say no more."

With that, he hurried away. Zant watched him go and considered the man's words. Knowing now that Manuel was sympathetic to his cause, Zant figured the man wouldn't urge him to go upstairs if he was going to be ambushed. But wait—was his repeated insistence that he go upstairs a warning in itself? After all, he'd seen the gun in Zant's waistband. And too, if Manuel'd been coached to send him upstairs, and hidden eyes watched to see that he did, then hadn't his face and gestures warned of his reception?

Zant looked up the long curving stretch of stairway. And then cast another glance toward the very quiet salon. His gnawing fear told him to get the hell in there. But Manuel insisted. . . . Zant looked again to the stairs and made his decision. Resettling his Stetson on his head, he pulled his Colt out of his waistband, kept close to the wall, and began his cautious ascent to the second floor. *All right, Manuel, but this better be important.*

* * *

"Ahh, Señorita Lawless, I hear Manuel speaking with someone. Perhaps my grandson has returned at long last. If it is him, I'm sure he will join us soon. And then we can all dine together."

Oh, thank you, God. Thank you. Letting out her breath, Jacey gave no other outward sign of her intense relief that Zant was here. Instead, she kept her poker-face gaze on her host and retorted, "Did you say dine or die?"

Señor Chapelo chuckled and shook his head. "One little letter to make such a difference, eh? I of course said 'dine.' "

When quiet descended on them, Jacey lowered her gaze to her skirt and smoothed the fabric, resettling folds and pleats. No way was she going to initiate polite conversation. If he wanted to talk to her, he could darn well open his mouth.

"Tell me, Señorita Lawless, how are your lovely sisters?"

Fear lanced through Jacey's gut and stilled her hands. She looked up, meeting the don's far-from-innocent expression. "Fine."

"Ahhh. They are fine. You know this, eh? Which reminds me, I believe I have been remiss in offering my condolences to you on the recent and tragic deaths of your parents. You must be deeply saddened."

You no-good, rotten, guilty-as-hell, son of a— "I am."

In the salon, seated across from her in his leather chair, Don Rafael crossed an ankle over his opposite knee. "As you say. And yet, here you are at Cielo Azul. Why?" He suddenly sat forward and pointed a finger at her. "And I want none of your sass and games this time, young lady."

Before she could temper her response, Jacey shot forward in her uncomfortable seat. "Games? The games are all of your making—playing the polite host, calling me your guest, making me wear these fancy dresses. But that's over. No more. I'm here because someone who works for you stole from me on the same day my folks were killed. But that yahoo made the mistake of leaving something that led me here. A piece of Kid Chapelo's spur. And the rest of that spur was in your office. So don't try to tell me you know nothing about it. Because you and I both know you're lying when you say otherwise."

Breathing hard, her lip curled in a snarl, Jacey held the old man's gaze. What she saw shining from those eyes scared her.

She recognized that her enemy was much more than cruel and ambitious. He wasn't even insane. He was evil. She'd thought it before, had even said it before. But not until this moment had she realized just what it meant.

Don Rafael's grim expression slowly changed to a knowing grin. Had he read her thoughts? "What exactly is it that you think I'm guilty of?"

Jacey sat back in her chair and gripped the armrests. "I hate to admit it to the likes of you, but I don't know yet. I just know you're guilty of . . . something."

"Of something. I see. Well, that's certainly enough to have me shot or hanged. I'm guilty of something, and you yourself—my accuser—admit you have no idea what." Through narrowed eyes, he considered her a moment, as if chewing on some thought. Then, he perked up and raised a finger. "I have it. Question me. Let's see where this leads. Perhaps we can clear up this whole misunderstanding."

Jacey's heart leaped. This was a trap. Her calculating thoughts narrowed her eyes. Aha. He'd brought up *her* family, knowing that would hurt the most. *Let's see how you like a dose of your own medicine.* "Good idea. Tell me about your wife, Zant's grandmother. What was she like?" *And how could she ever have loved a bastard like you?*

The old don tented his fingers together and looked thoughtfully up at the ceiling. "Ah, yes, my wife. Elena." He lowered his head and leveled his sharp stare on Jacey. "She was Spanish nobility, of course. Her family and mine arranged the marriage. We never met before she arrived for our wedding. She was beautiful, very young, very gently raised. Unfortunately, the harsh . . . rigors of life at Cielo Azul did not suit her health. She had the good grace to give me a daughter before she died. I never remarried."

Saddened for the girl and horrified at Don Rafael's callous words, Jacey sat up straighter. But feeling she was on the right track, that there was something here to uncover, something important, she persisted. "Tell me about your daughter. She died in an untimely manner, didn't she?"

Bull's eye. Don Rafael visibly tensed. But he nodded his agreement and gave every appearance of being calm and relaxed. "My daughter. Miranda. So much like her mother. Such a tragic figure. Despite my best efforts to see her married well, she had the poor judgment to fancy herself in love with a common outlaw, such as your father was. She saw him behind my back. And even bore Kid Chapelo's bastard when he wouldn't marry her."

He paused, as if he thought she'd like to defend her father. Jacey made sure her expression didn't change. Acknowledging her refusal to quibble, Don Rafael went on. "For two more years after Zant's birth, the Kid mistreated her. But she wouldn't come home, or allow me to help her in any way. Then, about a year after your father killed the Kid, when Zant was only three, my daughter took her own life. I then took in my little grandson, my only heir, and raised him as best I could. He is the only person I have ever loved."

Jacey never looked away. She heard the warning note in his voice with his last words. He'd not allow her, a common outlaw's daughter, to take his grandson away from him. With that realization came another. Don Rafael was being so forthcoming with his family history, he was answering all her questions, even encouraging her to ask them . . . because he didn't plan on her ever leaving Cielo Azul. Alive, anyway.

A trickle of sweat coursed slowly down between her bound breasts. Well, then, she didn't have anything left to lose, did she? Wanting to hurt him as much as he'd hurt her family, she blurted out the very first thing to pop into her head. "It's ironic—isn't it, Don Rafael?—how life seems to turn in circles. Your daughter gave birth to a bastard, as you called your only heir. His father was, as you say, a common outlaw. And now"—Jacey paused to laugh softly, as if at the irony of it all—"here I sit. The daughter of the common outlaw who killed your Miranda's one true love."

Don Rafael sat forward, looking like a wolf preparing to kill. "I'd advise you to make your point, Señorita Lawless." He all but spat her name.

Feeling the power had shifted, that she was now in control, Jacey smiled. "Be patient. I've had to be for nearly three months. Surely you can wait three minutes? Now, as I was saying, here I sit. Unmarried. Your grandson's lover."

"And the mother of my child."

Jacey jerked toward the salon's portal. *Mother of his child? Has he lost his mind?* From the corner of her eye, she saw

Don Rafael shoot to his feet. Sputtering and gasping sounds were all that issued from him.

But her attention stayed riveted on Zant, who continued when he had their attention. "Yes, Don Rafael. Another Calderon bastard. Or so it would seem. But certainly nothing is as it seems here, is it?"

Zant was dressed in the same denims and shirt he'd had on that morning. His revolver dangled from his hand, as if forgotten. But it was his face, his strong and handsome and beloved face, that brought her hand to her heart. As if just forced open against a too-bright light, his black eyes squinted with pain. Under his tanned and wind-lined complexion, she detected a pallor, an ashen grayness. His firm, down-turned mouth was limned in white.

An emotion, stronger than relief at seeing him, stronger even than the love she bore him, tugged at Jacey, making her ache with the need to hold him and protect him. She intuitively knew he'd just learned or gone through something that was tearing him apart. And from the way he stared unblinking at his grandfather, she also knew that Don Rafael was the cause of it.

With a swish and a rustling of her elaborate gown, Jacey came slowly to her feet. She knotted her hands at her waist, looking from Zant, who all but ignored her, to Don Rafael. He too looked only at Zant. The air thickened with the hate and hurt that radiated from them both. If she were able to make her feet move, Jacey knew she would flee from the room. Because something was happening here, something that had nothing to do with her.

But before she could make a move, the old man took an angry stride toward her. Jacey retreated, hitting her legs against the chair behind her. She fell against it, clutching at its high back for support. A gun was cocked. Wide-eyed, Jacey jerked in the direction of the sound. Zant had his revolver pointed at his grandfather.

"Stop right there. Or I'll shoot you where you stand. So help me God, I will." His voice could have been coming from upstairs, so vacant did it sound.

Jacey stayed frozen in place, and Don Rafael stopped where he was. His mouth worked futilely, but he finally found his voice. "My grandson, my heart of hearts, you would shoot me? After everything I have done for you? All of this that my family before me and, now I, have built—it will be yours. You do not want to shoot me. Not over her."

He pointed to Jacey but kept his gaze on Zant. "We can rid ourselves of her. It is not too late. Think of it—there is no child born yet. And look at her. She is a slut, a nobody, an outlaw's daughter. She would lie with dogs. She cannot be the mother of a Calderon. She is not worthy, and I won't allow it."

"*You* won't allow it? What you want doesn't matter. And she's a thousand times the person you are. So take a good look at her. Go ahead. This is the woman I love. In her belly is the future of the noble Calderons of Spain. Even as we speak, my son grows big and strong inside her. And he is a little bastard—like you made me think I was all my life. So, don't talk to me about everything you've done for me. You've done nothing but hurt and kill."

Jacey gasped, along with Don Rafael. Had Zant gone plumb loco? None of this made sense. She was not carrying his baby. And he knew it. And all this talk about bastards . . . or thinking he was one. What had he found out?

A subtle movement of Don Rafael's alerted Jacey. She pushed away from the chair and locked her gaze on the old man. The mask of gentility, of civility, was gone. His naked expression made her heart pound, made her palms slick with sweat.

With spittle forming at the edges of his snarling mouth, he started for her. Jacey had time only to stiffen and cry out before he was upon her.

She heard Zant yell a warning. But with the mighty roar of a bear, Don Rafael swung his heavy arm back and came down with all his strength, his huge hand catching her across her cheek. Her head snapped back, the side of her face exploded in pain, her ear rang with the force of the blow.

Shocked into numbness, with time moving forward at blinding speed, Jacey heard the sharp report of her head hitting the stone fireplace. Or maybe it was the deadly bark of Zant's gun. But then, it ceased to matter as she fell to the floor in a silk and taffeta heap. The light slipped away from her.

* * *

The bullet from Zant's gun pinged harmlessly off the fireplace. But Zant's heart hit the floor with Jacey. The way her neck snapped with the force of the old man's blow. The sickening thunk as her head hit the fireplace. The crumpled, unmoving, broken-doll heap she was now. As little as she was, she couldn't have survived such an attack. Don Rafael had killed her.

Momentarily stunned by the swiftness of his grandfather's strike against her, Zant could only stand and stare. But finally, every nerve ending in his body came to life. He stung, he burned, he raged with the need to hurt. Zant leveled his revolver on Don Rafael. He cocked the gun. This time, he wouldn't miss.

He looked the scared old man in the eye. And knew this twisted monster deserved to die. But suddenly, without warning, Zant's limbs felt weak, his heart drained of hateful revenge. Because it just didn't matter anymore. Not if Jacey was dead. None of this, not Cielo Azul, not the people here, not being the *jefe,* not leading a life that counted for something. None of it mattered without her.

He now realized, like never before, that he'd wanted to make something good happen at Cielo Azul . . . for her. He'd been trying to make himself worthy of her. But if he couldn't have her, then none of it mattered. He'd walk away, go back to the boozing and the women and the gunfights. Until finally, someday, a better gun than him would come along and blessedly take his life.

Without being aware that he was going to do it, Zant lowered his gun and spoke. Even to his own ears his voice sounded blank, flat. "You killed her. Move away from her. Now."

Don Rafael made an imploring gesture with his entire crouching body, as he callously, casually stepped over Jacey, as if she were no more than a kitten killed by a wolf. "Think, Zant. It's over now. We can bury her and go on as before. Only this time, we'll—"

"Say no more!" Zant sprang forward, covering the few feet between them as if they were mere inches. With his pistol still in his fist, he grabbed Don Rafael by his shoulders and flung him aside. His grandfather sprawled onto his leather chair. Zant pointed a finger at him. "Get out of my sight, you evil son of a bitch. In fact, clear out of Cielo Azul. If I see your face again, I'll kill you. And I don't want to do that because there's still something left of my soul, something good and forgiving, despite your years of trying to kill it."

With that, Zant turned away from his grandfather and knelt beside Jacey. He laid his gun down on the floor, pulled her away from the fireplace, and gently turned her over. His heart all but stopped. A thin line of blood trickled from her temple, her mouth slacked open, her black eyes were rolled back in her head. A tortured sob tore from the depths of Zant's soul. He pulled her limp body against his chest and held her there.

Not even the sounds of Don Rafael stirring behind him could make him look up. Jacey was still so warm, so soft. Maybe she wasn't dead.

Just as Zant found her pulse, just as joy spread through him, an explosion of pain in his head sent him sprawling forward atop Jacey.

Chapter Twenty

Manuel heard the gunshot in the salon. Hand to his mouth, his eyes widened, he looked from one servant's face to the other in the dining room with him. They silently pleaded with him. Manuel began herding them all outside. Panicked, they nevertheless grouped together and fled out through the courtyard. There they silently parted for Manuel, allowing him the lead. Then, as one, they raced for the heavy gate to the camp.

Manuel fought the slowing effects of fear on his starved lungs and pumping heart. He raced on. By the time he reached the gate set in the adobe walls, the only thing that kept him going when his legs wanted to collapse was his determination to reach Señor Blue. That and the herd of servants pushing him from behind. Tearing his flesh in his haste to open the gate, Manuel kept telling himself that Señor Blue would know what to do.

Upstairs, on the villa's second floor, Conchita, Paco, and Esteban all jumped at the echo of a gunshot from downstairs. Esteban clutched tighter at his grandmother. She looked to Paco. He gave her the signal they'd worked out earlier. She was to hide with the boy on the bed's far side. Conchita nodded and complied. Paco took up his place behind the room's door. From this position, he had the slim chance of surprising their guard, should this be the beginning of the end and he came in to carry out his orders.

Giving them added hope of living through the night was the knowledge that Señor Zant was home. But he was downstairs. They'd both heard him, seemingly only minutes before, speaking gruffly to their guard before his echoing footsteps told them he'd gone on to his room. But then, less than a minute later, he'd stalked back by their door, without hesitating, and had proceeded down the stairs. Had he fired the shot? Or had he been shot?

They had no way of knowing. They could only hope and do what they could to save themselves. So, tense and alert, the adults waited for the sound of the key turning in the lock. If this was truly the beginning of the *revolución,* and if Señor Zant was still alive, he may not have a chance to send someone to free them before one-eyed Norona, their guard, could kill them all.

Those were his orders. If trouble started, he was to kill them all three.

Down in the salon, Don Rafael stared down at the limp bodies of his grandson and the Lawless bitch. His fingers clutched Zant's pistol. The old man bent over to feel for a pulse. He found one, a good and strong one, in Zant's neck. Good. He'd hit him on the head only hard enough to knock him out, which was his intention. But sometimes, he didn't know his own strength.

How had it come to this? He shook his head. He had to save the boy from himself. And from this woman. He gazed at her, cocking his head from side to side. Was she really dead? On an impulse, he reached under Zant and felt her neck. A pulse beat there as well.

Don Rafael's eyes narrowed. The Lawlesses did not die easily. He raised the pistol, aiming it at Jacey's head. But just then, the front door opened. He jerked toward the sound. If they knew what was good for them, it had better be Miguel and Victor. They were late. If they'd been on time, none of this would have been necessary. Sure of himself and of the Colt fisted in his hand, Don Rafael hurried to the room's entry and peered down the hall. It was them.

Stepping out into their view, and frowning his displeasure at their lateness, he spat out, "Where have you been?"

Miguel opened his mouth, but then closed it, looking from Don Rafael's face to his right hand. To the gun. He frowned as he strode purposefully down the hall. As always, Victor was right behind him. "What has happened here, Don Rafael? Have you killed them?"

"No. They're alive. Help me get Zant upstairs before he awakens. Victor, you will stand guard over him. And Miguel, you will bring the woman and come with me." With that, Don Rafael turned and entered the salon.

On his heels, the two men rounded the corner, but while Don Rafael proceeded over to the two unconscious bodies by the fireplace, Miguel and Victor stopped where they were. And stared. Don Rafael turned back to them.

He watched them exchange a glance with each other. Then, without comment, they strode over to him. Victor easily lifted Zant, tossing him across his broad and heavy shoulder. Once Zant was lifted off his lover, his body no longer protecting hers, Miguel scooped her into his arms and stood with his burden. They both faced their chief, awaiting his next order.

"Victor, take Zant to his room, put him on the bed, and then find the key and lock the door. You watch him closely and you stay with him until I tell you differently. Do you understand that?"

Victor nodded dully and walked heavily across the room with his burden. He turned left, in the direction of the stairs to the second floor, and disappeared from view.

Satisfied, Don Rafael turned to Miguel and considered the fate of the woman in his arms. "And now, what to do about her? Ahh. I know. Take her to the chapel. We shouldn't be disturbed there. Wait with her until I join you. There are some things I need to get from my office, things Miss Lawless should find very interesting when she wakes up."

Zant became slowly, painfully aware of the world again. What had happened? He struggled to bring the memory forward. It wouldn't come. But as the darkness receded, as the stars cleared from his mind, he realized he was lying on a bed. Weakly he clutched at the covers under him. He then realized he was lying on his stomach. So he was lying on his stomach on a bed and his head hurt like hell.

What else? As if in answer, a sudden noise at his bedside, that of a chair scraping across the floor, stilled him. He wasn't alone. Zant opened his eyes. He saw two huge black eyes and a bulbous nose about an inch from his face. Zant jerked back in mind-numbing startlement. Waves of pain warned him not to move so quickly again. Carefully, he sat up. Holding his aching head, he took a second look. "Victor, what the hell are you doing?"

"I am watching you closely."

"I can see that. Back off some, will you?"

Victor promptly backed off, scooting the chair back.

Zant sat up a little straighter. "How long have I been out?"

Victor frowned at that one. "The sun was down when I brought you up here." He looked over his beefy shoulder to the night beyond the balcony's doors. "And it is still dark. So, five minutes. Maybe an hour."

"That's good, Victor. Just great. Can you get me some water?"

As the big lumbering man stood up and turned away, Zant clutched fistfuls of the bed's covers as the room spun. Just then, tepid water splashed into his face. As rivulets ran down his nose and chin and soaked through his shirt, he scrubbed a hand down his face. "What the hell was that for?"

With a dripping washbasin dangling from his hand, Victor replied, "I am getting you water."

"I meant to drink, you—" Zant cut off his own words. What did it matter? At least he was awake enough to realize that it was strange for Victor to be with him and not with—"What are you doing here?"

"Don Rafael."

A jet of fear and urgency stabbed at Zant's gut. It all came flooding back. He had to shake off this weakness in his limbs, ignore the pain in his head—put there by his loving grandfather—and get out of here. He had to find Jacey. She was alive. Or had been. But first, he had to get around Victor.

He eyed his companion. The simple giant was supposed to be sympathetic to him, but making the *pistolero* understand that he was, was another thing entirely. He'd been following Don Rafael's orders all his life. Could he go against his grain in just one night? Well, there was only one way to find out. "What are your orders, Victor?"

"I am to carry you up to your room and find the key and lock the door and watch you closely and stay with you until Don Rafael tells me differently."

Zant nodded. Victor's speech was probably word for word what Don Rafael had said to him. But he'd probably meant for Victor to lock the door from the outside . . . he chanced a peek at the door's keyhole . . . and not from the inside, like he'd done. The key was still in the lock. Zant looked up at Victor's dull, staring face and thought about the man's orders, the exact wording. It was worth a try. "Give me your gun, Victor."

Victor promptly handed over his gun. Not surprised, but still relieved, Zant hefted it in his hand, getting a feel for it. Nice. Balanced weight. Fully loaded. It'd do. He then looked up again at Victor, sizing him up. There was no way he could best this man in a fight. And he couldn't bring himself to shoot the unarmed giant in cold blood. But there was also no way Victor would allow him to leave this room . . . without him. So, "You ready to go?"

Victor's frown creased the skin between his eyebrows. "I cannot go. My orders are to watch you closely and stay with you until Don Rafael—"

"Tells you differently. I know. But I'm leaving now, Victor. If you want to follow your orders to watch me closely and stay with me, you're going to have to come with me."

Victor's frown intensified as he gave every sign of thinking this through. Zant seethed with the need for urgency, but he was helpless in the face of Victor's slowly turning mental wheels. Just when Zant decided that maybe he could shoot the man, his broad, swarthy face cleared. "Okay."

Zant slumped. "Good. Let's go." As he dropped his legs over the side of his bed and stood to test his balance, he reminded himself that Victor could just as easily go the other way on an order from Don Rafael. He'd have to watch Victor more carefully than the giant watched him.

Feeling increasingly steadier on his feet, Zant swiped his sleeve over his face to dry it more and then stuck Victor's long-barreled pistol in his waistband as he headed for the door. Victor tailed him like a huge puppy. Once at the door, Zant carefully turned the key in the lock. Before opening it, he looked over his shoulder and asked Victor, "Is anyone posted outside this door?"

"Me," Victor assured him.

Zant looked at him. Twice. He then shook his head, telling himself to pay attention to what was ahead of him, and not who was behind him. After all, he didn't know how long he'd been out or who might still be in the villa. One misstep could see him dead.

Opening the door, he eased out just enough to look down the hall. Sure enough, there was Norona. But he was practically hanging over the hallway's railing as he peered down to the first floor below. What or who was so interesting down there? Zant stepped back into his bedroom and spoke quietly to Victor. "I want you to go ahead of me. Norona's out there. He won't—"

"Norona is guarding my friend Esteban. If he hurts him, I will kill him."

Zant stared at the big man. Earlier Norona had told him he wasn't guarding anyone, that Don Rafael had posted him up here in case there was trouble. Obviously, Norona had lied. Sighing, hating the delay, but fearing to let any detail go, afraid it could cost him his own or Jacey's life down the line, Zant resigned himself to getting to the bottom of this. "Who is Esteban? And why's he in there?"

"He is Conchita's grandson. She is in there, too. She took the spur from Don Rafael's office and told Esteban to put it in the señorita's room. He came with Conchita when they did the lady's bath. He made sure he was the last one out and put the spur on the bed and then hid under it. He is very brave."

Stunned, Zant tried to absorb this startlingly significant story. "How do you know all this?"

"Esteban is my friend. He told me his story only today. He is not too smart, though. He fell asleep and then you and Paco scared him and he ran away. After he told me this, he hid for the day. But when Don Rafael said to find him, I did. I know Esteban's favorite hiding place."

Poor, dumb, simple bastard. He'd betrayed his friend, but he'd never be able to understand that. Zant thought quickly. He had to get rid of Norona, so he could free Conchita and Esteban. To leave them here was to sign their death warrants. "I want you to go ahead of me. When you get to Norona, take his gun and knock him out. We're going to free Esteban and Conchita—"

"And Paco."

Suddenly feeling he was more the simpleton here than Victor was, Zant repeated, "And Paco? He's in there, too?"

"Yes. Do not worry, Señor Zant, I will get them out."

Zant put a hand on the man's arm. "I don't doubt it for a minute. Let's go. We have to hurry."

Victor nodded and turned out of the room. Almost wedged up against the big man's back, Victor's gun in his hand, Zant followed his every long stride. When Victor reached Norona, he simply grabbed the unsuspecting man by his throat, lifted him off the ground, ignored his gagging and kicking, jerked the one-eyed guard's gun out of his holster, and sent him flying and screaming over the railing. He landed with a sickening thud on the floor below.

Only silence followed. No feet running to the scene, no screams, no yelling voices. No one climbing up the stairs. Stunned as he was by Victor's straightforward methods, a part of Zant's mind registered the fact that, except for them, the villa apparently was empty. That was good. And bad.

Recovering somewhat, Zant looked at the gun in his hand. It hadn't been necessary. When Victor turned to him, Zant took a cautionary step back. "Well, Victor, that wouldn't have been my first choice, but . . . effective. Very effective."

Victor nodded. "Here." He thrust Norona's gun at him and held out his bear-sized paw for his own. Zant didn't even blink before making the trade. "Now, Victor, let's get Esteban out. The key's in the lock, so—"

"Okay." Victor turned and kicked the door in. Inside, someone grunted, another one screamed, and a third one whimpered and cried.

Zant looked at the ruined door. "Or you could just kick the door in." He then hurried inside to see Paco holding his forehead with both hands. Apparently he'd been behind the door. He then saw Conchita and the boy Esteban huddled together across the room. Conchita's look of terror changed to one of joy. "Señor Zant! It is you! Oh, thank you, God. We are saved."

"Victor!" Esteban screamed. He pulled away from his grandmother, jumped up and ran to embrace his big friend. Victor happily pounded the boy's back with resounding thuds.

Fearing the long, gushing reunion that loomed, Zant raced over to Conchita and helped her to her feet. "Come on, get up. It's started. Hurry! Victor will take you to the camp. Go with him. Paco, you come with me."

Conchita pulled at his arm. "Miss Lawless—she is in the

chapel with Don Rafael and Miguel Sereda. You must hurry."

Surprised, Zant stared in momentary silence down at her. "The chapel? How do you know?"

"Paco saw them out the balcony doors. It is the only place they could be going. Don Rafael was leading the way. Miguel Sereda carried her."

Zant spun to Paco. "How long ago?"

Still rubbing his forehead, Paco answered right away. "About fifteen minutes, my chief."

Fifteen minutes! He might still be in time. "Victor, take Esteban and Conchita to the camp."

"No. I must stay with you. Those are my orders."

The man chose now to get stubborn. Zant looked at Victor, who was armed, and at Paco, who wasn't. "All right, you come with me. Paco, take them to the camp, get Blue, get yourself a gun, and meet me at the chapel."

"Yes, my chief." He pulled Esteban away from Victor and herded the boy and his grandmother toward the door.

"Victor and I will go ahead of you downstairs. I believe the villa's empty, except for us. Conchita, you're going to have to step over Norona down in the hallway. He's dead. Just be brave and do it. We'll stay with you as far as the camp's gate, but after that, you're on your own." He looked from face to face, trying to assess if everybody understood. Satisfied that they did, he nodded and said, "Let's go."

Jacey sat on a front pew of the tiny chapel. She refused to do so much as flinch at the blinding, throbbing pain on the side of her face. Or wipe away the trickle of blood that rolled down her temple to her jaw. She'd show these men no weakness. All she wanted was a chance at her knife. But against two armed men? Maybe she'd get one of them before she died.

She flicked her gaze up to the holy cross above the altar. She kept expecting it to fall from the ceiling, from having two such evil presences in its nave. Looking back down, she caught Miguel's gaze as he stood, feet apart, arms folded over his chest, to one side of his leader. The man's sly, leering grin made her gut roil.

Don Rafael stepped up to stand in front of her. "Now that you are fully awake, señorita, we can continue our conversation from earlier."

"Go to hell."

With a snarl of anger, Don Rafael drew his hand back, as if to slap her again. Jacey tensed for the blow and met his black-eyed gaze with her own unwavering one. Just as suddenly, Don Rafael chuckled and relaxed, bringing his arm down to his side. "No. You can no longer make me angry. But here, I have some things to show you that I think you will find very interesting."

With that, he walked over to a pew on the opposite side of the aisle and picked up something small that Jacey couldn't make out clearly. Her left eye was watering and beginning to swell shut. She kept blinking to keep her right eye free of tears. She waited in silence until he walked back over to her.

Into her face, he shoved a small painting of an elegant woman in a black velvet dress. A part of its frame was torn away. She sniffed but gave nothing away. *Great-grandmother Ardis.*

"Is this perhaps your mother?"

"No." Jacey marveled at her steady voice, when inside she was shaking.

Don Rafael raised the picture and rubbed his finger over the lady in the painting. "What a shame. I was so sure it was. Well, no matter." He tossed the picture aside. It hit the chapel floor with a clattering dance. More of the frame broke away. Ignoring it, Don Rafael sat down next to her and turned toward her. He rested a hand on the pew's back, not quite touching her.

Jacey refused to recoil from him. Or even to look at him. She stared straight ahead and right through Miguel Sereda.

"I know you don't believe me, Señorita Lawless, but I never bore your mother any malice. I never gave any order to harm her. My men tell me she was already dead when they arrived. Isn't that a mystery?"

Jacey couldn't help herself. She turned toward the monster and stared at him. "What about my father?"

Don Rafael made a gesture to indicate his innocence. "I swear on that cross right there that I never gave any orders to see him harmed, either. I never wanted their deaths. Or that of the old man out in the wagon yard and all those animals. It must have been a sickening sight."

Jacey thought of poor Old Pete and his dogs and cats and

chickens. They'd been slaughtered where they stood. "If you didn't order anything, and your men didn't do anything, were they there for a tea party?"

Don Rafael laughed and sought out Miguel's face as he pointed at Jacey. "Did I not tell you she is amusing? It will be such a shame to kill her."

Approaching from the adobe-wall side of the family's private chapel, and thankful for its remote location on the villa's grounds, Zant edged up to its propped-open doors and stealthily peered inside. At the altar, a torch burned brightly, casting shadows and light out through the low windows. Facing Zant was Miguel Sereda. But Don Rafael and Jacey, seated in a front pew, had their backs to him. Zant watched Jacey for a moment. She was sitting up and talking. Relief coursed through him.

With Zant and Victor now were Blue and Paco. Using hand signals, Zant indicated the positions he wanted the men to take. When Miguel turned around momentarily, he sent Blue and Paco scooting over to the other side of the open doors. And he stayed where he was with Victor at his back.

Zant assessed the situation in the chapel. Sereda was armed and, most likely, so was the old man. So, one false move or sound from him or his men, or going in too soon or too late, could cost Jacey her life. Zant had only his instincts and a prayer to help him pick the right moment. Until it came, all he could do was watch, listen, and wait.

"No, Señorita Lawless, there was no time for a tea," Don Rafael continued. "My men tell me that from their hiding place, they watched as your father exchanged fire with two gringos who were dressed in their best clothes, like . . . how do you say? . . . dandies? When your father got the best of these men, they fled from the ranch. My men waited for them to come near, and then they slit their throats. Do you remember Rafferty? Yes? Well, Rafferty was there, and he told me they then searched these men."

Sickened at having to hear of her parents' last moments from the likes of Don Rafael, but needing to know what had happened, and riveted by his story, Jacey asked, "What were they hoping to find?"

Don Rafael looked surprised by her question. "Why, for clues as to who they were and why they were there, of course. I'm sure they kept any money they found, but they did bring me that lovely woman's portrait I showed you. But that's neither here nor there. Done with their search, they bound the dead men to their horses and set them off in a gallop. Next they slipped down to the hacienda and surprised your father as he bent over your mother's dead body."

Jacey took a deep breath to stiffen herself against further tears. "Go on."

"As you wish. Rafferty says he shoved the very piece of spur you have around your neck into your father's face—so he would know who was asking—and ordered him to tell them where his daughters were. Señor Lawless refused and he then did a very stupid thing. He jumped up and hit Rafferty. The two men scuffled, and when my other men could get off a clean shot, they killed him. He fell over your mother's body. How tragic, no? Ahh, but you are crying again. Miguel, how can I be so cruel to her?"

Hot and sweaty with emotion, her voice thick with tears, Jacey blubbered, "I am not. Go on." Inside, her heart was melting, her strength was waning. Poor Mama. Poor Papa. They weren't killed together or even by the same men or for the same reasons. And there was no way she could let Hannah know this. Or Glory. In the face of Don Rafael's continued quiet, Jacey gritted out, "What were your men's orders?"

Don Rafael smirked. "Their orders, my dear señorita, were to bring you and your sisters here. Where you would die by my hand. After letting your father know who and why. But even the best-made plans often go awry, no?"

Left breathless by his bald pronouncement, and swearing that only one of them would walk out of this chapel, Jacey could only stare at the heavy cross suspended above Miguel Sereda. What about Hannah, alone in Boston? And Glory, dear God, alone at the ranch? Were they even still alive? Jacey turned to stare at the evil man sitting next to her. "Why me and my sisters?"

"I thought it would be obvious to you. I wished for your father—in the long, empty years ahead of him—to have no joy from his family. No daughters to love. No grandchildren. I wished for him to live a long time and to know the suffering one goes through after the death of a child. Suffering such as I have known."

"But why now? Why not years ago? We're grown women now."

The old don shook a finger at her. "Aah, now you see. So was my Miranda when she died. She was a beautiful woman, like you. But there is more. You see, you can blame Zant for some of this. It was only when I freed him from that prison, when I brought him home, that I realized he truly was lost to me, too. He wanted no part of me or his inheritance. He wanted only to drink and to fight his life away. He turned his face away from me. It was then I made my decision."

The glittering lights in his black eyes dimmed some as he smiled. "And now . . . such is life's irony . . . he has come back to me. I again have a family. While you, señorita, have none. I'm afraid you must suffer your sisters' fates. You see, I'd already sent men after them before Zant came home for good. And now, I have no way of stopping them. It's all very sad."

Jacey turned a snarling mask to her tormentor. "You sick son of a bitch. You're what's sad."

Don Rafael only quirked a grin as he cocked his head at her. "Am I? Well, then, let me show you something else. Miguel, will you hand it to me? Ahh, thank you." Taking it from Miguel, Don Rafael dangled a ruby necklace in front of Jacey's face. "Do you recognize this?"

Jacey's blood ran cold, even as her face heated up with fever. A ruby necklace. The world was full of ruby necklaces. But this one had to be Laura Parker's, mentioned in her journal, the journal being hand-carried to Glory. Seething inside, Jacey forced a calmness into her voice that she truly did not feel. "Why would I?"

He swung the necklace back and forth in a slow arc. "No reason. But it has a most interesting history. You see, the story of the Kid's death at your father's hands and the breakup of the Lawless gang filtered down to us here. Miranda was heartbroken. She wouldn't believe her lover was dead. With no choice but to prove it to her, I sent men to the deserted Lawless hideout. They dug up the body and brought it back here. I made her view it. Screaming and crying, she threw herself across his gruesome corpse. She then dug wildly through his shirt's pocket, saying she felt something. She pulled out this necklace and insisted the Kid had been bringing it to her when he was killed. She wore it every day thereafter until her own death.''

Jacey flinched at the horror of it all. And was glad that Zant wasn't hearing any of this. It would kill him. She realized Don Rafael was still talking and focused on what he was saying.

''All this is very long, and I apologize. But there's only a little more to go. Well, I heard later that the reason your father killed the Kid was because he'd murdered a family coming alone through Apache Pass. Apparently they had a baby, which your father found and took home with him.''

He looked into Jacey's face. But waited in vain for a response from her. Fearing and yet knowing what was to come, she could only stare at him. ''At any rate, I now believe this necklace belonged to that woman the Kid killed. And that baby is the girl you think of as your youngest sister. And this''—he dropped the necklace into his hand—''is your sister's birthright from her real mother. It is indeed sad that the two will never be reunited. You see, she is the one I especially want dead. She was the cause of the Kid's death and eventually of my Miranda taking her own life.''

Jacey's heart nearly stopped beating. She had to get out of here. Had to warn Glory. She should've never left her baby sister alone. Despite everythings she'd heard, Glory *was* her baby sister. Overcome with emotion, with the need for action, Jacey jumped up. Immediately, two guns were aimed at her. ''You're going to have to kill me right here, you lowlife scum. Because I'm going to my sister, and I'm leaving now.''

Don Rafael grabbed her arm with his free hand. ''No you're not. You're dying right here. I won't allow you to live, not with a Calderon bastard filling your belly. You are no better than my daughter, and she was a whore, shaming the entire line with her sin.''

''There is no bastard in my belly. I carry no one's child.''

He shook her arm violently enough to loosen Jacey's curls and increase the pain in her face. ''Lying whore. Zant himself told me this thing.''

''I heard him. It appears you're not the only one who can lie convincingly. But go ahead and shoot me. Right now, right here. Right in this holy place. My revenge will be knowing you'll rot in hell for such a thing."

Don Rafael's entire demeanor changed. He grinned evilly into her face. "Nothing so dramatic. I intend to make your death look like a suicide. I would not want Zant to wake up and learn I have killed his whore lover. I would only lose him again."

Jacey ignored his insult to focus on what he'd said about Zant. "Wake up? From what? What have you done with him?"

"Don't worry. He rests comfortably in his room. He'll have a headache tomorrow, but that will be all."

Realizing the moment was near, knowing she'd have to create a diversion in the next few moments or die, Jacey continued to taunt the old man. Maybe he'd let go of her and she could shove him into Miguel, who now stood just behind his boss. "What makes you think Zant would believe I committed suicide? Why would I?"

"I will tell him you thought he was dead. And killed yourself out of grief. Like my daughter did."

"He knows me better than that. He won't believe you."

Don Rafael's shout of laughter echoed insanely throughout the chapel. "But he will believe me. He's believed all these years that his mother took her own life."

Jacey froze. "What are you saying?"

"I killed Miranda myself. She would not get over her grief and marry the young Spanish don I arranged for her to wed. I had no choice. She continued to humiliate me. All she would do was cling to Zant and shower her love on him. I strangled her myself and took her child to raise as a proper Calderon. But he too defied me at every turn. Until now. Now he is truly my heir, and you will not stand in my way."

With that, he poked the gun into her back and began marching her down the center aisle. Miguel was two steps behind. Fear pounded in Jacey's heart and at her temples. Her throat threatened to close. Sweat beaded over her. It was now or never. And her gown hindered her more, only made it more difficult for her to reach her knife. But it couldn't be helped. Jacey began slowing her steps, began to resist Don Rafael's tugging on her.

Then, he did exactly what she wanted. Snarling a warning,

he let go of her arm and shoved her shoulder. Jacey whipped around and shoved as hard as she could against the old man's chest. With a startled cry he fell back against Miguel. Jacey dropped to the floor and rolled, tearing at the gown's yards of fabric, pulling the skirt up, desperately searching for her knife in its sheath. This would be her only chance.

Outside the chapel, Zant fought off Victor's restraining hold. "Victor, let go. I'm okay. I'm under control now." Finally jerking free, he called across to Blue and Paco. "Now. Let's go."

Zant leaped up from his hiding place, Norona's gun in his hand. The four men burst into the chapel, brandishing their weapons and yelling out warnings for Miguel and Don Rafael to freeze and drop their guns. Shocked by the suddenness of the attack, Don Rafael and Miguel did freeze. But they didn't drop their weapons. Instead, they both pointed them at Jacey, who was sitting on the floor, her skirt pulled up, her hand clutching her knife.

"Jacey, are you all right?" Zant didn't dare spare her a glance with his question. He watched instead the two guns aimed at her.

"I'm okay, Zant. Did you hear—"

"Every word." He raised his black-eyed, hate-filled gaze to his grandfather. "You rotten bastard. Let her go."

The old man cocked the Colt and aimed it at Jacey's heart. "I cannot. She will destroy everything I've done for you." He then spoke to Victor. "What are you doing here with him? I told you to guard him."

"I am, Don Rafael. See? I am still with him, like you said."

Don Rafael narrowed his eyes. "Good, Victor. Now, bring me his gun."

"I cannot. You have it."

The old man's complexion deepened to red. "The one he has in his hand, you simpleton."

"No. Don Zant is my chief. Not you. You hurt my friend Esteban. I don't take orders from you anymore."

Zant breathed out his relief. But a snarl curled his grandfather's lip. "Then you will die with the rest of them. I will see to it myself."

"No you won't, Don Rafael. Your days of seeing to anything are over.'' Zant lowered his voice to a hiss of hatred. ''I was never a bastard, was I? And you let me think it all those years. Did you think it would make me grateful? You told me, from the time I was a boy, how lucky I was to have such a wonderful grandfather who'd forgive me the circumstances of my birth. Didn't you?''

He drew in a breath, glared, and went on. ''And all that time, you knew that Kid Chapelo'd married my mother. How do I know? Conchita left their marriage certificate on my bed this afternoon. And you, you heartless shit, you killed my mother. Your own daughter. How could you?''

Zant grimaced, swallowing back the sick bile that rose to the back of his throat. ''Did you have me thrown into prison so you could rescue me? Was that supposed to make me more cooperative?''

Don Rafael shook his head no and raised his free hand to Zant. But it was Miguel who spoke up. ''No, he did not. I did that. I produced the false evidence that convicted you. Call it my gift to Don Rafael for all the heartache you have caused him.''

Zant was as stunned as Don Rafael's face showed him to be. When the white-haired old man spun toward Miguel, taking his gun off Jacey, Zant motioned for her to move over to him. She quickly came to her feet.

But Miguel grabbed her and held her to him, placing her between himself and everyone else. He put his gun to her temple. ''Not so fast, *amigo*.''

With a hiss of breath, Zant raised his gun to a neutral position. ''Don't even think it, Sereda.''

Miguel started to say something, but then got the strangest look on his face, like something had just happened that he couldn't quite believe. His arm fell limply away from Jacey. He staggered backward, clutching at his belly and looking at his own blood. He then looked up at Jacey, whose bloody knife remained fisted in her hand. The dying man raised his gun to her.

Zant snapped back into position. His shot took Sereda in the forehead and spun him around. The Mexican fell dead onto a pew, slid off, sprawling faceup on the floor. In the silence, Zant heard the sounds of running feet outside. But he stared impassively at the dead man and said, ''I owed you that.''

Behind him, Blue said, "Zant, you hear that running? We're going outside. Are you all right in here?"

Zant nodded. "Yeah. Go. I can handle this. It's my place." As his men departed, he watched Don Rafael, who now seemed not to comprehend what was happening. He looked old. His face seemed to have taken on more lines, his jowls drooped heavily, his clothes seemed not to fit his shrinking body. Suddenly, seeing him like this, Zant wasn't sure if he could or should kill him.

But then, Don Rafael straightened up. As if time had slowed, Zant watched in horror as his grandfather raised his gun again to Jacey. She froze, her eyes widened. Zant heard the hammer click back in place. Saw Don Rafael begin to squeeze the trigger. The gun erupted as Zant screamed out, "No!"

Don Rafael then very coolly swung the gun to Zant. And fired again. The bullet missed him, but Zant heard Jacey scream out. Blinded by rage, he aimed and pulled the trigger. At the same moment, Jacey's knife flew through the air. It lodged in the old man's chest a second after Zant's bullet hit him there as well . . . with a dull thunk and an explosion of blood.

Don Rafael fell to his knees The gun slipped from his fingers. He held his hands out to Zant.

Zant spared him only a glance as, holstering his gun, he rushed to Jacey. She was collapsing where she stood. He was seized with fright at the sight of her blood-spattered dress. Just as she would've hit the floor, Zant reached her. Kneeling with her in his arms, he stroked her hair, searched her for wounds. "Oh, my God, Jacey, are you hit?"

Clinging limply to him, drawing on his strength, she dully shook her head. "No. I'm just . . . weak. I'll be all right." Then, she suddenly found the strength, to clutch at his shirt. "Is he dead?"

"No. But he will be shortly." Zant pulled her closer, wanting only to feel her heart beat against his. Dimly he was aware of the sound of running feet outside the chapel. And intense gunfire.

Jacey suddenly pulled back. "Go to him. Go to your grandfather."

Looking down into her precious face, Zant frowned, not

understanding her insistence. Still, he looked over his shoulder. Don Rafael now lay on his side. He'd pulled Jacey's knife out of his chest. His blood pooled on the church floor. Zant turned away from the sight and sought Jacey's pleading gaze.

He shook his head, speaking just above a whisper. "Go to him? You mean . . . forgive him? How can I? You know everything he's done. All the people he's killed, all the lives he's ruined."

Jacey licked her lips and and nodded. Desperation edged her eyes. "I do know. And I don't understand it myself, Zant. There's just something in me that says you need to. Please, I'm afraid . . . for you."

Zant stroked her hair, begged her. "Don't make me do this."

Tears spilled out of Jacey's eyes and ran down her cheeks. Her voice breaking on a sob, she cried, "I can't. I won't. Just . . . search your heart. Do you want to carry hate around forever? Will there be room for anything else if you do? I came here hating, Zant. I came here wanting to kill. And I did. But now, I'm empty. I feel nothing. There's no love in my heart . . . for myself, for anything. All I have is my keepsake to take home, and a ruby necklace for Glory. Things, Zant. Just things. I know now they're not as important as what I carry home in my heart. I won't take hatred with me. It won't wash off like the blood on this dress."

With that, she pulled out of his arms and allowed him to help her stand. Taking a deep breath, squaring her shoulders, she looked up at him. "I'm going to him, Zant. I'm going to tell him I forgive him. It'll probably be the worst thing I could do for him. But it'll be the best thing I do for myself."

She turned away then, began walking toward the dying Don Rafael. After a few steps, she turned back to him. "Search your heart. And do what's right for you. Nobody can make you forgive him. But what you decide right now, you live with for the rest of your life." She stood still, stared quietly, and then added, "I don't think you hate him as much as you love him."

Zant stared after her as she turned and knelt beside Don Rafael. He saw her take his hand, heard her speaking softly to him. Then, as if not of his own will, Zant's feet moved. He took one step. Two. Three. And then he slowly knelt beside

Jacey and looked into his grandfather's lined old face. He saw the tears that rolled down his pale, papery cheeks as he stared up at him. Taking a deep breath, feeling the numbness slipping away, and the intense pain beginning, Zant reached out and took his grandfather's hand from Jacey.

She smiled and slipped her hand under his arm, resting her cheek there as well. Feeling her warmth and her nearness, and cradling Don Rafael's hand in both of his, Zant watched as the life dimmed from the old man's eyes. He pulled his grandfather's hand up to his cheek. "I love you," he whispered.

The gunfire outside the chapel stopped.

Chapter Twenty-One

Three days later, on a cool, crisp morning at the close of November, Jacey was ready to leave Cielo Azul. For good. Dressed as she was the day she left home, she tossed Knight's saddle across his broad back. Tethered outside his small corral, the danged gelding gave a mighty shudder that threatened to see the saddle in the dirt. Poking her bottom lip out, Jacey held it in place. But when she attempted to tighten the cinch, the big horse sucked in a gust of air and held it. "Dang you, Knight."

She attempted a second cinching of the saddle. Again, Knight bloated his stomach with his held-in air. Jacey poked her bottom lip out. "You asked for this." She kneed the horse's belly, forcing him to exhale. As soon as his girth deflated to normal, Jacey pulled the cinch tight. "Aha, gotcha."

Behind her, seated across the top rail of a facing corral, some *caballeros* chuckled and made a few comments in Spanish. Jacey spun around to glare at them. The men sobered appropriately, despite a few anonymous snorts of laughter. Frowning, Jacey pulled her saddlebags off the fence railing and flung them over Knight's back. He sidestepped. The overstuffed bags hit the sandy ground like a thrown broncobuster. Shouts of laughter came from behind her. Jacey whipped around, but the men had scattered to the four winds.

Her angry words died on her lips. Her glare vanished from her face. Zant was standing there. He hadn't been only a moment ago. Looking as cool and fresh as the morning air felt, and as tall and strong as the mountains behind him, he smirked at her. Clad in his denims, a blue shirt under his leather vest, his Stetson low over his brow, and his Colt strapped to his hip, he sipped gingerly at a cup of steaming coffee in his hand. He then teased her with a grin. "I figured I'd find you at the source of all the laughter. What're you doing?"

Words and courage failed Jacey. She spun back to Knight and fiddled with straps already in place. "What's it look like, Chapelo? I'm saddling my horse. The ornery son of a gun's been let run wild this past week. He doesn't want to leave."

Her hands stilled with her last words. She stared blankly at the quickly blurring saddle in front of her. She swiped a sleeve across her wet eyes.

"Leave? Where you headed?"

Jacey smoothed her shaking hand down the multicolored blanket under Knight's saddle. "Home."

"Home," Zant repeated, as if he'd never heard the word before.

Jacey moved up to Knight's head and clutched at his bridle. She stroked his soft muzzle. "That's what I said."

"Yeah, it is." He was silent a moment, but then he added, "You figuring on passing through Tucson?"

Jacey nodded. "That's where I pick up the trail."

"You stopping long enough to say good-bye to Rosie and Alberto?"

She nodded again. "Yep."

"And maybe go to church?"

Jacey frowned as she smoothed a lock of mane over Knight's forehead. She chanced a peek back over her shoulder. He was serious. "Church? The way I see it, Chapelo, I've been in church twice, and I've been dragged out twice, both times by somebody with a gun in his hand. I believe I'll most likely forgo church."

He nodded and pressed his lips together, as if her words required great thought. Then he said, "Figure you'll make good time getting home?"

Jacey turned back to Knight. Her efforts to draw in a deep breath forced her head up and back. "I figure I will. If I can beat the snows."

"Shouldn't be too much of a problem until you get close to Santa Fe."

What with the sudden lump in her throat, she could only

nod her answer. Knight chose that moment to nudge her, forcing her back a step. One step closer to Zant.

Apparently finished with being polite and friendly, Zant erupted in a snarl of anger. "Look at me, Jacey. If you're going to leave, then have the guts to turn around and tell me to my face. You haven't said one word in the past three days about this. Were you just going to sneak away? Is that how little I mean to you?"

Hands fisted at her side, her chin jutted out, Jacey turned to him. "I figured it'd be easier."

"For who—you? I never figured you for a coward, Jacey Lawless." Zant glared at her.

Despite his insult and her heart's wrenching beats, Jacey maintained her stiff, stubborn stance. "I've done what I came here to do. I've got my answers, I've got my keepsake back, and I've got the ruby necklace for Glory. Don Rafael is buried, Cielo Azul is yours, and the men who didn't take off or manage to get themselves killed are all loyal to you. You've got your life all set up here."

"What's stopping you from being a part of it? I've held you in my arms while you cried, while you fought me, and while you loved me, Jacey. And you held me when I needed it most. Was all that a lie?"

Jacey blinked, felt weak in her knees. "It was no lie. But there's . . . too much bad blood here. It's just *too soon* for us, Zant. I can't—" She paused, telling herself there would be no more beating around the bush concerning the fears that lodged knifelike in her heart. "All right, Zant, here's the truth. Don Rafael's men are still out there, still following his orders. So, what am I going to find when I get home? Are my sisters going to be dead? If they are . . . I have to tell you . . . I can't promise you how I'll feel. About you."

Zant's first response was to toss aside his coffee, cup and all. Then, his black eyes squinting under the low brim of his Stetson, he threw his hands up in a helpless gesture. "That's hard, Jacey. Too hard. I can't undo my bloodlines. Why are you making this impossible? Three days ago, you begged me to forgive my grandfather. And you were right. But now, where's the forgiveness in your heart—for me?"

Jacey lowered her gaze to her boots, but then raised her head to look him in the eye. "I'm not saying I'm right. I'm just saying it's how I feel. Three days are a long time to think, Zant. And I've made up my mind. I've got to leave, got to get home. If Glory's . . . still alive, I've got some hard news for her. It's only right she hear it from me. And if she's not alive . . . then I've got some burying of my own to do."

Her piece said, her heart full, she turned back to Knight and picked up her saddlebags. She threw them across the now docile gelding's rump and settled them in place. There. It was done. All she had to do was mount up. And leave. Still, she hesitated, unable to shrug off his presence behind her. Only a short distance separated them, but it was widening.

"Just tell me you don't love me. That's all I ask."

His softly spoken words hurt more than his yelling. Jacey's next breath came in shuddering gasps. Turning her head only an inch or so, just enough to direct her words over her shoulder to Zant, she said, "I can't do that, outlaw."

Then, without looking back, without another word, she mounted Knight, turned him, and rode out of Cielo Azul.

"*Rosie, venga aquí!* It is our Catarina!"

In the early evening of the third day after she left Cielo Azul, Jacey reined in Knight in front of Alberto's noisy Tucson cantina. And found she could smile again. Alberto's joy made her shake her weary head. She chuckled and waved back at him. His eyes lit up, and he threw his hands up as he danced a few steps. Suddenly, he sobered enough to cross himself and send a muttered prayer heavenward.

Jacey'd no more than dismounted before Alberto engulfed her in his warm and fatherly embrace. Stepping back, he looked her up and down, frowned, and chattered steadily in Spanish. His chiding tone told her plainly enough that he didn't like what he saw.

Jacey chuckled. "I am a sight, aren't I, Alberto?"

Blinking, Alberto switched to English. "I forget to use the English for you. And, *sí,* you are the sight for the eyes that hurt. We have missed you very much. We have said many prayers for you. And we have lit many candles." He then turned and bellowed into the cantina. "*Rosie! Venga aquí—ahora!* It is our Catarina!"

He'd no more than said it before Rosie came tumbling out of the cantina. A crowd of curious men wedged into the doorway behind her and at the windows. Laughing, crying, Rosie grabbed Jacey by her shoulders and smacked a loud kiss on both of her cheeks. Beaming, still holding her, she stepped back to look Jacey over, just as Alberto had. Her cheer turned to a frown as she spoke to her father. "She does not look well, no? She is skinny now."

Alberto raised a finger and shook it, his face appropriately serious. "We will put the fat back on her bones, yes?"

"No," Jacey broke in, making sure her voice was firm. If these two got rolling with a plan, she'd still be here come Christmas. "You won't. I'm staying just the night. I've got to get home as soon as I can."

Rosie's frown deepened as she released Jacey. "Your face says you have been through much, *mi amiga*."

To her utter embarrassment, Jacey felt her chin quiver and her eyes fill with hot tears. She blinked and jutted her chin out. "Yes, I have. And not too much of it good, Rosie."

Rosie stared sympathetically and then exchanged a look with Alberto. Apparently he understood her meaning because he nodded and made a shooing motion at the girls. Rosie turned to Jacey and held her arm out, as if she wanted Jacey to step into her embrace. Surprising herself, Jacey did just that.

"Come," Rosie ordered as she settled her arm around Jacey's shoulder. "Papa will see to your horse, and we . . . you and me . . . will go around back to your room. And then, you will tell Rosie all about it, no?"

Sniffing in earnest now, Jacey nodded her head. "No. I mean, yes."

Jacey slept later than she'd planned. As she quickly washed herself over the basin, she peeked out of the room's window and made a sound of disgust. The sun was already high above the horizon. Alberto'd sworn last night that he'd wake her at dawn. But he obviously hadn't. Now, by the time she dressed and saddled Knight, she fussed, it'd be danged near noon. She was losing precious daylight.

Tossing aside the washcloth, she dried off and quickly braided her hair. Getting dressed was only a matter of slipping back into . . . She reached for her split skirt and blouse and underclothes, which she'd tossed last night onto the chair . . . and stared. Her clothes were gone. The fury of her Lawless temper exploded over her frowning hot face. She stomped naked to the door, jerked it open, and yelled ''Rose!'' into the narrow and empty hall. No answer.

''Rosie,'' she bellowed again. ''Where're my danged clothes? If I have to, I'll ride out of here naked. I swear I will.''

That worked. The door from the cantina opened and Rosie stepped through. Her eyes widening, she shushed Jacey. ''Catarina, lower your voice. Already there are thirty men out there cheering and wanting to see you do just such a thing. Your clothes will be here in a moment. They are being brushed and readied for you, that is all.''

Rosie walked toward Jacey as she spoke. Jacey yanked the girl into her room and closed the door. Hands to her bare waist, she took out her frustration on Rosie. ''Why wasn't I awakened at dawn?''

Rosie frowned as she looked Jacey up and down. ''Please, Catarina, cover yourself.'' As Jacey jerked a sheet off the bed and wrapped herself in it, Rosie explained, ''My poor father and I were very much tired after last night. We too slept over. Only the thirsty men banging on the cantina doors awakened us. We meant to wake you as soon as we opened our business.''

Somewhat mollified . . . and feeling guilty, seeing as how she was the reason they'd been up most of the night, Jacey settled down some. ''I'm sorry I yelled. I'm just fretting about getting on the trail to home. When will my clothes be ready?''

Rosie looked everywhere but at her as she answered. ''Um, soon.''

Looking askance at her friend, Jacey narrowed her eyes. ''What the heck is going on, Rosie? Exactly when will my clothes be ready?''

Rosie shot a darting glance to the window behind Jacey and instantly brightened. ''They will be ready now. I will go get them.'' With that, she turned and yanked the door open.

Jacey jerked around to the window. Nothing there but the outside. She turned back to the open door and the dim hall beyond it. And frowned.

''I'm telling you for the last time, I don't want to go to church before I head out. It's already past noon, and I need to get going." Despite her protests, Jacey was already halfway to the mission church. "And why does everyone from the cantina have to go with us?"

She turned in her saddle to look at their following. A crowd of grinning horsemen tailed them. She looked again to Rosie and Alberto, both of them jostling along in their small, loose-jointed wagon. A sleepy old nag pulled it.

Handling the reins and watching the way ahead, Alberto spared her a glance. "Is it so much to ask, Catarina, that you do this one last thing for us? That you go with us and give thanks to the God who saw you safely through your troubles? And these men—any time they spend in a church can only do their souls good."

Guilt and shame lowered her gaze to her nicely brushed split skirt. "I suppose you're right." She raised her head and glared at her two friends' solemn yet wide-eyed faces. "But right after this mass, I'm leaving. You understand that?"

Two grinning faces and nodding heads met her words. Alberto then turned his attention to the looming white church ahead. "Here we are. San Xavier del Bac."

Jacey and her following reined in, dismounted, and tethered their horses in the otherwise deserted wagon yard. Taking a deep breath, she resigned herself to the next hour. What could it hurt? She then looked up to the towering spire of the holy building. And remembered the last time she'd been here. That Sunday when Zant'd stalked in and yelled for her and she'd left with him.

To her grateful surprise, the memory wasn't as painful as it was funny. Well, maybe being in church was just what she needed.

She turned to Alberto and Rosie, only to find that Alberto was making for the entrance and herding the men ahead of him. Rosie was rummaging around in the back of the wagon. She came up with two lace shawls and two small bouquets of flowers. Jacey frowned as she removed her slouch hat and took the offered shawl from Rosie and placed it over her hair. She tossed her hat into the back of the wagon and asked, "What're the flowers for?"

Rosie thrust the bigger bouquet into Jacey's hands. "For . . . you. And me. For an offering."

Jacey looked at the fall wildflowers in her hand, and thought for a moment of home. She roused herself and said, "All right. Let's go."

Rosie grinned and stepped in front of Jacey. "Me first. It's, um, tradition."

Getting steadily irritated, Jacey barked out, "Fine. Just go, will you?"

And go, Rosie did. Stepping along smartly, she got Jacey to the church doors in double time. Once there, she slowed to a step-pause-step cadence that made Jacey all but trip over her. As Jacey cussed under her breath, she followed Rosie as best she could. Organ music swelled at their entrance.

No more than two steps into the sanctuary, Jacey stopped cold. The church was packed. And everyone was standing and staring at her and Rosie. Jacey's mind raced. Was this Sunday? No. A church holiday? Well, how was she supposed to know? Then, what? She tapped Rosie on the shoulder and whispered, "Where're our seats? Everybody's staring at us."

Over her shoulder and out the side of her mouth, Rosie whispered back, "Up front. In the first pew."

"What?" Jacey's voice was no more than a croak. "I don't want to sit right up front." She nodded as she passed some of the men from the cantina. "Let's sit with them."

Rosie grabbed Jacey's arm. "No. We must go up front."

Whispering loud enough to make herself heard over the organ music, Jacey fussed again. "Why?"

Rosie jerked her up even with herself and pointed toward the altar. "There. That is why. Now, walk."

But Jacey couldn't. She'd taken root where she stood. That damned Zant Chapelo stood there by the same priest he'd scared the hell out of not too long ago. All shined up and in his best clothes, and with Paco and Blue and Victor all duded up and ranged alongside of him, the outlaw had the guts to grin at her.

Jacey put her fisted hands and her bouquet to her waist. Rosie looked back at her and frantically urged her forward. Oh, she'd go up there, all right. She go up there and wipe the smile right off that polecat's face. She'd been tricked into a wedding. They were traitors, all of them.

She called out their names in her head. Rosie, Alberto . . . she tromped forward, passing Rosie, and making for the altar gate. She looked from side to side, studying at the congrega tion. There were Conchita and Esteban and Manuel. She stopped short and stared at their smiling faces until Rosie fled past her. Dumbfounded, Jacey watched her friend stop and turn to stand beside the waiting priest.

Suddenly, none of it seemed real. Jacey turned in a slow circle, taking in the crowd, the music, the men and the women of Cielo Azul, the three groomsmen, her . . . groom. Oh, it was real enough. She stalked over to Zant and got right in his face. "Outside, Chapelo."

The organ music dribbled off on a sickly note and the church became deathly quiet. Even the chubby, ruddy priest dared only clear his throat.

Zant smiled down at her. "Can't. Not yet. Not until we're married."

"We—" Her voice was a squeak. Over a hundred sets of eyes bored into her back. She started out with a yell. "We are *not*"—and lowered her voice to a hiss—"getting married."

Zant grabbed her by her resisting arm and turned her to face the priest with him. He didn't seem to care how loudly he spoke or who heard him. "Yes we are. Preacher, I've been living in sin with this woman"—Jacey gasped right along with everyone else—"and I'm asking you to marry us and set that to rights. I fear she may already be carrying my child, and I—"

Jacey screeched and hit his arm with her bouquet. Dried petals drifted to the floor. "Will you quit saying that? I am not."

Zant looked down at her, his black eyes as affected by his grin as his mouth was. "You could be."

Jacey squirmed and cast a wary glance at the disapproving priest. "I'm not," she told him. She then turned back to Zant. "What about all that stuff I said at Cielo Azul? I still feel that way."

Zant sobered and slipped his hand down her arm to take her hand. "I know you do. And I respect that, Jacey. It won't be easy. There's bound to be some rough times ahead. But the difference is, I want to help you through them."

Feeling the tension of the churchgoers ease, hearing the murmurs, Jacey fought the love swelling in her heart and welling in her eyes. "I could end up hating you."

Zant smiled. "You won't. You love me, Jacey. You love

me, and you need me to help you through what's at home You stood by me at the worst moment in my life. Did you really think I wouldn't stand by you when your time came? We all''—he indicated Blue, Paco, and Victor, and then swept his hand over the congregation—''we all want to help you and be your family, too.''

And that was another question. Jacey leaned in toward Zant He bent over until his ear was to her lips. ''How'd you do all this?''

He grinned and whispered into her ear. ''We followed you up here. Early this morning, I told Alberto and Rosie my plan They delayed you until we got the signal to them that we were ready. Now, are you going to disappoint all these folks and embarrass me, or are you going to marry me?''

But Jacey had still another question. ''Who's minding Cielo Azul?''

Zant chuckled. ''Right now, my neighbors at Villa Delarosa But after the wedding, Blue's taking everyone home, except Victor and Paco—they're going with us. Blue'll be in charge until we get back from No Man's Land.''

With that, he straightened up, still looking down at her. Jacey quirked her mouth as she thought about it. ''Cielo Azul.''

''Could you come to think of it as home, Jacey?''

She searched her heart, thought of the folks there, and realized she was nodding. ''I might.'' She then searched Zant's face. ''But I'm not sure.''

He pulled her close to his side. ''Fair enough. We'll worry about it when the time comes, okay?''

Jacey nodded. But yet another question presented itself. ''Zant, why didn't you wait to see if I worked things out at home and then came back to you?''

Zant made a disbelieving noise and chuckled. ''And leave something as important as love up to your Lawless pride and reckless heart? I didn't dare.''

Jacey laughed. ''All right, outlaw. I'll marry you. But you may have some answering to do up in No Man's Land, what with your last name and all.''

Zant grinned again. ''Why do you think I'm changing your last name to mine long before I get there?'' He winked and mouthed, ''I love you.''

Her heart bursting, Jacey mouthed it right back.

Zant gave a whoop and turned her with him to the waiting congregation. "She said yes!"

A rising swell of emotion filled the church. Over every cheer, over the renewed burst of the organ music, drowning out everything else, except for Jacey's and Zant's love for each other, was the cry, "*¡Viva el jefe! ¡Viva la jefa!*"

TURN THE PAGE FOR
AN EXCITING INSTALLMENT
OF *SEASONS OF GLORY*,
THE NEXT ROMANCE
FROM CHERYL ANNE PORTER . . .

Mama's and Papa's dream had been for a better life for them all. But now . . . Mama and Papa were buried out back, alongside old Pete. And Glory's older sisters? They were gone from home, looking for answers, for vengeance. That left her in charge. Glory swallowed, keenly feeling the responsibility pressing squarely on her shoulders for every man, horse, cow, and blade of grass for miles around.

She couldn't do this. A prick of panic gripped her belly, urged her to run after Jacey and again beg her to stay. *No.* Glory stubbornly fisted her hands in her shawl's folds. *No. It's best to think about what I can do.* Which wasn't much, she admitted. After all, Papa'd seen to the day-to-day running of the ranch, the hiring and firing, the buying and selling of the cattle, the ordering of supplies. Jacey'd dogged his every step, so she knew all those ins-and-outs. But she was gone.

And Mama . . . *well, she tried to teach me,* Glory grimaced, seeing herself again dawdling so long over tasks that Mama would shake her elegant head, shoo her, and put the work in Hannah's capable hands. Thus freed—the memory now pricked at Glory's conscience—she'd fritter away the hours in her room, indulging her romantic daydreams of her own home, a loving husband, and her own beautiful children.

Just how you intend to take care of them, Mama'd fussed, *when you won't lend your hand to the simplest of tasks, I'll never know, Glory Bea Lawless.*

Oh, why hadn't she paid more attention, asked more questions? Because here she was now—nineteen and helpless. And in charge. *Well, surely I know something.* Glory bit thoughtfully at her lower lip. She'd helped Mama some with the bookkeeping. And got in the way when Biddy was baking. And she'd also . . . nothing else came to mind. Surprised realization stiffened her spine. *That's it? That's all I know?*

Glory blinked, found she was staring at Biddy's wide and capable back. Solace and reassurance rested with her. In a blaze of emotion, Glory hurried to her and clutched at her beloved nanny. Biddy's squawk of startlement at being grabbed from behind blended with Glory's heartfelt and sobbing cry of "You're the only one who hasn't left me, Biddy. I love you."

Biddy turned in Glory's embrace and hugged her tightly. "There, there, child. I love you, too. Yer sisters will be back. We must believe that. But right now 'tis you I'm worried about. Yer breakin' me heart—all that time ye spend at yer poor parents' graves. 'Tis not good for ye. Why, look at yerself—ye haven't eaten or slept properly for the past month. Are ye still havin' those nightmares?"

Nestling her face in the warm crook of her nanny's neck and shoulder, her world once again warm and secure, Glory nodded her head and sniffed inconsolably. Biddy patted her and held her until she felt strong enough to pull away. Glory smiled that she was okay and then turned to stare out at the wind-stirred tallgrass. "I keep . . . seeing them, Biddy. Mama and Papa. Just lying there. All that blood."

For long moments, Glory suspended thought, allowing the terrible pain in her chest to subside. Than she squared her shoulders against her sorrow and pivoted again to face Biddy. "I've been thinking about . . . well, everything. The ranch. Hannah gone, and now Jacey. Me—the only one left to keep the place going. Why, I don't have the first idea about how to do that. But Jacey seems to think I can. And it's not like I have a choice, is it? Because this ranch was Mama's and Papa's dream. They made it our home. And now I have to see that the dream lives. There's no one else but me to do it."

Having made that brave speech, she stood there, feeling alone and already bested by circumstances. Her shoulders slumped right along with her resolve. "Oh, Biddy, what am I saying? I don't know a thing about running a cattle ranch. It'll ll die because of me.'' The enormity of it all brought her ıands to her mouth. She stared teary-eyed at her grandmoth- rly nanny.

Who leapt into action. ''Now, child, don't take on so. You'll lo a fine job of it. And 'tis plenty of help ye'll have. Why, miley's been the foreman since yer father settled the place. le'll help you with the everyday ranching decisions. An' ourdough's out in the cook shack stirrin' up the men's break- ast this minute. He knows what supplies are needed and when) get them. An' there's me, darlin'. I'll be takin' good care f you. See? Ye'll be naught but an overseer until yer sister omes home.''

Heartened by Biddy's cheery picture, Glory smiled—and xhaled for the first time since Jacey'd announced yesterday fternoon that she was leaving. ''You're right. We'll be just ne. Hannah and Jacey will be so proud when they come ome. The ranch'll be better than ever.''

''That's the spirit, child.'' Biddy beamed with pride. 'Those are the first words ye've uttered in a month that show ome gumption.'' She clasped Glory's hand with both of hers. ' 'Tis proud of me baby, I am.''

''Now, Biddy, you can't go on calling me a baby,'' Glory hided, feeling stronger by the minute. ''I'm a grown woman charge of a cattle ranch. And I'm a Lawless. Papa's blood ows through my veins. And the way I see it, that more than ıakes up for whatever I don't know yet.''

Biddy stared a moment but then her expression changed, oftened. Her mouth puckered with some emotion. She pulled er hand free and covered her quivering lips with it.

Glory tensed. ''What is it, Biddy?'' What's wrong?''

Biddy shook her head, unsettling gray, wispy curls from her notted little bun. But then her expression became intense. She ripped Glory's arm with a fierceness that surprised her. ''Lis- n to me, child. Ye'll need other help besides that of a bunch f old folks who maybe canna protect you, should them mur- erers decide to ambush us again. So I'll hear no talk of Law- ss pride and how ye can take care of yer own without outside elp. 'Tis rubbish and will see us all dead. I want a promise om you. Should outside help come a-callin', promise me 'll accept it, Glory Bea. Promise me.''

Truly alarmed now—she hadn't considered the possibilit that the unknown men who killed Mama and Papa migh return—Glory cried, "I promise, Biddy. I swear it. Do yo really think they might come back?"

SEASONS OF GLORY—

Coming soon from Cheryl Anne Porter and St. Martin's Paperbacks!